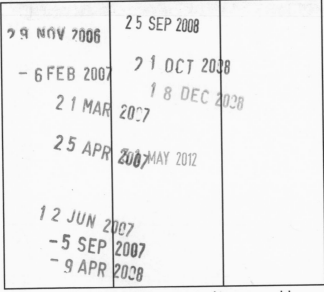
This book should be returned/renewed by the latest date shown above. Overdue items incur charges which prevent self-service renewals. Please contact the library.

Wandsworth Libraries
24 hour Renewal Hotline
01159 293388
www.wandsworth.gov.uk

Wandsworth

L.749A (rev.11.2004)

Also by Evelyn Hood

The Silken Thread
A Matter of Mischief
The Damask Days
A Stranger to the Town
McAdam's Women
Pebbles on the Beach
Another Day
The Dancing Stone
Time and Again
A Procession of One

THE SHIMMER OF THE HERRING

Evelyn Hood

LITTLE, BROWN AND COMPANY

A *Little, Brown* Book

First published in Great Britain in 2000
by Little, Brown and Company

Copyright © 2000 Evelyn Hood

The moral right of the author has been asserted.

A CIP catalogue record for this book
is available from the British Library.

HARDBACK ISBN 0 316 84919 7

Typeset in Times by
Palimpsest Book Production Limited,
Polmont, Stirlingshire
Printed and bound in Great Britain by
Creative Print and Design (Wales)

Little, Brown and Company (UK)
Brettenham House
Lancaster Place
London WC2E 7EN

This book is dedicated to
Isabel M. Harrison and Peter Bruce,
both of Buckie, and both descended from Moray Firth
fisher-folk. It is my pleasure and my privilege to know
them as good friends.

Acknowledgements

My thanks to Isabel M. Harrison, poet and historian, who generously gave me access to her own Buckie history collection; to Peter Bruce, who provided the title for this book; to Carol Thornton for her assistance in gathering research; to Sheila Campbell, chief librarian at Elgin Library; and to Ian Leith, chief librarian at Buckie Library. My thanks, too, to the volunteers who staff the Buckie and District Fishing Heritage Museum, the staff at Buckie and Elgin Libraries and the staff of The Drifter Museum in Buckie.

I am also indebted to the staff of the Scottish Fisheries Museum in Anstruther, Fife, particularly Alan Whitfield, model-maker at the museum, who helped me with research into details of pre-First World War steam drifters.

Without all those people, this book would not have been possible.

1

'You know your trouble, Weem Lowrie? You're lazy, that's what. Bone idle! Always were and always will be, and God forgive me for ever takin' you on as a husband,' Jess railed. 'Lyin' there and leavin' me to deal with all the worry of your own bairns – and me gettin' too old for the task. And look at the state of ye – am I never tae be done runnin' after you and tidyin' up your mess?'

She plucked irritably at the single weed that had dared to plant itself on the grassy green mound and put it into her pocket to dispose of later, then clambered to her feet and rubbed vigorously at the gravestone with the cloth she had brought specially.

A year after their carving the letters stood out clear and strong, claiming the six-foot rectangle of ground before them for William James Lowrie, fisherman of the parish of Buckie, born 1870, died 21 July 1911, beloved husband of Jess Innes and father of James, Bethany and Innes.

Her work done, Jess stepped back and surveyed the grave, head to one side. There was not a speck of dust on the stone, not so much as a fallen leaf on the grass. The mixed bunch of flowers she had brought from her tiny back yard had been arranged neatly in a glass jar and for the moment, at least, her man was neat, tidy and seen to.

'You're fine here, aren't you, Weem, where I can tend tae you?' Her voice was anxious, and she bit her lower lip as she glanced at the fields surrounding the small graveyard. It would have been more fitting for a man who had spent most of his life on the sea to be buried within sight and sound of its waves, but since the small fishing town of Buckie did not have its own graveyard, the Buckie dead had to be buried in Rathven Cemetery, on the hill high above their own small part of Buckie with its huddled houses and narrow cobbled streets. Jess took comfort in the thought that on days like today, with the high grey clouds scudding across it like ghostly sails, the great stretch of sky above the graveyard could well be likened to the ocean.

'Aye, you're fine.' She answered her own question. 'I just wish to God that your bairns could be put tae rights as easy as you are, Weem.' Even as she spoke she knew that there was no sense in talking to him about such matters, for he had always left the worrying to her.

She sniffed, used the cloth she had brought for the headstone to mop at the tears that had spilled over of their own accord, then put it back into her bag and brushed at the skirt of her coat.

'I'll be back next week, same as always.' Picking up the bag, she made her way out of the graveyard, straight-backed and with her head held high.

Fields of young corn to each side of the road rippled and swayed in waves beneath the wind; again, the similarity to the sea was obvious, but deep in her heart Jess knew that similarities would mean nothing to her Weem, for he had never had much time for the land. As she came within sight of Buckie, nestling on the shores of the Moray Firth and clustered for the most part round the harbour, guilt tramped alongside her as it had done since the day she had claimed her husband from the sea and laid him in the black earth.

Jess lifted her chin higher and quickened her step, trying to appreciate the bright yellow magnificence of the broom bushes by the road and the delicate beauty of the pink and white wild roses. The decision to bury her man in the ground instead of letting their son James return him to the huge rolling sea had been hers, made in the full knowledge that she must live with the consequences for the rest of her life. She had not realised, then, that it would cause such a deep rift between herself and her first-born, the son who was so like Weem in nature.

She had intended to go straight home, but when she reached the town she hesitated, then turned towards the huddle of houses known as the Catbow. As she neared her daughter's house a small, brown-haired tornado detached itself from a group of children and hurtled towards her, crashing into her knees and locking itself there with sturdy little arms.

'Granny Jess!' Rory Pate yelled up at her, his blue eyes wide and angelic in his dirty face. 'Where have ye been?'

'Tae London tae see the Queen.'

'Did she send me anythin'?'

'Aye, a facecloth and a bar of soap,' she retorted, rummaging in her bag. 'But I must have left them behind, so you'll have to have this instead.'

Rory's eyes lit up at sight of the liquorice strap and he released her knees to snatch at it with one hand.

'Is your mother busy?'

'No, she's just talkin' to Aunt Stella. I was playin' with the bairns, but they all got too tired and went to sleep. They're too wee to play,' four-year-old Rory said scornfully.

He accompanied her to the door then darted off again, leaving her on her own. 'Are you in, then?' she called, tapping gently at the door before lifting the latch. Most local women were free to walk into their own daughters' homes without having to announce their arrival. But then most local women did not have a daughter like Bethany.

All day Bethany Pate had dreaded a meeting with her

mother. She had been trying hard, without success, to
keep thoughts of her once-adored father at bay on this
first anniversary of his death, but despite all her efforts
he had pushed himself into her mind at every opportunity.
To make matters worse, her sister-in-law Stella had been
sitting in Bethany's small kitchen since early afternoon,
talking about Weem Lowrie.

'I'm just glad that James is away at the fishing, for
I don't know what he'd have been like if he'd been
home today.'

'He'd not have let it make any difference.' Bethany
had little time, even when she was in a good mood, for
Stella's assumption that because her twins weren't much
older than Bethany's step-daughter Ellen the two women
had a lot in common. It never seemed to occur to Stella
that Bethany, not having given birth herself, might not be
interested in continuous talk of bairns and domesticity.

'You don't know what he's been like since his father
went. He's not the same man at all. I never know what
way to take him.'

'James was always difficult. It's in his nature. It's a
family thing.' In Bethany's hands the knitting needles
flew along the row, turned and flew back, the points
stabbing into the thick wool. She was knitting a jersey
for her husband while Stella worked at a jacket for one
of the twins.

'Innes is a good civil soul, and your mother's the
same.'

'James inherited his nature from our father, same as
me.' It was all Bethany could do not to throw the knitting
into Stella's bland face. No wonder James was difficult at
times, she thought with a stab of pity for her older brother.
Having to spend his time ashore with a woman who could
talk of nothing but bairns and cooking, and bairns and
mending, and more bairns would turn any man morose.
And James had been moody to start with.

'But you'd think . . .' Stella began, then stopped short

as they heard the tentative tap on the outer door, and the voice from the street. 'It's her . . . your mother!' Her brown eyes, guileless as a child's, flooded with concern.

'I know my own mother's voice.'

'Should I say something about . . .'

'No!' Bethany put the knitting aside and got up to fetch a cup as her mother came into the kitchen, crooning at the sight of the three infants drowsing, exhausted from their games, in an intertwined, boneless heap on the hearth rug. They woke at the sound of her voice, reaching stubby arms up to her and chattering like a nestful of baby birds.

Jess sank on to the chair Bethany had vacated and managed to gather them all into her lap. 'Aren't ye the bonniest bairns in the whole of the Firth?' she asked them. 'And I'd not sell one of you for a thousand pound!'

'You'll not be able to take your tea now,' Bethany said irritably from the stove.

'I'll manage fine. I'm used tae bairns climbin' all over me.' With difficulty, Jess tucked sixteenth-month-old Ellen and fifteen-month-old Sarah and Annie into the crook of one arm and reached out with her free hand for the mug of sweet black tea.

'Sit nice now, my wee birdies, for Granny Jess.' She drank it down swiftly and handed the cup back. 'That was good. I'd a thirst on me.'

'Have you been walkin' to Rathven and back?' Stella asked.

Jess shot a look at Bethany, who devoted all her attention to washing her mother's empty cup. 'Aye, pet, I just took a stroll up the hill.'

'On your lone? Me and the bairns would've gone with you if you'd asked.'

'I'd not have you walking that distance when you're so near to your time.' The children were squirming to get down now and Jess was glad of the diversion. She lowered them to the floor, then pulled her own knitting wires from the leather pad known locally as a whisker,

slung from her belt. Buckie women never let a moment
lie idle, and if there was nothing of greater urgency for
their hands to do there was always knitting or darning.
'How are you keeping, Stella?'

'Well enough. Wearying for the time to come.' The
girl hesitated then said shyly, 'If it's a boy I thought to
call him Weem, after his grandfather.'

'But is that what James wants?' Bethany asked tartly,
returning to her chair.

'I've not asked him yet, I wanted to speak to Mother
Jess first.' Stella beamed at Jess, who hesitated, glancing
over at her daughter. Bethany, head bent, was intent on
her knitting.

'It's a kind thought, lass, but I think James should have
the final word on the matter.'

Stella's mouth drooped a little. 'He wasn't interested
in naming the lassies.'

'If it's a laddie that'll change.' Bethany's voice was
brittle. 'Sons count more than daughters. Sons can carry
on the family tradition and the family name. Daughters
aren't of much use.'

'You think so?' Stella asked nervously, eyeing her little
daughters and placing a protective hand on the great swell
of her belly. Then, putting her knitting needles away, she
began to ease herself up from her chair. 'I'd best go. The
bairns'll be gettin' hungry.'

'I'll come with you, and help you with the wee ones,'
Jess offered.

Outside Stella said, 'Bethany's in a right black mood
today. She snapped at me more than once before you
came in, and I can't think what I did to deserve it.'

'It's not your fault, pet. We've all got our ups and
downs.'

'Aye, I suppose so. I just thought it would be nice for
the two of us to spend some time together. Even with my
father and the bairns tae see to, the house seems awful
empty when James is at the fishin'.'

'Aye.' Jess felt sorry for the girl, knowing full well how hard it was to be head over heels in love with a man who did not possess a grain of romance in his soul. 'Why not come along to my house for a wee while?'

'Best not, my da'll be ready for his cup of tea.'

'How is he?' Mowser Buchan, a former fisherman, had been in poor health.

'Not too bad. The worst of his troubles is the way he's still pinin' for the sea, even though he's been ashore these three years past.'

'My own father was the same when he got too old to go out on the boats. Once the sea gets them it never lets go.' The words were out of Jess's mouth before she realised it and, as she walked the short distance to her own house after parting with Stella, they came clamouring back, filling her head until her ears rang. Worse still, they were being shouted not in her own voice, but in Weem's.

'Once the sea gets them, it never lets go.' How could any woman who knew the truth of that have kept her man's body back from the sea, which had been more dear to him than anything else?

'For love, Weem, for love,' she muttered, and didn't realise she had said it aloud until two little girls scurrying towards her hand-in-hand hesitated, looked at each other, giggled and gave her a wide berth as they ran past.

'Hello, Innes.'

'Zelda . . .' Innes Lowrie, intent on the piece of machinery on the bench before him, greeted the newcomer brusquely without turning to look at her. Unabashed, Grizelda Mulholland found a corner where she was out of his way and waited. She enjoyed watching Innes at work; she liked the gravity that overlaid his normally cheerful face, the narrowing of the dark eyes, the way his strong, long-fingered hands moved deftly among what to her were lumps of metal, but to him were objects of beauty.

After a few moments he straightened, wiping his oily

hands on a rag then turning to give her his usual broad
grin. 'What brings you here?'

'Johnny had to bring one of the carthorses to be shod
and wee Peter wanted to come to the smiddy to see the
work being done.' Zelda was employed as a maid at a
farm in Rathven, helping the farmer's busy wife to tend
the hens, make the cheese and see to the house and the
large family.

'Again? Wee Peter's been here that often to see
the horses shod that he must be able to do it himself
by now.'

'Bairns like smiddies.' She hoisted herself up to sit
on the rough wood of his workbench, swinging her legs.
'You're not complaining, are you? If I'm in your way
just say and I'll be off.'

'I'm not complaining a bit, Miss Grizelda.' Innes leaned
on the bench, enjoying the way the girl pouted at the
mention of her full name.

'Don't say that! Is it my fault my family have long
names? When I have . . .' She stopped short, flushing
and looking up at him from beneath her lashes, 'If I have
bairns they'll be given proper names like Ann and Mary
and John.'

'I think Zelda's a fine name.' Innes wiped the sweat
from his face with the rag he still held. Because the
blacksmith who employed him had his furnace positioned
against the brick wall between workshop and smiddy, both
places were always hot to work in.

'At least it's better than Grizzel. That's what my aunt's
called.'

'That wouldn't suit you, not with your bonny nature.'

Zelda flushed with pleasure at the compliment, then
poked a finger at the metal he had been working on.
'What's that? Part of a motor-car?'

'Just a bit from a reaper. I wish it was a motor-
car,' Innes said longingly. 'We don't see many of them
hereabouts.'

'Zelda!' A small boy appeared in the doorway, face flushed with heat from the blacksmith's fire. He stamped in and clutched at the maid's hand. 'I want to go home. I don't like it here!'

'Yes, you do.'

'I don't!' Peter insisted. 'You know I don't. Why do we have to keep coming?'

'Don't you be cheeky . . . And what are you laughing at, Innes Lowrie?' Zelda snapped, flustered by the little boy's revelations.

'Nothing at all.'

'That rag you wiped your face with has left dirt all over your cheek,' she said and flounced out, towing Peter behind her. In the doorway she turned. 'Will you come up to the farm for me later?'

'I can't tonight, my mother'll mebbe want me to go to Rathven cemetery with her. It's . . . it's been a year since . . .'

The girl took a step back towards him. 'Oh, Innes, I forgot about your father. I'm sorry.'

'It's all right. I'll come up tomorrow night?'

She beamed and nodded, then hurried off, leaving Innes to return to his work.

Jess was stirring the soup when the youngest of her three children arrived home from work. 'Are you all right?' he asked as soon as he came in the door.

'Why wouldn't . . .' she began, then changed it to, 'Aye, lad, I'm fine.' Then, eyeing his dirty overalls, 'Get yourself washed, now, your dinner'll be on the table in a minute.' She had never become used to the streaks of oil on Innes's dungarees, or the smell of it. 'Your clean shirt's over the back of that chair.'

Unlike her own mother, Jess had the luxury of a cold-water tap in her kitchen, but Innes, a thoughtful lad, always insisted on washing the day's grime off at the big sink in the outhouse. Whistling, he went out the back with a

kettle of hot water while Jess rattled the pots busily on
the stove.

Although she had always tried not to favour one of her
children over the others, her last-born was more precious
to her than his older brother and sister. For one thing, he
was still under her roof and therefore in her care: for
another, he was the only one of the three with whom
she felt comfortable. Innes had been a loving and giving
soul from the moment of his birth, whereas James and
Bethany had both shrugged off embraces from an early
age. Now that they were grown there were times when
she felt quite uncomfortable with them, while with Innes
she could say and do as she wished without fear of being
laughed at or criticised.

'I thought the two of us might take a walk up to Rathven
after,' he said casually when he returned to the kitchen,
sleeking his wet hair back with both hands and reaching
for the shirt.

'It's all right, laddie, I went to see your father this
afternoon.'

'On your lone? Did Bethany not think to go with you?'
he asked when she nodded.

'I didn't ask her. Would you mind just having your
own company when you go there later?'

'I'll stay in with you instead. To tell the truth, I paid
my respects this morning before work. Mebbe Bethany
went on her own, too.'

'Mebbe.'

'Then there's James . . .'

'He'd be too busy catching herring to remember.' Jess
put the soup bowls on the table and sat down. 'James has
his own life to live now.'

Weem had always predicted that he would die at sea and
rest there, but in actual fact he had died of a sudden, mas-
sive heart attack on board the *Fidelity*, the steam drifter
that he, his brother Albert and James jointly owned. James
had wanted to honour his father's wishes by putting the

body over the side there and then, but Albert had insisted on leaving the final decision to Jess.

Despite James's arguing and, eventually, his pleading, she had settled for a burial, unable to face the thought of losing her man completely to the sea, with no grave to visit. Since then James had scarcely had anything to do with her. It was as though she had lost a son as well as a husband.

2

─────◆─────

When her step-children were in bed and asleep and the dishes had been done Bethany pulled a shawl over her head. 'I'm just going down to visit my mother.'

Gil Pate, settled by the fire with his pipe and the newspaper, reached up and caught his wife's hand as she moved past his chair. 'D'you have to go out?' His strong fingers caressed the soft skin on the inside of her wrist.

'I feel that I should. It's a year to the day since my father went. She gets lonely.' It was an excuse she had often used in the past months, when she needed to get away from the house to walk by herself in the fresh air, away from the cloying domestic responsibilities.

'She not on her lone, there's still Innes at home.'

'He's never there – you should know what laddies are like.'

'Laddies have to go out looking for companionship,' Gil said, his fingers stroking and stroking. 'But a man has the right to find it there at his own hearthside.'

'You won't miss me for an hour. You'll have your nose in the newspaper for longer than that and the bairns'll not be any trouble. They're sound asleep and they'll stay like that till the mornin'.'

'I like to know you're sittin' on the other side of the fire, knittin' away, all bonny and contented,' he sulked.

'Just an hour, that's all.' She drew her hand away gently but firmly.

'If you must, you must . . . but don't take all night about it. It's time Jess realised that you're a wife now, and that's more than a daughter.'

Once over the doorstep Bethany drew the night air deep into her lungs with a great, shuddering sigh before walking briskly down the hill towards Cluny Harbour. At that time of year most of the Buckie fleet was fishing the waters round Shetland, Orkney and Caithness, and the few boats left in the harbour rode high in the water, occasionally nudging against each other. For a moment she drew the peace of the place into her soul. Then, turning away from the water, she moved in the opposite direction from her mother's house, keeping her head down and her shawl drawn close about her face.

The road to Rathven was quiet and all too soon the larger monuments in the cemetery were outlined against the cool blue-grey of the evening sky, then she had reached it and the iron of the gate was cold and hard beneath her fingers. She knew exactly where her father's grave lay; she could even see his stone from where she hesitated, clinging to the gate.

Over the past year she had often walked up the hill to this place, but she had never been able to take that first step into the cemetery. It was the same story tonight; before peace could be made with her father's memory she would have to come to terms with the conflicting emotions within her own soul. She would have to relinquish something – either the deep love she had had for the man from her earliest days, or the bitter rage born of knowing that he had used her love and trust to further his own interests, trapping her in the process with a man who meant nothing to her.

Bethany's fingers tightened painfully on the gate. Letting go of the rage meant that she must resign herself to becoming what Weem had made of her: a wife and mother with no other identity. And she could not do that. Not yet, perhaps not ever. She turned away from

the graveyard and started back down the road towards
home.

Once in sight of the Firth she could see the lights of a
group of sailed fishing boats sliding out of the harbour
below. Although its fishing fleet was second to only that
of Lowestoft in size, Buckie was badly situated for the
large fishing grounds, and during the busiest seasons its
boats were obliged to stay away from home for weeks at
a time, discharging their catches and re-coaling in more
accessible ports. The sailed boats, smaller than the steam
drifters and dependent on wind and weather, were less
able to reach the big fishing grounds and concentrated
on line fishing in the deeper waters of the Moray Firth.
The boats below, passing in stately procession though the
harbour entrance with their masthead lights twinkling in
the gloaming, would be back in the morning with their
catches.

Once out of the harbour they dipped and bounced,
moving apart and picking up speed as the wind caught
their spread sails. Bethany watched hungrily, longing to
be on board and heading for the open sea with no thought
for the land falling away behind her.

Back in the town she returned to the harbour, standing
at the very edge, looking down into the deep, still water
where as a bairn she had swum with the lads, heedless
of the future. She had certainly never anticipated that it
would bring marriage and a ready-made family. While
the other lassies had played with dolls and as they grew
from childhood dreamed of their own homes and their
own men and their own bairns, Bethany had had other
plans. Even though she knew that women did not crew
on fishing boats she secretly hoped that her father, who
could deny her nothing, might break the unwritten rule
specially for her. But Weem was as superstitious as any
fisherman and, on leaving school, Bethany was set to work
in one of the smokehouses, then became a 'guttin quine',
as the fisher lassies were known in the area.

Frustrated, she had then come up with another scheme. The guttin quine, employed by fish curers, coopers, or buyers, worked in three-woman teams, with two gutters and one packer to each team. Once brought ashore, the fish were emptied from baskets into the farlins, wooden troughs similar to the deep sinks used for washing clothes. Salt was scattered over the herring to make them easier to grip, and in seconds the gutters' sharp knives slit the fish open and scooped the entrails out. The gutted fish was tossed into a tub on one side of each gutter and entrails into a tub on her other side. The packer arranged the fish in the barrels; an outer ring and an inner ring, with a space between each fish to avoid damaging them. The layers were separated by handfuls of coarse salt.

The work was hard, and when the fishing was good the guttin quine might work at the farlins for twelve or fifteen hours, with only short breaks for meals. For this they were paid threepence an hour, plus tenpence per barrel, to be divided between the three women in the team.

It had occurred to Bethany that an ambitious, hard-working woman could take over the running of the teams, renting their services out, bargaining with the curers and coopers and possibly earning more money for the teams and for herself . . . money that, carefully and patiently hoarded over the years, might eventually enable her to buy her own boat one day and pick her own crew to work it.

With this secret aim in mind Bethany had set herself to work hard at the farlins. Once the herring were landed they had to be gutted, sorted, salted and packed as fast as possible. Usually there were one or two experienced women working alongside the teams, ready to step in and take over if someone had to drop out for any reason. Bethany, her hands as fast as her mind, had swiftly learned the art of gutting and by being in the right place at the right time she had become a supervisor.

The next step had been to gather the women together

and persuade them to consider working for themselves
instead of for the menfolk, but while she was waiting for
the right time, fate – in the form of her beloved father –
had stepped in and ruined everything.

Since childhood Bethany had had striking looks. Her
curly hair was long and thick, brown like her father's,
but with a rich mahogany glow to it that came from
her mother's colouring. She possessed her mother's good
bones and her father's clear grey eyes, which, in Bethany's
case, could change in an instant from warm velvet to the
hard, cold grey of slate or become as stormy as a wild sea
or glitter like silvered spray. Full-grown, she was slightly
on the tall side for a woman, with a body that was feminine
yet sturdy. Like her older brother James she was never
short of admirers, but while James, in his bachelor days,
enjoyed the attentions of blushing lassies, Bethany had
no time for the youths who sought to court her.

Her natural ability to supervise others, combined with
her youthful good health and her striking looks, had caught
the eye of her employer, a cooper by the name of Gilbert
Pate. Although Gil already had a wife, he would have bedded Bethany willingly if she had shown any signs of being
agreeable to it. The other women at the farlins had joshed
her about Gil's interest, some with amusement and others
(the younger ones who thought the cooper a good-looking
man) with a certain amount of jealousy. Unfortunately,
James had heard of it and had teased her unmercifully
in their father's hearing, something that Weem Lowrie
remembered when Gil's wife died in childbed, leaving
him in sore need of someone to look after his home and
his two children.

Gil was ripe for the picking and Weem Lowrie had
never been one to let a chance go by. Only months
after burying his first wife Gil had taken Bethany as
his second, and Weem and Albert Lowrie had secured
an arrangement to sell all the *Fidelity*'s future catches to
Gil and his brother Nathan, a curer, at a price that suited

all four men. Nobody had asked for Bethany's views on the matter. And now, she thought bitterly, it was too late to do anything about it. She had made her bed . . .

The unfortunate but apt phrase reminded her that time was passing all too quickly while she stood there, still as a figurehead, lost in her own thoughts. And time was no longer hers to squander. Shivering in the cool air, she wrenched herself away from the sea and went slowly back to the cottage where Gil was asleep in his chair, legs stretched across the hearth, his newspaper spread across his deep chest, his mouth open and snoring.

As Bethany closed the door he choked in mid-snore and struggled upright in his chair, wiping drool from his chin and glancing at the clock. 'You were a good while.'

'We got to talking.'

He reached up and touched her fingers as she went by his chair. 'You're chilled.'

'I went down to the harbour to look at the boats on my way back.' She picked up the poker and bent to stir life and warmth into the glowing range, but he put his paper aside and got up to take the poker from her.

'Leave it.'

'I'm cold.'

'I'll warm you in the bed,' Gil said huskily, his hands busy.

'The bairns . . .'

'There's not been a murmur from them all the time you've been gone.' He pulled her to him, one arm about her waist, his free hand catching hers and pushing it against his swelling crotch. 'They have your attention during the day. The night-time's mine,' he said into her neck.

'I'll just make sure they're settled, then I'll be back,' Bethany said and escaped to the small room at the back of the house, just large enough for two cribs. Rory and Ellen were both sound asleep, Ellen on her stomach and Rory on his back, arms and legs spread like the tentacles of a

starfish. They were good bairns and she was fond enough
of them, but in the same way she tolerated all young
things such as kittens or puppies. Watching Stella and
the other women she knew that she lacked their maternal
feelings. Perhaps if she had children of her own . . . but the
very thought made her flesh creep. Gil, who fortunately
seemed content with the two bairns he already had, had no
knowledge of the ways in which his young wife guarded
herself against an unwanted pregnancy.

'Bethany?' Gil, already in his long night-shirt, said from
the doorway. 'Come on, woman, I want my sleep.'

'I'm just going out to the privy first.' She lingered
there, in the smelly, spidery dark, hoping that he might
fall asleep, but knowing he would not. Young and healthy
and with a natural appetite for life and all it had to offer,
she had enjoyed her bridegroom's attentions at first, but
after a few months her duties as a bedded wife had become
tedious; why, she had no idea, but she suspected that it
might be because Gil was not of her own choosing.

When she returned to the warm, dark kitchen, lit only
by a faint glow from the range, Gil was awake and too
impatient to wait until she had brushed her hair out and
put her night-gown on. Bouncing rhythmically on the
mattress, her scalp pierced by straying hairpins, Bethany
stared beyond her husband's head at the ceiling and
thought of her father, who had engineered this marriage
to suit his own purposes.

Weem had been unable to understand why his beloved
daughter had become so withdrawn from him after her
marriage and it had hurt Bethany to see his bewilderment.
She had always assumed that one day, when the hurt had
eased and she was ready to forgive him for pushing her
into this marriage, they would become close again. Then
suddenly Weem was dead, and it was too late.

As Gil rolled on to his own side of the bed and began,
almost to once, to snore, she stared at the dull glow of the
fire and wondered if the continuous seething restlessness

within her would have eased and vanished if she had been able to make her peace with her father.

Busy as James Lowrie was that day, his father was not out of his thoughts all through the journey to the fishing grounds off Caithness. It was a relief when they were ready to shoot the nets not long after darkness fell, for it was an exercise that involved every member of the crew and gave them little time to think. In the rope locker, an area little more than a cupboard below-deck, the ship's lad feverishly paid out the messenger – the thick, tarry rope that held the nets. At the same time the huge nets themselves were being fed carefully from their hold on to the deck, where one man attached the corks that kept the nets suspended from the sea's surface, and the buoys that would indicate their position, while another passed the netting strop-ropes to James, who made them fast to the messenger and sent them on their way overboard – on the starboard side of the boat, since it was considered bad luck to shoot the nets to port.

'I'll stand watch,' James said two hours later when the others stretched cramped, weary limbs and looked longingly towards the galley, where the deckhand who doubled as a cook was already starting to prepare their supper.

The boat had been brought round head to wind and the mizzen set to hold her there. Below the surface of the water, their presence indicated by floats at regular intervals, some two to three miles of drift-nets spread out from *Fidelity*, hanging in curtains, waiting for the herring to swim into the trap set for them.

Albert Lowrie, square-built like his late brother, though without Weem's height, narrowed his eyes as he stared out into the darkness. 'It's a quiet enough night, she'll not move much. I doubt if we'll need any more swing-rope. You get below, Malky can stand tonight,' he told his nephew, but James shook his head and repeated with a bite to his voice, 'I said I'll watch!'

Albert shrugged then nodded to the other men, who tumbled into the galley at once, eager to get out of the wind that chilled now that they were idle. It was a relief to James when his uncle followed them. He was in no mood that night to be shut up with the others, listening to their endless talk. He lit a cigarette, drawing the tobacco deep into his lungs. It was dark apart from the carbine lamp fixed forward of the wheel-house and the oil lamp at the mast. Around him, he knew, a vast fleet was scattered over the fishing grounds, tossing on the heavy but regular swell, though in the darkness all he could see was an occasional masthead light and the quick froth of a wave-top now and again.

Like his father and sister, James loved the sea more than anything else. He loved its contrary moods – the worst of them as well as the best. He loved the sight and sound of it, its salty kiss on his lips, the harpy screaming of a gale in the rigging. When first he went to sea he had been taught his craft by his father on one of two sailed Zulu fishing boats owned by Zachary Lowrie, his grandfather. A shrewd and ambitious man, Zachary had put one boat in the care of Weem, the older of his two sons and the better fisherman, while he himself was skipper of the other with his younger son Albert as mate.

The arrangement had worked amicably until Weem, shrewd and ambitious as his father, set eyes on one of the first steam drifters in Lowestoft during an English fishing season. He had done all he could to persuade his father to sell both Zulus and invest in steam, but Zachary would have no truck with the newfangled 'steam kettles'. James could still remember every word of the quarrels that flew between them each time they met.

'D'you know the cost of one of these things? Three thousand poun' and more! I've never been in debt in my life, and I'll not be in debt in old age,' Zachary had thundered.

Weem stood his ground. 'You're well enough known

and well enough respected to get a good loan from the North of Scotland Bank. The sale of the two Zulus would pay off some of the money . . .'

Zachary took his pipe from his mouth and gobbed a mouthful of phlegm into the fire. 'They'd fetch next to nothing compared to the cost of a steam drifter!'

'. . . and once we're able to reach the fishing grounds in all weathers without fear of being becalmed,' Weem ploughed on doggedly, refusing to be diverted from his dream, 'we could soon make up the rest.'

'And there's you and Albert and the rest of the crew to be paid, and an engine driver and a trimmer to feed the furnace,' the old man pointed out. 'I'm fine as I am. Once I cover the cost of my sails the wind's free. So hold your tongue, Weem, for I'll not have any more of this nonsense, and that's final!' He humphed and bit so hard on the stem of his pipe that James expected it to snap in two, then he took it from his mouth to add, 'When I'm gone you'll probably win Albert round, for you always were a silver-tongued bugger and he's a fool, more interested in fathering bairns than makin' sensible decisions. But you'll never get me to change my mind.'

The door of the galley clanged back on its hinges and Jem, the younger of the two bastard sons Albert had brought on board the *Fidelity* as crew members, arrived on deck with a mug of hot tea and a sandwich big enough to warrant the title of doorstop.

'My da says I've to take over the watch if you want to go below.'

'I'm fine where I am,' James told him shortly and the lad, recently promoted from ship's boy to deckhand, shrugged and ducked back into the warm fug of the galley. As the door opened James heard the low rumble of voices from the cabin below, and the soft strains of his cousin Charlie's mouth organ. The rest of the crew would be clustered round the table in the small, pitching cabin, smoking and drinking mugs of strong tea sweetened with

condensed milk. They were welcome to it . . . Give him
the open air and the sea and his own company any day.

He ate and drank without tasting the food or noticing
the scalding sting of the tea, then hunched into the shelter
of the wheel-house to light another cigarette, sucking the
smoke deep into his lungs, blowing it out again on a long,
shuddering breath.

Zachary Lowrie had been right. Almost as soon as he
was in his grave Weem had talked his easy-going brother
into agreeing that they should replace the Zulus with a
drifter, which they would crew together, with Weem as
skipper and Albert as mate. There was one snag: as the
old man had pointed out, steam drifters cost a lot of money.
Between them the Zulus only cleared one-third of the cost
of a steamboat and although both Weem and Albert were
prepared to take on a hefty loan from the bank, the debt
would have been crippling.

That was when James became important to his father's
calculations. When he closed his eyes he could still see the
pub that the three of them had visited after inspecting the
Fidelity, which was up for sale and lying in Fraserburgh
harbour.

'She's a grand boat, we're all agreed on that,' Weem
had said, and the other two had nodded vigorously. 'But
the cost of her – the bank won't lend us all that money.
Who'd have thought good Zulus would raise so little?'

'The value of sailed boats has gone down, Da, because
more and more folk like us want to turn to the steam
drifters.'

'Aye.' Weem tugged thoughtfully at his beard, then
said, 'Another Zulu to sell would make all the difference.'

'We've not got another.' Albert's eyes were on the barmaid's round backside as she bent over a nearby table.

'No,' Weem said; then slowly, with emphasis on the
second word, 'No, *we* don't, but I was speakin' to Mowser
Buchan the other day. His chest's that bad that he's havin'

to give up the fishing, poor man, and him with his three lads drowned two years back and nobody left to sail his boat out for him. A fine Zulu lying idle in the harbour with neither a skipper nor a crew.'

'Mowser's surely not wanting to come in with us at his age?' Albert asked.

'No, no, the sea's done with the man, poor soul. But there's other ways. James, fetch more drink for us.'

'I'll go,' Albert offered swiftly, but his brother clamped a hand on his arm when he made to rise from the table.

'You'll bide where you are and leave that lassie alone. We're not looking to start trouble with the Fraserburgh men over any barmaid. James . . .'

Waiting for his turn to be served, James saw his father and uncle deep in conversation, heads close together. Once he was back at the table Weem said, 'I was just saying to Albert here that Mowser's daughter's not spoken for.'

James took a deep drink from his tankard and summoned Stella Buchan to mind. She had been in his class at the school: a quiet sort of lass, brown-haired and brown-eyed, not interesting enough to attract his attention. 'What about it?'

'A young fisherman like yourself could do a lot worse than buying a share in a fine steam drifter. Just think of the fish we could get to the shore in that beauty we saw today.'

'Me? I only earn what you pay me. How could I buy a share in any drifter?'

'If you'd a sailed boat you'd make enough from the sale of it to buy a share in that very drifter we saw less than an hour since.'

James choked on his drink. 'Are you talking about me offering for Stella Buchan?' he spluttered, wiping his mouth with one sleeve.

'She's a bonny enough lassie,' Albert put in, adding hurriedly, 'Not that I've had any dealings with her myself, you understand.'

'You hear that, James? Who's a better judge of women than your uncle, eh? Famed the length and breadth of the Moray coast.' Weem slapped his brother on the back and Albert grinned. Although he had never married, every one of his large brood had a different mother.

'I've no thought of marrying yet!'

'Have you no sense in your head at all? If you want to be in that bonny drifter when the next herring season comes round you'll get a ring on that quine's finger before some other young lad comes up with the same thought. I know Mowser would be proud to see the two of you settled together.'

'You've spoken to the man behind my back?'

'To clear your way, just. And it would suit him fine to know his lass had a good hard-working man to look out for her.'

'And what does Stella say to it all? I suppose you've spoken to her behind my back and all?'

'Don't be so daft,' Weem said in his most reasonable voice. 'All the lassies of marriageable age have their eyes on you, and Stella Buchan's no different. If you're half the man I think you are you'll welcome a wife with such a fine dowry.'

James, footloose and fancy-free, had fought against the idea, but in the end he came to realise that his father was right when he said that selling off three Zulus instead of two was the only way to raise enough money to buy the *Fidelity*. And he wanted the drifter just as much as his father and uncle did. He had wanted her from the moment he first saw her in the harbour at Fraserburgh. So he had married Stella Buchan, and the Zulu was sold within a week of the marriage. A week later he was a shareholder in the *Fidelity*.

'Albert giving up his own Zulu gives him the right to be mate,' Weem had explained to his son, 'but his heart's not in the fishing, like ours. He'd far rather be in bed with a woman than out on the boat, and once we've cleared our debt with the bank you and me can buy him out. Then you'll be mate, and follow me as skipper when I give up the sea . . . or when it takes me.'

But the bank loan was still outstanding on the boat when, in a cruel twist of fate, Weem's heart gave out one morning just after they had finished hauling in the catch. If only the man could have been struck down while working the nets moments earlier, James thought, sucking hard on his cigarette, he might have toppled over the side and been dragged to the seabed by the weight of his boots and his clothing. Instead he had collapsed on to the deck planks almost at his son's feet, and as a result he now lay in rich farming earth, away from the sound and taste and feel of the Firth he had lived on for most of his life.

'It's only natural for her to want to know where he is,' Stella had tried to explain to James before the funeral. Her three brothers had drowned during a bad storm and the misery of not knowing where they lay had tormented her mother for the rest of her life.

'It's not her right at all,' he railed back at her. 'He always said that when his time came he'd be with the sea!'

But she had not understood. And why should she, James thought wearily, reaching for another cigarette. She was only a woman, with no understanding of fishermen and the ways that were important to them.

3

James's hand had been stinging for some time before he realised that the glowing cigarette butt was clenched between two fingers, burning into the skin.

Cursing, he threw it overboard as the moon ripped another hole in the ragged clouds and peered at him, its light picking out the wintry-white glitter of spray on the crests of the heaving, tossing waves. A wind had come up and the boat was beginning to dance restlessly. He knew that he should call the others on deck, but he also knew that in the calm depths below the stormy surface the silver darlings were tangling themselves into *Fidelity*'s nets. If Albert Lowrie, sleeping soundly in his bunk at that moment, was made aware of the worsening weather he would head for shore, abandoning the catch. So James did nothing.

By dawn the sea was worse, and the first of the light showed that some of the boats in the distance were getting up steam and hauling in their nets hurriedly, preparing to run for shelter. The rest of the crew arrived on deck, pulling on jerseys and sou'westers as they tumbled out of the galley.

'Damn you, James, why didn't you call us up sooner?' Albert was having difficulty in knuckling the sleep from his eyes.

'It's just a wee swell. Plenty of time to get the nets inboard.'

'A wee swell?' Albert barked, staggering and grabbing for a handhold as the *Fidelity* reared up like a nervous horse. 'You damned young fool, you'll not be content till you drown the lot of us!' As he roared down to the engine driver and trimmer to come up on deck and lend a hand, and the steam capstan leaped into action, James grinned to himself, throwing away his half-smoked cigarette and moving to the starboard bulwarks, where he held on with one hand and leaned precariously over the side, heedless of the waves thundering in on the boat.

It was there, glimpsed beneath the water's foaming surface as the first net was coaxed slowly and steadily upwards . . . the faintly milky tinge that quickly became a silvery shimmer. Although he had seen that same glimmer rising towards him from below the waves on countless occasions, James's body still tingled with a surge of elation and excitement. It was what he was born for, what he and the others risked their lives for over and over again.

'It's a good shot today, lads!' he shouted over his shoulder to the rest of the crew, waiting in a line along the deck. 'Didn't I tell you when we got here that I could smell the herring?'

'You and your bloody nose,' his uncle grunted, his own eyes fixed on the dark sky above. The weather was closing in fast now, but as the seas raced in on her from all sides the boat fought back, twisting and rolling and righting herself every time, only to stagger as another huge wave crashed towards her, then rally and begin the struggle for survival again. Each time she rolled to port the deckhands dug their feet firmly into the angle formed by bulwarks and deck, twisted their hands into the thick wet mesh emerging slowly from the water, and leaned back with all their weight. The trick was to hold tight to the net, which was being lifted from the sea by the rolling action of the boat itself. Over she went, until she was close to lying on her port side, the men almost

horizontal on the steeply sloping deck, teeth gritted hard
and muscles screaming with the effort of pulling the net
along with them. The capstan roared as it hauled in the
great messenger rope inch by bitter inch.

When she had rolled as far as was safe the *Fidelity*
hesitated, as though making a choice between living and
dying; then, deciding, she began to reverse the roll.

The men came upright with her, then as she began to
pitch to starboard, threatening to take the emerging nets
with her, they leaned forward, clawing at the mesh, their
fingers slipping among the tightly packed fish. The steam
capstan spun faster now, gathering in foot after foot of the
messenger, then as the vessel reached the furthest edge of
her roll the net exploded on to the decking among them,
filling up every inch and forcing them back towards the
gaping maw of the hold while it spilled out its catch,
until the crew were knee-deep in hundreds, thousands,
of leaping silvery fish.

Now they began to work as one, each man concentrating
on his own given task. Jem caught up a wooden shovel and
began to scoop the herring towards the hold, as another
man deftly disconnected the netting from the messenger
rope. Two more detached the round canvas buoys and
tossed them into a corner of the deck, out of the way. In
the soaking dark rope locker the lad feverishly coiled the
dripping rope, while in the hold Charlie and the three other
men used their wide wooden herring shovels to scoop to
the sides the torrent of fish descending on them in order
to make room for the herring following on. When the net
was freed from the messenger it, too, went into the hold,
where the men disentangled those fish still caught by the
gills in the mesh, before bundling it up and clearing it
out of the way. Later it would be shaken out and folded
and properly stowed, but in the meantime the fight was
already on for the next length of netting.

'The weather's gettin' worse . . .' Albert shouted.

'There's time yet, and fish.' James tossed the words

brusquely over his shoulder. All that mattered was getting the fish aboard. Even with the assistance of the steam capstan, the job of bringing a good catch inboard was back-breaking work. Spray and sweat mingled to run down the crew's faces, their necks, their backs beneath the layers of warm clothing. Their oilskins dripped salt water and their feet skidded on the slippery fish scales.

Albert roared an oath as he almost fell after his heel landed on a lump of jelly-like substance that had fallen from the net. 'Watch what you're about, man,' he barked at a young deckhand who had just managed to free a hand and was about to scrub some spray from his face. 'There's scalders in the nets – touch your face and you'll burn your eyes out!' Scalders were a type of jellyfish that covered the fishermen's hands with a toxic stinging slime, which passed to anything they touched. The only solution to the agony of burning eyes or mouths was to wash the afflicted areas with fresh water, but when the nets were coming inboard there was no time for such niceties.

A wave larger than the others caught the boat, lifting it up, then letting it slide down a long, steep flank. It rolled sickeningly and a mass of green water poured inboard. Down and down the boat went, dropping fast enough to leave James suspended almost knee-deep in the sea. For a long, breath-stopping moment he hung on to the net, waiting, then the deck came back up with all the strength of the next wave beneath it, slamming against the soles of his iron-nailed boots with a solid thud that vibrated right through him to the top of his skull. He grinned, relishing the stomach-churning thrill of the experience. One of these days he and the boat might well part company in such a sea, and he would either topple forward into the net, among the thrashing fish, or be carried straight to the seabed far below by the weight of his iron-studded boots. If that should happen he would not struggle, for it would be what fate had intended for him all along.

The next time the boat rolled Albert, too, was left

suspended in the water for long seconds before the deck heaved up beneath him, sending him staggering. He immediately announced that they were heading back.

'But the hold's not full,' James yelled against the banshee howling of the wind.

'I'm not minded to lose the boat for the sake of a few more cran of herring. We've enough fish. Jocky, Claik, down below with ye and get these engines going.'

'When did a fisherman ever have enough!' James shouted, and was ignored.

As they passed those boats still fishing the great stretch of the bank, every vessel heeling over sharply as its crew wrestled with the nets, James felt humiliated to be heading for safety. In his father's day, he raged inwardly as he and the others stored the buoys and, retrieving the nets from the hold, piled them to one side after the last of the fish had been shaken free, the *Fidelity* had been known to wallow back to port with her hold filled to capacity and her decks piled so high with baskets of fish that she was more often below the water than above it. To his mind it was a crime to own and skipper a good steam drifter like *Fidelity* and not use it properly. Albert, damn him, might as well own a wee rowing boat and a few lobster pots, for he'd no proper understanding of the way to treat a good vessel.

Davie Geddes came to mind, a man in his early sixties, still wiry and strong but beginning, by his own admission, to slow down. 'A man has to be fast on his feet and quick with his thinking if he's to face the sea on its own terms,' he had said when he and James met in the public house a few days before. 'Although the Lord's been good to me, I believe He's decided that the time's come for me to spend more of my energy on doing His work instead of my own.'

'You're looking for another crew member?' Unlike most fishermen, James was not a strong Christian and sometimes he found such talk confusing.

'I'm looking for a mate, lad. Johnny's the same age as myself, and to my mind there's nob'dy else in the crew ready to take on such responsibility yet. Since the Lord never saw fit to bless the wife and me with sons, I'm looking for a good man to sail with me during the next season so's he can get to know the boat, then he'll take it over when I leave. A man like yourself, James, though I doubt if you'd want to leave the family boat.'

Davie raised his brows when James said that he might be willing to make the change, but merely said, 'No hurry. We'll both think on it and pray for guidance, and when the answer's been given to each of us we can talk about it.'

It was a good offer; Davie's boat was sailed but sturdy, with years of good use in her yet. However, James knew that there would be a third member in the partnership – the God that Davie introduced into almost every sentence he spoke. James had heard that the old man led his crew in prayer before the nets were shot, and after they were hauled, no matter how great or small the catch. Davie's mate and partner would be expected to be a regular church-goer, which would please Stella, who had tried in vain when they first married to persuade her husband to attend Sunday worship with her.

Then there was the prospect of leaving *Fidelity* and giving up all hope of being her master. Putting a hand briefly on the mast as he straightened from working on the nets, James felt the heart of the boat throb and sing through the timber beneath his palm. His father had fallen in love with her at first sight, wooed her like a lover and bonded so strongly with her that flesh and wood had become one. James ached to do the same. It would be hard to leave her.

Once the work was done it was James's turn to rest. Bone-weary though he was, he tossed in his narrow bunk, the thud and judder of the engines echoing through his skull. Although the steam drifters were faster and their engines removed the punishing physical work of hoisting and trimming sails, they were not as comfortable as the sailed boats. Steam drifters tended to pitch and jar, while the constant noise from the engine made sleep difficult.

He sighed and crossed his arms behind his head. The bunk was narrow and uncomfortable, but at least he was alone in it. At home Stella would be asleep in their marriage bed, her soft rounded body heavy with their coming child. Or she might be awake, tending one of the twins or making a hot poultice for her father's chest. She had a sweet, caring nature but she was not the right woman for James Lowrie. He had never met the right woman, and perhaps he never would.

'There's times, Jess, when I fair envy you with your bairns and your grand-weans,' Meg Lowrie said as Innes went to the back yard to change out of his dirty overalls and get washed. 'Times I cannae help thinking that if things had been different I might have had young ones of my own.'

'Life treated you badly, Meg.' Jess touched her sister-in-law's large knuckly hand. Meg's young husband had been lost at sea just two weeks after their wedding and, since his body had never been recovered, she had never had the chance to say her last farewell or to have him laid to rest in a decent Christian fashion.

'Ach, it's the way things go.' Meg, never one to brood, shook off the sympathetic touch. 'At least I've always had my health and my strength. But I'd not have minded a nice laddie like your Innes. It was a great disappointment to Weem when the boy refused to crew on his boat.'

'He didn't refuse, Meg.' Jess fought to keep the anger from her voice. 'He did his best but he was so sick after those two voyages that I couldn't let him try again. If anyone was in the wrong, it was Weem for taking it so badly.'

'Everyone gets sick at first. It passes.'

'Not the way Innes was. If I'd let him go back to sea the way Weem wanted, the laddie might have died! And it's not as if he's a failure,' she insisted to Weem's sister, just as she had insisted it to Weem himself over and over again. 'Look how well he's done since, apprenticing himself to the blacksmith in Rathven, then being set up in his own wee workshop.'

'Aye, well, there's no sense in hashin' over the past, nor in you and me falling out over what might have been. I'd best be off, for I've got my own things to get ready for Yarmouth.' Meg groaned as she heaved her bulk from the chair, clapping a hand to the small of her back when she was upright. 'Packin' herrin's awful sore on the back. I'm fine when I'm sittin' down and I'm fine when I'm on my feet, but see that bit in atween? I feel as if someone's been usin' my spine to poke the fire!'

'D'you want me to come along tonight and rub some liniment on your back before you go to bed?'

'Would ye? That would be awful good of ye,' Meg said when Jess nodded. 'That's the worst of living alone – there's nob'dy tae give me a good rub when I need it.'

'You should be thinking of giving up work at your age.'

'Away you go . . . What would I do with myself if I wasnae at the farlins durin' the fishin'? Anyway, when we're away from home and livin' a'thegether in lodgings, there's aye someone there to rub my sore joints for me.' Meg laughed gustily. 'You should see us some nights, all standin' round in a circle with every one of us rubbin' away at the woman in front of her. We must be a sight!'

She was still chuckling wheezily when the latch was lifted and James walked into the kitchen. 'Is Innes about?'

'He's out the back. He'll be here in a minute.' Jess was flurried at the sight of her first-born, who only came to her house when necessary, now. The way he had breenged in as though he owned the place reminded her painfully of his father.

'I'm just sayin' to your mother, James, it's been good fishin' so far,' said Meg, seemingly unaware of the tension between mother and son.

'Aye, it has.' His grey eyes studied the air around the two women, never settling on one or the other.

'You'll be glad to get back to your own house for a wee while,' Jess put in. In the two months since the anniversary of Weem Lowrie's death the herring shoals had moved south to the Moray Firth, which meant that the Buckie men were able to work out of their home port for a short time before following the fish down the east coast to England. 'How's Stella, and the new wee bairn?'

'Fine.'

'I'll have to go and see them. What did you cry the wee one?' Meg wanted to know.

James's mouth opened then shut again, and it was left to his mother to supply the answer. 'Ruth. You're all right with the name, James? Stella said you'd not settled on one before you went to Caithness, and since she'd to get the wee one baptised . . .'

'It'll do,' James said. Then as Innes came into the kitchen, 'I've been waitin' for you,' he snarled, clearly relieved to be spared any more conversation. 'Come on outside for a minute.'

'What in the name's up with that man?' Meg asked as the brothers went through the street door.

'He's vexed at fatherin' another lassie.'

'There's nothin' wrong with lassies, I'm one myself,' Meg said vigorously, booted feet planted apart on the floor. She didn't look very feminine, being as sturdy and square-built as her two brothers, with a froth of grey curls rampaging over her head and round her weather-beaten face. 'And he should mind that every lassie that's birthed could be the mother of another good fisherman one day, not to mention becomin' a bonny worker at the nets or the farlins when she's old enough.'

'I know that, but after the twins were born Weem took

to jibing at James, and telling him that he'd not be a man until he'd fathered a son . . .'

'Ach, Weem's been dead and gone more than a year since! James is never still frettin' about it?'

'Things fester with him.'

Meg peered into her sister-in-law's face. 'God save us, Jess, you're not tellin' me that he's still angered with you because you put our Weem in the ground?'

'You surely saw for yourself just now that he can scarce bear to look at me, let alone talk to me.'

'That's nonsense!'

'But it's true that Weem always said the sea would take him in the end . . .'

'Aye, he did, but when his end came the sea thought otherwise. I'll have another cup of that tea if you don't mind, but I'll stand to drink it, for sittin' down again's not worth the bother. If the sea had wanted my brother it would've taken him and that's all there is to it,' Meg went on as Jess hurried to refill her cup. 'Just as it's wrong to claim a body back from the sea, it's wrong to put one in unwanted. James should know that.' She sucked noisily at her tea.

'Sometimes I think I made the wrong decision, Meg, but I couldn't bear the thought of being left with no grave to visit.'

'I know what you mean and you're quite right.' A shadow passed over Meg's face then cleared away as she said, 'It's time the lad let bygones be bygones.'

'You'll not say anything to him, will you? He's still missing his father and I don't want things to be made worse.'

'That's another thing he'll have to get over . . . and the rest of them as well. To tell the truth, Jess, I never thought it right for a man to be as caught up with his bairns as our Weem was.'

'He loved them, and they worshipped him!'

'That's what I mean. Birthin' and raisin's a woman's

job. It's the man's task tae provide for them, then set them to work when they're old enough.'

'Weem did provide for them, and very well too.'

'I never said he didnae.' Meg set her empty teacup down. 'But it sometimes seemed to me that everyone in this house was daft over the man, and he revelled in it for he was aye fond of himsel', was our Weem.'

'With good cause, for there were few men on the Moray coast to match him. And there was no harm in his children loving him, surely.'

'Fathers are for mindin' and respectin', no for lovin'. Albert's young ones never fussed over him the way Weem's did.'

'That's because Albert never raised any of his bairns, being a bachelor,' Jess pointed out a trifle tartly. 'They were all reared in different houses by their own mothers.'

'Aye, but at least he acknowledged every last one of them, and those two lads that work on the *Fidelity* with him are a credit to him. Just as your bairns are a credit to you, Jess,' Meg hastened to add. 'Give James time. He'll settle down and become his own man once he's got this nonsense about his father out of his head.'

'He'll have to,' Jess agreed. Her sister-in-law's words had hurt and worried her more than she was prepared to let on. It was true that Weem's children had adored him from birth, and he, unlike most men, had always found time for them. Jess had more than once consoled herself with the thought that even if her restless, energetic, handsome man ever tired of her – and she used every womanly wile she knew of to make sure that that didn't happen – he would never turn his back on his beloved children for the sake of another woman and another bed.

She had had no inkling, then, of the problems that would come later, as James, Bethany and Innes grew up and Weem, an ambitious man, began to use them to suit his own ends.

4

'Why me?' Innes felt as though an icy hand had reached deep into his body and caught his bowels in a painful grip.

'Who else?' James asked impatiently. 'You're good with engines . . . better than Jocky, for all that he thinks he's the best engine driver in the whole fleet.'

'I work with farm machinery and delivery vans, and mebbe a car now and again, not with drifters.' Innes, who had thought the September day mild until then, shivered and wished that he had had the sense to take his jacket from its hook as he followed his older brother out of the house.

'God's sake, man, an engine's an engine and you'd not want us off down the coast to Yarmouth with a faulty boat, would you?' James peered into his brother's face then gave a short bark of laughter. 'Is it being on the water that worries you? The boat's moored, and there's that many drifters crammed into the harbour with her that she couldnae sink even if the keel was ripped out of her. You'll be safe enough.'

The jeering note in his voice didn't bother Innes, for he had been so used before his father's death to hearing it day in and day out, every time Weem spoke to him. What bothered him was knowing that he couldn't refuse to go aboard the *Fidelity* and see to her engines, because she was the family's boat and he, together with his uncle, brother, sister and mother, was part-owner.

'Well . . . will you do it?'

'Aye, I'll do it.' The words came out with an effort, for his tongue felt as though it had swollen in his mouth. 'When d'you want me there?'

'Good man.' James's big hand landed painfully on his shoulder. 'Now's as good a time as any.'

Now! Innes swallowed hard, though there was nothing to swallow since his mouth had gone bone-dry. 'I'll . . . I'll have to get my jacket.'

'I'll see you down there, then.'

'Come in and wait. I'll not be a minute.'

'I've got things to do,' James said, and hurried off. The irony of the situation wasn't lost on Innes and, if he hadn't been so upset and worried, he might have been amused at the realisation that they were both scared: he at the prospect of going on board *Fidelity* and James at the thought of having to return to the house and make conversation with their mother.

Going back through the low doorway, Innes ran up against Meg's bulk on the way out and had to skip aside like a rowing boat giving way to a steamship. As she passed she gave his shoulder an affectionate pat, her hand as heavy and as strong as James's.

'I'll see you afore I'm off to Yarm'th, Innes,' she said, and went striding down the street, her steps as long as any man's.

In the kitchen Jess had set the flat-irons to heat on the range and was kneading the dough that had been left to rise. 'Where are you off to?' she wanted to know when her son, who had gone through to the back yard without a word, re-appeared in his oil-stained work over-alls.

'James wants me to have a look at the *Fidelity*'s engines.' His tongue still felt as though it belonged to someone else.

Jess looked up, consternation in her face. 'Is that what

he was here for? Will you be all right?' she asked when he nodded.

'I'll be fine. The boat's in the harbour, just. I'll mind and jump off if they start putting to sea.' He tried to make a joke of it, but knew as he felt the smile falter and tremble on his lips that he had failed miserably.

'Innes . . .'

'Keep my dinner hot, I'll be back for it,' he said swiftly and went out before she could say anything else. He had sheltered behind her skirts before, as his father had never tired of reminding him. Now he had to stand on his own two feet.

It wasn't easy. With every step of the short walk to the harbour the days, weeks and months seemed to fall away from him. He went from being an eighteen-year-old garage mechanic to a bairn in the old battered perambulator that had had the life knocked out of it by James and Bethany before he ever drew breath.

He had been too young at the time to put a sentence together or to toddle more than a few faltering steps, but even so he still remembered that bonny summer's day on the shore as vividly as if it had happened the week before. He remembered James hauling him out of the perambulator, clutching him round the waist, lugging him over the rocks to a little inlet where the water waited, lapping gently. Normally when older brothers and sisters tossed them into the sea the local bairns spluttered, floundered, then instinctively began to swim. But for some reason this instinct was lacking in Innes, who had spluttered, floundered, then gone down like a stone.

He could still recall with painful clarity the sea's dark-green chill and the way he had been imprisoned in it as though stoppered in a bottle made of thick, cold glass. He remembered the salty bite of the water flooding mercilessly into his mouth and his eyes, and filling his lungs when he tried to suck in air. He remembered the flashes of red light before his bulging eyes gradually dimming into blackness, and he very dimly remembered James, kneeling on the rocks and reaching deep into the waves, catching hold of him and hauling him out by the seat of his rompers.

He had been slung face down over a rock and his back pummelled until water rushed from every orifice in his body and, at last, his traumatised lungs managed to suck in their first breath of air. He had then been tossed into the perambulator by his irritated brother and trundled home, soaking and shivering, curly black hair plastered to his round little skull, too shocked to cry until James wheeled him into the kitchen and Innes caught sight of his mother, his beacon of safety. Then the floodgates had opened.

Innes had never again gone swimming, even when he was much older and all the other lads stripped off on hot summer days to plunge in from the rocks, or from moored rowing boats in the harbour.

'Ach, it's no loss,' his father, sorry for him at first, had said when James and Bethany jeered. 'What use is swimmin' to a fisherman anyway? If you go off the boat, the sea fills your boots and takes you down whether you can swim or not. You're better to go peaceably.'

His rough kindness only made things worse for Innes, for the words burned themselves into his brain through all the years of growing up. Like his brother and his father, and his forebears for generations before him, Innes was destined to be a fisherman when he turned fifteen. There was no question of getting out of it. And he knew, through the days and years, that when the time came he would, sooner or later, feel the cold, salty water rushing into his heavy, nail-studded boots as he went down and down into the green bottle that had been waiting to reclaim him.

As he turned the corner and saw the harbour he stopped short, the breath leaving him. All four basins were crammed with vessels, mainly steam drifters but with a sprinkling of the sailed Zulus that had been the mainstay of the Scottish fishing industry before steam arrived. There were so many of them that it would have been difficult to squeeze in a toy yacht – every one of them swarming with men painting, or cleaning out the holds, or storing the great drift-nets aboard.

The very sight of the boats brought a rush of sour bile into Innes's mouth and he had to turn his head aside and spit it out against a wall. His first terrible trip to sea had been at the opening of the season, and from the moment the engines started, the stench of fish and stale sea water from the bilges had set him vomiting even before they cleared the harbour entrance.

'Ach, it's always like that when the boat's been lying idle,' his cousin Charlie had told him as Innes hung over the side, retching. 'It's a filthy stink, but once she's been washed through by a couple of good hard seas it'll clear.'

It was true that by the time she was halfway to the fishing grounds the boat smelled much sweeter, but that stink had lingered on in Innes's memory for all of that voyage and all of the next, and for months after his father had given up on him as a seaman. Now the sight of the boats cramming the harbour vividly brought back the memory.

He would have turned tail and run for home there and then if James, who had been waiting for him on the harbour, hadn't grabbed at his arm. 'Come on, then.'

'Where is she?'

'There, can you not see her at the other side? We were lucky to get her by the harbour wall. We'll go across the other boats.'

Innes shied back. 'I'll walk round.'

'Oh, for . . .' The grip on his arm tightened, forcing him towards the nearest boat. 'It's quicker this way. Don't worry,' James said, the sneer back in his voice, 'I'll see that you don't get your precious feet wet!'

To James, who would have swum the harbour without a second thought, crossing it by scrambling from boat to boat was no trouble at all; but Innes – his stomach lurching with every faint movement beneath his feet, every rasp of hull rubbing against hull, every glimpse of black water below – felt as though an eternity passed before he finally arrived safely on the deck of the *Fidelity* to be met by his uncle Albert Lowrie and the engine driver, who was black with oil.

'I've tried everythin' but I'm no sure that I've got it right,' the man said. 'You'd best come below and see for yersel'.'

Engines, Innes told himself as he scrambled down into the boat's bowels. Just think about the engines. Sure enough, at the sight and smell of the compound steam engine everything else faded into the background and the mechanic in him took over.

Half an hour later, when his uncle Albert said, 'You're a grand clever lad, right enough,' Innes, on his knees among the engine parts, lifted a hot, oil-streaked face and grinned up at him. The problem had been found and resolved and he had enjoyed every minute of the work.

'It wasn't that difficult.'

'You'll come and have a drink with us.'

'Of course he will.' James, who disliked the smell of oil and the cramped conditions of the engine room, was in a hurry to lead the way back on deck.

Following him, no longer occupied by thoughts of the machinery, Innes suddenly became aware of the slap and thud of water against the wooden hull only inches away from where he stood, and of the slight motion of the boards underfoot. Memories rushed back, swamping and paralysing his mind. All at once the low-roofed space he stood in was no longer the engine room but the rope locker, a tiny cupboard immediately below the forrard deck, where the messenger warp had to be coiled as it brought the nets inboard. Whenever he thought of Hell he visualised it as that little cupboard where he had crawled round and round in the cramped darkness, wretched with sea-sickness, tugging at the thick, wet, slimy rope that smelled of the sea's depths and fought against him, almost as though it wanted to return there, pulling back out of the slot it had been fed through, slithering over the deck and splashing into the waiting waves and down to the seabed. And the worst horror of all was that it seemed to Innes as he wrestled with it that the rope wanted to take him with it.

Hour upon hour he had struggled, his arms feeling as though they were being wrenched out of their sockets, his lungs labouring in the stuffy, smelly atmosphere, his clothes slick and filthy with grease and dirt. It had been like being buried alive; the stamp and clatter of feet on the deck just above his head as his father, his brother and the rest of the crew fought to drag the big nets, heavy with sea-harvest, inboard had become the sound of people jumping on his coffin lid to hold it down and keep him imprisoned within. And all the time the boat rolled and tossed, throwing Innes against the wooden walls and then, before he could gather his wits, hurling him back, to sprawl against the coiled rope that took up more and more of the limited space as it continued to slither in.

The mercy, if there was any at all, was that he had already emptied his stomach long since, so although he retched continuously there was nothing left to bring up. Had there been, he would have had no option but to crawl through it.

As he now followed James out on to the deck the nightmare of remembering went on. Once the nets had finally been hauled aboard and he was allowed to stagger on to the deck to breathe in some fresh air, the sight of the tossing sea, the desperate leaping of the silver herring as the last of them were shaken from the nets into the hold, and the frosting of fish-scales and blood on his fellow crew members' hands and clothes, faces and hair had set Innes's tormented stomach off again. He remembered his father's big hands plucking him off the

deck where he sprawled and holding him over the side of
the boat, suspended above the sea while the icy spray was
tossed into his face with each roll of the drifter. And even
worse than the conviction that he was going to fall from
his father's grasp and be sucked down was the contempt
in Weem Lowrie's voice from above Innes's head, 'For
God's sake will ye behave like a man instead of a wee
lassie? I'm sick with shame over ye!'

Aware of the familiar clenching in his gut, desperate
to get off the boat and on to solid land, Innes now strode
across the deck, almost falling headlong over a rope being
coiled by his cousin Charlie, Albert's oldest by-blow.

'Mind out,' the man said, amiably enough, but the
only voice Innes could hear in his mounting panic was
his father's. 'Call yourself a son of mine? Call yourself
a Buckie man? If ye cannae go to sea ye might as well
go to Hell!'

Fortunately the boat's holds were empty and she was
riding high on a full tide, which meant that the deck and
gangplank were more or less level with the harbour wall.
Even so, halfway along the narrow plank Innes stumbled
and almost lost his balance. Arms flailing, he looked down
and, at the sight of the water below, his mind froze with
sheer terror.

'Not so fast, man,' his uncle admonished from far away,
then a hand thumped him between the shoulder blades,
propelling him willy-nilly along the last section of plank
to stumble on to the flagstones. 'You were takin' it like
a bull at a gate,' Albert Lowrie said amiably, fetching up
alongside his nephew. 'That's no way to do it.'

James, scorning the plank, balanced a foot on the
bulwarks and gained the harbour with one long stride.
'Aye, Innes, you shouldnae be showing off like that,' he
chimed in as he landed lightly beside them. 'You might
have fallen in and got yourself all wet.'

He too sounded amiable, but Innes knew without having
to look that his brother's grey eyes were glittering with

contempt, an expression that he well remembered. Even Bethany had looked at him like that, bitterly resenting the fact that her younger brother should hate the sea when she, who loved it, was denied his chances just because she was a girl.

Innes clenched his fists in his pockets and wished that he had the courage to knock the sneer from James's face. 'I'll have a drink . . . if you're putting a hand in your pocket to buy it for me,' he told his brother grimly.

'Good man. Charlie, Jem, you're comin'?' Albert hailed his sons. 'And fetch Jocky and the rest along with ye.'

The small public house was filled with fishermen standing shoulder to shoulder, as close-packed as herring in a barrel. Used as they were to living in crowded conditions at sea, none of them was bothered about the darkness and the lack of space; at first Innes was keenly aware of it, but his first pint, hurriedly downed, hit the pit of his stomach and sent a calming glow through him, easing tense muscles. When Albert insisted on buying another round, Innes nodded and held out his empty tankard, aware of his brother's watchful eyes, knowing that James fully expected him to turn tail and run for home as soon as he could. After what he had been through, he needed a good drink.

When Innes and his drinking cronies emerged two hours later night had fallen. Bidding the others an affectionate farewell, he reeled and lurched along Main Street, weaving from one side of the narrow road to the other. He had done it. He had gone on board the *Fidelity*, and he had repaired her engines and had drunk shoulder to shoulder with the fishermen. Taking two shots at the latch before managing to lift it, he gained entry to the house in a fine mood.

It was well past the dinner hour, but Jess said nothing as her son wafted into the kitchen on an alcoholic cloud. This had happened so many times in her life with Weem

and James, who worked hard, pitting themselves against
the might and moods of the sea and were entitled, in her
view, to take their ease in their own ways when they
were ashore.

'You fixed the engines, then?' she said calmly, putting
his dinner on the table.

'Aye.' He had slumped down in a fireside chair, heedless for once of his dirty overalls, and was making a stab
at taking his boots off. 'James and Uncl' Al . . . Uncl'
Albish took me for a wee drink after.' He belched, gave
up on the boots and leaned back in his chair. 'I'll see to
these later.'

'It was the least they could do, since you were such
a help to them.' Jess knelt down and unlaced his boots
with practised skill. When she stood up she saw that
he had fallen asleep, his head lolling against the back
of the chair, one arm hanging over the side, his mouth
wide open.

She covered his food and put it back in the oven, then
picked up her knitting, marvelling at the way grown men
could revert to the innocence of their childhood when
relaxed in sleep.

He gave a slight snore, then came another, louder this
time, while Jess's hands flew over the wool on her lap, the
knitting growing fast. Soon she would walk along the road
to Meg's single-roomed home and rub her sister-in-law's
aching back, but for the moment it was pleasant to sit
quietly with only the ticking of the clock and her son's
snoring for company. It was a bit of a worry about her
good chair and his dirty overalls, but she was reluctant
to disturb him.

She didn't grudge him the drink or the dinner, carefully
prepared and now ruined, for she knew what an effort it
must have been for him to go on board the *Fidelity* that
afternoon to see to the engines. Although every fisherman,
even Weem and James, suffered from sea-sickness when
they first began their trade, it had been different with

Innes. Weem had refused to listen to her when she voiced her fears after the boy came home from his first trip, tense and nervy, his eyes little more than haunted pits in a white face.

'We all have to find our sea-legs, and he's no different,' Weem had insisted, and Innes was dragged off on another voyage. This time when he returned he was unable to eat or sleep, waking the rest of the family from their own much-needed slumber with his nightmares. Noting how he jumped and quivered at every sound, especially his father's voice, and seeing the way his hands and mouth trembled when they should have been in repose, Jess had refused to let Innes return to the boat. It was one of the worst quarrels she and Weem had ever had, but she had won, though he never forgave her for coming between him and his son. Although Innes had then found work in the garage and had done well for himself, Weem had never stopped thinking of him as a coward, hiding behind his mother's skirts.

At least, Jess thought, getting up to fetch the ointment needed for Meg's sore back, she had made sure that Weem – who had loved his children so deeply when they were small, and had used them with such a lack of understanding once they reached adulthood – did not manage to destroy Innes the way he had destroyed James and Bethany.

5

'James thinks this year's fishing'll be just as good down in England,' Stella said as the Lowrie women – Jess, Bethany, Meg and Stella herself – mended the nets.

'It's to be hoped so.' Meg plied her needle busily. 'We could all do with a good bit put by for the winter.'

The four of them were in James's net loft, sitting cross-legged with a great stretch of net spread over the floor between them. From below, where old Mowser had been coaxed into keeping an eye on the five children, they could hear the continuous murmur of Rory's voice. As they worked, the women frequently wiped their hands on their aprons, and Stella had set two buckets of fresh water within easy reach, for the men had seen a lot of scalders among the summer catches. When the nets dried, fragments of jellyfish still adhering to them turned to a powder that stung the hands and burned like pepper if it got into unwary eyes.

September was a busy month, for the English winter fishing was about to begin and provisions had to be arranged, nets checked and mended, engines overhauled or, for those who still used the graceful, efficient Zulus for their fishing, sails readied in preparation for the journey south to Grimsby, Lowestoft and Yarmouth.

Jess had always found net-mending a soothing occupation and she loved the companionship and the bustle at this time of year. Once, she had gone south too as one of the guttin quine, until the year when Weem Lowrie first noticed her in Yarmouth. A year later, when he left in his father's sailed Zulu for the fishing grounds, Jess had had to wave him goodbye from the harbour wall, with small James straddling her hip and the tears choking her at the thought of being without her man for weeks.

'We'll have a cup of tea,' Meg suggested, putting her needle aside. She made to get up then stopped, wincing, one hand flying to the small of her back.

'Is that lumbago bothering you again?'

'Just a wee twinge. That salve you put on it made a difference.'

'Sit where you are and I'll see to the tea.' Jess put her own needle down and went to the ladder. The children, bored with their games, greeted her with yells of joy and Mowser, brightening at the sight of her, got out of his chair remarkably quickly. 'I'll just take a turn for you,' he said, and made for the ladder, pathetically eager to play his part in the preparations.

Growing old was a terrible thing, Jess thought as she measured tea into the big pot. Bad enough for a woman, but worse for a man who had once fought the sea as a living, only to find himself eventually reduced to the status of child minder. Mowser Buchan had been a fine, handsome man in his time, but the loss of all three of his sons in the one storm, followed within a twelvemonth by the death of his wife, had taken a heavy toll on the man. Years of hard work had carved themselves deeply into him, and now he was bowed, slow-moving and suffered badly from bronchial problems. The luxuriant moustache that had given him his nickname was still there, but nowadays it was yellow from the pipe Mowser smoked and dominated the shrunken face behind it.

The womenfolk, normally never allowed to set foot on a fishing boat for fear that they would bring bad luck and poor catches, came into their own when the boats were

being 'rigged out' for the journey south. Then they were
allowed to go on board, armed with buckets of water and
scrubbing brushes, to turn out cupboards and clear every
corner of dust and dirt. It was a matter of pride with
them to keep the Scottish fishing boats free of diseases
that thrived in dirty conditions.

For once, working together at the net-mending and then
cleaning out *Fidelity*, Jess and her daughter were freed of
the awkwardness that had crippled them since Bethany's
marriage. They even laughed at times as they carried the
long sacks of chaff that served as mattresses up on deck
to air them, before giving the cabins fore and aft a good
redding out.

Slipping sidelong glances at her daughter as they brushed
and scrubbed, Jess knew that this was where Bethany was
happiest, on board the *Fidelity*. Like her father and her
elder brother she was a child of the sea, treating it with
respect but without fear. Jess would never forget the day
a neighbour had come to her door to ask if she knew that
three-year-old Bethany was swimming off one of the creel
boats in the harbour with the laddies. Rushing from the
house with Innes in her arms, Jess had discovered her
daughter, stripped to her drawers and semmit, balancing
precariously on the edge of the boat while James and some
other boys cheered her on, treading water. As Jess watched
in horror, Bethany had leaped into the deep black water,
surfaced, paddled like a dog to the mooring rope, then
moved deftly hand-over-hand along it back to the boat,
where she clambered aboard, punted up from behind by
two of the boys, and went through the whole process again.

To Jess's fury Weem, coming back from the fishing
grounds to find Bethany moping and scowling because she
had been forbidden to swim again, scooped his beloved
daughter into his arms and told her that she was a fine
wee lassie and her daddy's pride and joy. He even gave
her permission to return to her swimming and, as she
scampered off, barefoot and wearing one of Jess's pinnies

pinned between her legs in place of her underclothes, he shrugged off his wife's protests.

'She's got courage, that one. I'm right proud of her.'

'She's only a baby yet. She could drown!'

'If the sea takes her it'll be because she belongs to it,' Weem said calmly. 'You know that, Jess. We don't want to mollycoddle the lassie.'

By the time she started school Bethany was an accomplished swimmer and more of a daredevil than most of the boys. Most of her time was spent at the harbour, and when her father was home she hung on his every word.

It was a pity, Jess thought as they shook the chaff mattresses out on the deck, then dragged them below to the bunks, that Bethany hadn't been born the boy and Innes the girl. It was a cruel twist of fate that had given him such a fear of the sea and her such a love of it. When she was grown, the girl had tried repeatedly to get her father to take her on a fishing trip, but without success.

'Women don't belong on the boats,' he said each time she asked, coaxed or demanded. 'It would bring bad luck, same as meetin' the man in black . . .' The word 'minister' was never mentioned in Weem's house, let alone on board his boat, for fear of bringing bad luck to the fishing.

'Why should James get to go to sea and not me?'

'Because you're a girl,' taunted James, now out of school and sailing with his father.

'I'd be better than you!'

'You'll still be part of the fishin',' her father had tried to console her. 'You'll work at one of the net factories, and when you're old enough you can go to the farlins with your Aunt Meg. And that's an end of it,' he added sharply as Bethany opened her mouth again. Later, he had told Jess, 'That lass of ours is gettin' too big for her boots. You've spoiled her.'

Jess, knowing her man well, had not bothered to argue.

'At least the cabins smell a sight better than they did,' she said now, as they climbed back to the deck.

'Aye, for a wee while. You go on ahead,' Bethany said as they were about to cross over the intervening boats to get to the harbour. 'I'll just give the wheel-house another going over.'

Alone in the small wheel-house, she put her work-reddened hands on the wooden spokes, settled her feet firmly into the decking and closed her eyes, giving herself over to the gentle motion of the boat and the soft thud of water against the hull. For a long time she stood there, motionless, and she might have stayed all afternoon, heedless of her duties ashore and of the children, waiting for her at Stella's house, if booted feet hadn't thudded on to the deck.

'Still here?' James asked, surprised, as she emerged from the wheel-house. 'I thought you'd be done long since.'

'I was just finishing. That's you ready to go south, then?'

'Aye, if Uncle Albert can be persuaded to stir his fat carcass.' His mouth took on a sour twist. 'If it was left to him, the boat would never leave harbour.' He looked restlessly around the deck, then at the other boats crammed into the harbour. 'And if it was left to me we'd be at sea all the time.' He gave her a quick, conspiratorial grin. 'I never was one for the fireside and bairns.'

'Neither am I,' Bethany said sharply, irritated by what she saw as his smug attitude. 'But some of us have no other choice.'

The grin faded. 'What's wrong with you now?'

'Think it out for yourself,' Bethany snapped, scorning the point where the next boat rubbed gently against *Fidelity*. Instead she moved to a spot where there was quite a gap to cross, then placed one foot on the gunnels and leaped out across the black water below, her skirt swirling about her legs. Running across the deck, she repeated the leap a few more times until she had crossed the other boats and gained the harbour.

As she reached the street a cart passed with several chattering children perched on its load of nets. The carter, a man who had often let Bethany and James ride his cart on top of the piled nets when they were younger, called out, 'Want a lift, lass?'

All at once the thought of going back to Stella's house to collect her step-children was more than Bethany could bear. She almost ran to clamber up on to the narrow seat by his side, then common sense prevailed. It would not be the done thing for Gil Pate's wife to behave like a foolish bairn in public.

She shook her head, then stood in the middle of the road watching the cart trundle away towards the cutching yard, where the nets would be dipped in tanks of boiling water and tannin to season and strengthen them, then spread out or hung up to dry.

Then, slowly and reluctantly, she made her way back to Stella's house.

James, watching his sister storm off the harbour, saw her pause when the carter called to her. For a moment, as her lithe body lifted and half-turned on her toes, he thought that she was going to run to the cart and climb aboard the piled nets. But instead she settled back on her heels and stood watching as the cart went on its way. When it was out of sight she turned and walked slowly away, head lowered, all the fire and anger quenched.

He tried to fathom out the mystery of what had happened to Bethany as he went below to the fore-cabin, which smelled strongly of soap and disinfectant underlaid by the odour of fish and bilge water. Once she had been as good as any lad, clambering over the rocks without a thought of danger, swimming off the boats in the outer harbour basin, climbing trees and fishing, playing kick-the-can and football while all the other lassies were

contented with their dolls and peevers and skipping ropes.
She had been a bonny fighter too, had Bethany. Nobody
ever picked a fight with her more than once. Even James
himself had had his nose bloodied by her small, sharp-
knuckled fists.

It had been a grand childhood, but in growing up they
had also grown apart. He had been too busy making the
transition from laddie to man, too cock-a-hoop and full
of himself to give much thought to his sister.

His mouth twisted derisively at the memory of himself
only a few years ago, swaggering about Buckie in his
good blue jacket and his cheese-cutter cap, enjoying the
way the lassies fluttered their eyelashes at him when he
went to the dancing. He had had his pick of them in those
days, and he had made the most of his popularity. And
now look at him!

It had all gone sour since the very moment of his
father's death. James groaned and slumped back on the
narrow bunk, remembering Weem, washed and dressed
in his good suit by the womenfolk, then laid out in his
coffin quiet and still, with two pennies to close his eyelids
and a patterned kerchief tied about his jaw.

The neighbours had crowded in to pay their respects,
bringing with them dishes and bowls of food, and when
they were gone and Jess had been persuaded to rest, James
and his uncle and Innes and Gil Pate had kept Weem
company. All through that long, silent night James had
been unable to take his eyes from the open casket or close
his ears to the clamour of his father's voice, reproaching
him for bringing him back from the sea and forcing him to
be the centrepiece of this circus of ritual mourning, when
he should have been beneath the waves, at one with the
fish that had been his livelihood.

When James had returned to the house after the funeral,
uncomfortable in his best suit with its stiff collar and his
shining, tight-fitting black shoes, Bethany had opened the
door to him, her mouth hard and her grey eyes glowing like

two hot coals as though she, too, blamed her brother for not having had the courage and the wit to bundle their father's body over the side of the boat when he died, even if it had meant locking his arms about the corpse and going down with it. She had stepped back without a word and he had walked past her and into the kitchen, coming face-to-face with his mother and turning away at once, unable to look her in the eye and forgive her for the wrong she had done Weem Lowrie.

The chasm that had opened between him and his mother was one thing, but Bethany's rejection was another. It bothered James, who was sorely in need at times of someone to talk to openly and honestly. Innes, having turned his back on the sea, did not count, but Bethany might well have been that person if she hadn't changed so much.

It might not just be him that she disliked now, he reasoned. She tended to glare at everyone these days, even poor Gil Pate, a decent enough man and a good, providing husband. Women! Stella and his mother and the bairns and Bethany . . . the sooner he was off to Yarmouth, the better.

Back home, he went up to the net loft after he had eaten. There was nothing left to do . . . *Fidelity*'s nets were all mended and neatly stacked for the trip down south, and the ropes checked and coiled, but he enjoyed pottering about the place inhaling the smell of ropes and creels and baskets and canvas, free of the need to make conversation.

'Can I give ye a hand, son?'

James felt his heart sink as old Mowser came wheezing and gasping up the narrow ladder.

'I was just having a look at the lines.' In an attempt to look busy James dragged out a basket of the long lines used for catching white fish – cod, ling, skate, whiting, haddock and halibut – in the early part of the year before the herring began to run, and pretended to be inspecting it closely.

'I'll see to them while you're off in Yarm'th, never worry about that.' Mowser settled himself on the scarred old box that had once carried all his clothes and personal possessions when he was at sea, scrabbling in his pocket for his pipe, matches and baccy pouch. When the pipe was packed and lit and drawing to his satisfaction he blew a long stream of pale smoke towards the rafters, gave a thoughtful 'Aye . . .' and launched into a monologue of memories, as he always did whenever he caught James's attention for a moment.

The smell of the tobacco mingled pleasantly with the other aromas in the loft and the old man's wheezy voice, interrupted now and then by a bout of coughing and spitting, was not intrusive. He didn't need to be listened to, for he was quite happy to ramble on without any contribution from his audience. Gradually James gave up the pretence of work and settled on the floor with his back against the wall, elbows on knees and hands idle for once, letting Mowser's creaky voice wash over him without bothering to listen.

Below, he could hear the twins squealing and giggling as Stella bathed them before the kitchen fire. The baby began to cry and was hushed, and after a while he heard his wife singing a lullaby, an indication that the twins were in their bed and close to sleep.

'. . . one of the worst storms I ever encountered.' Mowser's frail voice drifted in the air like his pale-blue tobacco smoke. 'Three boats lost from this coast on that one night, one of them takin' my uncle and two cousins with it. And me just a laddie new to the sea, certain sure that I'd be down deep among the fishes come the morn . . .'

James felt a stab of pity for the old man, dependent on his daughter's husband for bed and board, with nothing to do but while the long days away down by the harbour, where he exchanged memories with old fishermen like himself and watched younger, fitter men take the boats through the entrance and out towards the horizon.

But at least Mowser had food and shelter, a fireside to sit by at nights and money for baccy. Unlike Weem, he had reached a good age and survived a lifetime spent at the whim of the sea. One day if he lived long enough, James reasoned, he himself would be in the same position. And it might well be the very same position, for the way things were going there would be no sons to be taught the way of the fishing. He might well have to live under a son-in-law's roof as Mowser did now, feeble and dried up and dandling grand-bairns on his knee.

He scrambled to his feet, suddenly anxious to get out of the house, then said diffidently, 'D'you want to come down to the pub for a drink?'

'Eh?' Mowser blinked at him, then his lined face lit up. 'Aye, son, I'd like that fine.'

Albert, at the bar, greeted them noisily and insisted on buying their drinks. The three of them retired to a table, but half an hour later Albert announced that he had to go.

'A wee matter of business,' he said, with a wink and a leer.

'Daft bugger,' Mowser said blandly when Albert had gone. 'I had him as a deckhand on my own boat once, as a favour to his father. Albert wasnae long out of school at the time, and he'd already got a lassie in trouble. Since her father was on the same boat, and he was too good a man to lose, I took Albert till the fuss died down.' He shook his head. 'I was glad to get shot of him – a useless loon, and lazy intae the bargain. The only part of him that was willin' to work was in his trousers.'

'He's not changed.'

'Why d'you put up with him then?' Mowser asked bluntly.

'I've not much choice, seeing it's the family boat and he's older than me.'

'Did your own father's share not go to you?' the old
man asked, and James shook his head.

'I already had a one-third share, from selling . . .' He
stopped short, and Mowser nodded.

'I know, lad, from selling my boat. A bonny Zulu, she
was. The way things have worked out you might have
been better keeping her and turning your back on the
Fidelity.'

James looked at him with new respect. 'Aye, I should
have, but we never know what lies ahead. Anyway, my
father's share went to the rest of them – my mother and
Bethany and Innes.'

'And that's why you're stuck with Albert. I've often
wondered.' Mowser drained his glass noisily and set it
down. 'Have you never thought that if you could get
the three of them to go along with you, you'd have
two-thirds of the boat? Then you'd be able to put Albert
in his place.'

As James stared at him in dawning realisation, Mowser
sniffed, scrubbed the back of a knotted hand across the
underside of his thick yellow moustache and pushed the
glass across the scarred table. 'I'll have another pint, son,
since you're in a buying mood.'

'It was nice of you to take Da out for a drink,' Stella
said when the old man had gone off to his bed. 'He fairly
enjoyed it.'

'He's good company.'

She smiled at him across Ruth's head as the baby sucked
noisily, starfish hands the size of seashells spread over the
blue-veined curve of her mother's full breast. Suddenly
sated, she fell asleep, her slack mouth falling away from
the nipple; Stella used one corner of her shawl to wipe a
dribble of milk from the little chin.

'You're fretting to get to Yarmouth.'

'The sooner we go, the more herring we catch and the
more money to see us through the winter.'

'Aye.' She gave a little sigh, and he knew that she was thinking of the weeks ahead, without him. But that was the way it was for a fisherman's wife. 'Are you coming to bed?' she asked, drawing back the curtain that hung by day across the wall-bed, and reaching in for her night-gown.

'In a minute.' James poked the fire into a red glow, half-aware of the soft sounds of his wife undressing. Then he got abruptly to his feet and reached for his jacket.

'You're not going out at this time of night, surely?' In the long gown, with her hair loose and falling about her shoulders, she looked like a lassie just on the verge of womanhood, rather than the mother of three children.

'Just for a wee while.'

He knew, as he went out of the door, that she would still be awake when he returned, unable to sleep until he was home. The knowledge that she cared for him so much was one of the many burdens he had to carry.

6

Gil had every right to go out in the evenings. Men who worked hard to support their families were entitled to relax once the long day's work was done, their stomachs full of good food cooked by their womenfolk, a pint mug in their hands, in the company of other men. It was what Bethany's own father had done almost every evening when he was ashore and, until her own marriage, she had taken that male right for granted.

Now, throwing down her knitting and staring round the kitchen's four walls, she asked herself if it was fair. It was true that her man had been working all day, but so had she: cooking and cleaning and washing and ironing, blacking the range and scrubbing the front doorstep and seeing to his two children. And where was the relaxation for her? Here she was, bored and alone, with no chance of getting out of the house for a breath of fresh air and nobody to talk to. Not that she wanted any more of the sort of talk she got from the likes of Stella, all about bairns and recipes and knitting patterns.

Rising to pace about the small room, she thought longingly of the days when she had been free to earn her own money and live her own life. It had been hard work, in the net factory during the winter months and at the farlins during the summer and autumn herring fishing, but it had been good, too, specially at the farlins, with the fishermen and coopers and curers and buyers all around, and the other women, with their lively minds and quick tongues. At the end of the day, hands stinging and back aching, she had slept soundly, drugged by the fresh air and happy in the knowledge that she had done a good day's work and earned a day's wage. Now, although she was kept busy from morning to night, she had lost the deep, almost exhilarating exhaustion of the old days and her sleep was continuously broken by demands either from Gil or from one of his children.

By the time he rolled in through the door, flushed and smelling of beer and in high humour, she was almost at her wits' end with frustration.

'I'm going to take a turn down by the harbour.' She reached for her shawl.

'At this time of night? I'm ready for my bed . . . and a bonny, willing wife to share it.' His voice and his look were both heavy with meaning.

'In a minute. I'll not be long.' She put a hand to the door latch, anxious to get out before he delayed her further. He had had a lot to drink; she estimated that he would be asleep and snoring in ten minutes, which would suit her fine.

'Make sure of it.' He collapsed into his usual chair and made an unsuccessful stab at untying his shoelaces. 'Give me a hand with them before you go, pet,' he begged plaintively, and when Bethany left the door and went to kneel before him he put a hand on her bright chestnut hair, his fingers slipping round to stroke her cheek. 'My wee birdie,' he said thickly, then, 'I was speakin' to your James tonight.'

'And drinking with him, I'll be bound.' One shoe was off, but the lace of the other was knotted. Bethany pulled at it, cursing below her breath.

'Your Uncle Albert's fair driving him mad. He thinks he could do better.'

'He probably could. He's a good seaman, James.' But

not as good as she would have been, given the chance, she thought, fiddling with the obstinate lace.

'You know how James owns a third share in th' boat, an' you an' yer mother an' Innes hold another third between ye . . .' Gil paused, brow knotted, trying to puzzle out the next part of the sentence.

'Aye, and Uncle Albert has a third share. What about it?'

'Well, James thinks . . . and so do I, mind, so do I,' Gil slurred solemnly above her head, 'that if he'd control over the other third – the shares you an' yer mother an' Innes have – that would make him a maj-majority holder. Then he'd be able tae give Albert the orders for a change. D'you see what I'm trying to tell ye?'

'Of course I see, I'm not stupid.'

'I knew you'd understand, lass. You always had a good head on your bonny shoulders.' Gil reached down to caress the shoulders in question. 'So I told him he was welcome to make use of your share.'

Bethany left the knot and sat back on her haunches, staring up at him. 'You told him what?'

'That he could have your share of the boat. That way he's got a bit more say in the run . . .' He stopped as she jumped to her feet.

'What right do you have to say a thing like that? Behind my back, too. How could you!'

'Eh?' Her husband peered myopically up at her through a drunken haze.

'James already has a share in the *Fidelity* and he's not having mine as well. It's all I've got, d'you not see that?'

'But you'll still get the money, pet, I made sure of . . .'

'You daft gowk, it's not the money I care about, it's the boat! Here.' Bethany stooped, picked up the shoe she had just taken off his foot and tossed it at him. It cracked against his shin and bounced to the floor. 'You can just put that on and go and tell him you'd no right to make decisions for me!'

Gil rubbed at his leg. 'I'll do nothing of the sort. D'you think I want him to see me as a weakling who takes orders from his wife?'

'He can see you any way he likes, but he's not getting my share of the *Fidelity*!' Knowing that if she stayed a moment longer she would probably strike him, Bethany stormed out of the house, ignoring Gil's shouted order to stay where she was. As she slammed the door behind her she heard the wail of a child wakened abruptly from sleep. Let him see to his own bairns for once, she thought, striding off into the night. She had had more than enough of domesticity.

Although most of the houses she passed were in darkness, a light still burned in James's kitchen window. Bethany raised her fist to give the door a hefty thump, then paused. She was in the mood for a good quarrel, but if she started one in front of Stella and her father she would upset them, not to mention rousing the children. Best to wait until the next day and catch him on his lone. There was no fear that her anger would cool completely in the interim; it glowed in the depths of her mind like a fire that had been banked up to nurse its heat for hours and burn brightly again when needed.

She turned away and went on along the coast road, making up her mind to walk until she was too tired to think. That way she would be sure to stay out until long past the time Gil was asleep, which suited her, for the thought of being fondled and used by him that night was beyond bearing.

Heartened by his conversation with Gil the night before, James went first thing the next morning to the smiddy – an apt place, he thought as he heard the jingle of a harness and the nervous stamp of hooves in the blacksmith's shop, for wasn't he here with the intention of striking while the iron was hot?

There was a smile on his face as he marched into the

adjoining workshop to put his proposal to his younger brother, but it faded when Innes, having heard him out, said uncomfortably, 'I don't know, James.'

'Why not? We all know that you've no interest at all in the boat.' James could have bitten his tongue out as he saw the colour rise in the younger man's face. 'Not that that's wrong,' he hastened to add. 'Each to his own. And I give you my word that if you put your share of *Fidelity* in my name I'll see to it that you get your money just the same.'

'I'm not bothered about the payment, for mine all goes to Ma.'

'Well then! You're a landsman, Innes, and I'm a seaman. I earn my living and support my family from my work on that boat, and that's why I need to have more say in the way she's used.' James swallowed and ran a finger round his collar. 'How can you stand the heat in here? And there's scarce room to move. It's like being buried alive.'

'I'm used to it. Here . . .' Innes poured water from a jug into a chipped mug. 'You need to drink plenty, it makes the heat more bearable.'

The water was lukewarm and tasted stale, but at least it moistened James's dry throat. He drained the mug, wondering what sort of man Innes was to want to spend his days in this place. To his own mind the cramped, wet rope room below the *Fidelity*'s foredeck held more appeal.

Innes fidgeted nervously with a spanner. This workshop was his own private world, where he was happiest, and now James, who had never before entered this place, was destroying the peace he always found there. He wished that his brother would just go, but instead James wiped his mouth with the back of his hand and returned to his argument.

'When the boat was first bought, Da and Uncle Albert and me were equal partners, all of us free to speak our minds and have our say. But now that Da's gone and

Albert's running the boat his way there's wrong decisions being made. Albert hasn't got half the brains Da had.'

'Or you have?'

James flushed at the note in his brother's voice. 'I'm a good fisherman and there's plenty folk would tell you that,' he countered sharply. 'And I've more sense than Albert, for my father taught me well. Bethany's already agreed to give me her share, and with yours and Ma's I'll own more of the boat than Albert does. Then I'll be the skipper and he can go back to being the mate. He'll not mind that – it's always been easier for him to let others make the decisions.'

'If that's the way of it, why don't you get him to give you his share and be done with it?'

James's face reddened further. 'Don't be daft, he'd never do that. I'd have to buy it from him, and where would I get the money? We're already owing the bank more than enough.'

'So Uncle Albert would want paying, but the rest of us wouldn't?'

'You're closer kin than he is and I've already said that you'll still get your share of the catches, so it'll make no difference to you. Stop playing the fool, Innes, I've got work to do. What d'you think?'

Innes gave him a swift sidelong glance. 'Have you spoken to Ma about this ploy of yours?'

'I thought it right to come to you first, seeing as you're the only other man of the family now.'

'But you spoke to Bethany.'

'I saw Gil; it's the same thing.'

'I'd like to see what Ma thinks before I make my mind up.'

James fought to keep his irritation from showing. 'She'll tell you just what I'm telling you.'

'I'll give you my answer tomorrow.'

'Once you've asked Ma's permission?' Tools rattled as James, his patience nearing its limit, thumped his fist down

on the bench. 'Innes, you're eighteen years of age, you're
a man now! D'you still have to consult your mother before
you so much as wipe your own backside?'

His brother's face tightened. 'I just want to know her
views on the matter. You look out for Stella and the bairns,
and Bethany's got a husband to care for her and see to her
interests. Ma's only got me.'

'You?' James gave a scornful laugh. 'She doesn't need
you to look out for her. It's more likely to be the other
way round, for when it comes down to the truth she's
twice the man you are.'

'That's enough, James.'

'Prove me wrong. Make your own mind up here and
now.'

'In my own time, I told you that.'

'In Ma's time, you mean.'

'Get out of here,' Innes suggested, his voice level.

James felt his hands curl into fists. He yearned to
give way to impulse and give his brother the thrashing
he deserved, but as Innes picked up the spanner again,
tapping it against the palm of his free hand, common
sense prevailed. A brawl between them would not bring
him the shares he needed.

'Gladly,' he said with an effort. 'I've no liking for the air
in this place. How any man can work in a black hole like
this I don't know!' And he stormed from the workshop,
blundering into the blacksmith on his way in.

'What's the matter with him?' Tam Gordon asked his
employee.

'Nothing.' Innes turned back to his work.

'We could hear the two of you in the smiddy. A quarrel,
was it?'

'Just brothers talking,' Innes said levelly, and after a
moment Gordon shrugged and returned to his own work.

He should never have gone to Innes first, James told himself angrily as he stormed back into the town. It had been

courtesy on his part, a belief that the menfolk of the family should settle the matter of the shares between them, without troubling the women. But how could anyone expect a coward to understand the importance of a good fishing boat? His father had been right when he said that Innes was only half a man; and to be honest, James had been relieved when his mother had interceded and refused to allow Innes to go to sea for a third trip, thus putting an end to the embarrassment of him. Although their father was convinced that eventually Innes would find his sea-legs, it seemed clear to James that he never would.

And now this useless brother of his had refused him the shares he needed, which meant that he must now confront his mother, something he had hoped to avoid.

He smoothed down his jacket, set his cap more firmly on his head and drew a deep breath. Since it had to be done, best to get it over with now.

Jess was calm enough on the surface as she sat at the kitchen table and heard her elder son out without interruption, her expressionless face and folded hands giving no indication of her inner turmoil.

James was having a hard time of it, stammering and stumbling over the words he had clearly tried to prepare before coming to her door, his own hands locked tight together on the scrubbed table, his eyes travelling all over the kitchen but never coming closer to hers than the edge of her ear or the point of her shoulder.

When he finally came to a halt there was a long silence, so long that he eventually had to ask, 'Well?'

'James, I'll not give you my share in the boat.'

For the first time he looked full at her, shock in his eyes. He opened his mouth to speak, closed it, then tried again. 'Why not?'

'Because it's mine and I don't want to give it to anyone, not even you.'

His eyes turned to chips of ice. 'It's because I wanted

to put my father in the sea, isn't it? Because I wanted him to have a proper ending – the ending he wanted for himself. But that would have put him out of your reach, and you couldn't bear to let that happen.'

It was the first time in a year that he had spoken to her so harshly and Jess felt as though each word was being used as a stick with which to beat her. 'As far as I'm concerned,' she said slowly and clearly, 'that business is over and done with and not to be mentioned between us again. I told you . . . my share is mine. It's all I have of the *Fidelity* and I want to keep it.'

'But I've said that you'll get your money at the end of each season, just like now. D'you not trust me?'

'Of course I trust you,' she flashed back at him, roused to sudden anger. 'The whole world can trust you, for you're mine and Weem Lowrie's son. This has nothing to do with trust.'

'Until I can stand face to face with Uncle Albert as an equal I'm nobody on that boat, just another crew member,' James argued desperately. 'The man's not fit to skipper *Fidelity*. You know that when my father ran the boat we were the first to reach the fishing grounds and the last to leave. If any vessel went into port loaded down to the gunnels with the fish spilling out of her holds and over her decking, it was the *Fidelity*. That never happens now, for Albert's too lazy to make his crew work and at the first sign of poor weather we're hauling the nets in and running for safety every damned time. If there was any justice my da would have made sure that all of his share went to me, as the head of the family after him.'

'If the Lord hadn't seen fit to take him so suddenly he might have done that. But it happened differently, James.'

'You know fine and well that some of the money that went into her came from the sale of old Mowser's boat.' James jumped to his feet and stormed about the little kitchen.

'Aye, I know that. That's why you got your own third share of the drifter.'

'That was the only reason I married Stella, to get the boat as her dowry.'

'God forgive you for saying such a thing, for she's a good wife to you, James Lowrie, a loving wife and the mother of your three bonny bairns.'

'My three bonny lassies – not even a son to call my own – and oh, did my da not make a joke out of me because of that, after what I did for him!' James glared down at his mother, who sat still, hands locked together on the table before her. 'You were as bad, for you stood by and let him push me into a marriage I never wanted, just so's he could get his hands on Mowser's sailboat.'

'My heart hurt for you then and it still sorrows for you now, if the truth be told, for it was wrong of Weem to use you and Bethany as he did. But when were you or me, or any of us, able to make that man change tack when he was set on a course of his own plotting?'

James spat out a contemptuous laugh. 'You managed it well enough for your precious Innes!'

'He was ill and getting worse. The fishing was going to kill him.' Her voice shook slightly and she firmed it with an effort. 'If he'd done one more trip, it's a body you and Weem would have brought back to me, and I couldn't let that happen. Marrying Stella didn't kill you, James, but it's made you into a bitter man, and that's not my blame. Mebbe it's time you learned to appreciate what you've got instead of hungering after what's passed you by.'

There was a short silence, during which the air between them simmered with James's rage. The only noise was the rattle and rustle of coals in the grate and it seemed to Jess that they were shifting nervously, as unsure as she was of his next move.

Then James said, low-voiced, 'If you care anything for me, Mother, you'll save me the way you saved Innes. You'll let me use your share in the boat.'

Jess longed to give him what he wanted. It might help
to atone for the harm that Weem had done the lad; it might
even heal the great rift between herself and her first-born.
But on the day she had pledged before the minister to
cleave to Weem Lowrie for the rest of her life she had
made a commitment that, in her eyes at least, would last
to the grave and beyond.

The *Fidelity* had been Weem's life, and relinquishing
the small part of it she still retained would be like letting
his memory slip through her fingers. She couldn't do that
for anyone.

'No,' she said, and heard her son's boots scuff across the
stone-flagged floor. The door opened, letting a draught of
cold air into the kitchen.

'I wish to God that I'd put the man into the sea when
I had the chance, for you didn't deserve to have him,'
James said bitterly before the door closed.

7

The *Fidelity* slumbered in the harbour, rocking slightly to the rise and fall of the water, snug among the other boats. Most of them had crewmen aboard, freshening up the paintwork, seeing to the engines, checking the gear in preparation for the English fishing trip, but James was alone on the *Fidelity*, working with the nets in the small, claustrophobic net room.

The lack of space didn't bother him, for he saw the drifter as far more than just a boat; she was mother, sister, friend, lover, wife and child, filling all those roles better than Jess and Bethany, and Stella and his three little daughters, ever could. Every time he put to sea he entrusted his life to his own skills and to the drifter, and in all weathers and situations she had looked after him and brought him safely back to harbour. Now he was letting her strength soothe him and ease the emotions roused by the jarring encounter with his mother.

When someone jumped on to the deck and a voice yelled his name, he cursed and would have stayed where he was if Bethany hadn't shouted again.

'I'm here.' He began to crawl out of the net room, but yelped in shocked surprise as Bethany caught at the front of his jacket, dragging him the rest of the way, then releasing him so that he landed clumsily on the deck.

'Ye daft bitch, what are you doing?' He scrambled to

his feet, painfully aware of laughter from the men on the
adjacent boats.

'Me? It's you that's up to no good, James Lowrie!' It
had been years since he had last seen his sister in such
a rage. 'What d'you think you're doing, taking over my
share in this boat without so much as a word to me?'

'Folk can hear you!'

'I'm not bothered.' Bethany deliberately raised her
voice. 'Let the whole town know how my husband and
my brother plotted to rob me!'

'To what?' He grabbed her arm and hustled her along
the deck to the galley. 'If you're going to talk nonsense, then talk it down in the cabin where nobody can
hear you.'

She glared, then flounced to the top of the vertical
metal ladder leading to the cabin. He followed her down,
scorning the rungs and descending by the uprights, his
open palms and the insides of his ankles controlling
his slide.

In the cabin he said angrily, 'I've stolen nothing from
you.'

'You talked Gil into saying you could have my share
when you know fine it's not his to give away. That's theft.'
Bethany's voice had dropped – always, James recalled
from the time when they were youngsters together, a bad
sign. He remembered his cousin Charlie warning a newcomer to their circle, 'Watch Bethany, she might just be a
lassie, but when her voice goes down her fists come up.'

'But Gil's your husband and we agreed that . . .'

'I'm not a dancing bear with a rope round my neck
and no voice of my own. I'm part-owner of this boat,
not Gilbert Pate. He'd no right to speak for me!'

'You'll still get your money, I promised that to Gil . . .'

'You're not having my share!' Her eyes, grey like his
own, had the same cold, threatening, leaden look that
James had seen in the sky and the sea just before a bad
storm came shrieking over the horizon.

'Will you listen to me? Just sit down there for one minute and listen,' he insisted as she stood her ground, glaring.

For a moment he thought that he was going to have to take her wrists and force her, then she eased herself to the edge of a bunk, her back straight and her chin up.

'Now, I've lost count of the times this past season we've run for the harbour with the holds only half-full, just because Uncle Albert saw the weather getting a wee bit rough. We've all lost money because of that man . . . you've lost money! Weem Lowrie would've gone down with the boat sooner than turn back to land while the fish were still coming into the nets.'

'We all have to put up with fools now and again – why should you be any different? At least you can change things if you must.'

'That's what I'm trying to do, but there's not one of you willing to help me!'

Her eyes narrowed. 'You mean that Ma and Innes won't let you have their shares either?'

'They don't understand, but I thought you would.' He sat on the opposite bunk. 'You understand the ways of fishing more than they do. I can only get the better of Albert if I've more say in the boat than he does. Can you not see that?'

'Why should I help you when you never helped me?'

'Helped you how?'

'When I left the school and wanted to crew on the boat, you made a fool of me!'

'For God's sake, Bethany, how could a woman be part of the crew on a drifter? I'll grant you,' he added hurriedly as her eyes darkened, 'that if things had been the other way about you'd probably have been as good a seaman as me . . .'

'Better!'

'. . . but it didnae happen that way,' James forged on. 'Listen.' He leaned forward, elbows on knees, his head close to hers. 'We can work together on this, you and me. Let me use your share, and make Ma and Innes see sense, then mebbe between us we can buy Albert out once the boat's paid up. That's what Da planned, only he never lived to see it.'

'The two of you were going to buy Uncle Albert out and share the boat between you?'

'That's right,' James started to say, then realised that he was walking into trouble. 'I mean, it would still have been the family boat, but . . .'

'But you'd have been the skipper.' She got to her feet. 'And no doubt you'd have made sure that the rest of us had no share at all then.'

'That's nonsense!'

'You should know, for you talk plenty of it.'

'Ach, Bethany!' He caught at her arm as she made for the ladder. 'Another two years of good fishing should see us clear of the bank – less than that, mebbe . . .'

'If you'd wanted my help you should have asked me, not gone to Gil behind my back.' She wrenched her arm free, eyes blazing. 'You can just keep your thieving hands off my share of this boat, James.'

'You bitch!' he spat at her as she grasped the sides of the ladder. She tossed a cold smile at him over her shoulder.

'I've been called worse,' she said, her skirt belling out briefly as she floated up the narrow rungs. Her booted feet clattered across the deck, then the boat shifted slightly as she jumped on to the harbourside.

Alone again, James hurled every curse he knew at the opposite wall, then scrabbled in one of the cupboards and brought out a half-empty bottle of whisky. He had believed Gil's assurances that Bethany would not mind handing her share over to him, had convinced himself that – of all the family – she, his childhood companion, would understand his frustration. He had even been relying on her to talk his mother and brother round. And now she had betrayed him.

When the bottle was empty he crawled into one of

the narrow bunk beds (more like coffins, some said, but adequate for a crew that spent most of its time on deck anyway) and fell asleep.

When Innes came home from work, his normally cheerful nature subdued and his eyes wary, Jess decided not to beat about the bush. 'James visited you today, didn't he?'

'You too? Did he ask for your share in the boat? And did you agree?' he wanted to know when she nodded.

'No, but you must make your own decision.'

'I'd as soon give my share to you, then you could use it as you wish.'

'I don't want it.'

'Neither do I.'

'Then give James the right to use it as he asked.'

'If you believe that, why didn't you give him yours?'

'I'm keeping my part in the boat because of what she meant to your father. It's different for you. Sit down to your dinner now. You'll be going out afterwards?'

'I said I'd meet Zelda at the farm.'

'If you take my advice,' Jess told him, 'you'll put James and the boat out of your mind and just think about that bonny wee lassie of yours. There's no need to hurry with a decision, whatever your brother says.'

James woke in darkness. Someone was shaking him violently, pulling and dragging at him. 'James . . . James, you fool, wake up!'

He tried to sit up, bumped his head on the underside of the upper bunk and realised that he was on the boat. 'Wha' . . . who . . . Is it time to haul the nets?' he asked, bounding out of the bunk, then clutching at his aching head.

'We're not at sea, you daftie! It's me, Charlie.' A match scraped, its flame searing into his eyes. He screwed them tightly shut and when he opened them again, cautiously, the lamp on the table had been lit.

His cousin, dressed in his best clothes, blew out the match and put it in the tobacco tin kept for that purpose, before bending to lift the empty whisky bottle from the floor. 'God sakes, man, we could hear your snores before we even came on to the boat.' He wrinkled his nose. 'And the place smells like a pub. How long have you been sleeping?'

'Not long.' James rubbed hard at his face with both hands. His head felt twice its usual size and his throat and tongue were swollen and dry. 'We? Who else is here?'

'Just me and . . . a friend,' Charlie said evasively.

'A lass? You've brought a lass on board?'

'There's no harm in it when we're in harbour.'

'That depends on what you're up to.'

'Nothing worse than what you've been up to. Go on home to your wee wife and leave me to my own business.'

James straightened, holding on to the top bunk for a moment until his head stopped swimming. 'You must be desperate. These bunks are narrow for sleeping in, let alone what you've got in mind.'

'Mebbe so, but the table's just fine.' Charlie winked, then said, 'Go on now, she's waiting on the deck and I want you out of here before she decides to go home to her ma and da.'

On deck, the girl was nothing more than a pale, blurred face hovering in the shadows, and a faint nervous giggle when James, about to leap on to the next boat as usual, missed his step and went floundering. He would have fallen overboard if Charlie hadn't thrown an arm about him.

'Easy now, Jamie. Over we go.' He escorted his cousin to the harbourside then leaped back on board to where his companion waited.

As James made his unsteady way along the harbour, bumping into the sea wall one minute and perilously close to the water's edge the next, a ribbon of giggles followed

from the *Fidelity* – the unknown girl's light and musical
trill mixed with a deeper undertone, sleepy yet sensuous.
Charlie was his father through and through, James thought
blearily. Even down to the lassies and the laugh.

'Are you sure you should go?' Jess asked anxiously.

Meg Lowrie, sitting on a small three-legged wooden
stool in her back yard, her skirts kilted over her knees
and her legs spread wide so that she could plant one foot
on either side of the large tin box that she and Jess were
packing, shaded her eyes against the sun and squinted up
at her sister-in-law.

'What else would I do with myself?' she wanted to
know. 'Sit at home and order the serving lassies about?
Or mebbe starve to death, since there's no money comes
into this house bar what I earn myself? Were those two
clean semmits where I told ye?'

'Yes.' Nothing in Meg's one-roomed house was ever
where she expected to find it but Jess, who was good
at running lost objects to ground, had found the vests
beneath the extra winter blankets. 'I'd look after you,
you know that well enough,' she said as she knelt on
the piece of old carpet brought out to protect her knees
from the stone flags. 'I just don't think you should be
going off to Yarmouth with your back still troubling you
the way it is. What do you say, Bethany?'

Bethany, busily stuffing fistfuls of clean fresh chaff
into a large sack that had been washed and re-washed
until it was soft and pliant, paused for a moment and
rested on her haunches, running the back of one hand
over her hot face. It was a perfect early-October day, mild
and golden and soft as silk. 'I say she'll do as she pleases
no matter what you say about it. At least I've made you
a comfortable bed to ease your back when you're not at
the farlins, Aunt Meg.'

'Thanks, lass, I'll bless you when I'm lying on it.'
The three of them were preparing for Meg's departure

for Yarmouth. Now she peered into the trunk. 'I think that's my kist packed and ready now.'

'I put in that roll of flannel: don't forget to wrap it round you underneath your bust bodice for added warmth. And get someone to pin it so's it keeps right all day. And there's three jars of that liniment that does you so well.'

'Aye aye, I'll be fine. Don't fuss me, Jess!'

'You're too old to be working with the herring, you know that.'

'If you want me to give it up you'll have to find a young husband willing to keep me in comfort.'

'You'd not want the trouble of a young husband, Aunt Meg.'

'Mebbe not, but I'd no' mind findin' that out for myself.' Meg chuckled wheezily then put her hands on the edge of the open kist and began to lever herself up. 'Time to make a cup of tea. We've earned it.'

'Sit on where you are and enjoy the sun a bit longer.' Bethany got to her feet, dusting her skirt down. 'I'll see to the tea if you sew up the end of the mattress, Ma.'

'Give the nice china an airing for a wee change,' Meg called after her as she went into the house, a single dark room crammed with the possessions that her aunt had collected during her lifetime. On a hot day like this the two small windows and the street and yard doors were all open wide to catch any fresh air there might be. Ellen still slept, slumped at one end of the horsehair sofa in the boneless way of cats, dogs and young humans, while Rory, at peace for once, sat on the floor near the open yard door, intent on threading a collection of buttons on to a length of fishing line.

The best china was kept in the corner cupboard, cups and saucers and plates and ornaments all lavishly hand-painted, with most pieces gilt-edged and bearing the name of one of the fishing ports Meg had worked in. Bethany chose the one that had been her special favourite from childhood, a cup and saucer covered with fat red and pink roses, with *A Present from Lowestoft* inscribed round their rims. For her mother and aunt she selected presents from Grimsby and Whitby.

'Me too,' Rory clamoured as she poured the strong tea. She put a little into a mug and topped it up with water, and he went out into the sunny yard clutching it to his chest while she followed with the fancy cups, crowded together with a battered tin teapot on an equally battered tin tray.

For a while the women sipped at their tea in silence, enjoying the peace and warmth of the afternoon, then Meg, never one to stay quiet for long, said thoughtfully, 'I'd miss it if I didnae follow the herring. To tell the truth I don't know what I'll do with myself when I get too old for the work.'

'You'll stay home and keep me company. There's plenty going on when the boats and the fisher lassies are away,' Jess told her robustly.

'Mebbe, but there's far more where we are.' Seeing Meg's eyes grow vague, Bethany knew from her own experiences that already her aunt's heart was moving south, towards the busy English harbours. 'All the folk from every place in the country, and the friends you met last year . . . And the crush of boats, and the gulls screamin' for the fish guts and the gossip from all the different ports. And the folk from further away too – the Russians and the Germans and the Hollanders, and dear knows who else.'

She chuckled, digging her niece in the ribs. 'D'ye still mind what it's like, Bethany, walking down King Street in Yarmouth on a Saturday night with the week's work done, all of us dressed in our best?'

'Of course I mind it. I've not been away from the farlins that long, Aunt Meg.' Bethany's voice had an edge to it and Jess, always alert for trouble where her daughter was concerned, glanced at her apprehensively. Meg was too busy with her own thoughts to notice anything amiss.

'And the mission. I love the mission,' she said dreamily.

'Singing away at those lovely hymns and listening to the
pastor's sermon, then the men comin' back afterwards tae
the lodgin's for a cup of tea and a good gossip . . .'

In the shaded room behind them Ellen woke and began
to cry, frightened at finding herself alone in an unknown
place. Bethany got up and went in to her and Rory
followed, clamouring for something to eat. The little
party in the sun-washed yard was over.

Meg's talk of Yarmouth had stirred memories in Jess as
well as in her daughter. It was a bonny evening, and when
her work in the house was done Jess walked out along the
shore road towards Portessie, where she had been born
and raised.

The evening was still, the water grey-streaked and
velvety. A soft mist blurred the horizon, and the sky
was pewter, lightened towards the west by the last rays
of the hidden sun. Portessie's huddle of cottages, their
windowless gable ends facing towards the Firth, were like
a group of old wifies settling down for the night. Everything was calm, until suddenly the dolphins appeared,
swimming up the Firth as they did every evening, their
sleek bodies breaking the surface of the water as they
played. She went down on to the shore and sat on a
rock to watch them frolic. When they had gone and the
surface of the sea had stilled again she sat on, her mind
filled with those days at the farlins in the bustling English
port, the Saturday evenings when, their work done, the
lassies walked along King Street arm in arm.

It was in King Street that Weem Lowrie first spoke to
Jess, skilfully separating her from the others, walking her
back to her lodgings, kissing her in the soft shadows of
a house end . . .

Her middle-aged body quickened now, remembering,
and her eyes filled with tears. Alone on the shore, in the
soft grey gloaming, she sobbed out her longing and her
hunger for Weem.

8

In the weeks before the Scottish fishing fleet, more than 1,200 strong, went south Gilbert Pate and his workmen toiled from dawn to dusk on the barrels that would be needed as soon as they reached Yarmouth. Once there they would be required to produce a further sixty barrels a day to hold the herring, most of which were salted and packed on the quayside for consumption in Germany, Russia and the Low Countries.

As well as the men working in his cooperage, Gil employed ten teams of gutters and packers, a total of thirty women in all to be hired and transported to the accommodation arranged for them in Yarmouth.

Here, Bethany was invaluable to him. Calmly and efficiently she dealt with the women, getting each of them to sign on with the Pates for the season in return for a small advance payment known as 'arles', seeing to it that their chaff mattresses were uplifted and taken to Yarmouth by cart and arranging their accommodation in the two lodging houses Gil always used. The women themselves would be driven by lorry to Aberdeen; from there they would travel by rail to their destination.

The *Fidelity* was one of the first boats to leave Buckie on the journey south. Stella stood by her mother-in-law on the harbour wall holding the twins, and even the baby, up in turn to see their daddy go off to England. The twins waved energetically and Stella wagged Ruth's little hand to and fro, while James gave a terse wave in answer before turning away to get on with his work.

As the drifter slid through the harbour entrance and dipped a demure curtsey to the open sea, Jess knew without having to look that her daughter-in-law's eyes were damp.

'If the herring keep running the way they have this year, we'll all be well set up for the winter when the boats come home,' she offered.

'Aye, but a good season means they could be away for longer than usual.' Stella's voice was muffled.

'Lassie, your own father was a fisherman; you know what the life's like. I mind how much I missed my Weem when he first sailed away and left me at home,' she prattled on, collecting a twin in each hand so that Stella was left in privacy, hampered only by the baby, to scrub the tears from her eyes. 'But you've the bairns to see to, and your father as well. And there's always some neighbour or other in need of a helping hand. The time'll pass fast enough, then there's the homecoming to look forward to.' She smiled, remembering past homecomings.

'My father always looked forward to coming home to us,' Stella said, then, hurriedly, 'I mean . . .'

'You don't have to watch your tongue in front of me,' Jess assured her. 'I know fine that my James is never content unless he's on the sea.'

'He went about like a bear with a sore head when his uncle refused to take the *Fidelity* to the fishing off Northumberland in September,' Stella confided.

'As I mind it, Albert had other things on his mind,' Jess said drily. Half the town knew that during September Albert had been paying a lot of attention to a well-set-up middle-aged widow in Buckpool. 'It fairly put the man's nose out of joint when that woman settled for a farmer in Fochaber. Though from what I hear, she made the most of Albert's attentions before comin' to her decision.'

Stella hesitated, eyeing her husband's mother, then said

in a rush, 'James is thinking of working for someone else when he comes back from Yarmouth.'

Jess stopped in her tracks. 'He'd never leave the *Fidelity* – she's the Lowrie boat.'

'I don't think he'd be happy away from her. I'd not want him to make a mistake he'd regret.'

Guilt swept over Jess. If only she had given James the right to use her share in the *Fidelity* when he asked; if only she had persuaded Innes and Bethany to do the same . . . But what was done was done, and she had learned early on in her married life that there was no sense in fretting over the past. The only way was forward.

'He's probably thinking the better of it already. I'll walk back with you and have a wee visit with Mowser,' she said briskly.

Stella followed Jess along the road, wondering if she had said too much. The one thing she had not disclosed, and never could disclose to anyone, was her constant fear that one day she might lose James. Not to the sea – as a fisherman's daughter she could cope with that if she had to – but to another woman.

She knew well enough, for she was no fool, that he had only married her to help his father buy the *Fidelity*. She hadn't minded being part of the bargain, for since they were both at school she had secretly adored James Lowrie, hiding her passion behind her clear brown eyes and serene nature as she watched him courting the prettier, bolder girls in the area. She had never dreamed of becoming his wife, but when it happened – not because of her beauty or charms, but because of her father's sailboat – she had been the happiest girl on the Moray coast.

She had believed, naïvely, that once they were man and wife James would grow to love her, but instead he had become even more distant. Even when they lay together, even when he was inside her, part of her body, she knew that for him their union was no more than the satisfaction of needs, both material and animal.

Here, in Buckie, where everyone knew everyone else, and there were no secrets, she was more sure of James. But each time he followed the herring up north or down the English coast Stella worried and fretted until he came back to her.

Normally easy-going, though he had a fiery temper when roused, Gil had driven Bethany mad with his fussing and panicking and it was with a sense of relief that she stood on the harbour wall, Ellen straddled over one hip and Rory's hand firmly in her grasp despite his efforts to wriggle free, and watched her husband leave Buckie.

As the boat, its holds crammed and its deck piled perilously high with barrels, went through the harbour entrance into the open sea, she suddenly scooped Rory up, tucked him under her free arm and began to run, chanting, 'Ride a cock horse, to Banbury Cross . . .' with both children clinging to her and giggling helplessly as they were jostled and swung around. By the time she gained the street her tawny hair, pulled free of the loose knot at the nape of her neck, flew in curly strands about her face and her skirt clung to her pistoning thighs.

Older women, sedate and proper in black, hair trapped beneath the shawls and scarves most of them wore, even in the house, tutted and raised their eyebrows, whispering their disapproval as Gil Pate's scandalous second wife raced by. But Bethany paid them no heed, panting out the rhyme about the lucky lady with her fine white horse again and again; she timed it so that, as she reached the house and swung sideways to allow Rory to lift the latch, they burst inside to 'To see a fine lady . . .' and ended up in a heap on the wall-bed with '. . . upon a white *horse*!'

The three of them rolled together on the bed, tickling and screeching and kicking their legs until finally, worn out by the fun, they collapsed in a tangled pile. At times like this Bethany enjoyed her step-children; they reminded her of puppies, smelling of sun and fresh air and soap, and something that could only be described as the sweet perfume of babyhood innocence. They were soft-covered bundles of wiry energy with the ability, at a second's notice, either to spring into action or collapse in limp, vulnerable sleep.

But such moments were all too few. Apart from the fact that Gil didn't like to see his wife behaving like a wild bairn, too much of her time and energy were taken up by the constant drudgery of feeding, washing and having constantly to keep watch over the children. From now on there would be no solitary walks by the sea for her, for there would be no Gil sitting by the fire, reading his paper and smoking his pipe and available, albeit grudgingly, to keep an eye on his son and daughter for a precious half-hour. Rory and Ellen were in her sole charge now and their needs would fill her every moment, sleeping as well as waking.

Even as the thought came to her, Ellen, worn out by the fun, began to grizzle and Rory pulled at Bethany's arm, chanting, 'I'm hungry!'

When the children were in their beds and she finally had a moment to herself, Bethany found it impossible to settle with her knitting and her mending. It was always the same when Gil was away from home, and yet it wasn't as though she missed him. On the contrary, she relished her freedom. For a month at least she would be able to lay down the burden of being a wife, freed from the need to have his food on the table at exactly the right time; free to sprawl bonelessly, like the children, from one end of the bed to the other if she so pleased, and to sleep the night long without being plucked and groped at, or wakened from dreams of freedom and the sea to satisfy his sudden urges.

Prowling around, she suddenly realised that the house itself was the cause of her unease. It was Gil's home, not hers; it bore his stamp at all times, and Bethany's place in it was only on sufferance, as his wife. Even when he was away for any length of time, as he was now, the house refused to be hers, subtly reverting instead to the days when it had been the domain of her predecessor. The pictures on the walls had been chosen by Molly Pate and the fancy curling shells and the gold-edged hand-painted dishes in the parlour's glass-fronted corner cabinet had been brought home by Gil for Molly's pleasure. Molly's hands had crafted the rag rug that lay before the fire and the cushions on the two fireside chairs. Molly had chosen the wallpaper and had even stitched the patchwork quilt that covered Bethany and Gil every night. She had birthed the two children now asleep in the tiny bedroom, and she had died through Ellen's arrival in the world.

Every day Bethany dusted Molly's wedding portrait, which stood at one end of the kitchen mantelshelf, and her own at the other end. Both prints were strikingly similar; the bride seated and Gil standing, a big hand clamped on his new wife's shoulder in what was probably meant to be a protective gesture but looked, to Bethany, more like a public declaration of ownership. In the first likeness he was youthful, with a full head of dark hair and a curve to his cheeks and chin. Molly's thin shoulder seemed to be weighted down by his hand, while her neat features were solemn and somewhat anxious, as though she had just become aware of the responsibilities she had taken on.

Moving to her own wedding portrait, Bethany noted the distant expression on her pictured face and the way her body was poised on the chair as though planning to leap up, throw off the restraining paw from her shoulder and dart out of the picture entirely. This, she thought, was understandable, given that the marriage had been arranged by her father and had not been her own wish. In this second portrait Gil's hair had shrunk to a thick fringe skirting a bald head and the youthful chubbiness had given way to the onset of middle-aged fat; although still in his mid-thirties, he was the type of man who had a brief youth and a prolonged middle-age.

Bethany sighed and turned both portraits to the wall. She could, of course, have made changes about the house to suit her own taste. Gil had suggested this when they first wed, but she had done nothing, having no interest in domestic virtues. As a result she now had little option but to continue to live as an interloper in her predecessor's home.

Returning to her chair, she picked up her mending then put it down again, still too restless to settle to it. Instead she opened the door and stood leaning on the frame for a long time, her face lifted up to the dark night, eyes closed, drawing the salt air deep into her lungs. The chill wind made her shiver, but she wrapped her arms tightly about her body for warmth, refusing to go back into the house. She would have given everything she had to be where Gil was now, out on the water, facing away from Buckie and looking towards new adventures.

'It's awful cold,' Zelda was saying at that moment, up on the hills above Buckie. 'I'll have to go in before I'm chilled to the bone.'

'Am I not keeping you warm?'

'You're certainly trying hard enough – you're near squashing me to death.' She wriggled out of Innes's arms and sucked in a deep breath. 'That's better.'

'There's always the barn . . .'

'And have me going into the house with straw all down my clothes and in my hair, so's the mistress can tell what I've been up to?'

'I'm not saying we'd get up to anything, I just mean that we'd be away from the wind in the barn.'

'What's the sense,' Zelda wanted to know, as contrary as any other woman, 'of us going into the barn if we're not going to get up to anything?'

'Then we will, if that's what you'd like.' Innes clamped an arm about her and tried to ease her towards the great dark shape at the other side of the farmyard. 'I'm willing enough.'

'I know you are, Innes Lowrie, but I'm not. Not yet.'

'Och, Zelda!'

'It's not the right time or the right place.'

'If it's marriage you want I'm more than willing.'

'Really?' She peered up into his face. 'You mean it?'

He touched her cheek with his free hand, loving the curve of it against his palm. 'I'd marry you tomorrow if I could.'

'It's not just the – you know – the need for me that's got your tongue, is it?'

'Zelda, my need and my tongue aren't so close together that one can rule the other.'

'Oh!' She bounced away from him. 'You're coarse, Innes Lowrie!' she accused, her voice rippling with shocked laughter.

'Mebbe, but I'm honest too. And I mean it . . . we'll get married if you want to.'

She came back to him, close enough to play with the buttons on his jacket. 'Where would we live?'

'There's room in my mother's house.'

'I couldn't!'

'She'd not mind. She likes you.'

'But I couldn't . . . you know. Not in the same house as your mother!'

'What then?'

'We'll have to save, both of us, until we can afford a wee place of our own.'

'That'll take a long time.'

'The sooner we start, the faster we'll save.'

'And in the meantime there's always the barn.'

'There is not! I'm not going to roll in the straw like any common slut!'

'Zelda . . .' he pleaded.

'I'll have to go in, it's time,' she said as the bells of a church clock splintered the chilled air.

'Not till you give me a proper kiss,' Innes insisted, and pulled her into his arms. She melted against him for a moment, her mouth softening beneath his, then as the fire kindled in his loins and his hands became more urgent, she pulled away.

'I'll see you on Saturday afternoon?'

'Aye.'

'And we're agreed to start saving?'

'We are.'

She flitted away from him, then returned to brush his mouth again with her own in a soft butterfly kiss. 'I love you, Innes Lowrie,' she said.

He waited until the farm door opened, spilling a flood of lamplight over the flags, then closed again before turning for home, striding out not only because it was too cold to loiter, but because the burning, throbbing swelling between his thighs made great steps essential. He didn't mind the discomfort at all because it was part of being a man and the cause of it had said she loved him, and they had committed themselves to a future together. And the fishing fleet had gone, taking James and his cool contempt with it. And tomorrow a man who lived in one of the big houses was bringing his motor-cycle into the workshop for repair. Life was very sweet.

As he marched homewards Innes began to whistle.

9

'You should never have tried to pull that kist out from below the bed, not when it was all packed, Aunt Meg. You knew I'd see to it for you if you'd just let me know.'

'I'm not in my dotage yet, Innes,' Meg Lowrie snapped. 'I can still do things for myself.'

'So we see.' Jess's voice was dry and her sister-in-law flounced from her in high dudgeon. It wasn't easy to flounce when huddled in a chair, but she achieved it by tossing her head and turning away slightly. Even that movement caused her to draw her breath in sharply. 'See here, Meg, there's no sense in us arguing about what's over and done. We need to get you right again, so Innes is going to fetch the doctor to you.'

'He'll do nothing of the sort! We're leaving tomorrow – all I need is some ointment and mebbe a hot toddy to comfort my bones, and a good night's sleep.'

It was obvious to both Jess and Innes that Meg needed more than ointment and a night's sleep. Her face was drawn with pain and she winced with even the slightest movement. They had both come running, leaving their dinners half-eaten on the table, after a summons from a neighbour who had heard Meg's shouts for help and found her lying on the floor.

'If you'll just give a hand to get me into my bed, and give my back a wee rub before you go . . .'

'You'll sit where you are until we hear what the doctor has to say.'

'I'm not spending my hard-earned silver on a physician!'

'Nobody asked you to. I'm paying the man and to my mind it's money well spent, for it'll buy me peace of mind. Innes, off you go.'

'I'll not see him!' Meg roared. Innes, at a loss to know what to do, hovered by the door, looking from one woman to the other.

'You've little choice. He's coming and I doubt if you're up to hiding from him below the bed, alongside that heavy kist of yours,' Jess shot back.

'You're a right thrawn bitch, Jess!'

'I'm a Lowrie . . . we're all thrawn. Innes, do as you're told. Now, is there anything you need before the doctor comes?' Jess asked as her son escaped, glad to be away from the arguing.

Meg remained silent until the door had closed behind Innes, then she said, her voice suddenly shaky, 'You could mebbe bring the chamber-pot out from below the bed. I couldnae say anything about it in front of the laddie, but I was tryin' to fetch it when my back went. I just didnae feel up to going out to the privy in the yard.'

Tears of humiliation glittered in her eyes and Jess felt a great wave of compassion for this strongly independent woman, who was suffering as much from the shame of having to depend on others as from her pain. 'Oh, Meg!'

'Never mind "Oh, Meg",' came the sharp rejoinder from the old woman huddled on the chair. 'Just fetch that damned pot, will ye, for I'm wetting my breeks like a bairn at this very minute. I thought Innes would never leave us!'

'I'm sorry you've got this landed on you the very day before the lassies go off to Yarmouth, Bethany, but the doctor'll not hear of Meg leaving her bed just now. Not that she can, poor soul, for she's twisted like a hairpin. I think it's the end of her days at the farlins.'

'She must be in a right taking about it.'

'She's bellowing like a bull gone daft The sooner she realises that shouting doesn't mend anything, especially old bones that have been hard treated for years, the better,' Jess said feelingly. 'The thing is, I was trying to think who you could get to replace her. There's Isa Thain – her bairns are up in age, and her mother lives with them, so she can see to them all while Isa's away. I know she'd like to earn a bit more money,' she added, then as her daughter stared past her shoulder, her eyes like grey mist and her fingers worrying her lower lip, 'Bethany? Are you hearing me?'

'What?' Bethany blinked, then said with an attempt at a casual air, 'Isa Thain. I'll go and see her now. I was just thinking,' she added diffidently, 'that mebbe I should go to Yarmouth myself.'

'You? But you've got the bairns to see to!'

'Gil's mother would take them . . . or she could come here, instead of them having to go to Finnechtie.'

'And what d'you think she'd say about you running off and leaving them?'

'Ach, that woman finds fault no matter what I do. She can't see past Molly's memory,' Bethany said bitterly, 'and she's never thought I was good enough for her son and her grand-weans. Anyway, if I'm not here I won't be troubled by what she says.'

'Mebbe not, but I'll have to listen to her.'

'Ignore her. She's not worth bothering over.'

'But Meg's a packer and you're a gutter. How could you do her work?'

Bethany hesitated for only a second before saying, 'I'll still hire Isa if she's willing, then I can supervise and help out with the gutting like I used to. Isa's got a sharp tongue in her head and some of the other lassies might not get

on with her, so it would be as well for me to be there to
keep the peace. Gil's no use with the women, he's got
the wrong manner entirely – I should know, I worked for
him myself – and since Aunt Meg's not going to be there
to keep things right he'll need me.'

'He won't like the idea of his wife working at the farlins
alongside the other quine, like any common fisher-lassie,'
Jess said, but realised that she had made a mistake as soon
as she saw the sudden spark in her daughter's eyes, the lift
of her chin and the way her shoulders straightened.

'Why not?' Bethany demanded. 'I am a fisher lassie,
one of the best. And Gil can say what he likes. He doesn't
own me and neither does his witch of a mother. I'm going
to Yarmouth and that's an end to it.'

That night when the children were asleep she climbed
the wooden stairs to the loft, which was filled with all
the accoutrements of the cooper's trade. The tin trunk
she had used in her days at the farlins was in a corner,
stowed beneath a bench. Bethany manhandled it down
the narrow staircase into the kitchen, where she knelt to
open the lid.

The deep trunk was almost empty, apart from a few
items covered by a folded length of canvas, which she
opened out and spread over the floor. Moving the kist
to the middle of the canvas she began to unpack it:
a small tin box for her soap, facecloth, hairbrush and
comb; a bundle of clean rags, held together with lengths
of twine and used to safeguard her fingers against injury
from her own knife or from sharp herring bones; her long
waterproof apron and sturdy leather sea-boots, both kept
in good condition by regular applications of linseed oil.
And at the very bottom, carefully wrapped in a piece of
oilskin, was her gutting knife, honed and polished.

Bethany took it out of its wrapping and turned it about
so that the blade caught the light. She hefted it in her hand,
loving the way the handle fitted with easy familiarity into

her palm and handling it with the respect it demanded, for although it had not been used for a year the blade was still razor-sharp. Then she wrapped it up again and laid it back in the trunk. Time was moving on, and the trains carrying the guttin quine south were due to leave the day after tomorrow.

Isa Thain had agreed to travel to Yarmouth. Tonight Bethany planned to do most of her packing, and tomorrow morning she would walk to Finnechtie to see Gil's mother. She had no doubt at all that the woman would be pleased to have her grandchildren to herself for several weeks, and even more delighted to have a grievance against her son's second, unsuitable wife.

Once the arrangements were made she would spend the rest of the day cleaning the house from top to bottom. Whatever else the older Mrs Pate might have to say to the neighbours about Bethany in her absence, she would not be able to claim that Gil's young wife kept a dirty house.

While lamps were being blown out in the neighbouring houses and her neighbours were settling into their beds, she flitted about gathering clothing, toiletries, a long, thick woollen scarf to put about her head when she worked on the open harbours, warm stockings and underwear to keep the worst of the Yarmouth early-winter winds at bay. She tore up more clean rags to protect her fingers and packed sewing needles and threads, scissors and thimbles, her knitting wires and wool.

When they followed the boats north to places such as Lerwick, the fisher lassies even packed wallpaper and curtains into their kists in an attempt to make the long, dreary huts where they lived more homely, but in larger ports such as Lowestoft, Grimsby and Yarmouth, where they lodged in houses, there was not the same need. This meant that Bethany had room for her best dress and a lighter, pretty scarf for Saturday nights, when the fishing – for the Scots crews at least – ended until after midnight on Sunday. On Saturday evenings the fishermen and the lassies socialised.

When the kist was full and she was quite certain that she had remembered everything, she threaded a large needle with thick, strong thread and gathered the ends of the canvas sheeting together. In and out the needle flashed and when she was done the kist was protected by a snugly fitting canvas jacket. Rising stiffly to her feet, she inspected it from all sides, nodding her satisfaction, then undressed and fell into bed where, snug beneath the quilt made by her predecessor, she nursed her new-found sense of freedom.

When the motorised lorry blared its horn outside the house two days later Rory, who often embraced adult knees but was too manly to approve of hugging and kissing, clamoured to be lifted up. When Bethany obliged he put his arms tightly round her neck and whispered into her ear, 'You'll not be long, will you?'

'I'll be as quick as I can,' Bethany lied. The children both liked their grandmother well enough, but it was clear that the little boy was not at all certain of being left in her charge. Putting him down, Bethany took Ellen from the older woman's arms and buried her face in the child's silky hair for a moment. She had never loved them as much as she did now that she was deserting them. 'Be a good lassie now, for your grandma,' she told Ellen.

'Of course she will, I'll see to that.' Mrs Pate took the little girl back and captured Rory's fingers with her free hand. 'Tell my son he can rest assured that his children will be properly fed while they're in my care. And I'll give the house a good redding out too.'

'I see to it every week.'

'Mebbe so, but I've my own ways and I like to observe them wherever I may be,' the woman said inflexibly, then nodded towards the lorry with its cargo of excited guttin quine. 'You'd best be off, since you insist on going. You can tell Gilbert I'll be writing a letter to him directly.'

Bethany could make a shrewd guess as to the contents of the letter, and she was certain that Gil would disapprove of her actions just as strongly as his mother did. But the die was cast and she was escaping from her life in Buckie for a while, and that was all that mattered.

The driver clambered down from his cab and ambled over. 'Here, Bethany, I'll take your kist for you,' he offered.

'You will not! If I can't lift my own kist, how d'you think I can manage with the barrels at the farlins?' She bent and caught the heavy tin trunk in exactly the right grip, remembered from earlier days. There was a cheer from the women standing on the back of the lorry as she hoisted it up and began to walk towards them, grateful that there was only a short distance to cover.

When she reached the lorry, willing hands reached down to take the kist from her and carry it to the back to be stacked with the rest, while other hands seized hers and hauled her up. The driver helped her on her way by cupping his own hands over her backside and pushing, grinning at the remarks the women were yelling down at him.

'I'm just bein' a gentleman,' he protested in mock-innocence. 'Just doin' my duty by the ladies.'

'Duty? The last man that put his fingers where you put yours when you punted me up, Walter Lochrie, had tae marry me,' a hefty middle-aged woman boomed back, and as the lorry-load erupted in gales of laughter Bethany saw her mother-in-law, her face the picture of outrage, whisking the children into the cottage out of earshot.

As he was dragged in, Rory twisted round for a last look and a final wave before the door slammed.

Although weeks of hard work in harsh conditions lay ahead of them, all the women were in high spirits, waving and calling to passers-by and singing whatever came to mind – hymns, choruses, even popular nursery rhymes – as the lorry covered the miles to Aberdeen, where the railway station was thronged by fisher-lassies from all over the area, crowding on to the special trains awaiting them. Once on board they found seats, gathered their possessions about them, took their knitting needles from the padded leather whiskers strapped about their waists and settled down to knit and gossip the hours and the miles away.

'Here . . .' Isa, sitting beside Bethany, offered her a screw of paper, 'have a sookie sweetie. Your Gil's surely not going to be pleased to see you working on the farlins again,' she went on as Bethany prised a sticky humbug free of the lump and popped it into her mouth. 'He surely thinks his wife's too grand to mix with the likes of us.' The spiteful undertone that accompanied so many of Isa's remarks, and which had more than once led to ill-feeling when she worked at the farlins with the other women, could clearly be heard.

Bethany licked her sticky fingers. 'That's my business, Isa, and his. All we want you to do is work hard, the way you can when you put your mind to it.'

'All *we* want?' The woman emphasised the second word. 'So you're comin' along to make sure your man gets his money's worth out of us, is that it?'

'I'm going to Yarm'th to work, the same as the rest of you, and to make sure that we're all of us getting our money's worth,' Bethany said lightly, aware that all those within earshot were listening with keen interest. 'Thanks for the sweetie, Isa, it was kind of you.'

When they finally arrived in Yarmouth Bethany was taken aback to find Gil himself waiting on the platform for his teams. She had not expected to see him until the next day at the farlins and had given herself up to enjoying the noisy journey, instead of planning what she would say to him.

She thought at first that his arrival was simply bad luck,
but when he came striding straight towards her down the
platform, scattering women to left and right, she realised
that he had already known she was on the train.

'Look at the face on him,' Isa whispered into her ear.
'I told you he'd not be pleased!'

'Right, there's carts waiting, get your boxes out as fast
as you can,' Gil told the other women roughly, then he
grabbed his wife's arm and pulled her aside. 'What d'you
think you're doing here?'

'I suppose you got a letter from your mother? She didn't
waste any time.' The woman must have been writing her
letter even while Bethany was walking back to Buckie
after asking her to look after the children.

'She did her duty as she saw fit, and she was right to
do it. I wrote at once to tell you to stay where you belong.
Did you not get my letter?'

'It must have arrived too late,' Bethany said, thanking
the fates for their timing.

'Well, you can just go home tomorrow.'

'I'll do nothing of the sort! I've come to work at the
farlins.'

'I will not have my wife working along with the guttin
quine!'

'Why not? I'm one of the best, as you well know. I'm
here because my Aunt Meg's ill with a bad back, so I had
to ask Isa Thain to take her place, and it's lucky for you
that she was able to do it at such short notice. She's a
good worker, for all that she's got a tongue sharp enough
to gut the herring with if she ever lost her knife, and
can cause trouble among the other women . . .' Bethany
babbled on, trying to prevent Gil from talking, then as
she looked up at him and saw the anger in his eyes she
finished lamely, 'Anyway, since Aunt Meg's usually the
one to keep an eye on the teams, and I used to do that
myself before we wed, I thought it best to come here in
her place.'

'I hope you got the payment back off your aunt now that she's not working for me this season.'

'I told her to keep it, since she's bad enough to need a doctor.'

'You did, did you? So how d'you think I can afford Isa if I don't get my money back from Meg Lowrie?'

'I paid Isa her seven shillings from your wee bank,' Bethany told him, and his eyes bulged. His wee bank was a large treacle tin hidden in a far corner of the house loft.

'That's my money and it's private!'

'Not from me – I'm your wife. And Aunt Meg's had my share, since I didn't pay myself any arles.'

'That's as well, for you're not staying.'

'I am, Gil. You're going to need me at the farlins, and the bairns'll be fine with your mother until we get back home at the end of the season.'

'But the town's packed with folk from all over. I don't know if I can find somewhere for us to stay.'

'No need for that; you'll lodge with your men the same as always and I'll bide with the lassies.'

'But . . .'

'There's no but about it, Gilbert, I'm here and I'm staying. And we're all worn out after the journey. If you want us at the farlins tomorrow morning in time for the boats coming in you'd better take us to our lodgings and no more arguments!'

10

Yarmouth's vast harbours were packed and still the boats came up the river on their way back from the 'brown ledges', as the nearest fishing ground was called. The steam drifters, with smoke belching from their tall, narrow stacks, were first at the quayside, with the benefit of their engines, but the first of the sail boats with their great dipping lug sails hauled in and their high mainmasts lowered were close behind. All the boats were low in the water, weighed down by the fish known as the silver darlings; all were impatient to open up their holds and get the fish ashore in great baskets. Buyers and sellers were just as impatient, and as each catch was landed men swarmed to inspect it and bargain over it.

The Buckie guttin quine had settled into their new lodgings the previous evening with the ease of women well used to setting up home wherever they happened to find themselves. They had been allocated two former sail lofts in adjoining houses, which together formed a great long space below the sloping roofs of the two-storey buildings. Iron-framed cots were lined down each side, two stoves in the middle provided warmth and the means of cooking, and there were double stone sinks at either end and three long narrow tables, flanked by a collection of wooden kitchen chairs and stools, down the centre of the room. The beamed lofts were claustrophobic, with little space for movement, but since the women would spend most of their time at the harbour this was not a problem.

Their chaff mattresses had already been delivered and it had not taken the women long to make up their beds with the blankets and quilts they had brought in their kists. The kists themselves served as bedside tables, while the food they had brought with them was handed over to their landlady to be stored in the cool, stone-flagged pantry on the ground floor. Not that there was much danger of foodstuffs being spoiled at this time of year; the women knew that most nights they would be obliged to sleep with all their clothes on for warmth, and it was not unknown for water left in basins or jugs overnight to be frozen hard in the morning.

Bethany slept well on that first night and by half past six the following morning she and the others were preparing the farlins: the gutters positioning the fish barrels to one side and slightly behind them at the long wooden troughs, while the tubs where the offal was thrown were put to the other side; the packers checking the big tubs of coarse salt and bringing up empty pickling barrels. Usually farlins consisted of long, shallow tables, but this year the Scottish women were working at the deep farlins, tubs some three feet in depth, each of them only long enough to take four gutters.

Despite her announcement to her mother and to Gil that she was going to be there to lend a hand wherever needed, Bethany had managed to persuade one of the older gutters to change places with her. Now she was on a three-woman team with Isa as the packer and Kate, a young woman on her second season, as her fellow gutter.

When the coopers arrived a short time later Gil made no attempt to speak to his wife, although she was aware of his gaze following her every movement. At one time she had been one of his best gutters but now, she knew, he wanted her to fail, to be forced to admit that she had lost her old skills and to return home where she belonged.

She was damned if she would give him that satisfaction, she thought as she wrapped clean rags round her fingers, deftly using her teeth to knot the twine about them. Catching his gaze on her, she deliberately faced him for a long moment, her eyes holding his, then she turned her back and went to help one of the other women manoeuvre a tub of salt into place.

Waiting for the fish to arrive was the most tedious part of the women's work and the hardest for Bethany. Like the others, she took her knitting wires from the leather whisker slung as always at her waist, but all the time she was knitting, her stomach churned with nerves beneath her thick jersey and her oilskin apron, and inside her sturdy boots her toes curled and uncurled restlessly.

It wasn't just Gil who bothered her, it was the other women as well. Once she had been their equal, but things had changed now that she was married to their employer. She knew from the sidelong glances being cast in her direction that some of them resented her and suspected that she was in Yarmouth as Gil's spy.

It was a relief when the clanging of a bell signalled the arrival of the first boats from the fishing grounds and the women put their knitting wires away, hurrying to their places. It wasn't long before the first carts appeared, piled high with baskets of herring. As the silver stream spilled into the deep farlins and the packers scattered double handfuls of coarse salt over them for easier handling, Bethany tightened her hold on her sharp knife and prayed behind set lips that the old skills had not deserted her.

She needn't have worried, for almost as soon as she slid the blade into her first fish it was as though she had never been away from the farlins. In four seconds the fish was split and gutted, the offal tossed with a twist of the wrist into the barrel slightly behind her and to one side, and the prepared fish put into a tub on the other side; then the knife was into the next fish and she had settled into the old, practised rhythm.

By the time daylight came, bringing with it the buyers and the carriers, Bethany and Kate were working as an effective team while, behind them, Isa scooped the gutted fish from their barrels and packed them in tiers consisting of two circles – inner and outer – laid in such a way that the fish did not come in contact with each other. Then she threw generous double-handfuls of salt over each layer before starting the next. A cooper assigned to their section was on hand to inspect each barrel as it was started, to make sure that the fish were being properly packed, then he covered the barrel when it was full and rolled it off to one side. After a few days, when the fish had settled, the salt brine would be run off through a bunghole, the barrel opened and topped up with more layers of herring, then more brine would be added before it was finally sealed.

Someone further down the line began to sing a popular hymn in a rich, clear contralto and Bethany joined in along with the others, singing her heart out as her hands flew about their task, feeling as though she had come home after a long absence. The hours flew by and one hymn followed another as basket upon basket was emptied into the farlins in a never-ending silver stream.

'This is going to be the best year yet,' Effie, gutting in the next team, called down the line.

Bethany looked up at the mountain of herring still waiting to be shovelled on to the farlins when space permitted. 'And the busiest,' she said, and Effie took a second to wipe the back of one hand over her brow, decorating her forehead with a mixture of glittering scales and fish slime.

'There's no harm in being busy. It makes it harder for the devil to put mischief into our hands.'

'He'd be a fool if he tried,' Bethany pointed out. 'The knives'd have his fingers gutted and into the barrel for packing before he knew what was afoot.'

The constant hard work kept the women reasonably warm and only when they began to walk back to the lodgings for their midday break were they aware of the stiff cold wind.

'There's somethin' to be said for that big wall of barrels all round us,' Isa said as they linked arms and ran for shelter. 'They fair keep the wind away.'

'But not the rain.' Effie looked up at the lowering sky. 'We'll get soaked before the day's done. Here, I'm fair ready for that soup!'

They had made two big pots of soup the night before and several of the women had been sent back to the lodgings earlier to heat it up and cook some fresh herring. After working all morning in the fresh air they fell upon the food as soon as they gained the big lofts, stuffing it into their mouths in a rush to satisfy their hunger before hurrying back to work. A long afternoon lay ahead of them, and judging by the pile of fish still waiting to get into the farlins, they would be working until late in the evening, too.

As they returned to the quay they met James, who stared when he spotted his sister among the others. 'Bethany?'

'Aye, it's me all right.' She stopped, letting the others walk on without her.

'What are you doing in Yarm'th?'

'What does it look like?' She indicated her oilskin apron and her boots with a sweep of the hand. 'Aunt Meg's not able for the work this time, so I'd to hire a new packer. I thought it best to come down to see how she settled in.'

'Gil said nothing about that when I spoke to him yesterday morning.'

'He didn't know. I only arrived last night.'

'What about . . .'

'The bairns,' Bethany said with a touch of irritation, 'are being well looked after by Gil's mother.'

'You'll be finding the work hard after being away from it for a year.'

'I'm managing fine,' Bethany retorted, and went on her way.

James watched her go, head high, shoulders squared and
booted feet striding out across the stone flags as though
she owned the place, then shrugged, yawned and hurried
to catch up with the other men. It had been a long night
and he was more than ready for a good sleep, then a meal
and a drink with the rest of the lads before setting out to
sea again.

The rain stayed away and the clouds cleared; as the afternoon wore on a knot of onlookers arrived to watch the
fisher-lassies work, marvelling at the way their bandaged
hands moved so fast that each movement blended into the
next. The women were well used to these audiences and
paid little heed to them, apart from occasionally involving
them in their talk. Today a well-dressed middle-aged man
caused great excitement among the crowd as he set up a
tripod and camera.

'D'you fancy being one of these fillum actresses,
Bethany?' Effie wanted to know as he began to take
pictures.

'I'd as soon fill another barrel and get paid for it.' It
was going to be grand to have her own money again,
Bethany thought, her knife flickering and the barrel at
her back filling steadily. Gil was generous enough, but
he always needed to be told what every penny had been
spent on and whether she had got value for money. Even
her annual share from the *Fidelity* was banked by him.
This was her chance to make some money of her own.

She was determined to avoid the trap some of the
younger quine fell into – spending all their wages at the
Yarmouth picture houses and theatres, or on clothes for
themselves and gifts for family and friends back home.
She intended to save every penny and enjoy for as long
as possible the sense of independence that the money gave
her. She was aware that Gil would do all he could to make
sure that she would not get back to Yarmouth again.

As afternoon met evening and the sky darkened, the

photographer packed up his equipment, tipping his hat to the fisher-lassies as he left. The buyers, having made their deals, were long gone and the watchers began to drift off. The women had another meal break and this time when they returned to the farlins they trudged, where earlier they had stepped out in linked lines. After almost everyone else but the coopers had gone, they toiled on in the light of oil lamps, for the fish had to be gutted and pickled while it was still fresh.

With no more boats coming in, the level of fish in the farlins fell rapidly, but for the tired gutters the work became harder. Now they were required to lean into the deep tubs, and by the time the last fish had been gutted and packed, and the final barrel covered and rolled away, the women were stiff and exhausted, longing for the freedom to return to their lodgings.

The fishermen had landladies to cook their meals and, for extra payment, wash their clothes, but the guttin quine, being women, were expected to do all that for themselves on top of the long day's work.

Once they had satisfied their hunger they divided by mutual agreement into two groups, one taking on the housework and the other, Bethany included, doing the washing. Tired though they were, they laughed and joked and sang as they scrubbed and wrung out the clothes before putting them through the big mangle, glad to know that the first day's work was behind them.

Trudging back upstairs with a bucket of damp cloth-ing, Bethany was uncomfortably aware of a knot of pain between her shoulder-blades. 'When the washing's hung up I'll need to get one of you to rub ointment on my back.'

'I'll do it, if you do the same for me,' offered Kate. 'I feel as if a carthorse has been dancing a reel on my spine.'

'At your age?' one of the older women scoffed. 'Lassie,

you've got years ahead of you yet. Leave the sore backs to us old ones.'

'At least you're used to these deep farlins. My back's not had time to get accustomed!'

Arguing and teasing, they gained the top of the stairs and burst into the loft, where the washing lines still had to be strung from the rafters and the clothes draped over them. Bethany, anxious to be accepted by the others, caught up one end of the clothesline and stepped on to one of the narrow beds. Balancing precariously, she managed at her first try to toss the rope over one of the cross-beams that ran at intervals down the room. A bit of jiggling brought the end back down to her hand so that she could catch and tie it. Triumphant, she was about to jump down and repeat the process halfway down the room when one foot slipped and she only just saved herself from plunging on to the floor below, or, even worse, crashing on to the edge of one of the tables, by jerking her body up so that she could catch at the cross-beam directly over her head.

'Bethany!' Kate squeaked. 'Are you all right?'

'I'm fine.' Bethany, heart thumping from the fright, managed to get her other hand over the rafter to secure her grip.

'Hold on, I'll fetch a stool for you to stand on.' But when Kate came scurrying back with the stool, Bethany, both hands clamped on the beam, said breathlessly, 'Leave me be for a minute. This is the first time all day that my back's stopped hurting.'

'Don't be daft, lassie, come on down,' one of the other women ordered.

'I mean it.' She ducked her head between her upraised arms and grinned down at the knot of women below. 'It must be something to do with the stretching. It feels grand!'

'Here, let me try it.' Kate scrambled on to a table and, by standing on tiptoe and stretching her arms up,

just managed to take hold of the beam above her with
both hands. 'Oh here, you're right, Bethany. My back
feels grand.' She swung her legs to and fro. 'It's like
being a bairn again, playing at climbing trees.' Then,
peering down at the uplifted faces, 'You should try it,
it feels good.'

'Ach, why not? Give me a hand, someone,' Effie
ordered, kilting her skirts to reveal sturdy, slightly bowed
legs.

'Don't be daft, why would you want to be hanging
from rafters like a bat at your age!'

'If it takes the ache from my bones, Isa, I'll try anything.' With help, Effie clambered on to a chair, then on
to one of the tables and finally, to resounding cheers from
below, she managed to hook both hands over a beam.

'Catch me making a fool of myself like that,' Isa
sneered. 'You look like a monkey in a cage.'

'At least I'm a monkey with a contented spine. Try it,'
Effie urged, and within five minutes all the women except
Isa were hanging from the rafters, blissfully stretching
their aching spines.

'Like fish hanging from a pole in the smokehouse.' Isa
threw herself down on her bed and glared at them. 'And I
can see right up your skirt, Effie Jappy. I can nearly tell
what you had for your dinner.'

'You know what I had for my dinner – the same as you,'
Effie snapped back at her. 'As for the rest, I've nothing you
havenae got yourself, only it's in better working order.'

'And how are you going to get back down?'

'This way.' Bethany, her arms beginning to ache, edged
her way hand-by-hand along her beam. When she was
directly above one of the beds she let go, and although
the bed-frame squeaked alarmingly it took her sudden
arrival without collapsing beneath her. The younger and
more agile women followed suit, then between them they
managed to ease the older quine down.

'Oh my,' Effie gasped when she reached the floor, 'that

was as good as a party! I'm going to do it again tomorrow
night, and so are you, Isa Thain, even if I have to hoist
you up myself.'

'If you're going to hoist anything up you could start
with the washing,' Isa told her sourly. 'It'll not dry by
itself in those buckets.'

'I knew you'd be calling, Mistress Lowrie, to find out if
the children are all right.'

'I know they're fine with you, Mrs Pate, and very well
looked after,' Jess told the woman courteously. 'I only
came to ask if I could do anything to help.'

'I raised my own five with no help at all, so two are
no trouble. You'll have a cup of tea.' Phemie Pate made
it sound more like a command than an invitation.

'I'd not want to put you out.'

'You're not. The housework was done by eight o'clock
and the bairns washed and fed long before then. Have you
got no manners at all, Roderick Pate? Say good morning to
your Grandmother Lowrie,' the woman admonished Rory,
who was looking unusually subdued.

'Gran . . .'

'What sort of word is that? Only lazy tinks use that.
Say it properly now, the way I told you.'

'Good morning, Grandmother Lowrie,' the child muttered, giving a stiff little bow.

'Good morning, Ro . . . Rory,' Jess said firmly, ignoring the hissing intake of breath from the other woman.
'And good morning to you, Ellen.' Even the baby, she
noticed with dismay, looked subdued. Both children were
immaculately dressed, with not a crease or a dribble to be
seen. 'Are you not going out to play today, Rory?'

'He's been doing his letters. But now that your Grandmother Lowrie is here I suppose you'd best get out from
under our feet. Mind now,' Phemie warned as Rory made
a bolt for the door, 'you've to stay close to the house,
and no rough games, and keep your clothes clean. And

mind . . .' She broke off as the door closed behind him,
then sniffed and said disapprovingly, 'These children need
to learn their manners.'

Jess felt her hackles rise. 'I've always found them to
be very pleasant bairns. Did you say Rory was doing his
letters?'

'Indeed.' The woman handed Ellen a rag doll. 'Play
quietly with that, now, and don't make a mess. I made
sure that Gilbert and his brothers and sisters were well on
with their letters and their figuring by the time they went
to the school, and it's stood them all in good stead. There's
Gilbert and Nathan both with their own businesses, and
my three lassies well married to good, hard-working God-
fearing men. You'll have a scone, they're fresh made this
morning.'

She split the scone, put a tiny scrape of butter on it
and handed it to Jess on a plate. 'I'd expected you here
before now.'

'I had to see to my sister-in-law before I could get
out. I'm staying with her just now, because she's a bad
back and can't do a thing for herself. Otherwise I'd have
offered to . . .'

'I mean, I expected you here before today.' Mrs Pate
set two cups of strong black tea down and settled herself
in her son's seat at the head of the table. 'To make certain
that the children were being well cared for.'

'I knew that without having to call in.'

'Gilbert knows it too. It's eased his mind, I've no
doubt about that.' The woman sipped like a bird at her
tea. 'Though it would have been best if his own wife
had been here to see to his wee children. She's still very
young, of course, I pointed that out to Gilbert when he
first thought of taking her for his wife. And young women
need a stern hand if they're to be taught to observe their
duties. I know my daughters did. Ellen, stop sucking at
that doll's hand, only dirty lassies do that.'

11

'I could do nothing but sit there and let her criticise my Bethany,' Jess raged to Meg an hour later. 'How could I speak up for the lassie when I know as well as Phemie Pate does where her duty lies? Anyway, I'd not want to quarrel with Gil's mother in his own house in front of his own children. But it was hard to keep silent, Meg, very hard.'

'Just mind that it's none of your business,' Meg advised. She was in her fireside chair with all of Jess's cushions stuffed behind her back, for Meg had none of her own. 'Let the woman have the pleasure of feeling like a martyr if that's her way. As long as the bairns are all right . . .'

'You could say so, if being all right means being fed and looked after, but the two of them looked as if they were in prison instead of their own home. Poor wee Ellen was scared to move. They'd been scrubbed till their faces were shiny. I should have taken them myself, but . . .' Jess stopped suddenly and her sister-in-law completed the sentence for her.

'But you'd me to look after.'

'Now don't you go thinking such a thing, Meg Lowrie. You're not able to see to yourself and I'm happy to do it. And if you were fit you'd have been down south at the farlins and Bethany would have been here, so I'd still not have been looking after the bairns.' Jess paused, realising that there was no sense to be made of her laboured efforts to keep Meg from feeling guilty about the situation, then rushed on, 'The whole place smelled of carbolic. I hope Bethany sees sense and comes home soon.'

'No doubt she will. You're probably fretting about Innes, too – you're a right mother hen, Jess.'

'Innes can manage fine without me for once. Look at your Albert, he's lived alone for years and it's done him no harm.'

'Our Albert and your Innes are nothing like each other.' Meg wriggled in the chair, then gave a contented sigh as she found a comfortable position. 'Albert's a randy pig and Innes is a nice quiet laddie. Our poor mother's heart was fair broken with Albert and his shenanigans . . . sometimes it seemed that every knock at the door brought some poor man to say that Albert had been misbehaving with his lassie. You're fortunate, Jess, you can trust Innes.'

'Are you certain sure it's all right?' Zelda whispered, staring round the kitchen as though she expected Jess to pop out from below the wall-bed or behind one of the high-backed fireside chairs.

'I told you, my mam's staying with my Aunt Meg at nights because of her bad back. We've got the house to ourselves.'

'If that's true, why are you whispering?'

'Eh? Ach, it's you,' Innes said aloud, irritated with himself. 'You're behaving like a cat on hot coals!'

'Well, no wonder. Just think how it would look if your mother came in and found us like this.'

'Like what?' he asked innocently. 'We're just standing here in the kitchen.'

'I doubt if that's what you brought me here for – to stand in the kitchen.'

'That's true,' he admitted, suddenly tired of the game. 'Oh, Zelda, you've got me so's I don't know whether I'm on my head or my heels. I can't concentrate on my work for thinking of you.'

'You think it's any easier for me? You're like the chicken-pox, Innes Lowrie: you've got me fidgeting and thinking about you all the time until it's hard to get my work done properly.' She side-stepped deftly as he reached for her. 'Listen!'

Innes froze, his ears stretched to their utmost, certain that Zelda had caught the sound of his mother's step on the path outside; but all he could hear was the slow, comforting tick of the pendulum clock that had been on the kitchen wall since before his birth, and the occasional whispering shift of a coal in the range. Nervously he eyed the girl in the middle of the room, head tilted back, so still that she might have been a statue.

'What?' he whispered at last, unable to bear the tension any longer. 'I can't hear anything.'

'That's what I mean.' She looked over her shoulder at him. 'It's so quiet in here!'

'Zelda, you gave me the fright of my life! Of course it's quiet, there's only you and me in the place.'

'You're lucky, Innes. You've seen for yourself what our house is like . . . so many folk crowded into it that there's never any peace to think.'

'Aye.' Zelda had taken him several times to the small tied farm cottage in which she had been born and raised. From the moment they stepped through the door she was claimed to calm a fractious toddler, nurse a crying baby, help a perplexed younger brother or sister with school homework, peel potatoes or wash the pots. The Mulholland house was a seething mass of bodies, no matter what time of day it was.

'And it's so nice, too.' She flitted about the small kitchen, looking at her own reflection in the gilt-edged mirror, stroking the neat folds of the curtain drawn across the wall-bed, peering in through the glass front of the display cabinet at the painted china dishes. Seeing her delight and pleasure in the things he had always taken for granted, Innes felt his very bones melt with love for her.

'We'll have a place like this ourselves one day.'

'Will we? D'you mean it?'

'I promise you.' He did mean it. No matter how hard he had to work, no matter what he himself had to do without, he meant every word.

'Oh, Innes!' She flew at him, holding him tight and covering his face with kisses. 'I love you!' Then, as his mouth became more urgent and his hands began to roam, she drew back. 'Where do you sleep?'

'In the loft.'

'Show me.'

Now that the prize was almost his, Innes hesitated, though his body ached for her. 'You're sure?'

She cupped his face in a work-roughened palm. 'I'm sure,' she said, and with trembling hands he lit a candle then led her up the narrow stairs to the loft area.

Since his father's death James had taken away most of the ropes, nets and lobster pots and the lines and tools Weem had used, but there was still a clutter of bits and pieces and the air still held a smell of sea water and tar and pipe tobacco. Although he feared the sea, Innes found the mixture of smells comforting, for it reminded him of his early childhood, when his father had been his safety and refuge, his delight and his god.

The candle flame flickered and danced as he led Zelda along the side of the loft, their heads bent beneath the slope of the house roof, to where one-third of the space had been partitioned off to form an extra room. This had been Bethany's bedroom before her marriage, but now it was Innes's domain. Apart from the bed, covered by a patchwork quilt of Jess's making, there was a small table, one chair, a cupboard where Innes kept his clothes and a shelf holding the few books he had managed to buy. The books were all about engineering and the walls were covered with pictures, cut from magazines and newspapers, of cars and lorries and motor-bicycles.

When the lamp was lit Zelda took in the entire room

with one swift glance, then went to look out through both windows, the one at the back overlooking the yard and the houses beyond, the one at the front showing a glimpse, over house roofs, of the Moray Firth.

'You've got this all to yourself?' Her voice was awed. 'I've never had a place of my own, or a bed of my own. There's always six or seven of us at home, and at the farm I have to share with the dairy lassie.'

'I shared with James until he got wed.' Innes felt the need to apologise for his good fortune. 'And there's only me left now. That's why I said we could get married and live here until we could get a place of our own. There's room up here for two of us.'

Zelda looked round enviously, then heaved a sigh and shook her head. 'I couldn't, not with your mother downstairs.'

He reached out and touched her lips with the tip of one finger, very gently. 'She's not downstairs now,' he whispered and a radiant smile lit up the girl's round, expressive face.

'No, she's not,' she agreed, and moved into his arms.

Now that she was sure they were alone her nerves had gone, and she returned his kisses with a passion that first astonished then excited him. In all the time they had spent together, always in the open, she had been willing yet reserved. Now, indoors and safe from discovery, she changed completely, sighing and moaning, pressing her soft body tightly against him, her mouth and hands just as adventurous and daring as his. When Innes, driven to distraction by his need for her, lifted her and carried her to the bed and began with trembling fingers to unfasten the buttons of her blouse, she didn't push his hands away as he had expected but reached down to unfasten her skirt before wriggling out of it like an eel.

The entire Mulholland clan was dark-haired and dark-eyed – a throwback, Innes had heard some say, to gypsy blood. Kneeling on the bed above Zelda, seeing her bathed in lamplight, he wished that he had the words to express the glowing skin shades before him. Her face and throat and arms could only be described in his limited vocabulary as being a soft golden colour, matched by the gold flecks that the light picked out in her dark eyes, while her smooth, plump body was the rich, creamy shade of the flowers that blossomed in hedgerows in early summer.

'Do I please you, Innes?' Her voice was suddenly uncertain.

'Please me? Oh, Zelda . . .' His voice shook and to his horror he felt unmanly tears prickling behind his eyelids. Now of all times, just when he felt more like a man than he had ever done! He raised a hand to dash them away, but Zelda pushed it aside and reached up for him.

'Come here, you silly,' she said, suddenly in complete control of the situation, knowing instinctively what to do. She drew his head down on to magnificent pillowy breasts tipped with large, dark nipples and held him there, stroking his hair, the nape of his neck and the length of his back through his shirt for the few minutes that his tears flowed. When he lifted his head again, sniffing, she kissed the last of the moisture from his eyes, then said, 'And now I want to see you.'

Once he was naked to her gaze it was Innes's turn to tremble and wonder if he was good enough, but only for a moment before she said, 'Come here, my handsome lad!' and drew him down on to the bed, turning over on her side so that they could lie facing each other, breath mingling and bodies touching.

'Have you ever . . . ?'

'No, have you?'

'Never once?'

'I never found a lass I wanted to lie with, till now. Are you certain . . .'

She gave his arm a little slap. 'You just be quiet, Innes Lowrie, and let me enjoy myself.'

'But you've told me more than once that you wanted to wait till our marriage bed, and this isn't it.'

'I know, but you can be very persuasive,' Zelda said comfortably, nestling closer and sliding her upper leg over his flank. The touch of her skin against his sent a tremor through his already trembling body. 'This is close enough. Women just know these things.'

Then suddenly, just as he felt that he had made sure of her, her soft body went rigid within the circle of his arms.

'What's that?'

'What?'

'That!' she hissed, and now Innes heard it too, the sound of the street door closing and movement in the kitchen directly below.

'Dear God, it must be my mother back home!'

'You said . . . !'

'I thought she was staying the night with Aunt Meg. She's been sleeping there for the past three days!'

'What are we going to do?' Zelda began to scramble over him in an attempt to get out of the bed, but he pushed her back.

'Stay still, then she won't hear us.'

They lay for a moment, two naked bodies locked together, but with all their sexual excitement drained away by the fear of discovery. There was more movement from below, then Jess called from the foot of the loft stairs, 'Innes, are you there?'

'I'll be down in a minute,' he yelled back, and Zelda jumped so violently that she almost tossed him off the narrow cot on to the floor.

'I thought we were supposed to be quiet?' she hissed, raising herself on one elbow as he leaped up and began to snatch at his scattered clothes.

'I had to answer; she might have come up to see for herself if I hadn't.'

'What are we going to do?'

'Stay still.' He dragged his jersey over his head, emerging to say, 'I'll be back as soon as I can.'

'I can't stay here all night. I have to get back to the farm.'

He turned in the doorway, a warning finger to his lips, then went out, closing the door behind him.

Down in the kitchen his mother was ferreting about in the large canvas bag she used to store all her mending and knitting things. 'I thought you'd still be out with Zelda.'

'Mrs Bain wanted her back early, so I thought I'd just go to my bed and get a good early start in the morning.' He had never in his life lied to anyone, but it turned out to be quite easy, given the right circumstances. 'Is Aunt Meg all right?'

'As all right as she can be. I just came back for some wool she needs. Here it is. You've not touched the pie I left in the oven.'

'I was looking something up in one of my books. I'll eat later.'

'Are you all right? You look flushed.'

'I'm fine. Really,' he added hurriedly as she reached up to put a hand on his forehead.

'I shouldn't be leaving you on your own like this.'

'Mother, I'm old enough to look after myself. And Aunt Meg needs you.'

'Well, don't study too much, and get to your bed early. And be sure to eat all of that pie for you're still a growing lad,' she said, and at last she took the wool and left.

Zelda had crawled under the blankets and pulled them over her head. When he drew them away she blinked up at him and mouthed the words, 'Is she gone?'

'Off to my Aunt Meg's for the night. She only wanted to fetch some wool she'd forgotten.'

The way her breasts lifted and tautened when she heaved a sigh of relief brought the warm tingle back to his loins. 'I thought she was going to stay here all night and I'd not be able to get out. I thought she was going to find me.' She raised herself on one elbow. 'What d'you think you're doing?'

'Taking my clothes off again.'

'You think we can . . . be the same as we were after the fright we've just had?'

'We're really alone now. And my ma says I have to get to my bed early.' He grinned down at her. 'She says I'm still a growing lad.'

'I can see that.' She reached out and laid a hand lightly on his groin, exciting him beyond bearing. 'Put the lamp out, then.'

In the darkness they kissed and touched, coaxing each other back to the heights they had reached before being interrupted.

'D'you know what to do?' Innes whispered, desperate for relief but not certain just how to achieve it.

'I've only ever seen animals together.'

'Well, what do they do, then?' Animals or humans, it was all the same to him at that moment.

'We'll work it out somehow,' Zelda said against his chest.

12

'Thank God that's the first week near over.' As one of the coopers covered the barrel she had just completed and trundled it out of the way Isa snatched a minute to drink from the bottle of cold tea she had brought to the farlins. 'I'm chilled to the bone. I wish I'd been born a cooper!'

She scrubbed the drizzling rain from her face and looked longingly over to where Gil and his men were hard at work beneath the shelter of a makeshift tarpaulin. In contrast to the shivering fisher-lassies, the men were sweating and stripped to their shirt sleeves, for they were in close proximity to a blazing fire that was used to bring tubs of water to the boil. The steam from the heated water was needed to shape the staves for the barrels. 'Why is it that men always get the best jobs?' Isa girned.

'Never mind, hen, the first week's the worst,' one of the other packers called over to her. 'You'll be bright as a linty once you've had a wee rest and a bit of a party. You know fine that Yarm'th's the great place to be.'

'I'm not so sure.' Isa squinted up at the heavy grey sky, then stoppered her bottle as one of the other lassies rolled an empty barrel to her. 'Here we go again . . . you'd wonder who eats all these fish.'

'Folk with sense. There's nothing like a good herrin' to keep a body fit and well,' Effie told her. 'Look at me for a start. You'd never guess that I'm really a hunner and thirty.'

'I'd have put you at nearer a hunner and thirty-five,' Isa said sourly.

'Ye're as old as ye feel,' Effie told her, then suddenly broke into song. '"Twenty-one today, I'm twenty-one today . . ."'

'"I've got the key of the door, never been twenty-one before,"' Bethany roared along with the others, her knife slicing through the herring with renewed vigour. It was Saturday morning and, as far as the Scottish men and women were concerned, there would be no work the following day, for Sunday was the Lord's Day and the Scottish boats would stay in the harbour no matter how well the herring were running. The fisher-lassies could have worked every day of the week, for they were renowned for their skills and in great demand, but they agreed with their menfolk – Saturday evenings and Sundays until midnight were sacrosanct.

Once the boats had been cleaned and made ready to go out immediately after midnight on Sunday, the crews were free to enjoy a well-earned rest, but the fisher-lassies, as women, simply exchanged one job of work for another. Before they sat down to their evening meal on Saturday buckets of water brought up from the wash-house were set to heat on the stoves; then, after they had eaten, one group went off to the shops with money contributed by all to buy tea, sugar and milk, bread and cheese, cold meat and a large selection of fancy cakes, while those left behind cleaned out the loft, scrubbing the two long tables as well as the great expanse of wooden flooring. The pots of water on the stove were constantly re-filled, and when the others had returned with their purchases they all turned to the task of washing clothes and bed-linen and cleaning the skylight windows.

'To think I was complaining about the cold earlier,' Isa puffed. 'The sweat's runnin' off me now!' By the time the loft was as clean and neat as they could make it they were all hot, sticky and uncomfortable, and more than ready to strip off their working clothes and take turns in the three tin baths provided by their landlady.

As they dressed in their best they discussed plans for the evening. Some opted for a visit to a music hall or to the cinema, but most planned to take the evening air and either meet up with the menfolk or enjoy a wander through the streets, peering in shop windows to see the wares on offer.

'I wish we could get a fiddler and an accordion player and have a nice wee dance to ourselves,' young Kate said regretfully. 'That's what I like about going to the islands.'

When they followed the fishing fleets north, to places such as Orkney or the Shetlands, the lassies lived in isolated wooden huts and had to make their own entertainment, which usually took the form of late-night dancing with the fishermen. In large, well-populated ports like Lowestoft and Yarmouth, where the lassies were under the eyes of landladies, there were no parties other than a fairly sedate gathering after the mission church services on Sunday.

'Away ye go,' Effie boomed. 'It's much nicer bein' able to look in the shop windows and visit the music hall.'

'At least in the islands you know where your man is when he's not at sea,' Kate grumbled. 'In Yarm'th my Charlie could be up close with any of these English lassies.'

'I don't blame you for frettin' over that,' Effie conceded, 'since he's Albert Lowrie's lad.'

'He's not like his father that way,' the girl flared, her face flushing, then the colour deepened as Effie immediately shot back, 'Then why are you worryin' yourself about where he might be when he's ashore? Anyway, the big ports are safer for you, lassie. More than one nor'-east bairn's been started in the islands during the herring season. Best for you young folk to be where the landladies and the rest of us can keep an eye on you.'

That night most of them ended up strolling along King Street, where they soon met up with their menfolk, smart in their blue suits and black jerseys. Arm-in-arm in groups or couples they promenaded in slow and stately fashion along the street, stopping every few yards to greet old friends. During the Yarmouth fishing season there could be as many as twenty thousand people in the town, and as they all followed the herring along the coast year after year, coopers and lassies and fishermen from all the ports got to know each other well.

It wasn't long before Gil fell into step beside Bethany, threading her arm firmly through the crook of his elbow. 'So how d'you feel after a week back at the farlins?'

'Grand. It's as if I'd never left. You'd see for yourself that I was keeping up with the rest of them.'

'I wasnae watching.'

'I noticed that,' she said drily, and he cleared his throat and walked on for a while in silence before saying, 'I've had some letters from my mother.'

'And I've had letters from mine, saying that the bairns are fine.' She didn't add that Jess thought the children were missing her and perhaps being too firmly disciplined. She had only skimmed that part of the letter and refused to let herself dwell on it.

'Of course they are, with my mother minding them. But she's not happy about you being here and neither am I.'

'That's too bad, Gil, because I'm staying.'

'Is it something I've done? Are you trying to punish me?'

'Of course not!'

'Then why d'you make a fool of me by going back to the farlins?'

'It has nothing to do with you. I'm making sure that everything's fine and Isa's settling in, that's all. And it's nice to be earning my own money again.'

'That's another thing – folk'll be thinking that my own wife has to go out to work because I cannae support her.'

'If they're daft enough to say that, let them. We both know it's not true.'

'Why d'you need to work for your own silver?' he burst out, stopping and turning her to face him. 'Do I not give you everything you ask for?'

'You do.' And he always wanted to know exactly what she wanted it for, too. 'It's just that I was always used to keeping myself and I miss having money of my own in my pocket. And it's nice to be back at the farlins, Gil.'

'It's . . . it's nice to see you there,' he admitted, turning to walk on. 'Looking so brave and so bonny, with that gutting knife in your hand and the pretty colour of your hair peeping out from under the scarf about your head.' His arm tightened so that her hand was wedged close against his side. 'It fair takes me back to the days before we were wed. I never thought then that I'd have you for my own one day.'

'Neither did I, Gil.' Young and innocent, enjoying her life and her work, she had had little idea in those days of the plans being hatched in her father's head. She shivered a little as the wind leaped out at them from a narrow lane as they passed. The ranks of the walkers were beginning to thin out as some couples slid quietly into the darkening night on private business of their own and others turned back towards their lodgings. 'I'm going back now,' she said. 'It's been a hard week and I'm tired.'

'I'll walk with you. I just wish we could be together,' he went on as they turned. 'I've been looking around, but there's not a room to be had in the entire place.'

'I told you I wanted to stay with the other lassies. If I moved into lodgings with you they'd say I was too stuck up to bide with them.'

'Never mind what they'd say,' Gil growled, squeezing her arm so tightly that pins and needles began to shoot through her fingers. 'It's driving me mad being without you, Bethany.'

'You'd have been without me anyway if I'd stayed home with the bairns.'

'That's different. It's seeing you every day that's unsettling me.'

'You're just saying that to get me to go home.'

'Back home,' said Gil, 'is the last place I want you to be right now.' Then as they reached the door that led to the attic stairs, 'Come here a minute.'

Before she realised what was happening he had deftly pulled her off to one side and into the narrow lane that ran up the side of the lodging house. High walls on either side cast deep black shadows and as Bethany's feet skittered and slid over the uneven, unseen cobbles he looped an arm about her waist to hold her upright, using his superior strength at the same time to urge her deeper into the darkness.

'Gil . . .'

He pushed her against a wall and slathered damp kisses over her mouth, all along her jawline, then down to her throat, one hand fumbling at her breast and the other tugging her skirt, pulling it up to her thighs. 'Bethany lass,' he mumbled through the kisses, 'I'm on fire for you . . .'

'Gil . . . no, Gil, not here. Not like this.'

He lifted his head and the dim light from a gas lamp in the nearby street glanced off his eyes so that they glittered down at her. 'This is all we have, thanks to you,' he said, arousal souring the edge of his temper. 'So this it has to be.'

'It doesn't have to be at all!' She pushed him away but he was ready for her, anticipating her attempt to slide along the wall and round the corner to the house door.

'Bein' in Yarm'th's mebbe good for the both of us,' he said breathlessly, his hands sliding inside her blouse, and up her thigh.

*   *   *

Bethany paused on the attic landing to pin up her hair, now straggling about her neck, and make sure that her clothes were in place before venturing in. It was not necessary, for although some beds were still empty all the women in the attic were already asleep.

She stripped swiftly and used her skirt to scrub at her face and body, rubbing Gil's touch away before rolling into bed, drawing the blanket right up to her ears and relishing the pleasure of being alone at last.

On Sunday morning the women were up early to put on their best clothes, make the beds, take down the washing lines and put the clean laundry out of sight. Then they made up piles of sandwiches and arranged them and cakes on the long tables, for on Sunday afternoon it was traditional for the fisher-lassies to entertain their menfolk.

When all was ready they pinned on their hats and went off to the morning service in the mission, which as always was packed with worshippers. The service was long, but Bethany enjoyed every minute of it, for it wasn't often these days that she got the chance to go to worship. Although most fisher-families were keenly religious, neither she nor Gil was a great church-goer, for he usually lay late in his bed on Sunday mornings, while Bethany had the children to see to and a big midday meal to cook. But in Yarmouth it was different, for the mission services were social as well as religious gatherings.

She saw Gil as soon as she went in, sitting with the other men and turning round each time he heard the door open. He grinned at her, the smug grin of ownership, and she gave him a brief smile and a prim nod. She was surprised to see James – who, to Stella's distress, had not set foot inside the church since the day of their marriage – sitting among the congregation, his hair sleeked back and his face impassive.

'I never thought you'd be here,' she said when she met him and Gil outside afterwards.

'I was with Davie Geddes. He sets great store by religion.'

'Why should you want to please Davie Geddes?'

Gil clapped a hand on the younger man's shoulder. 'It seems that Davie's looking for a mate for his boat.'

'You've already got a boat, James.'

'Uncle Albert has a boat, not me.'

'But . . .'

'Are we going to the loft or are we not?' Gil interrupted. 'All that hymn singing's made me hungry. You'll come back with us and have something to eat, James? Religion's great for the appetite!'

James hesitated for a moment, then shrugged and nodded, striding up the road ahead of them, the studs in his sturdy boots striking sparks from the cobbles.

'You were in a right hurry to get away last night,' Gil said low-voiced as they followed.

'I was tired, and you got what you wanted, didn't you?'

'Watch your mouth,' he hissed in a panic, eyeing his brother-in-law's broad back. 'D'you want the whole place to hear you?'

'Speaking for myself, I'm not bothered. And as far as the rest of our stay here goes, there'll be no more hiding up dark alleyways for me or you, Gil Pate. I'm not a loose woman and I'll not be treated like one. You'll have to wait until we get back to our own house,' Bethany said haughtily, and ran ahead to catch up with Isa, Kate and Charlie.

The loft was filled with folk all afternoon and Bethany had no chance to speak to James. She caught sight of him now and again, talking mainly to the other men, though at one point she saw him in conversation with one of the younger lassies. By the time she had managed to work her way to the corner where she had seen them the girl was on her own.

'Has our James gone already?'

Maggie, a known flirt, shrugged and pouted. 'How should I know? I never thought he was all that fond of Stella, but I didnae realise that he's got no time for any woman at all.'

'If you'd taken the trouble to ask I could have told you that my brother cares about two things: himself and his boat,' Bethany said flatly. 'He didn't say where he was going?'

'To the devil, for all I care.'

'There's plenty men in Yarm'th, Maggie, some of them single. Don't waste your time on our James.'

Finding him at last by the table, picking through the scattered remains of the food, Bethany took his arm and towed him to an empty bench. 'That nonsense about Davie Geddes's boat – you're not really thinking of leaving the *Fidelity*, are you?'

'I'm a free man, I can do anything I choose.'

'What would Da think about it?'

'If he wanted me to stay on the *Fidelity* for the rest of my life he should have left me his share, since I'm the only one in the family to work on the boat.'

Bethany bit her lip. 'Mebbe I was too hasty. You can have my share if it matters so much to you, and I'll talk to Ma and Innes as soon as I get home. I'll write to them now if you want.'

'It's too late, d'you not see that?' James glared at her from beneath shaggy black brows, just like their father's. 'None of you cared enough about me – not him or you or the others. I'd as soon go my own way.'

'You'll not be happy on another boat.'

'I'm not happy where I am, so where's the difference? Stop fretting about what Da would want, Bethany. He was never worth it and he didn't give a damn for you and me when we were grown.'

'He did!'

'He used the two of us to serve his own purpose and he doesn't give a damn now for us or for the boat, because he's dead and buried in the earth and feeding the worms. And they're welcome to him!' James said savagely and walked off.

She stayed where she was, shocked by the strength and ferocity of his bitterness, but even more shocked by the realisation that she recognised and understood it, for it burned in her as well as in her brother.

'Bethany . . .' Gil arrived and drew her into the corner, away from the others. 'Listen, I've been speaking to a man who lives on the edge of the town, and he says that his landlady might have a wee room to rent.'

'How many times do I have to tell you that I'm biding here where I belong?'

'Mebbe I'll just take the room and find another lassie to share it with me, then. There's plenty of them about.'

'You're right, and no need to look far, either. Try Maggie,' Bethany suggested coldly. 'She's always looking out for a man.'

In Buckie, Jess continued to spend her nights with Meg, who found it hard to start moving in the morning without a good back rub. This meant that Zelda could spend her nights off in Innes's bed, with nobody any the wiser, since Mrs Bain, her employer, thought that she was with her parents; they, in turn, were under the impression that she was sleeping at the farm.

'My mother says that Mrs Bain should pay me more than she does, seeing as she keeps asking me to stay on,' she giggled into Innes's shoulder.

'And what did you say to that?'

'I told her that it was only for a wee while, until the bronchitis leaves Peter's chest, and it wouldn't be a good thing at all to anger Mrs Bain by refusing.'

'It'll be just for a wee while too,' Innes mourned. 'My mother's good with bad backs.'

Zelda, cosy in the nest they had made for themselves within the blankets, sighed. 'I'm going to miss being here with you, Innes Lowrie, all snug and warm. It wouldn't be the same in a draughty old barn or,' she shivered deliciously against him, 'a drystone dyke.'

'But you'd not deny me, surely?' he protested, alarmed at the thought. He couldn't get enough of Zelda's warm, silky body, with its exciting curves and hollows; for the first time in his life he felt truly alive and the thought of being without her loving was more than he could bear.

'I should . . . but I don't know that I could deny you, now,' she confessed.

Making a sudden deft move that flipped her on to her back with him poised above her, he grinned down at the pretty face on his pillow.

'The thing to do,' he said, 'is to make the most of the comfort we have now, and the time we've got left.'

13

With most of the boats at the English fishing grounds the village was achingly quiet. Mowser Buchan and the other old men, who spent most of their time down at the harbour, had nothing to look at but the horizon and nobody to speak to but each other. The womenfolk, once they had scrubbed and polished, and beaten rugs and told each other what a blessing it was to be able to get the work done now that the menfolk weren't getting under their feet, found time heavy on their hands for once.

Walking by Cluny harbour on her way from Meg's to her own house, Jess mourned to see the place so silent and empty, with only a handful of smaller boats berthed in one or other of the basins. The harbour had been built at the end of the previous century on the site of The Salters, an old boat haven, to cope with the rapid growth of the herring trade. The deep-water refuge, capable of sheltering hundreds of boats, looked quite desolate now that it was offering protection to only a few of the smaller fishing boats and a commercial sailing ship unloading its cargo of timber in the outer basin.

The tide was out and, in the last of the four inner basins, a few children had clambered down the iron ladders set into the stone walls to play happily on the mudflats. Smiling, Jess stopped to watch them climb in and out of the beached rowing boats, their voices ringing in the cold air. Rory was not among them – they were all

older than him, but the little boy had an adventurous spirit
and normally he would have shinned down the vertical
ladder with the best of them. Instead he would be at home,
poor wee mite, firmly under his grandmother's thumb and
hating every minute of it.

Jess decided that that very afternoon she would offer to
take both children off Phemie Pate's hands for an hour or
so. They would walk along by the shore and climb around
the rocks and look for crabs in the pools. Pleasant though
the outing would be, the thought of it already depressed
her, because of the looks she would no doubt see on their
two little faces when the time came to return them to their
grandmother. She wished with all her heart that Bethany
had never gone to Yarmouth, or that she would come home
early instead of waiting until the end of the season, but she
knew full well that having tasted freedom, her rebellious
daughter would not be in a hurry to return to the duties
of a wife and mother.

Perhaps if she birthed a bairn of her own, Jess thought . . .
then dismissed the idea. Bethany had never been mater-
nally minded and perhaps it was just as well that Gil
seemed content with the two he already had and showed no
signs of wanting to father more. Although Jess herself had
never had the desire or, thank God, the need to prevent a
pregnancy, she knew that some did, and she suspected that
her healthy, childless daughter was among that number.

'I only ever mind seeing you once with such a long
face, Jess Innes,' a voice said just behind her, 'and that
was the last day we set eyes on each other.'

She turned sharply to see a sturdy, squarely built man
not much taller than herself, his weather-beaten face dominated by bright sea-green eyes with a youthfulness in them
that denied the grey in the thick eyebrows above.

'Jacob?' Shock stole her voice away and the word came
out as a mere whisper. 'Jacob MacFarlane, is that you?'

'You mind me then?' The skin about his eyes crinkled
up in a huge smile and he seized one of her hands in

his. 'Och, Jess, it's grand to see you after all those years!'

'But . . .' A glance took in the silver-topped cane in his other hand, and the caped Ulster coat protecting him against the sharp wind. 'In the name of God, Jacob, where have you been?'

He gave a great boom of laughter that sent nearby seagulls, foraging for scraps among the crab pots, leaping for the sky with shrill screams of vexation, and made the children on the mudflats stop their play and stare up at the two figures high above them. 'Fishing out along the rocks with a pole and a string and a bit of bait on a pin, Jess. Begging a hurl on top of the nets being carted off to the cutching yards. Running a message for my mother,' he said in delight. Then, as she stared at him, uncomprehending, 'You said that just the way you used to say it when we were bairns playing together. It was for all the world as if we'd seen each other not an hour since.'

'And I'll say it again. Where have you been . . . all these years?' she added.

'Oh, such a lot of places, Jess. England, The Netherlands, Russia. Here and there.'

She looked again at his fine clothes, which could have been made specially for him. 'You'll have given up the fishing?'

'Long since, though I've stayed in the trade one way or another,' he said, then shivered as a particularly keen gust of wind swept along the harbourside. 'It's far too cold to be standing here.'

'I'll need to be on my way home anyway.'

'Then I'll walk with you if I may.' He took the shopping basket from her and turned to match his steps to hers.

She was still trying to come to terms with the shock of seeing him again. 'What are you doing in Buckie?'

'I've come to see you, Jess.'

'All the way from Russia and The Netherlands just to see me?'

'Not entirely,' he admitted. 'I'd to visit Aberdeen on a matter of business, so I stayed with my sister Minnie and her man. You'll remember Minnie?'

'I do indeed.' The MacFarlanes and the Inneses had been neighbours in the village of Portessie, just along the coast from Buckie, and their children had grown up together, more like brothers and sisters than friends. 'How is she?'

'Hearty. She asked to be reminded to you. It was Minnie that told me about Weem passing away,' he added soberly. 'I was sorry to hear it.'

'Aye, well – it comes to all of us in the end.'

'Somehow I never thought of it as happening to Weem Lowrie.'

'Nor did I,' Jess said huskily. Then, as she heard the intake of breath that meant that he was about to say something else, she jumped in quickly with, 'I always mind Minnie's lovely long black hair. She was a beautiful lassie.'

'She's a bit heftier these days, with not a bit of black left in her hair, though it's still as thick as ever. Just like my own.' Jacob took off his curly-brimmed bowler hat to reveal a healthy shock of grey hair. 'But she still has her looks. There's only the two of us left now, me and Minnie.'

'Is that right?' There had been five MacFarlane children; Jess knew that the other sister had died young, in childbirth, and that Jacob and his brothers had all left home as young men. She had not heard any more of them, not even of Jacob.

'Minnie managed to keep in touch with us all, and give us news of each other, though I never saw any of the others once we were scattered across the face of the globe.'

'Have you been along to have a look at Portessie yet?'

'I'm not sure that I want to. Some memories are best left in the past and the place has nothing for me.'

'It's not changed.'

'Mebbe I will take a look, if you'll come with me.'

'Surely, if there's time before you're off again.'

'There's time all right. I've taken a room in the Commercial Hotel, for I might be doing business in the area. And I'd welcome the chance to catch up with all your news.'

'There's little of that, since I've only moved a few miles from the house where I was born and raised.'

'There's different ways of travelling and I'm sure a lot's happened to you since we last met.'

They had reached Jess's door; she hesitated, then said, 'I'd ask you in, but my son's been staying on his lone in the house for a week or more and there's no knowing what state he left it in this morning. And I have to visit my grandchildren.'

'You have grandchildren, Jess? I wondered.'

'Five of them. Three belong to my son James and two are step-children to Bethany, my daughter.'

He handed the basket back, his eyes locked on her face, as though he was trying to absorb the look of her and hold it in his memory. 'Children and grandchildren. You see, Jess, you have travelled far in your own way. And I want to know all about your journeying.'

'You could come for your dinner tomorrow night about six,' she blurted out, made suddenly and ridiculously shy by the intensity of his gaze. 'You'll meet Innes, he's still at home with me.'

He put a hand to the brim of his hat. 'I'd be delighted to accept.'

'You've lost the Doric,' she accused.

'Fit like, Jessie quine?' The traditional north-east greeting was accompanied by a huge grin. 'Caal wither, is't no? My natural speech has had to bide quietly in the background, because I've spent most of my life talking to folk that would never have understood a word of it. But it's not left me, I can promise you that. I still use it for thinking.'

The house was tidy enough and Innes had even made
his bed before going off to work that morning. Thinking
herself lucky that it was her youngest who had been left
to fend for himself, and not James or Bethany, Jess
dusted the place and set the table, then started preparing
the evening meal.

Her mind was so full of Jacob and his sudden arrival,
after all those years when she had heard nothing from
him or about him, that she had peeled three times the
quantity of potatoes needed before she realised what her
hands were doing. She clicked her tongue in annoyance.
Now she would have to put most of them into a bucket
of water in the wash-house, to use over the next day
or two.

She had bought three plump herrings for the dinner,
one for herself, one for Innes and one to be taken along
to Meg, but on second thoughts she covered them with
a plate and put them away in the larder, then retrieved
some potatoes from the bucket and added them to the
pot on the stove. They could be cooked today and fried
tomorrow. Jacob would probably enjoy a traditional meal
of fried potatoes and herring coated in oatmeal. Tonight
she would use the mince she had bought for the next
day.

Innes was surprised and disconcerted when he came home
from work to find his mother bustling about the kitchen
and the table set for two.

'You're not going to eat at Auntie Meg's then?'

'Not tonight. She's more able to move around now and
I told her I'd take some dinner along after I got the pots
washed.'

'So you're sleeping at her house tonight?'

'Aye, but I think this'll be the last time I'll have to leave
you on your own, for she's well on the mend, providing
she takes proper care of herself.' She lifted the lid from
a pot and stirred its contents, then turned and flapped her

hands at him. 'Off you go and get washed, the dinner's nearly ready.'

His mind was in turmoil as he went to the wash-house. Only one more short night with Zelda in his arms, one more morning of waking to see her hair spread over his pillow and her pretty, sleep-flushed face close to his. He washed hurriedly and put on clean clothes, then returned to the kitchen feeling like a condemned man who has just been told the date of his execution.

'Are you sure about leaving Auntie Meg alone at nights? I don't mind seeing to myself.'

'You're a good lad,' Jess said with a sudden rush of affection. 'You've not once complained about being left on your own, and you're the first man I've ever known to make his own bed without being forced to it.'

'Och, that? It's easy enough done.'

'To tell the truth, I'm hankering after my own bed and I think me and Meg are getting on each other's nerves. I'm sure she'll be as pleased as me to get back to her own ways, for it's never a good thing to have two women in one kitchen. Mind you,' she went on as she helped him to more potatoes, 'neglect hasn't done you any harm. You're looking right well these days.'

'I've not been neglected, Mother. You've left a good supper out for me every night.'

'And from now on I'll be here to put it on the table for you and eat it with you, too. Oh . . . there'll be a visitor coming for his dinner tomorrow night,' she added casually.

'Who's that?'

'Jacob MacFarlane, a man I knew before you were born. His family lived next door to mine in Portessie, but they all moved away once they were grown.' It was the simple truth; no need for Innes to know that she herself had been the cause of Jacob leaving the Moray coast.

'So what brings him back?'

'Some kind of business. We met at the harbour this

afternoon.' The tea was well mashed by now; she got up and brought the teapot from the stove to the table, pouring the liquid – black in the way the fisher-folk liked it – into two big cups. ''Are you meeting Zelda later?'

'Aye,' Innes said casually, reaching for his cup. 'I said I'd look in at the farm to see if she'd an hour off.'

On her way to Buckie, Zelda would pass an old ruined cottage where they sometimes met. Innes got to it in good time and waited, sheltering behind one of the better remaining walls. When he heard footsteps approaching he called softly so as not to scare her, then stepped out to meet her as she ran towards him, a small shape in the dark night. As he caught and held her he felt as though his heart was breaking, and she was just as dismayed when he told her the news.

'Oh, Innes, what'll we do?'

'I don't know, lass.' He buried his face in her hair. 'It's like being taken to the gates of Heaven, then having them slammed in your face just when you think you're going to be allowed in.' His voice was muffled.

'We'll have to save every penny we can for a place of our own.' She drew back slightly. 'You still want to wed me, don't you, Innes?'

'Want to? It's all I do want, but it's going to take so long to get our own place, Zelda.'

'It's like walking – you keep at it, and then one day you find that you're there.' She reached up and kissed him, her nose cold against his face. 'We'll just have to think about that all the time. What about tonight?'

'My mother was at the house when I left, but she should be gone by now. She's spending one more night with Auntie Meg.'

'And Mrs Bain says I can stay at home tonight, so we're all right.'

'For the last time!'

'Since that's the way of it,' Zelda said firmly, linking

her hand in his and pulling him away from the cottage's tumble-down walls, 'then we must make the most of it, my bonny lad.'

Once Innes had gone out, Jess swept and scrubbed and polished until the house was as clean as she could make it. Jacob, with his fine clothes and his elegant way with words, must have been in some grand houses in his time. Perhaps to his eyes the cottage she had shared with Weem and their children would seem very small and shabby, she thought, then caught herself up sharply. What did it matter what he thought? This cottage had served her and her man and children well. It was clean and neat, with not a thing in it that hadn't been paid for, and if Jacob MacFarlane had become too grand for the likes of a fisherman's dwelling place then that was his problem. If he had stayed in the close huddle of cottages that was Portessie this was just the sort of home he would have had himself, and he would have been contented enough with it.

If he had stayed . . . Jess sank on to her usual fireside chair, the duster still clutched in her hand, remembering. He would have stayed, would have been happy to stay and spend the rest of his life fishing the Firth and the seas around Britain, if it had not been for Weem Lowrie.

There had never been a spoken pledge between her and Jacob, but for as long as she could remember there had been an understanding between them as they progressed from babyhood to childhood, then to young adulthood. Even although Jacob, the shyest of the three MacFarlane boys, had never gone beyond a few sweet gentle kisses when they happened to find themselves apart from the others, Jess had been content in the knowledge that one day – when they both felt the time was right – there would be more than kisses.

But the future was never certain and for her everything changed unexpectedly, with a surge and a rush that had swept all sense from her head and her heart. Working

at the farlins in Yarmouth, she had met up with Weem
Lowrie, who had no time at all for gentle kisses. Weem
took what he wanted, and as soon as he set eyes on her
he wanted Jess Innes.

Even now, with her body thickened by childbearing and
a lifetime of hard work, the pit of Jess's stomach clenched
and she caught her breath sharply as she recalled those
Yarmouth nights when Weem had contrived to get her
on her own. She remembered the sweet confusion and
delight into which his loving had spun her, thrilling and
bedevilling her. She remembered lying awake in the
lodgings when the other lassies were asleep all about
her, savouring over and over again the precious moments
she had shared with him.

And she remembered with bitter clarity the day she had
told Jacob that she was carrying Weem's child.

She had expected him to turn from her, disgusted and
repelled, but instead he had stood his ground, those sea-
green eyes of his blazing. 'He'll not wed you, Jessie, his
sort never do. But I'll marry you gladly, bairn and all.'

'He's said he will. We've set the date.'

He had argued, begged, then when he realised that she
was lost to him the light had gone out of his eyes and he
had cried, standing before her, hands by his sides; cried
silently but with his head up, making no attempt to conceal
the tears. When she tried to offer comfort, appalled by the
hurt she had dealt him, Jacob had stepped back, shaking
his head, refusing to let her touch him. Finally he had
wiped the moisture from his cheeks with a rough motion
of one hand and said, 'You really think the likes of Weem
Lowrie can make you happy?'

'I hope so.'

'He'll break your heart,' Jacob told her in a flat, empty
voice. 'He'll never be able to love you as I do.' Then he
had gone to seek out Weem, who had laughed at him and,
when Jacob flew at him, had beaten him soundly down on
the harbour in front of a crowd of men.

The next day Mrs MacFarlane came to the door, distraught, to tell Jess that Jacob had gone. It was clear from the woman's voice, and from the bitterness in her eyes, that she knew why her son had left and where to lay the blame. Jacob had never returned and within a year both his brothers had followed him; one, Jess heard, to crew with him on a fishing boat out of the English port of Whitby, the other to join the Navy. By then Jess had married Weem and was settled in Buckie, with wee James to care for and Bethany on the way.

Jacob had probably been surprised to find out from his sister that the marriage between Jess Innes and Weem Lowrie had survived until death, she thought, rubbing absently with the duster at an imaginary mark on the polished table. And that Weem hadn't broken her heart after all.

Then, remembering the rift between herself and James, now that her husband's bones lay in Rathven Cemetery instead of at the bottom of the sea, and her own aching sense of guilt over what she had done to Weem, she wondered if perhaps Jacob had been right after all.

14

Jem, who had been left on watch overnight, was too inexperienced to read the weather signs properly. The sudden squall had arrived out of nowhere, giving Albert Lowrie no time to bring in his nets and run for shelter. When the crew – alerted by a wave that lifted the boat high, then slammed it down again, bouncing them out of their bunks – raced on deck, the wind, screaming out of the dark, slapped them hard and took the breath from their lungs.

'Ye bloody loon!' Albert screamed at his son as, with a rending sound only just heard above the scream of the gale, the mizzen ripped, to hang in tatters. 'Why did ye no' call me up long afore this?'

'I didnae think . . .' The words were ripped from the lad's mouth. His eyes were wide with the horror of what was happening, the shock of its suddenness.

'You'll have plenty to time to think when you're down below, lookin' up at them nets above ye!'

'Never mind that now,' James yelled. He had been thrown hard from his bunk when the first wave struck, and he could almost feel the bruising coming up on his right arm. Even so, he felt his body tingling, coming alive, joyously preparing to meet the sea on its own terms and win. 'Get the capstan started, stand by to haul or we'll lose the lot! Jem, into the hold with you.'

Lights from the other vessels strewn across the fishing

grounds were sparking out and in again as the boats slid down into the well of the waves, then fought their way back up to the crests. The grey-black water was lanced with ragged white flashes as the gale snatched at the tips of the waves, ripping and tearing them into foam.

The boat danced, bucked and shied, and the crew had a fight on their hands to bring the first net, well filled with herring, to the surface. Each time the *Fidelity* rolled hard to starboard, dipping beneath the water and taking in green seas that swirled round their legs, threatening to pluck them from the deck and hurl them into the deep, the men hauled back hard; they deftly pinned the messenger to the bulwark by one knee, so that when the boat lifted again her bulk and weight lifted the net a little further out of the water.

When the dawn light came it was cold and grey, and only served to reveal the full extent of the storm. At times it seemed that there was no sky at all, only great walls of water bearing down on the boat like hungry grey wolfhounds, their foam-white teeth bared and eager to crunch and smash the drifter and her crew into oblivion.

James wondered, during a brief respite while they braced themselves and waited for the roll of the boat to aid them in easing the nets a little further from the sea, whether the inland folk who enjoyed a nice herring for their breakfast or their dinner ever gave a thought to how it was caught. Then, as the boat lifted and he felt his muscles and sinews stretch to snapping point and his joints threaten to come apart under the terrible strain of holding on to the net, habit took over and all thought fled.

Yelling above the sea's thunder and the sharp whine of the winds, James struggled to spur the others on, while he himself worked harder than he had ever worked before, desperate to get all the fish in before his uncle's nerve went. But he did not manage to save the final net, for Albert insisted on emptying it so that it could be hauled in easily while the boat turned to run before the heavy seas,

leaving behind a great mass of dead fish tossing belly-up
on the mountainous waves.

'Bloody dogfish!' Albert grunted as he spotted several
great holes in the empty net. Dogfish fed on herring,
and when they found themselves trapped along with
their quarry they used their vicious teeth to tear their
way free.

'The nets'll mend, but there's no recovering the fish
we left behind,' James told him.

'We've got plenty.'

'We could have had more.'

'We could have been at the bottom of the sea . . . and
more likely would be, if you had your way,' his uncle
snapped at him and stamped below, leaving James to
clear the few herring that had been brought aboard with
the final net.

Disentangling a limp fish and flipping it into the hold,
he decided that he had no option in the next season but
to become a member of Davie Geddes's crew – a fisher
for the Lord, as Davie proudly put it. That part would not
be easy, for James had never been one for religion, but
he would have to learn to thole it. At least Stella would
be pleased, he thought morosely.

It would also mean making a move from steam to sail,
but that didn't trouble him for he had learned his trade
on the sailed boat that his father had skippered before the
Fidelity and some of his most exhilarating experiences had
happened there. James grinned, recalling one storm more
vicious than the one they were running from, when the
boat had been tossed on raging, white-capped seas like a
leaf being carried down a rain-flooded gutter. The wind
had screamed like a harpy through the rigging, causing
the sails to crack like thunder and belly out until young
James, half-thrilled and half-terrified, was certain that he
could see the powerful mast bending like a bow beneath
the strain of trying to hold on to them.

That voyage was his third, and as the storm grew instead

of abating, he became convinced that they were all – boat and crew – set for a watery grave and that he would never see land, or his mother or Bethany, again. The fear mounted until he wanted to scream it aloud, to beg the wind to go away and the sea to leave them alone. He wanted to demand that his father take him home at once and stop frighting him, but when he turned to look at Weem, steady as a rock behind the wheel, fighting to keep his boat afloat and get his catch home, James's fear ebbed, replaced by the knowledge that his father would not let him die. In any case, if drowning was the right death for Weem Lowrie, then it was the right death for his son, too.

When at last the storm let up and they had time to draw breath, Weem asked, 'Were you frighted, son?' And James had shaken his head violently. 'No.'

To his surprise, his father said, 'Well, you should have been, for it's only right for men like us to be afraid of the sea's tempers. You need to give her her place, James. She's like a woman, and you'll find out for yourself when you're older that women need to be respected sometimes, and gentled sometimes, and coaxed sometimes. Aye, and pushed sometimes too, but you have to be sure of them before you can go the right way about that. You'll learn.'

Learn he had, about the sea and about women too. And he had had more success with the sea, since the 'herring fever' – a burning desire to fish all the seas of the world in search of the silver darlings – was in his blood.

He would bide his time, and when he was master of Davie Geddes's sailed boat, James swore to himself, he would show all of them – Albert Lowrie included – how a real fisherman went about his business.

'Is that all the barrels you've filled?' Gil came storming down the line of women. 'What's the matter with the lot of you?' He pointed to the mountain of herring waiting to be shovelled into the farlins when there was room. 'There's more boats due in and more herring on the way, and I'm not minded to be kept on working here all night just because you're too busy chattering.'

'The work's being done all right.' Bethany took a min-ute to straighten her aching back and draw her forearm across her brow to clear it of sweat, which chilled as soon as it burst from the pores. 'We can use our hands and our tongues at the same time.'

It was almost midday, cold and grey with a sharp wind, and not many people lingered to watch the lassies work, but those who did pressed a little closer, interested in the promise of a quarrel. Ever since Bethany had refused to move into lodgings with him, Gil had been in a black mood, watching the women at the farlins like a hawk hovering over a dovecote, bullying and nagging at the slightest opportunity. They were all, Bethany knew, on a short fuse.

Even the buyers, eyes narrowed and faces absorbed as they studied the barrels already packed, mentally trans-ferring the fishermen's and fisher-lassies' work into profit and loss, sensed the air of tension and drama and edged a little nearer so as to be in on any confrontation.

The other women had the sense to keep on working, though their eyes were watchful and their faces tight with a resentment that Bethany could feel as keenly as she could feel the wind trying to burrow beneath the layers of wool she wore below her big oilskin apron.

'Well, use your hands a bit more and your tongues a bit less. Wait . . .' Gil rounded on Isa, who had just finished spreading the first layer in her barrel and was scooping up a double handful of salt to scatter over it. 'Are you packing those barrels properly?'

The woman's face, reddened by the cold, took on a deeper hue. 'Of course I am.'

'I'll not have my customers getting short weight or having the fish spoiled because it's not packed right.' He elbowed her aside to check the barrel for himself. 'Fish that's been properly packed should stay right where it is, even if the barrel's shattered round it,' he blustered on, glaring round the farlins. 'Mind now, I'll not have poor workers in my teams!'

As he stalked away Isa made an obscene gesture behind his back and mouthed an oath, then glared at the others. 'There's nothin' wrong with my work!'

'Of course there isnae, lass. What's up with that man of yours, Bethany?' Effie wanted to know. 'He's been going round all this week with a face like a skelpit arse.'

'Asking for a skelpit arse, more like,' one of the women muttered and a peal of laughter rippled up and down the farlins.

'How should I know what's wrong with him?' Bethany bent again to her business, the knife in her hand flashing through one fish after another.

A gutter further down the line leaned forward to ask sharply, 'Have you been clyping to the man?'

'What would I have to clype about?' Bethany was enraged by the suggestion that she might tell tales. 'I'm here to work, the same as you.'

'So you say.' The muttered words were pitched just loudly enough to reach her ears. Despite the cold she felt her face burn.

'We could do the work better without his nagging. I've never known Gil Pate so bad-tempered before. It's not as if we're all that well paid for standing out here in all weathers, while the coopers stay warm by the fire.' It was clear that Effie, well respected among the fisher-lassies, was deeply offended. 'He wants to watch his tongue – where would he be if we decided to stop work?'

A murmur of agreement ran along the row of women and Isa chipped in with, 'I've a good mind to look for work with one of the other coopers.' She shot a venomous glance at Bethany.

'You'd not do that, surely. It was me who brought you

here to take my Aunt Meg's place.' Bethany's natural
impulse was to tell the woman to do whatever she wanted,
but if she did that they would all be against her. 'Stay for
my sake, Isa.'

'I don't know. Fourteen years I've been a packer and
nobody's ever shouted at me the way he did today.'

They were all good workers, tried and tested and loyal
too, but Bethany knew that today Gil had pushed them to
the limit, and one more contrary word from him would
be enough to make them down tools and return to their
lodgings. Unless something was done, and done quickly,
he would lose not only his teams, but also the fish that
must be pickled before it spoiled.

On impulse she pushed her gutting knife into her pocket
and left the farlins, marching over to the great mountain
of barrels that had been left to settle, then be topped up
and covered in readiness for the carters. She tugged at
one, but to her frustration it was too heavy for her to
manage on her own.

'Duncan . . .' She beckoned to the nearest cooper.
'Over here.'

He came at a run. 'What is it, missus?'

'Give me a hand to take that barrel back to the farlins.'

'Eh?' He gaped at her. Then, as she roared at him, 'Do
as I say!' he hastened to ease the barrel upright. The two
of them manoeuvred it across to where Isa stood, then
Bethany held out her hand.

'Now, give me your hammer.' Duncan automatically
did as he was told. By now all the women had stopped
work and gathered round, the loiterers pressing close
behind them.

'Give me room,' she ordered, gripping the heavy hammer in both hands. The look on her face and the tone in
her voice swiftly cleared a reasonable space around her.

As she hefted the hammer, wondering if she was going
to manage its considerable weight, Gil burst through the
growing crowd. 'What's going on here?'

'Since you're so set on finding out if Isa's packed the barrels properly, we'll do it the right way. You've said often enough that if a well-packed barrel fell apart the fish should stay in place without it.' Bethany lowered the head of the hammer and adjusted her footing in the mud. 'I'm testing Isa's work for you.'

'You're what? Stop this nonsense at once!'

She ignored him, glancing instead at the other woman. 'All right, Isa?'

'Aye . . . oh, aye. You go ahead, lassie. I've got nothing to worry about, and I doubt,' Isa flashed a malevolent glance at Gil, 'if that barrel needs much of a dunt to make it fall apart.'

Fidelity had outrun the sea storm, and now James, worn out from the night's struggle, was on his way to the nearest pub after making sure that her decks had been cleared and cleaned and all made ready for her next voyage. Noticing an unusual number of people hurrying across his path, seemingly heading for the farlins where the Scottish fisher-lassies worked, he slowed and hesitated. Then, as a cheer went up from somewhere beyond the clustered backs, he gave in to curiosity, pushing his way through the growing knot of folk until he came across his cousins Jem and Charlie.

'What's up?'

'It's your Bethany,' Charlie told him gleefully. 'It's as good as a turn in the music halls – she's taking a hammer to one of Gil's barrels and he's near havin' apoplexy.'

'What?' James used his square shoulders to carve a path deeper into the crowd, until he was stopped short by the fisher-lassies themselves who, their work now forgotten, were standing in a tight group at the end of one of the farlins cheering and shouting. Stretching to his full height, he had a good view over their scarved heads of Gil, who did indeed look as though he might collapse with a stroke at any moment, and Bethany, clutching

a large hammer. Between them stood a full barrel of
herring.

'Come on now, Bethany, you show him!' one of the
women shrilled, and as the rest took up the chorus Gil's
crimson face deepened to purple.

There was no going back now for Bethany. She straddled
her feet, shifting her hips to balance her body properly,
and began to heave the hammer up and back. The cloths
tied round her fingers to protect them during her work
helped her to grip the broad wooden shaft, and once she
had started the lift it gathered momentum.

'Bethany . . . !' Gil appealed to her, his voice almost
drowned in a burst of cheering from the onlookers as the
hammer-head swung up and back, forcing her to shift
her foothold again quickly in order to avoid being pulled
backwards by its weight.

Gil cast a despairing glance at his men, but although
they were as interested as anyone else they all made a
point of avoiding eye contact with him. None of them
was willing to try to get the hammer away from Bethany
or to fall foul of her supporters.

He looked back at his wife, then as the hammer set out
on its downward path, he shouted, 'Wait! Stop!'

It was too late to halt the hammer's momentum, but
Bethany managed to twist her body round slightly, just
far enough to avoid her original target, the upper rim
of the barrel. The hammer-head sliced viciously through
the air between husband and wife and thudded into the
ground, narrowly missing one of Gil's feet, before she
let the shaft slip from her hands and staggered back to
lean against the farlins, breathless. A roar of approval
burst from everyone but Gil; even the coopers standing
behind him, out of his sight, were applauding.

'You'll accept that Isa can pack as good a barrel as
anyone, then?' Bethany wheezed, one hand pressed tightly
to her chest.

'Aye, I suppose so . . . if it'll get the lot of you back to work. Come on now, or I'll dock your wages,' he bellowed, swinging round on the women. As they scurried back to the farlins he snatched the hammer up in one hand, as though it weighed nothing at all, and drove his own men, suddenly subdued, back to their duties by the brazier.

'That lassie's got spirit,' commented a man standing by James. 'She's a bonny fighter – and a bonny looker, too.'

'She's my sister,' James told him coolly, then pushed his way through the crowd to stand by Bethany. 'Are you all right?'

'What are you doing here?'

'Watching the circus act,' he said drily. 'I'm asking, are you all right?'

'I'm fine, though I think I've stretched my arms a good inch or so.'

'You could have done yourself damage trying to throw that thing around. It's over-heavy for a woman.'

'Gil had to be taught a lesson. He's been right crabbit all week and the women have had enough of him.'

'He's been taught, right enough. If you were a man I'd buy you a dram for what you've just done.'

She smiled wryly at him, the first smile he had seen from Bethany for many a long day. 'I wish I was a man,' she said, 'for I could fairly do with that dram.'

Word of Bethany's stand against Gil swept over the vast harbour and that night gutters and packers from the other farlins arrived at the Scottish fisher-lassies' lodgings, eager to hear the true facts of the story. As Isa said, the place was as full of visitors as it was on a Sunday afternoon.

'It's high time one of us stood out against the menfolk,' one of the local women said. 'They never think of the way we've to stand at the farlins in all weathers, or the

back-breaking job and the hours we work. And what do
we get for it?' She glared round at the great crowd of
women filling the loft. 'A pittance, that's what. Tenpence
for every barrel filled. Tenpence to be shared between
three women.'

She put her huge hand on Bethany's. It felt as strong
and heavy as a plank of wood and it was covered with
scars gathered during years of hard work at the farlins. All
gutters packed their cuts with a poultice made by chewing
pieces of bread; it was an effective treatment, but as the
edges of the wounds were kept apart it resulted in heavy
scarring. 'If the man that employs you tries to make you
suffer for what you did, pet,' the woman said, 'just you
let me know. Sal Whitton's my name and everyone in
Yarmouth knows where to find me. It's time we took a
stand together and looked after our own.'

'He'll not do anything to Bethany,' Isa scoffed. 'He's
her own wedded husband.'

Sal's eyes widened. 'You gave your own man a showing
up in front of all those folk? You've more courage than I
thought.'

'She has that,' Kate said proudly.

'Husband or none, I mean what I say – if he does bother
you, then let me know. We'll not have any man causing
grief to one of the fisher-lassies.'

'To be fair to Gil, he's not usually a bad employer,'
Effie spoke up. 'But he's had some flea in his lug all
this week. I don't know what's amiss with him.' She
dug Bethany in the ribs with a sharp elbow. 'Mebbe
he's missing his comforts, what with you biding in the
loft with the rest of us. Men can get awful narky when
they've to go without.'

'If that's all it is, tell him he can move in with us and
welcome,' Maggie suggested. 'We don't mind the two of
you being nice and comfy right here. We could do with
a bit of entertainment at night.'

'That's kind of you . . . I'll tell him about it right away,'

Bethany shot back. 'And I'll mind him that while I'm a guttin quine I work in a team, so he'll need to take on Kate and Isa, too. That should put a smile on his face.'

It was a relief to hear the scream of laughter thundering up and down the length of the room and to know that she had managed to turn aside their animosity towards Gil. Bethany regretted the way in which she had humiliated him, but sometimes humiliation was the only lesson men like Gil understood. There had been no need for him to bully her fellow workers just because of his frustration and anger with her.

Some of the visitors had brought food and others had brought bottles; as time passed the evening developed into a party, with the women roaring with laughter as they vied with each other over what they would like to do to the men who worked them so hard and valued them so little. Sal in particular had a sadistic turn of mind and every time the door opened Bethany glanced over nervously, hoping that Gil wouldn't take it into his head to come looking for her. If he walked in on all those women in the mood they were in, there was no knowing what might happen.

15

Gil Pate sulked among the other coopers for the rest of the day and after work he went with his brother Nathan to the White Lion, a public house popular with Scots fishermen, to drown his sorrows. By the time James met up with them Gil, egged on by his brother, was in a surly mood.

'I suppose you heard all about it?' he grunted as soon as James sat down opposite.

'I did better than that. I saw it for myself.'

Gil, elbows on the table, glared up at his brother-in-law from beneath his eyebrows. 'What's the matter with that woman?'

'How should I know? She's your wife, not mine.'

'She's your sister.'

'We've scarce exchanged more than half a dozen words in the past year.'

'I've not heard much more than that from her myself. She's a sullen bitch, with a right temper on her.'

James shrugged and took a deep drink before saying, 'You must have known that before you married her, so why did you take her for your wife?'

'Because she's the sort of lass every man wants to find in his bed when he wakens in the morning,' Nathan suggested with a snigger. Gil glowered at him.

'You watch your mouth! I married her because my bairns needed a mother.' He started to lever himself to his feet.

'And you needed some comfort for yourself.' Nathan was undeterred. 'You cannae fool us, man. You couldnae keep your eyes or your hands off that lassie, even when your bairns had a mother.'

Gil had begun to move away from the table, but now he turned suddenly and leaned on the scarred wooden boards, bending so that his face was close to his brother's. 'I told you, Nathan, guard that tongue of yours. If you don't, I'll take it out of your throat and wrap it around your neck with my bare hands,' he said softly, menacingly, then elbowed his way through the crowd.

'Has he eaten anything?' James wanted to know and Nathan shook his head.

'He wasnae in the mood for eating, just drinking.'

'You should get some food inside him. The drink on an empty stomach's making him dangerous.'

'It's not the drink; it's that sister of yours that has him so's he doesn't know where he is. He's right, she is a sullen-tempered bitch.'

James thought of Bethany as he had seen her that afternoon, angry and determined, struggling to lift the heavy hammer up high enough to strike the barrel. He recalled the almost comic little dance-step she had had to perform in order to avoid the barrel as the hammer began its downward sweep and Gil roared his submission. He remembered her faint, wry grin and felt his own temper beginning to stir.

'I've got no quarrel with Gil when he miscries her, for she's his woman and he's got a right to say as he pleases. But I'll not take it from you, Nathan.'

The man shrugged indifferently, but said no more. Soon Gil rejoined them and James started trying to get him to go back to his lodgings, where his evening meal would be waiting. But his brother-in-law had other ideas.

'I'll not put a morsel into my mouth till I've sorted this business out with Bethany,' he announced, staggering to his feet again.

'Tonight? Best leave it until tomorrow, when you're rested and clearer in the head,' James said, alarmed.

'I cannae rest till I speak to her . . .' Gil set off towards the door with James in pursuit and Nathan tagging along behind. Outside, the fresh cold air hit the cooper and he reeled, clutching at a lamp-post for support as his knees gave way beneath him.

'I'll be all righ'. I'll be . . . all righ',' he said peevishly, swatting James away as he tried to help.

'You'd be the better for some hot food in your belly and a good sleep. Come on now, Nathan and me'll see you to your lodgings.'

At first Gil showed signs of going along with the idea, but they had scarcely peeled him from the lamp-post and set off, with Nathan guiding his erratic steps on one side and James on the other, like a couple of tugs assisting a big ship downriver to the open sea, when he changed his mind.

'Bethany bides this way.'

James caught him as he tried to change direction. 'I know, but you live this way.'

'We should be together, James. A man and his wife should be together, d'you not think so?' Gil clutched at him. 'It's not right for a woman to sleep apart from her own legal husband, not when they're in the same town.'

'Mebbe not, but your lodgings are nearer than hers, so come on.'

'I found a room for the two of us together, James, but she wouldnae share it with me. And I miss her! My wee Bethany – I miss her!' Alcoholic tears sprang to the cooper's eyes.

'You're daft, man. If your woman refuses to share your bed, you should seek elsewhere for what you want,' Nathan broke in. 'I know the very house – we'll get something to eat first, then you can come with me. The lassies that bide there know how to make a man welcome, for a price. You'll come too, James?'

'I've never had need of company I'd to pay for.' James felt his skin crawl at the very thought. His own marriage might not be what he wanted, but he thanked God that he had never been driven to lie with whores and prostitutes.

'It's just you and me, then, Gil. There's women in that house can do things you've never dreamed about,' Nathan said eagerly.

'I don't want other women, I want Bethany!' Gil wailed, but his brother lost patience with him.

'God knows why. There's my mother having to go to Buckie to look after your bairns because your precious Bethany won't do it. And here's you in a right state because she'll not share your bed. How can you speak of her like that, right after she made a fool of you in front of the whole harbour . . . ?'

'Leave it, Nathan,' James warned, but he was ignored.

'I'm telling you, Gil, you're best off without her. A decent woman wouldn't have done what she did to you today. If you must go to her then go, but for God's sake don't slobber over her. Give the bitch a good hiding and then mebbe she'll make a better wife.'

Nathan's tirade ended in a strangled squeak as the cooper's big hand caught at his throat. 'Up here, you,' Gil stormed, dragging the smaller man into a pend. 'I told you already that I'll not have my wife miscalled.'

'Gil!'

Gil paid no heed to James, for he was too intent on making his way along the passageway, reeling and bouncing off the walls as he went. Since he was still gripping Nathan's throat the curer, too, was staggering against the damp stone walls, yelping at every thud.

'Gil!' James dived after them and caught up with them in a dark back court. After a moment's determined wrestling he managed to free Nathan, who slumped against the wall of the court, choking and wheezing. 'Stop making a fool of yourself, man, and get off home!'

Gil, breathing heavily, concentrated on steadying himself. 'Home? My home's in Buckie with Bethany and my bairns, not in this place!'

'Get back to your lodgings, I mean. Things'll sort themselves out in the morning.'

'A'right, James, a'righ',' Gil held up his large hands in an appeasing gesture. 'Back to the lodgings. A'righ'.' He began to stagger towards the pend then added, just as James thought he was getting somewhere, 'But first I'm going to teach our Nathan to keep his tongue off my wife!'

'You'll not, for I'll not let you. There's been enough carrying on today as it is.' James moved to stand before Nathan, who was still bent double, catching his breath.

'Then I'll see to you first and him after,' Gil growled, and swung his arm up and out in a wide arc, using his big knotted fist like a club. James dodged to one side, hearing a shout of agony as his heel, in its sturdy, iron-studded fisherman's boot, landed four-square on Nathan's toes. He felt a breeze brush against his face as Gil's fist swept through the air then continued on its way. In his drunken state the cooper was forced to go with the swing of his arm, his feet slapping and stumbling all over the place in an ungainly dance until they tangled with each other and sent him down with a crash.

As James watched, ready to dodge again if need be, and Nathan hopped about on one foot, cursing, Gil began to pull himself to his knees. He had almost managed it when his stomach suddenly and violently rejected the drink he had been pouring into it all evening. For several minutes he spewed helplessly before toppling sideways, very slowly, to the ground.

'You damned near broke my foot,' Nathan yelped.

'Think yourself lucky, for Gil would have done worse if he'd managed to hit you. Gil?' James bent and shook his brother-in-law's shoulder. It felt slack beneath his grip. Gil began to snore softly.

'He did enough, banging me off that wall and trying to squeeze the life out of me. The bastard,' Nathan added, darting towards the inert mass on the ground. As the toe of his boot found its mark, Gil's body quivered and he grunted and tried to lift his head. Then it fell back and he started snoring again.

'That's enough! I'll not have you beating the man when he's not able to defend himself!' James put himself between the brothers for the second time. 'I hope you're fit, for we're going to have to carry him back to his lodgings. I doubt if he'll stir till morning. At least he didn't fall face first into his own vomit. If he had, he could have lain here all night far as I'm concerned.'

As he and Nathan laboured to get the big cooper on to his feet, James realised that at least he had achieved his original purpose. His sister would not be troubled by a visit from an irate husband tonight.

'That,' Jacob MacFarlane said contentedly, 'is the best meal I've had since I last tasted my mother's cooking.'

'It was nothing much, but I'm glad you enjoyed it.' Jess tried to hide her pleasure.

'Nothing much? If I could just know for certain that they serve fried potatoes and herring in oatmeal in Paradise, I'd go there happily when my time comes.' Jacob edged his chair back from the table and caressed his stomach with both hands. 'You're a fortunate man, Innes, to get food like this as often as you do.'

'Aye,' Innes agreed with a wan smile. Fortunate indeed, when his mother was going to sleep in her own house from now on, keeping him and Zelda apart.

'Are you all right, son?' she asked, peering at him. 'You're awful quiet.'

'I'm fine. I was just thinking, there's a job needs finishing back at the smithy. The farmer's coming to fetch it tomorrow, so if I could manage to see to it tonight . . .'

'D'you have to?' Jess asked as he got to his feet.

'Can it not wait until the morning? We've a visitor, Innes.'

'Don't mind me, lad, just you go ahead. Your mother and me have a lot of talking to catch up on.'

'Well, if it's all right . . .' Innes muttered, reaching for his coat. There was no job to be finished and no Zelda to cuddle either, for she was wanted at the farm that night. But his mind and his body were both in turmoil and he felt that if he didn't get out into the night air he would suffocate.

'He's a fine lad,' Jacob said when the door closed behind Innes.

'He's a good son and I think the world of him.'

'More like you than Weem, I would say.'

'James and Bethany were Weem's bairns from the start.'

'I'm looking forward to meeting them.'

'They're both in Yarmouth for the fishing and they'll not be back for a good few weeks yet.'

'I'm not in any hurry to leave the Firth.'

'Have you not got work to go back to? Or a family, mebbe?' she probed gently.

'I never married, Jess, and there's nobody waiting for me anywhere. As to the other, I work for myself now, so my time's my own.' He stood up and stretched luxuriously. 'And I've got some business in mind for the place where I was born.'

'Sit in at the fire while I see to these plates and make another pot of tea.' As she cleared the table and stacked the used dishes Jacob took his pipe and tobacco pouch from his pocket. There was a long silence as he tamped tobacco carefully into the bowl of the pipe, then she heard the scratch and fizzle of a match being ignited. It was so like having Weem back home again that her heart ached a little, and sang a little.

The pipe was going well and his head was wreathed

in sweet-smelling blue smoke by the time the tea was ready. Jess filled two thick cups and handed one over before sinking into her own chair, inhaling the aroma of the tobacco.

'What are you smiling at, woman?' Jacob wanted to know, smiling himself as he set his cup carefully on the hearth.

'I just can't believe that it's you sitting there, as large as life. I never thought to see you again.'

'You mean you'd put me out of your mind and forgotten all about me?'

'Never!'

'That's good to know, for I never forgot you, not for one single day.'

The intensity of his gaze was disturbing, but familiar. Even in childhood Jacob had had that strange ability to sit or stand for hours, just looking and looking at something that gave him pleasure – the sea, a bonny boat, her own face. She recalled, now, how he had been able to sit watching her, never seeming to tire of it. In those days it hadn't bothered her because she knew him so well, but now, after all those years apart, it was different. She reached for her knitting, anxious to have something to fix her own eyes on.

'Tell me what happened to Weem.'

'Another time, mebbe.'

'Then tell me about that lad's brother and sister.'

'James is mate to Albert, Weem's brother. You'll mind him?' she asked, then, when he nodded, 'He's skipper of the *Fidelity* now. She's the Lowrie boat, a steam drifter. Weem and Albert bought her a few years back.'

'A drifter, eh? That was a good move.'

'Bethany's married to Gil Pate, the cooper. One of his teams was a woman short this year, so she went down to work at the farlins. She and James are more like Weem than like me.'

'Thrawn, and determined to get their own way.'

'Aye,' Jess agreed and let the matter drop, relieved when Jacob began asking her about people he remembered from his childhood. When he rose to go he said, 'I hope I can call on you again, Jess.'

'Of course you can, and welcome. I'm glad to see you back,' she said on impulse.

'I should have done it a long time ago, but mebbe it's as well that I waited until now. Before might not have been the right time.' He stood in the doorway, looking out into the dark night towards the Firth, listening to the shushing of waves on the rocks. Then he looked back at her.

'You know, Jess, sometimes you have to leave a thing behind before you can find out how precious it is to you,' he said, then clapped his curly-rimmed bowler hat on to his greying head and disappeared into the night, while she was still wondering what he meant.

Gil took Bethany aside in the morning when she arrived at the farlins, drawing her behind a pile of barrels that afforded some privacy. She was aware, as she followed him, of the other women's watchful eyes.

'Well? Are they going to work for me today or are they going to tear me limb from limb?' he asked with a weak attempt at humour.

'They'll work for you, but you'd be advised to stop nagging them. Not that you're in a fit state to do any nagging today,' she added. He looked terrible. One side of his face looked as though it had been scraped along the ground, and his eyes, sunk into his head, were half-shut against the morning light. 'You've been drinking, haven't you?'

'Can you blame me? You made a right fool of me yesterday, Bethany!'

'I stopped you making a fool of yourself, more like. D'you not realise that if you'd pushed Isa any further the whole pack of them would have walked away from the farlins, and me with them, leaving you with no way of getting the herring into your precious barrels? You'd have had to go cap in hand to the English lassies for help, and that would have made an even bigger fool of you, man.'

'My teams wouldn't have walked out on me.'

'Look at them, Gil!' She threw her hand out to indicate the women huddled in groups near the farlins, all of them busy with their knitting wires but furtively watching their employer and his wife, trying to guess at what they might be saying to each other. 'Look at the place where we're going to be working for the next eight hours or more. We're ankle-deep in mud and sand and fish guts, and Maggie's had to go to the mission station so that the lady dresser can see to her hands. She scarce slept last night with the pain of the cuts and the ulcers she's got from working with the brine. And you think they'd rather be true to you than think of themselves? It was just fortunate I was here . . .'

'Fortunate, you call it? You nearly smashed one of my barrels, you damned near smashed my toes with that hammer . . .'

'I had to do something to turn their anger away. And just because I'm determined to stay with the other women, instead of sharing a bed with you, it's not right to take it out on them.' She peered up at him again. 'You've not been fighting as well, have you?'

He rubbed a hand over his face roughly, mashing his nose almost flat. 'I fell against a wall on my way home.'

'The wall fell against you, more like,' she said as the clang of a cooper's hammer against iron caused him to wince and bite his lip hard. 'You should be in your bed, sleeping it off.'

'I wish I could get back to my bed, pull the blankets over my head and never get up again. This is the best fishing season we've had in years, but for me it's the worst.'

'Just stop fussing at the women on the farlins and everything'll be fine. I'd best get back to work.'

'Wait.' He pulled a crumpled sheet of paper from his pocket. 'This letter came this morning. It's from my mother.'

Angular and grim-looking, ground deep into the texture of the paper as though written with a knife instead of a pen, Phemie Pate's handwriting was just like the woman herself. The children were well, she wrote, though she had found them sadly out of control and it had not been easy to train them into proper ways. The house had been cleaned from roof to doorstep and she herself was managing to hold her head high in Buckie, though it was not easy when the whole place was gossiping about her daughter-in-law traipsing off to Yarmouth without a thought for the well-being of the young innocents left in her care. The cold winds from the sea were screwing wickedly into Phemie's old bones and she would be grateful to her son if he saw where his duty lay and sent his errant wife home at once, thus enabling his mother to retire to her own house to recover from the burden of the duties thrust upon her, which she had accepted as the lot of a good Christian woman and devoted mother.

'I'm not going home until the work here's done.' Bethany pushed the letter back at him.

'But the wee ones . . .'

'I know from my own mother that they're fine. She takes them out most days to give Mrs Pate a rest and she'd be the first to tell me if anything was wrong.' She was heart-sorry for the little ones and felt guilty about the way she had landed them with their grandmother, but having read the letter she was more determined than ever not to return home in disgrace. 'She'll be having a grand time playing the martyr to the other old gossips. She doesn't want me back, she wants you to feel guilty. And it'll not do the bairns any harm to be with her for a few weeks. After all, she's the one that raised you and Nathan.'

'I know,' he said glumly. 'That's why I wish you'd go home.'

'I'm better here where I can look after your interests.'

'Look after . . .' Words failed him.

'You nearly had trouble on your hands yesterday, and it's not just the Scottish lassies that are getting tired of the way they're treated; it's all the women.'

'God, they're never satisfied unless they're causing bother!'

'That's not true! It's all right for you, under shelter and working beside your nice warm fire. We're out in the snow and rain and the bitter wind, and we work long, hard hours, Gil. Back-breaking work too, specially on the deep farlins.'

'Keep your voice down, they're all looking at us!'

'It costs nothing to look,' she snapped, but lowered her voice as she went on, 'I'm only here because Auntie Meg's got terrible pains in her spine from working at the farlins for years for just three or fourpence a barrel. Would you work for that amount?'

'You get wages, too.'

'A few shillings, just. And most of that goes to pay our lodgings and buy our food. Some of these women go back to their families at the end of the fishing with scarcely any money to show for their work.'

'If they were paid better they'd work less, it's always the way.'

'If they were paid better – and treated better by the likes of you – they'd mebbe be more willing. Have you never thought of it that way? I'm telling you, Gil, there's trouble in the air and that's why I'm not going back home until the English fishing's over!'

16

'I never thought to see this.' Jacob MacFarlane's voice was sombre. 'Poor Weem.'

'It comes to us all.' Jess had to fight the impulse to kneel and smooth the grassy mound over her husband, as she would have done had she been alone. She felt uncomfortable with Jacob there, but he had asked her to show him where Weem lay.

'Aye, it does, but Weem – there was something about the man that made you think it would never happen to him.'

'I wish . . .' she began, then shut her lips tightly against the next words.

'You wish you'd taken more thought before you decided to put him here? I'm not a mind-reader, Jess,' he added with a faint smile when she gaped at him. 'Your Meg told me about the stramash between you and your oldest lad when Weem died.'

'Meg's tongue's hinged in the middle. It's the fuss you make of her,' Jess scolded, 'it's turned her head!' In the few weeks since he arrived in Buckie Jacob had been accepted by the local people and had completely charmed several of them, including Jess's sister-in-law.

He laughed, a great hearty laugh that made a passer-by turn to see who could be finding humour in a graveyard. 'The man who could turn Meg Lowrie's head isn't born yet and probably never will be.'

'Then you're the closest there is to him at the moment. Not three weeks in the place and you've already got her telling you all the family secrets.'

'You don't mind me knowing about young James falling out with you over where to lay Weem to rest, do you? Meg knows that we've been friends since before we could walk, and there was no harm meant.'

Jess shrugged. 'There's no point in minding things and I'm sure she told you the right way of it. But I sometimes think mebbe I should have let him be taken back to the sea, Jacob. Most of all I find myself wishing that Albert had just let James have his way at the time, then I'd have been spared this misery of wondering and worrying over whether or not I'd done right by the man.'

He reached out to rest his hand lightly on her shoulder. 'You did what you had to do and, if I was you, I'd put the whole business out of my mind. Now, d'you think we should be getting back down that road? You promised to take Rory and Ellen out this afternoon. And,' he added, the laugh bubbling back into his voice, 'I need to have another wee practice at charming Mistress Pate.'

'You'll never manage it – not even you!' Jess had been amused at Jacob's fruitless attempts to break though Phemie's grim exterior.

'I'll keep on trying, though I'm wondering if there's anything at all behind that face and those folded arms, apart from a lump of granite or an iron pillar. Poor bairns . . . At least we can give them a happy hour or two.'

'It's good of you to spend so much time with them, Jacob.'

'Och no, I enjoy that wee laddie's chat.' He had managed to coax back some of the natural bounce and cheeriness that Rory had lost since his grandmother took charge of him. With the children Jacob behaved like a child himself, playing football with Rory and squatting beside him to study crabs and dead jellyfish – even buying him a little wooden boat that they sailed together in the rockpools. The four of them had walked for miles, with Rory scampering ahead and Ellen, when tired, being carried on Jacob's broad, comfortable shoulders.

'Were you content, you and Weem?' he asked as they set off down the road towards Buckie, leaving the graveyard behind.

'We had our quarrels, but I've no complaints.'

'Or regrets?'

'There's little sense in looking back along a road you've already walked.'

'If I'd stayed and we'd wed, I might still be a fisherman. Mebbe I'd have been father to your three.'

'Innes, mebbe, for he's a gentle, caring lad, something like yourself at his age. But never the other two,' Jess said emphatically. 'Never James and Bethany.'

'You worry about them, don't you?'

'Aye, I do that.' Jacob and Jess had spent a lot of time together since his arrival, talking and reminiscing, and getting to know each other again. There was no sense now in her denying the truth. 'They're hurting, Jacob, both of them. I can see it, but I can do nothing about it. They're neither of them happy. There's plenty who'd be content with what they have, but not James and Bethany. They've got such an energy about them. They're like . . .' she sought for the right words, 'like two bottles of fizzy drink that were shaken hard before they were opened. I've the feeling that one day the anger's going to burst out of them and the longer I wait for it to happen, the more I fret.'

'They're grown folk, Jess, not your worry now.'

'Don't be daft, man,' she snapped at him. 'Women can never walk away from their own bairns. The fretting just gets harder as they get older.'

They walked in silence for a few minutes before he said, 'I'm looking forward to meeting them.'

'They'd have been home by now if the fish hadn't been running so well.' Although it had been years since she herself was a fisher-lassie at Great Yarmouth, she vividly remembered the big harbours and the farlins. The fish supply would be slowing down now, close to the end of the season. There would be an air of finality about the place, as the days grew shorter and the weather colder, and people who had renewed old friendships prepared to say goodbye for another year.

In fact, rather more was happening in Yarmouth – events that Jess could not have begun to imagine. A few days later Meg, now completely recovered from her back trouble, came running to tell Jess that the impossible had happened. All the fisher-lassies in Yarmouth (English, Scots and Irish alike) had reached the end of their patience, and had gone on strike.

It was a splendid rebellion, fuelled by years of grievance among fisher-lassies from all over Britain's coasts. At first they were content enough to grumble among themselves as before, then the bolder women began to discuss ways of improving their lot. Finally the day came when a group of women stopped work and marched around the harbours, waving banners hurriedly made from whatever cloth came to hand.

That, as Effie said when the Scottish women raced back to their lodgings to root among their own trunks in search of lengths of cloth waiting to be made up, was the beauty of being women, with the ability to stitch and hem their own banners in no time at all.

As they paraded through the streets, singing lustily and waving their banners, the gutters and packers gathered quite a following, even among some fishermen. Female workers from the smokehouses joined them and in a few days, with the strike showing no signs of abating, union officials came hurrying from London to hold meetings with the lassies, then with the curers and smokers, who were all in a state of shock at what had happened.

With the farlins untended and the stockpile of barrels
empty, the unsalted fish still on the harbourside had to
be carted off hurriedly to be iced or eaten before it went
bad. With nobody to gut, pickle or smoke their catches
the fishermen were forced to cool their heels while their
boats lay idle, crowded into the quays as tightly as matches
in a box.

Since her husband was a curer and an employer, it
was generally agreed (to Bethany's disappointment) that
she should play no active part in any of the negotiations.
She would have enjoyed the challenge and the excitement
of it all – indeed, she would have welcomed a good
confrontation – but Sal, who had become one of the
women's leaders, put her foot down. 'When this is over
and settled, as it must be one way or another, you've still
to go back home and live in peace with your man. You've
played your own part already; best leave the rest to us.'

So Bethany had to content herself with attending every
meeting and rally, spending her free time in writing
to her mother, her Aunt Meg and James's wife Stella.
After a lot of thought she wrote a brief note to Rory,
carefully avoiding any comments that might anger her
mother-in-law, who would have to read it to the little
boy. She wasn't even sure that he would know she had
tried to make contact – it all depended on the woman's
mood when the letter arrived.

She went to the shops and bought toys for the children;
a soft rag doll for Ellen and a brightly painted train in a
box for Rory. And she became so bored with her idleness
that she began to wish secretly that the strike would come
to an end. It was hard to hear the others talk, in the lofts,
about the parades and the speeches when she herself was
unable to take part.

But the strike dragged on, day following day with neither
the fisher-lassies nor their employers giving ground. Moun-
tains of stinking, rotting fish had to be carted away to be
used as fertiliser in the Norfolk fields, upsetting for the

women, who could scarcely abide the knowledge that good food was going to waste for want of their skilled attention. But as the strike leaders pointed out, if the lassies backed down now they would never win extra money or the respect of their employers.

Bethany had managed to keep out of Gil's way and he had not sought her out, but one evening when she was walking about the town on her own, trying to work off her growing restlessness and boredom, he stepped out of a public house just as she passed its door. They stopped short at the sight of each other and then, realising that flight would be undignified, Bethany said formally, 'How are you, Gil?'

The floodgates were immediately loosened. 'How am I? You must know how I am, woman! How could you do this to me?'

The genuine hurt in his face was hard to take. 'I've done nothing – it's all of us, all the lassies from right round the coast. We've struck because we've finally had enough, Gil. Have I not been trying to tell you that since I came here?'

'Never mind what you've been telling me; it's what you've been telling the rest of those bitches that I'm interested in!' She could smell the drink on his breath, and a fine mist of spittle sprayed across her forehead as he spoke.

'I've told them nothing. I didn't need to: they've got the sense to know when they're being treated wrong.'

'Oh aye? And even if some of them were too daft to know it, you made it very clear that day you threatened to break one of my barrels, didn't you?' he said savagely, then as she shrugged and made to turn away he caught at her arm. 'Why did you have to make such a fool of me in front of the farlins and all the rest of the folk there?'

'I told you before, I was only trying to save you from causing trouble. The way you were going that day it was a wonder the strike didn't start right there and then.'

'It's not just my livelihood that's being threatened by this senseless strike, d'you realise that? It's yours and the bairns' too, and Effie's and Kate's. Have you ever thought of Rory and the wee lassie having to go without, because of you and these other women?'

'I doubt if it'll come to that.'

'For God's sake, woman, you're my wife!'

'Let me go, Gil!' His fingers were digging painfully into her forearm and when he made no move to release her, Bethany stopped trying to pull herself away and suddenly swung in towards him, catching at one of his lapels with her free hand.

'I know I'm your wife, Gil,' she said into his face. 'I know it every minute of every day and every night. And I know that it's not my choice, it was yours and my father's.'

'Eh?' he said, bewildered and confused. 'How can you say such a thing? Did I not come out and ask you to wed me, fair and square?'

'And did you not speak to my father first, and arrange with him that you and your brother would buy all the fish the *Fidelity* caught from then on, if I agreed to have you?'

He thrust her away. 'Weem and me made a business deal. It had nothing to do with us marrying.'

'Mebbe you can make yourself believe that, Gil Pate, but not me. Never me. My father was clear enough about it at the time. He told me what to say when you came courting and I did what he wanted, because God help me . . .' it was Bethany's turn to sound bitter, 'I thought the world of the man and I always did as he said. You didn't win me, Gil – you bought me!' She spat the words at him.

It was out in the open; it was said and it could never be unsaid. She took a step back, then turned and ran.

It wasn't Gil she was escaping from, it was herself and the words that chased her, buzzing round her head like a swarm of angry bees as she ran through the streets and on to the harbourside, right along it to the entrance, with nowhere else to go other than into the River Yare below.

Briefly, staring down at the water sliding in and out of the harbour, she considered it, but the thought was rejected almost as soon as it arrived. Bethany had been born with a great hunger for life and a curiosity, always, as to what lay around the next corner. No matter what befell her she could never let go of her existence voluntarily.

She stood still, as motionless as one of the carved figureheads that had graced the old sailing ships, one hand clutching at the scarf that the wind tried to whip from her head, quite alone in the dark, windswept harbour. When her heartbeat had slowed and her lungs had stopped labouring she turned her back on the open river, walking to the other side of the harbour wall to look down on the great mass of boats, sailed and steam, squeezed into every available inch of space. Winter had arrived and soon most of the boats would be moving out of the harbours and into the open sea, homeward bound, while the lassies packed their kists and clambered aboard the lorries and carts waiting to take them to the railway station. Soon, whatever the results of the strike, she would have to go back to Buckie, back to being Gil Pate's wife. His wife, bought and paid for.

Bringing the truth out into the open did not change things after all.

The tide was out and the boats themselves lay quite a distance below her, dark and silent and empty, for after scrubbing down the decks and putting the fishing gear away there was nothing left for any of the crews to do but wait on shore until the strike was settled and they could put to sea again.

Bethany could tell *Fidelity* even in the dark; with a swift glance along the windswept harbour wall to make sure that she was unnoticed, she kilted her skirt and stooped to catch hold of the topmost rung of the iron ladder set into the stones. It was no trouble for her to cross the three intervening boats in the dark, but as she bridged the space between the third boat and the Lowrie vessel a wave swept into the harbour from nowhere, making the boats lift and dip and jostle together. Thrown off balance just as she was poised to jump, Bethany tumbled on to *Fidelity*'s deck, landing heavily on both knees. She rolled, cursing beneath her breath, then scrambled to her feet and limped into the small galley.

Closing the door, she felt for the big box of matches that was always kept by the stove, then made her way cautiously towards the hatch leading down to the fore-cabin.

The small space smelled strongly of wet oilskins, tobacco and herring, both fried and raw. At sea, when the crew were on board, the engine throbbing on the other side of the bulkhead and the stove in the galley above lit, the cabin would be stuffy, but tonight there was a bleak chill about it.

Even so, Bethany wriggled out of her jacket and hung it carefully over the porthole so that nobody happening to walk along the quay would see a telltale gleam of light from the vessel. Then she struck a match and lit the lamp. Replacing it on its hook, she sat down on the edge of a bunk and hauled her woollen stockings off so that she could examine her knees. They were both red; tomorrow they would probably be bruised, if she didn't remember to bathe them well before going to bed. She flexed and straightened them a few times to ward off the stiffness, then wriggled her way on to the bunk and rested her head on the hard, flat pillow, closing her eyes and drawing the boat's calm serenity into herself.

She was almost asleep, soothed and contented for the first time in many a long day, when the thump of boots on the deck above brought her upright, her eyes flying open. She waited, holding her breath and hoping that whoever it was had only come aboard to check on the nets or the pile of canvas buoys on the deck; then her heart plummeted as the footsteps crossed the deck and she heard the galley door open, then shut. Bethany put the lamp out, and as the new arrival began to come down the ladder to the cabin she huddled back on the bunk, pulling her stinging knees to her chin and locking her hands about them, trying to make herself as small and unnoticeable as possible.

17

It seemed to James Lowrie that the whole town was in turmoil, with not a corner to be turned without a man running into groups of morose fishermen, forced to cool their heels ashore, or fisher-lassies on the march with their flags and their shouting. The only place where he could get some peace and quiet, and time to himself, was on board the *Fidelity*. There was a half-bottle of whisky in the cabin and James was in a mood to get drunk.

He was irritated to find that whoever had used the galley matches last had not put them back in their usual place. James had no need of a light, since he felt more at home on the boat than anywhere else, but as he made for the ladder he promised himself that the guilty man would pay for his negligence in the morning. Uncle Albert was at fault again: a lax skipper meant a lax crew, and carelessness could easily cost lives on a fishing boat.

Sliding down the ladder to the cabin, he frowned as he heard a sudden shifting, scuttering sound from below. Although rats were seldom found on the Scottish fishing boats, where cleanliness was an unwritten and well-observed rule, the vessels in Yarmouth's basins were moored so closely together that it would be quite easy for vermin to travel from land to boat, and from boat to boat.

James deliberately dropped down on to the cabin deck with a great thump of booted feet, but the panicky squeaking and scampering he had expected failed to materialise. Instead, he was certain that the clatter of his arrival had been met with a sudden, soft intake of breath.

'Is that you, Charlie?' That was all he needed – the fool bringing a lassie back to the boat just when James needed some time to himself. 'Charlie?' There was no reply, but as his eyes became accustomed to the gloom he saw the glimmer of a face within the dark cave formed by the upper and lower bunks opposite. He lunged forward, and as his outstretched fingers closed on a shoulder he yanked back hard. 'Out of it, you!'

His prey kicked and struggled, fighting like a cat. Blows rained down on James's shins, but they were too light to have any effect. He thought the tussle won when he got a grip on the interloper's narrow shoulders, but then a sudden, painful and most unexpected crack on the chin jerked his head back and made him see stars for a second or two. Enraged, he shook his prisoner hard and a howl filled the small cabin.

'Let go of me!'

James stopped. 'Bethany?' he said into the darkness.

'Of course it's me!' She brought her hands up to push herself away from him and he heard a thud as she collided with the upper bench. 'Oh, my head,' she lamented. 'And you stood on my foot – you've broken it, you big daft fool!'

The salty taste of blood was strong in his mouth; he explored with his tongue and found that the blood came from a small abrasion, where the inside of his lower lip had been smashed against his teeth by his sister's hard head.

'Never mind your foot,' he snapped as he fumbled for the hanging lamp. 'Where did you put the matches?'

'Here.' Her voice was sulky. Groping in the dark, he located the box in her hand and managed to light the lamp. Its glow revealed Bethany, crouched on the edge of a bunk and nursing a bare foot.

'Let me see.' James hung the lamp up, then examined her foot, moving each toe gently. 'It's not broken, but it's going to be bruised. And so's my mouth.' He put a hand to his lips, but there was not enough blood to stain his fingers. 'You always did have a hard skull,' he recalled.

'It serves you right, sneaking on board and frighting me like that.'

Recalling his decision to get drunk, he stood up and took the bottle from the overhead cupboard, swilling liquid into a cup. 'I'm the one with the right to be here. You know fine that women don't belong on fishing boats.'

She glared up at him. 'I've a share in *Fidelity* too. I can go on board her any time I like.' She looked like a tinker-lassie, sitting on the bench with her skirt tangled about her bare legs, her hair wild and her grey eyes glittering silver malice at him in the lamplight.

James hesitated, then offered the cup to her. 'D'you want a swallow?'

'I wondered when you'd mind that you owed me a dram. At the farlins,' she reminded when he frowned at her, puzzled. 'You said if I was a man you'd buy me a dram.' She took the cup in both hands and drank deeply, choking on the raw spirit. He thumped her back as she coughed, and when the paroxysm was over she shook her head when he reached for the cup. 'Fetch another for yourself, I'm having this one.'

He did as he was told and took a long drink before sitting down opposite her. 'D'you not think that you and the rest of the lassies have caused enough trouble, Bethany, stopping work on the farlins and forcing us to keep the boats in the harbour, when they should be out at the fishing grounds?'

'Would you work for what we're paid?'

'That's different. You've got Gil to keep you.'

'There's plenty of women at the farlins have to keep themselves, and some have bairns to support and all,' she flared back at him. 'Most of these lassies are married to fishermen. What happens to them when their men are lost at sea? D'you never stop to think on that?'

James threw himself back into his own corner. 'Life's not easy for any of us. We have to make what we can of it.'

'Or what other folk make of it.'

'Listen, I came down here for a drink and a chance to think. If you want to talk, go and find someone else to natter to.'

She glowered at him but made no move to go, and when he reached for the bottle she handed her cup over silently, waiting for it to be re-filled. James wondered about the wisdom of letting his sister drink, then decided that since she was Gil's wife it was Gil's responsibility, not his.

As though reading his mind, she took a gulp from her cup then said suddenly, 'I met Gil in the street just now. I threw it in his face about the way we wed. I wish I hadn't, for it changes nothing.'

'What d'you mean, the way you and Gil wed?'

'You know . . . Da marrying me off in return for Gil and Nathan buying all the *Fidelity*'s catch.'

'You're havering.'

'I'm not. It was the same for you . . . marriage with Stella in return for her father's sailing boat, so that Father and Uncle Albert could buy the *Fidelity*.'

James shifted uncomfortably on the bunk. 'It's the whisky talking. You've had more than enough.'

'So you wanted her, then?' When he didn't answer she gave a soft, mirthless laugh. 'I was thinking, before you came in . . . D'you mind that time in Cluny harbour when Charlie dared me to dive off the wall and swim under one of the big Zulus?'

He remembered as clearly as though it had happened the day before. For a full minute he had waited and watched for her to surface from the dive; when another minute went by, then another, he began to picture himself running along the road, bursting into the kitchen to tell his mother that

Bethany was drowned. He had been on the point of hurling herself into the basin when she surfaced like a cork from a bottle, her face puce and her mouth gaping open for air.

Even thinking of it brought back the terror, the conviction that she had gone for ever. Aloud he said, 'I mind the smug grin on your face when you came up the ladder.'

This time her laugh was genuine. 'As soon as I got to the top you pushed me back into the basin.'

'No wonder, it was a daft thing to do in the first place.'

'Have you ever known me walk away from a dare?'

'You're saying that Da dared you to marry Gil?'

'No, but that's the way I felt at the time. I didn't realise that it was for the rest of my life. We're a sorry pair, James, caught in a net as tightly as any herring.'

'You don't know what you're talking about!'

'Do I not?' She had been leaning back on the bunk, but now she sat up, arms tight round her knees. 'Tell me you're contented with the thought of spending the rest of your days with Stella.' Then, as he said nothing, 'No use in it anyway, for I always know when you're lying, James Lowrie.'

He finished his drink and stood. 'It's time we were both out of here.'

'I meant what I said to you in the loft. You can use my share in the boat and I'll get Mother and Innes to agree to it too, as soon as we get back.'

'What difference would it make?' he asked wearily. 'Albert's older than me and he's got more experience, for all that I'm the better fisherman. I'd still have to dance to his tune. I've made my mind up to going to Davie Geddes's boat for the great line fishing. That's something else Albert won't do: take the boat out to catch the white fish before the herring run again.'

'You're young yet and Albert won't be going to sea for much longer. His heart's not in it.'

'And he might be thrawn enough to hand the boat

over to Charlie, or the two of us together. I'm best out of it.'

She slapped a hand down on the bulkhead by her side. 'But this is the Lowrie boat!'

'What difference does that make?'

'If I'd been born a man, I'd show you that it makes all the difference!'

'If you'd been born a man, it might be you and me quarrelling over her and neither of us any better off than we are now. It's time we were both out of here,' he said again.

'You go if you want, I'm staying for a while.'

'You're not.' She had ruined his moment of solitude and he was not of a mind to let her have hers. 'Where are your boots?'

'I don't know.' She huddled back into her corner as James knelt down and felt beneath the table until his hand came up against a leather boot.

He held it out to her. 'Put it on.'

Ignoring the boot, Bethany leaned forward and put her hand on his wrist. Her fingers were icy cold.

'James,' she said with sudden urgency, 'don't leave *Fidelity*. If you do . . .' She swallowed hard then said, low-voiced, 'It'll be the end of us all.'

'Of course it won't!'

'It will,' she insisted. 'There's something about the *Fidelity* . . . she's part of us and we're part of her. If you're not with her, then we'll just drift apart. We'll be like . . . like dead things.'

He had never heard her speak like that before. It was nonsense, but at the same time her words, and their intensity, sent a shiver down James's backbone. Looking up at her face, only inches from his as he knelt on the floor, he saw to his astonishment that her eyes were filled with a sparkling golden mesh of unshed tears. As he watched, one perfect tear spilled very slowly over her lower lid; leaving a shining trail behind, it navigated her high cheekbone, then began to slide down the soft curve of her cheek, glittering in the lamplight as it went.

Even as a very small child, scarcely able to totter across the kitchen floor without falling over, Bethany had confronted adversity and even pain with a scowl on her face and her two hands fisted by her sides. This was the first time he had ever seen her cry, and for some reason the sight of that single tear affected him so strongly that he could scarcely breathe, let alone speak. As it reached the corner of her mouth, James leaned forward, giving way to an impulse stronger than any he had ever felt before, the tip of his tongue sliding out from between his lips to catch the droplet. Drawing back, savouring the saltiness on his lower lip, he saw Bethany's silvery eyes widen.

'James . . . ?' she said, her breath warm on his cheek. Then the boot, forgotten, fell from his fingers while his free hand reached out to cup the nape of her neck and draw her close.

It was scarcely a kiss, more of a delicate, preliminary brush-stroke on an artist's virgin canvas, but as far as James Lowrie was concerned it was like a match put to a pile of dry straw. The mere sensation of her mouth against his, the smell of her skin and her hair, caused such a strength of emotion to flare up that he drew back hurriedly, startled and confused.

If Bethany had been as appalled by what had happened as he was, then perhaps his sudden, inexplicable lapse might have ended there, never to be mentioned again. But instead the astonishment in the wide clear eyes just inches from his turned to realisation and she leaned in towards him, kissing the corner of his mouth and then the angle of his jaw. James gasped with pleasure, then took her face between his two hands, claiming her mouth with his. And suddenly they were on the bunk, locked together, and the two fires had become one, all-consuming and not to be denied.

*   *   *

The fisher-lassies returned to Buckie from Great Yarmouth like warriors arriving home after a great battle, waving exultantly from the open-bed lorries to those who had gathered to meet them and heedless of the biting-cold December winds. For they had won; they had beaten the buyers and the curers who, in order to save the last of the winter's herring catch, had been forced to agree to pay an extra tuppence per barrel from then on.

'And I wasnae there for all the excitement,' Meg Lowrie lamented. 'All these years of workin' at the farlins and I wasnae there!'

'It can't be helped,' Jess tried to console her. 'Think of the extra money you'll make next year.' Meg had found work in a net factory, and when the line-fishing season came during the opening months of the new year she would work in a smokehouse. The fisher-lassies enjoyed the winter work; hard though it was, they were at least warm and dry and under cover

'You must come and tell me all about it,' Meg ordered her niece. By chance she, Jess and Jacob had been in the street when the cart carrying the women who worked for the Pates arrived from the railway station at Aberdeen, and they had intercepted Bethany as she alighted. Jacob had left the women to their talk, while he gave the lorry driver a hand with some of the heavy kists.

'There's little to tell, for I didn't do much more than marching with the rest of them and going to the union meetings.'

'Your man must have been in a right state about it all,' Meg gloated.

'Aye, he was. How have the bairns been?' Bethany asked her mother.

'Fine. Phemie's very conscientious.'

'I'm sure she is. But now I'm back,' Bethany straightened her shoulders and lifted her chin, 'she'll no doubt be more than ready to get back home. Walter,' she put a hand on the driver's arm as he returned to his vehicle, 'when d'you go on to Finnechtie?'

'After he's had a wee cup of tea at my house,' Meg said. Then, raising her voice, 'And the lassies, too, for I want to hear about Yarm'th.'

'She'll never have room for all these folk in her wee house,' Bethany said as the women flowed off the bed of the lorry to follow Meg along the street.

'She'll manage – and she'll get all the gossip she didn't get from you. Bethany, this is an old friend of mine, Jacob MacFarlane. He was once a Portessie fisherman.'

'And I don't know a single one of those lassies from the lorry.' Jacob came forward. 'Times change too fast, Jess. Mrs Pate, I'm delighted to make your acquaintance.'

'And I'm pleased to meet you, Mr . . . er . . .' Bethany cast a confused glance at her mother, then said hurriedly, 'If you'll excuse me, I've the bairns to see.'

'That,' Jacob said as he watched her hurry to her own house, 'is the most beautiful woman I have ever seen on all my travels . . . apart from yourself, Jess.'

'She's got Weem's looks.'

'I see a look of you there too.'

'Mebbe so, but in nature she's his to the very marrow.' Jess had been waiting anxiously for the day when the winter fishing ended and Bethany came home where she belonged, but now she wondered if things were going to settle down after all. There was something in her daughter's eyes, in the way she had scarcely noticed Jacob, that told Jess that the trip to Yarmouth had raised more problems than it had solved.

As soon as she stepped across the threshold Bethany knew that Euphemia Pate had stamped her own mark on every inch and thread of the house. Standing in the middle of the kitchen, waiting to welcome her daughter-in-law home, the woman was like a black-clad spider in the middle of a web.

'Gilbert's not with you?'

'He'll be back tomorrow or mebbe the next day. He'd to stay in Yarmouth on a matter of business.' After the fishing season came the bargaining and planning for the season to come, and the settling of accounts.

'The bairns havenae been too bad, I suppose . . . in the circumstances,' Phemie said dourly. 'And I gave the house a good reddin' for you from ceiling to floor. It was in sore need.'

'That was good of you.' Bethany spoke through stiff lips. The woman made her skin crawl. 'Rory, Ellen . . .'

She dropped to her knees, holding her hands out to her step-children, who hovered behind their grandmother. They stayed where they were, peering out from the shelter of Phemie's black skirt.

'You've not forgotten me, surely?'

'Bairns forget easily, that's why it's never a good idea to go off and leave them,' the harsh voice said, every word sounding like a condemnation in itself.

Looking at the little faces, sullen-eyed and withdrawn, Bethany shivered. Was it true that Rory and Ellen had forgotten her – or were children, in their purity and innocence, able to see further and deeper than adults? Could those four dull, narrowed eyes have looked right into her soul and seen there the shameful secret she had brought home with her?

'They'll get back to themselves soon enough,' she said with false cheeriness. ''Specially when they see what I've brought back for them.'

Even that failed to move them or warm the look in their eyes. Bethany put her bag down, rubbed her hands nervously together and said, 'It was very good of you to look after them for me, Mrs Pate. You must be wanting to get back to your own house.'

'I should mebbe wait for Gilbert to come home. After all, it's his bairns I've been entrusted with.'

Horror filled Bethany at the idea of spending one night,

possibly two, under the same roof as this woman – in the same bed, for there was no other place to sleep. 'No.' She put a steely edge on her voice. 'No, Mrs Pate, I'll not presume on you for one moment longer. Walter Lochrie's going on to Finnechtie within the hour and he said he'd call for you. We've time for a cup of tea before you leave.'

Hearing the older woman's sharp intake of breath, and seeing the way her nostrils flared and her eyes hardened, she knew that Gil would be told as soon as he came home how his wife had mortally offended the mother who had birthed and raised him, and who had given up weeks of her time to care selflessly for his motherless bairns. But Bethany didn't care. She desperately needed time to herself, time to think, before Gil came home. At that moment she would have taken Phemie Pate by the scruff of the neck and run her all the way home, if there had been no other way to get rid of her.

'I've no need of the tea. I'd not be able to drink it in a place where I'm not wanted!' Phemie said. Then, as Bethany stood silently before her, hands clasped over her skirt, head up, her eyes fixed on some point just beyond her mother-in-law's red-rimmed left ear, Phemie gave another offended snort and snatched her jacket up.

As the door closed behind her Bethany let her breath out in a long sigh of relief. The children were still where their grandmother had left them, holding hands tightly. Determined to break the ice, Bethany advanced on them and scooped Ellen up. At first the little girl resisted, clinging to Rory's hand, and when Bethany finally managed to lift her the small body felt stiff. Then all at once she threw her arms about Bethany's neck, holding her tight.

'There's my bonny lassie. You've grown since I went away, you both have.' Smelling the scent of baby skin beneath the aroma of carbolic soap, Bethany realised to her surprise how much she had missed the two of them. 'Well now, let's see what I've brought back from Yarmouth for my good wee bairns.'

She carried Ellen over to her usual fireside chair, collecting her bag on the way. It took a moment or two to loosen the little girl's arms, but finally Ellen consented to sit on her lap, one hand tightly clutching Bethany's blouse. Rory watched from a distance, unblinking, as she opened her bag and rummaged through its contents. She had never known him to remain still for so long.

'Here we are. This is for Ellen . . .' She pulled out a rag doll, made out of bright patches of cloth and with yellow wool for hair, and dandled it before the child's eyes. Ellen automatically began to put her free hand out towards it, then pulled it back again, started to stick her thumb in her mouth, screwed up her face and shoved the hand behind her back. Bethany retrieved it and arranged it firmly round the doll.

'There we are, I'll hold on to you and you hold on to your new babby. Is she not pretty? And what do we have for Rory?'

The little boy, still motionless, watched as she dipped into the bag and brought out a handsomely painted wooden engine. 'That's for being such a good boy for Grandma.'

She held the toy out, but to her astonishment Rory merely put both hands behind his back.

'Rory?' When he remained where he was, his small round face set hard, she repeated in a voice sharp with apprehension, 'Rory Pate, come here at once and take your new toy!'

He came in a furious rush, his face suddenly flushing as he barrelled across the small room at her and collided painfully with her knees. Snatching the train from her hand, he threw it across the room with all his might. When it landed harmlessly in Gil's cushioned chair the little boy rushed at it, grabbing it up and throwing it again, this time into the hearth, narrowly missing the meagre fire. There was a great jangling of fire-irons, and one wheel came off the engine and bounced into a corner as Rory made for Bethany again, punching and pummelling at her legs and arms.

'I don't want your toy!' he shrieked at the top of his voice. 'And she doesnae want that!' Rory snatched the doll from Ellen and threw it after the train before returning to the attack on his step-mother.

'We hate you!' he screeched as he pummelled. 'We don't want you here! This isn't your house. Go away, go away, go away!'

Ellen, screaming with terror, locked her arms round Bethany's neck again, kicking back at her brother when he took a handful of her skirt and tried to wrench her away from Bethany.

'Leave us alone!' he roared. 'Go back to your own house, this isn't your house!'

Appalled by the ferocity of the attack, Bethany could do nothing at first but let the punches and kicks land painfully on her shins, her arms and her feet. Then, feeling Ellen beginning to slide from her grasp, she tightened her grip on the little girl, while trying with her free hand to hold Rory at bay. But there was no denying him; it was as if he was determined to force her out of her chair and out of the house. Finally realising that pushing him away was not the answer, she managed to scoop an arm about him and drag him on to her lap, where he continued to punch at her, his small knotted fists landing painfully on her breasts and shoulders. A blow in the throat drove the breath from her and caused her to see stars; she ducked her chin down for protection while pulling him closer, too close for punching.

'Rory, Rory . . . !' The noise of his shouting and Ellen's terrified wails filled Bethany's head. She felt as though she had a whole cageful of monkeys on her knee, but she didn't dare let go. 'Sshhh, pet, hush.' She resisted the temptation to raise her voice above the clamour, lowering it instead to speak directly into his ear. 'What's wrong? You've never hurt me before, you'd not hurt anyone. Hush, Ellen, everything's going to be all right.'

At first it seemed that he couldn't hear her, for he kept fighting, tugging painfully at her hair when he realised that he could no longer draw his arm back far enough to hit her. Tears of pain rolled down her cheeks but she held on, talking and talking, refusing to let either of the children go. Finally, just as she was beginning to wonder if her own strength was going to hold out much longer, the little boy went limp against her, sobbing as though his heart would break.

'Rory?'

'I h-hate you,' he hiccuped. 'You w-went away and left us w-with Grandma Pate, and Ellen cried and c-cried and sh-she wanted you and you w-weren't there!'

'Oh, pet! Oh, Ellen! I'm sorry, I'm sorry!' The full enormity of what she had done to the children suddenly broke over Bethany and her own tears of pain gave way to a great flood of misery. The three of them clung together, weeping and rocking, united in their grief.

18

By the time the children were comforted all three faces were so swollen with tears that they looked, as Bethany shakily pointed out, like three canvas buoys that had been painted bright red. The idea made Rory laugh, the first natural chuckle she had heard from him since arriving home and the first, she suspected, that he had uttered since she had gone to Great Yarmouth.

She bathed their faces and her own, then filled bowls with bread and milk, scattering sugar liberally over each helping. After they had eaten she gathered them back into her lap, reading stories and playing with them until they were limp with exhaustion and ready to be carried into the smaller room and put to bed. Even then they both clung to her when she tried to go back into the kitchen and she had to stay with them until they fell asleep. Ellen succumbed within five minutes, but Rory fought sleep with the same grim determination he had used against Bethany earlier, never taking his gaze off her face and forcing his eyelids open every time they began to droop. When exhaustion finally took him she stayed by his narrow little bed for a long time, watching his swollen face and listening to his breathing, which was interrupted occasionally, like Ellen's, by an involuntary hiccup.

Back in the kitchen she tidied the place, then washed herself and changed into her night-gown before retrieving the brightly painted engine and hunting for the wheel. The wood was undamaged; she would ask Innes to repair it tomorrow. She sat stroking the engine, staring drearily into the fire. The toy would mend easily, but it would be much harder to repair the damage she had done to Rory and Ellen.

She should never have gone to Great Yarmouth. She had put herself first as always, abandoning the children to their grandmother's harsh regime, leaving them without a backward glance because, fond though she was of them, she always thought of them as Molly's bairns, not hers. But they were hers; by marrying their father she had undertaken to care for them. And instead of caring she had tried to recapture her own freedom, going off to Yarmouth to be a guttin quine, shaming poor Gil with that silly business about the barrel, not to mention . . .

Her thoughts veered sharply away from the scene in *Fidelity*'s cabin, but she forced herself to remember, to face the pain and the shame of it.

They had rolled and tumbled on the narrow bunk like wild animals, she and James, kissing and holding and babbling wordlessly, shameless in their burning hunger for each other. When at last they came to their senses it was too late.

'God, Bethany, what did we think we were doing?' Moving like a man in a dream, James had lurched on to the opposite bunk and buried his face in his hands. 'What did we think we were doing?' he asked again, his voice muffled.

'I don't know, but it's never going to happen again.' She was pulling her blouse straight as she spoke, tidying her hair with shaking hands. 'It was the drink, it turned us mad.'

She pulled on her stockings, pushed her feet into her boots, found her jacket and dragged it on. 'I'll go first and you stay here for a while so that nobody sees.'

At the foot of the ladder she paused, her back to

him. 'It was nothing, James, just a nonsense. It'll not happen again.'

'It will not!' he said, his voice hard. 'Away you go . . . hurry!'

She kept to the shadows as she moved along the harbour, the shame and horror of what had just happened choking her, so that she had to keep swallowing in a vain attempt to clear her throat.

She thought to walk the town's quieter streets until the other women at the lodgings had gone to their beds, for she couldn't bear the thought of having to look at them, speak to them, behave normally after what she had done. But when she reached the town itself she found the place abuzz with excitement and every street filled with shouting, singing, exultant fisher-lassies.

The strike was over, and they had won.

Bethany suddenly realised that she was rocking and keening to herself in her fireside chair in her husband's kitchen, fresh tears running down cheeks already rough and sore from earlier weeping. She got up and walked about the room distractedly. She and James had only seen each other once since that night and, after the first glance of recognition, they had carefully avoided speaking to or looking at each other, or touching. Above all, they must never touch again, they both knew that.

It would be years before she forgot that night; perhaps she never would. But it was in the past, she told herself firmly as she put the lamp out and got into bed. It was a mistake, but it was over and she must put it out of her mind in case, one day, Gil or her mother or Stella looked into her eyes, saw the memories there and guessed what she and James had done.

She stretched out in the empty bed and closed her eyes, worn out with travelling, with the confrontation with Gil's mother and comforting the children. Tomorrow Gil would be home, but tonight, thankfully, she was on her own. All she wanted was to sleep, but instead she tossed and turned in the big wall-bed, thinking, despite all her efforts, of James; of the sweetness of his mouth, the throaty murmur of his voice in her ear and the burning warmth of his lean, hard body beneath her hands.

Without realising what she was doing, she began to caress her own body beneath the demure folds of her gown in a desperate search for relief. And when at last it came to her, the man she gave herself to in her fevered imagination was not her husband.

The day the boats began to come back from the English fishing grounds was always a day of celebration in Buckie, just as it was in every fishing community up and down the coast. The menfolk were home again, and they would remain on shore for several weeks, since there was little fishing to be done now that the herring were gone. The turn of the year was a time to settle accounts and plan for the future, and with a good season behind them there need be no worries about food or fuel, or paying rent over the winter.

When the first boats were sighted the entire village turned out, including babes in arms and old folk hobbling with the assistance of sticks and crutches – even using brooms for support if there was nothing else to hand. They thronged the harbour walls, spurred on by the hysterical screaming of the seabirds that flew in their hundreds to meet the boats and escort them in.

Bethany and the children, exhausted by the traumas of the previous day, had slept late. When they woke she hurriedly did what had to be done about the house, then bundled Rory and Ellen into their warmest cloth-ing and took them off for a long walk along the coast and up the fields to Rathven; she carried Ellen most of the way and Rory, too, in the crook of her free arm when he began to grizzle and complain. When they were hungry she gave them the bread and cheese she had stuffed into her pockets before she left home, and when they were thirsty there was cold tea to drink from a bottle.

From the fields above the village the three of them saw the first of the boats come in, nudging over the horizon in a line that gradually opened out as the boats came closer. More and more appeared behind the leaders until the Firth was dotted with a huge flotilla.

As they neared the coast some split off, making for other communities, but most headed purposefully towards Buckie, crowding the waters outside the harbour, waiting patiently at the entrance for their turn. One after another, all morning and afternoon, they came in, the men hurrying ashore to be greeted by their families. Tomorrow they would return to clean the boats and check the nets, the ropes and the buoys, but today there was no more work, only celebration.

As the *Fidelity* nosed her way past the lighthouse at the entrance to Cluny harbour, James felt his belly curl with apprehension. While the drifter moved into the first of the inner basins he busied himself about the deck, taking quick glances at the crowds on the walls above. He spotted Stella with the baby in her arms and the twins at her knees, and his mother, beaming her relief at seeing boat and crew home safely, and nodded to them before his gaze travelled on, searching for a head with hair the colour of beech trees in autumn sunlight.

To his relief his sister was not among the crowd above, but even so he remained on his guard, just in case he caught sight of her unexpectedly and gave himself away to those watching.

He was the last of the crew to leave the boat and, when he did, Stella was waiting at the top of the ladder. 'James . . . oh, James, we've missed you!' she said fervently, forcing herself to hold back, aware that James, like his father before him, believed that shows of affection belonged behind closed doors in the privacy of a man's own home.

'Here . . . give her to me,' he said gruffly, holding out his arms for his youngest daughter. 'You'll be tired holding her all this time.'

The baby, cocooned in so many shawls that she was like a large, soft clothes-peg in his awkward hands, stared up at him with startled eyes, then blinked twice before breaking into panic-stricken yells.

'She's too wee to mind who you are,' Stella apologised, taking the bundle back and joggling it soothingly. 'She's a wee thing strange with folk just now, it's only her age. But you know your daddy, don't you?' she added to the twins, who looked solemnly at James. All three of them, he suddenly realised, were like their mother. There seemed to be little of him in the children he had fathered.

'You're safe home, then.' His mother arrived, accompanied by a sturdy grey-haired man and smiling the tentative smile she had adopted since their quarrel over his father's burial. 'I hear the fishing was good.'

'Good enough.' James eyed the stranger standing just behind Jess; not so much standing, he thought with a sudden sharpening of interest, as hovering in a protective sort of way. 'Who's this?' he asked bluntly.

Jess drew the man forward. 'Jacob MacFarlane. His people were neighbours to mine in Portessie and he was a fisherman like yourself.'

'But not any more, eh?' James eyed the outstretched hand. It was broad and thick-knuckled and Jacob MacFarlane's face was weather-beaten, but James was willing to wager money that it had been a while since the man had had to do manual work for his living.

'Not any more, though I'm still in the business.' His handshake was firm and hearty. 'I'm a buyer now.'

'A buyer? Were you in Yarm'th?'

'I'd men there and I was at Lowestoft myself for part of the winter fishing.' His voice was cultured, but there

were strong undertones of the Moray coast lilt. 'So . . .'
His sea-green eyes studied James with interest. 'You're
Weem Lowrie's lad. I can see the likeness.'

'You knew him?'

'Aye, I knew Weem well when we were about the
age you are now. And I'll hope to make your better
acquaintance too while I'm bidin' in Buckie.'

James nodded. 'For the meantime, though, I'd like fine
to get home and have something to eat,' he said, and
turned away to swing one of the twins up and offer
his big hand to the other. She surveyed it doubtfully
and then, urged forward by Stella, gingerly grasped one
finger.

'Who is this Jacob MacFarlane?' James asked his wife
later.

'I know no more than you do. He arrived a week or
two back.'

'I mind him well,' old Mowser chimed in from across
the hearth. 'The MacFarlanes lived in Portessie and they
had three or four lads, all of them good fishermen. But
they went off to other places one by one and I never heard
what happened to any of them.'

'He says he knew my father.'

Mowser puffed at his pipe, sending a cloud of pale-blue
fragrant smoke into the air above his head, then took the
stem from his mouth. 'Everyone knew your father and,
from what I mind, Jacob MacFarlane had cause to know
him better than most.'

'What d'you mean?'

The old man chuckled. 'Jacob and your mother were
sweethearts all the time they were growing from childhood, right up until Weem set eyes on her. That was the
end of it for poor Jacob. I heard that they even fought
over her, but your father was more than a match for
most of the lads round here. Jacob was sent off with
a flea in his lug and nob'dy heard sight or sound of

him till he turned up again the other week, dressed like a gentleman and with a silver-handled cane too, someone said.'

'I saw it,' Stella said from the stove. 'And a bowler hat. He's a right handsome man when he's all dressed up. He's been spending time with your mother, James.'

'Mebbe he's courting her now that she's a widow,' Mowser suggested.

'Don't be daft, they're both far too old for that sort of thing!'

The old man laughed, a wheezing, choking sound. 'Age has nothing to do with it, lad, as you'll mebbe find out in your own good time. And Jacob still looks to be a lusty man.'

'That's enough now, Father.' Stella's voice was sharp and the colour rose to her cheeks. The old man wheezed once more, then pushed the pipe-stem into his mouth, like a baby with a comforter, and went back to staring into the fire and thinking his own private thoughts.

James got to his feet. 'I'll wash before we eat.'

'The outhouse is cold. You can wash in here for once.'

'There's nothing wrong with the outhouse.' He rummaged in a drawer for a clean shirt.

'There's water heating in the kettle. It'll not be a minute . . .'

'You can bring it out to me when it's ready.'

The outhouse walls were old and full of cracks that let in the wind. The only time the place was warm was on washdays, when the fire had been burning for hours beneath the boiler and the draughts blew steam off the water's surface. James pulled his shirt off and dropped it on to the stone flags before fetching the soap and bringing the old tin basin from its usual place, upturned over the empty boiler.

As he ran cold water into it from the tap, Stella came in with the heavy kettle clutched in both fists.

'You don't really think that man's courting my mother,

do you?' James asked as he took it from her and emptied
it into the basin.

She had picked up his soiled shirt and was folding it
neatly. 'That's just Da blethering, pay no heed to him,'
she said. Then, after a moment, 'Though mind you . . .'
She laid the shirt on top of the basket of clothes waiting
for the next wash-day. 'She's young enough yet, your
mother, and bonny in her own way. It might be a good
thing if it was true.'

'Of course it wouldn't be a good thing!' James was
appalled.

'Why not? Bethany has Gil and Innes has Zelda, and
you and me have each other and the bairns. Why shouldn't
your mother have someone to care for her?'

'Because . . . because she doesn't need anyone else!
Come here, woman . . .' He reached for her as she opened
her mouth to argue further, pulling her tightly against him
and kissing her hard.

When he released her she was pink and flustered.
'What's got into you, James Lowrie? You've never done
that in the wash-house before!'

'I've been away a long time, that's all. Are you complaining?'

She giggled, daring to stroke both hands down the hard,
cool planes of his bare chest. 'Not a bit of it.'

'Good.' He kissed her again and this time she responded,
clinging to him and reaching up to draw him closer. When
he released her she would have moved back into his arms,
but he gave her a little push towards the door. 'Off you
go and see to the dinner, for I'm starved. I'll be five
minutes, just.'

When she had gone he turned back to the basin, gripping the edges tight, staring unseeingly through the grimy
wash-house window to the little garden where, in spring,
summer and autumn, his wife and his father-in-law raised
vegetables.

Stella's kisses had been warm and womanly, but she

wasn't Bethany. Holding her did nothing to rouse the fire that had consumed him only a few nights ago in *Fidelity*'s cabin. Nobody could bring that back, except . . .

Cursing, he emptied the hot water from the basin into the boiler, replaced it with cold water from the tap, then set to work lathering the soap. Scrubbing his face and neck, his chest and arms, and spluttering water all over the wash-house's stone flags, he pushed all thoughts of Bethany from his mind.

19

Gil Pate was in high spirits when he got home, for it had been a good season and he was in profit.

'And that's even after those damned witches you threw your lot in with forced me and the rest of the employers to pay them more.'

'Then it shows that you could well afford it. Be fair, Gil,' Bethany protested, 'we deserved that money.'

'Aye, mebbe so,' he agreed grudgingly. Then, always one to get in the last word if he could, 'It's just fortunate for all of us that the fishing was so good, else you and me and the wee ones would've been hard put to it to find food for our bellies this winter.'

She bit her tongue and said nothing. Gil and his brother were both known to be shrewd businessmen, comfortably off by local standards. There was little fear of them or their families having to go without.

It was common practice on the Moray Firth for fisher-men who owned their own boats and gear to sell their catches to certain curers at pre-arranged prices. The curers advanced the money needed to equip the boats, and at the end of each fishing season it fell to the curers to work out the total earned from the catches. Once that was done and an amount allocated to each boat, the skipper and mate deducted the vessel's expenses – coaling, paint, oil, repairs and food – before dividing the remainder between their crew.

Since Gil and Nathan Pate were sole buyers for all the fish caught by a number of Buckie boats, Bethany had to put up with being plagued by a whole series of meetings round her kitchen table as representatives of each boat met to go through the books with the Pate brothers.

So harassed was she by the meetings, which seemed to take place one after another, that she quite forgot that eventually James would be involved. On the day she opened the door to find him on the step, her mind went blank and her knees turned to water. She clutched at the door frame to keep herself upright.

'What are you doing here?' she hissed, mindful that Gil, who had gone to the privy at the back of the house, could walk in on them at any minute. 'Have you not got the sense to keep right away from this house?'

He frowned at her. 'What are you havering about now? We're here for the meeting . . .'

'Don't stand there blocking the way in, man,' Albert's voice boomed from behind him. 'Get in, I'm freezing to death in this wind!'

He gave his nephew a hearty push and James was propelled in through the doorway, almost knocking Bethany down. She backed away hurriedly as Albert stamped into the kitchen and Gil came in from the back yard.

'Have you not offered our visitors a drink, Bethany? Sit down, sit down, Nathan'll be here by and by.' He bustled about, fetching a bottle and glasses while Bethany began to get the children ready to go out. All she could think of was getting away from the house, which seemed to her overheated mind to be filled with James's presence.

'I hope you're away to make your peace with my mother,' Gil said pointedly. There had been a coolness between them since he had returned from a visit to Phemie Pate the day before, his ears ringing with complaints about his wife's ingratitude and ill manners. Bethany had resented his instructions to apologise as soon as she could, telling him sharply that she would make her own

mind up about it. Now, anxious to have a reason for her
hurried flight, she said, 'Aye, that's what I had in mind.
I'll be away for a while.'

'We can manage without you,' Gil told her indifferently. He was a man among men now, and for that
afternoon at least Bethany had been relegated to the
ranks of all women – handmaidens and servers, who got
in the way at times like this.

Nathan arrived just as she was about to leave. Outside,
Bethany took a long, deep breath of the cold December
air, then gripped the handle of the perambulator tightly.
She would go to Finnechtie and force herself to apologise
humbly to her dragon of a mother-in-law. Perhaps the walk
there and back, and the punishing treatment she would no
doubt receive while there, would help to calm the turmoil
that had leaped up within her when she opened the door
to James.

'That's better,' Gil said when the door closed behind his
wife and children. 'We couldnae settle to business with
the bairns running about the place, and women are best
kept out of these matters anyway.'

Nathan downed half the whisky in his glass in one
swallow. 'You're right there. Let a wife know how much
you're worth and she'll not be satisfied till she's got every
last penny of it out of your pocket.'

'Why d'you think I never wed?' Albert threw in his
contribution. 'Enjoy the benefits without sufferin' the
pain, that's what I always say.'

'Are we here to settle the wages or just to give our
tongues a good airing?' James asked sharply. His fists
were clenched in his pockets and it was an effort to stay
seated, when all he wanted to do was walk away from
their silly bragging – especially Gil's.

'God save us, here's a man still new enough married
to be missing his wee wife when they're apart,' Albert
sneered, holding his glass out to be re-filled. The other

two started to laugh, then as James half-rose from his chair the laughter subsided and Nathan reached out to put a hand on his arm.

'Sit down, lad, we're just about to start on the business. Are we not, Gil?'

'Aye, and fine business it was, too.' Gil opened the books he had written up, with much licking of pencils and muttering, and James settled back into his seat as the meeting started in earnest.

Once the *Fidelity*'s expenses were cleared and a sum set aside for the bank in repayment of the loan still outstanding on the boat the remainder was divided as usual into three parts – one for the crew, one for the upkeep and repair of the nets, and one for the boat, to cover loss, wear and tear. This year, since the boat did not require any major repairs, the third part of the money would mainly be used for a dividend payment among all the crew. As the nets had belonged to Weem, and had been bequeathed by him to James, he fell heir to the money set aside for them.

'What would have happened, Albert, if you'd had a bad season and you'd not been able to pay the bank?' Nathan asked as each man stowed his share away. 'You've not got a house to bargain with.'

Drifters like the *Fidelity* cost as much as £3,000 to buy and as bankers, unlike fishermen, were not obliged to take account of the weather or of the years when the shoals of fish simply did not appear as expected, they demanded their loan repayments even when the catches were poor. Most skippers on the Firth owned their homes, and many a good Moray man had lost the roof above his own and his family's heads because the loan could not be honoured, through no fault of his.

Albert winked. 'If ye don't have a house ye cannae lose a house.'

'Then they'd take the boat and sell her to cover their losses,' James said. 'Probably for less than she's worth.'

His uncle, who had been re-filling his glass from Gil's

bottle more often than the others, shrugged. 'They'd be welcome to her, as far as I'm concerned. At my age a man doesnae know how many years' work he's got left in him anyway, and at least I'd still have my snug wee lodgings and we'd be free of the loan . . . eh, James?' He clapped his nephew on the shoulder.

'And me and Charlie and Jem, and the rest of them, would be out of work.'

'Ach, you'd all be taken on elsewhere, no bother.'

'I don't see why that would worry you, James, since I've heard,' Nathan added with a sidelong glance, 'that you're of a mind to leave *Fidelity* anyway.'

'James? Never!' Albert finished his drink and swiped the back of his hand over his mouth.

James cleared his throat. 'Davie Geddes is looking for a mate.'

'You'd work for that pious creature? I've heard that he gets his crew together to pray before they shoot the nets,' Albert mocked, 'and again after they've hauled them in. That would never suit the likes of you, lad!'

'Davie's thinking of giving up the sea. He wants to keep his boat, and leave it in good hands.'

'So it's a fine skipper on a sailed boat you'd be?' Albert pointed a finger at his nephew. 'You stay with the *Fidelity*, laddie, she'll be yours one of these days. Patience, that's all it takes, patience.' Albert struggled to his feet, using the table-edge as a lever. 'You'll have to excuse me, gentlemen. I must convey my compliments to a certain lady further along the coast,' he said with a huge wink.

'And that's all he'll manage to convey to her, judging from the state he's in,' Nathan grinned when the man had staggered out.

It had been a difficult afternoon for Bethany. As soon as the children realised that they were on the Finnechtie road and bound for their grandmother's house, Ellen had set up a thin wail and Rory had stopped short and refused to go another step. Bethany had had to put up with their whining and squabbling all the rest of the way to Phemie's cold, immaculate house.

Once inside, the children had both stayed close to Bethany, holding on to her clothing and scarcely speaking to the older woman, who made plain her belief that as soon as she had arrived back from Yarmouth their step-mother had set to and speedily re-introduced them to her slovenly ways, removing all the training that Phemie had painstakingly instilled in them. She received Bethany's apology for her behaviour on her return from England with tightly pursed mouth and steely eyes, grinding out by way of acknowledgement, 'I'll say this for my Gilbert, he knows how to exercise control over his own household.'

It was so unfair, Bethany seethed as she walked home after a very uncomfortable hour, that even when she had choked out the required apology Gil had got the credit for making her do it.

To her relief he was alone in the house when they arrived, cheerful after his afternoon's discussion and mel-lowed by the bottle that he and the others had emptied while attending to their business. The children, whose spirits had risen with every yard that left Finnechtie further behind and brought Buckie nearer, rushed into the house to greet him with boisterous affection and in no time at all the three of them were scrambling about the floor in some energetic game.

'Your James is in a right strange mood these days,' Gil said thoughtfully that night when the children were in bed.

Bethany kept her eyes on her darning. 'What sort of mood?'

'He's never what you'd call the best of company, but since he came back from Yarm'th he's been downright thrawn. He found fault with almost everything that was said today. And mind he spoke of leaving the *Fidelity*

and going to be mate for Davie Geddes when we were
in Yarm'th?'

'That was just talk, he'd never do such a thing.'

'You're wrong there, for he's set on it. He spoke of
it in front of Albert this afternoon.' Then Gil knocked
his pipe out and stretched his muscular arms above his
head, yawning. 'Ah well, we've all got to see to ourselves and leave others to their own ways. As long as
we're comfortable . . . and we are that. Life's good to
us, Bethany, and with you by my side it can only get
better.'

Gil's good fortune, it seemed, was set fair. A few evenings
later, not long after he had returned from his day's work,
Jacob MacFarlane paid an unexpected call.

To Bethany's embarrassment, Gil was washing himself
in the kitchen when the visitor knocked on the door. 'Come
on in, man,' he said cheerfully through a faceful of suds.
'I'll be done in a minute.' Then, to his wife's horror,
'You'll take some dinner with us?'

'I'd like that fine.' Jacob's face was red with the keen
wind that was blowing in from the Firth that night.

'It's nothing grand,' Bethany said automatically, her
mind racing as she tried to work out how to stretch the
food, 'but of course you're very welcome.'

'I can think of nothing better than a good home-cooked
meal on a night like this. Thank you both for your
kindness.' Jacob, unperturbed by his host's naked, hairy
chest and the basin of soapy water on the table, stripped
his coat off, sat himself down by the fire and lifted
Ellen on to his lap. When she looked at him doubtfully,
wondering if she should weep or smile, he gave her
his fob watch to play with, and when Rory immediately rushed over he was presented with a small multi-
coloured pebble.

'That,' Jacob told him solemnly, 'is very, very special.
It comes from Portessie and it's been all over the world

with me, and you are to look after it while I'm in your house.'

As she worked at the stove Bethany heard his voice ramble placidly on, the sound of it punctuated now and again with questions or squeals of laughter from the children. Every time she glanced round she seemed to meet the man's bright-green gaze. While they ate, he appeared happy to answer all Gil's questions, telling them of the years after he left the Firth, working his way all down the east coast of Britain, crewing on boats out of Johnshaven and Arbroath, Anstruther and Port Seton, Grimsby and Whitby and Lowestoft and Great Yarmouth, never staying in any one place for much longer than a season.

'I was restless and I was young and answerable to nobody. I'd a mind to see the world.' From Yarmouth he had gone further afield, working for a Dutchman for several years.

'That job took me all over The Netherlands, and to Germany and Russia too, so I stayed with him for several years.'

'Always as a fisherman?' Bethany asked and his gaze, never far from her, returned at once.

'At first, then the man that paid me started using me as a buyer. That's how I got to know about the other side of the business – pickling and smoking herring. Eventually I'd saved enough and knew enough to set up in business for myself. As you well know, the Russians, the Germans and the Dutch all have a great love of pickled herring.'

'They have that, and thank God for it,' Gil agreed heartily, pushing his chair back from the table and slapping his stomach with both hands to indicate that it was full and satisfied. 'You'll take a wee dram, Jacob?'

'I will that. And you'll have a cigar?' The visitor brought out a handsome cigar case and both men moved to the fireside as Bethany set about the business of putting the children to bed. By the time they were tucked up and she was clearing the table, Jacob had got down to the reason for his visit. He was looking for people who could supply herring, both pickled and smoked, and where better, he had asked himself, than from his own part of the world?

'When Jess told me that you and your brother ran just such a business between you, and that you were a cooper into the bargain, I knew that I'd been right to come back to my own birthplace,' he finished.

Gil's face was radiant. 'You could do no better than me and Nathan,' he agreed eagerly.

'You'd probably need to expand. I know you already take all the fish that the Lowrie boat can catch, and buy from other boats too, but you'd need to be the sole buyer for a good deal more. I could mebbe find the extra money you might need as an equal third partner. Of course, I'll have to see round the cooperage and the curing yard and the smokehouse first, and take a look at your books.'

'That's no trouble,' Gil said at once, and Jacob got up, holding out his hand.

'First thing tomorrow, then, at your yard?'

'I'll look forward to it.' Gil shook his hand heartily, then Jacob offered it to Bethany.

'Thank you for a delicious meal, my dear. You're a fortunate man, Gil Pate.'

'I know that!' Gil was so pleased with himself that when the visitor had gone he paced about the kitchen, unable to sit at peace. 'This could be the making of us, lass. I'll be a rich man, you wait and see. You and the bairns'll want for nothing . . . And mebbe I'll be able to take you to one of these fine new houses they're building in Cliff Terrace. You'll be the mistress of a grand house, Bethany, with mebbe a wee serving maid for you to order about . . .'

'Gil, will you just wait until Mr MacFarlane's had a chance to look at the yard and the smokehouse?' she protested. 'He might not like what he sees, or he might change his mind.'

'Not a bit of it, he's a man of integrity. When he gives his word he'll keep it.'

'He didn't give his word tonight, he just spoke of what might happen.'

'He as good as gave it – and I've you to thank for that.' Gil lunged, lifting her right off her chair and into his arms.

'Me? Put me down, you daft loon!'

'I will not.' He danced about the room with her, jiggling her so vigorously that she had to wrap her arms about his neck to prevent herself being tossed to the floor. 'Yes, you. The man could scarce keep his eyes off you.'

'Don't be daft!'

'I know what I'm saying. And I can't blame him for it, for you're my own bonny wee dove,' he said into her hair. The generous tumblerful of whisky he had downed before bidding their host goodnight bathed her in fumes that made her eyes water. 'It's all thanks to you!'

At the same moment, in a farm stable near Rathven, Innes Lowrie was saying feebly, 'You're not!'

'You think I'd make up a thing like that?' Zelda's voice was thick with fear.

'But . . . how could it be?'

She made a sound that was half-laugh, half-sob, and pummelled at his chest with knotted fists. 'How d'you think? Have you forgotten that week I slept in your bed every night while your mother was looking after your auntie? Though devil the sleeping you did, Innes Lowrie, you randy bugger! And now you ask me how it could happen?'

'I didn't mean . . . I just thought that . . .'

'You just thought it was all fun, and now that there's a result you're trying to pretend that it was none of your doing?' Now she was kicking his shins as well, her booted feet landing sore blows. Tears ran freely down a face twisted with fear and fury. 'Well, I didn't force you, though if you keep on denying me I can always tell my father that it was *you* forced *me*. Then see what you'll get!'

'Zelda . . . Zelda!' he repeated as the blows and kicks continued to rain down. When she ignored him he was forced to use his superior strength on her, catching her wrists and trapping them above her head, then rolling his full weight on top of her and locking his ankles over hers to hold her legs still, so that she was held flat against the pile of straw.

Subdued, trapped, she went limp and began bawling like a child in her misery.

'No, Zelda, it's all right, lass,' Innes implored, kissing the wet face that tried to twist away from beneath him. 'It's all right! I'll marry you, of course I will. You surely didn't think I'd abandon you at a time like this?'

'You d-didn't believe me!'

'It was the surprise of it. Somehow I didn't think . . .' he began, then found the sense to stop before he made things worse.

The precious nights they had spent together had been a delight and a joy that he treasured and would always treasure, no matter what the future might hold in store for him. But somehow he had not associated them with the making of a bairn. That was a business for adults, and Innes had not yet become accustomed to thinking of himself as a grown man.

'I just never thought of it,' he said lamely.

She wriggled free and sat up, rubbing both hands over her tear-streaked face. 'Well, you'd better start, for I'm not facing my father alone over this!'

'You won't have to, I'll be with you. I'll always be with you, Zelda,' he said earnestly. 'You and me and our bairn – we'll be together no matter what.'

'But where will we be? Here?' Zelda threw out her arms to indicate the small stable.

A sturdy building with straw piled in one corner to

make a comfortable couch, it had become their favourite meeting place during the cold winter nights. It was already inhabited by two placid cart-horses, and their big bodies threw off enough warmth to make the place seem cosy in comparison to the bitter weather outside. It was private, too, for once the animals were bedded down for the night nobody came near the place.

'Mebbe a stable did Mary and Joseph well enough, but it's not what I want for my bairn,' Zelda warned.

'Of course you won't have to live here. I'll find somewhere,' Innes said desperately. 'I'll look after you, both of you.'

'Oh, Innes!' She threw her arms round him and kissed him.

'How long . . . I mean, when . . . ?'

'I'd say another seven months.'

'We've got quite a long time, then,' he said with relief. A lot could happen in seven months.

'No, we haven't, for I'll be showing soon. Mistress Bain's already suspicious. I've been ill in the mornings, and it was her questioning me about it that made me realise what was wrong,' Zelda explained. 'We'll have to wed as soon as we can, Innes, and to do that we'll have to tell my mother and my father.' Her voice faltered. 'You know what my father's like. He's going to be so angry with me!' The tears began to roll down her face again.

'If he's angry with anyone it should be me, not you.' Innes held her tightly, his cheek against her hair. 'When he knows that we're to be wed he'll not mind.'

'You think so?' Her voice was doubtful. 'And we still don't know where we'll live.'

'I'll see to that, too. I'll see to everything,' Innes promised. Even in the midst of sudden shock he was certain of one thing: that he loved her and would do anything for her. 'If you want, we'll go to your house and tell your father the truth of it right away.'

'Tonight?' She drew away from him.

'The sooner, the better.' Speaking for himself, he would rather get things over and done with.

'I'm not walking over there tonight! It's bitter cold outside and I've to be back in the farmhouse in an hour's time.'

'When, then?'

She bit her lip. 'A week or two wouldn't matter. Can we not wait until after Ne'erday's over before we tell anyone? That'll give us time to get used to the idea ourselves, and start making plans.'

'I'm not sure I can keep quiet for another two weeks.'

'You'll have to. Anyway,' her arms slid round his neck and her voice deepened slightly, 'there are other things for us to do tonight.'

'But, is it all right, with you . . . ?' Innes asked, bewildered at the sudden change of mood.

Zelda let herself fall back on the straw, drawing him down with her. 'It's as safe as it'll ever be,' she assured him throatily, the tears and fears forgotten now that she was sure of his support. 'The harm's already done and there's no reason why we shouldn't enjoy ourselves while we still can.'

20

After inspecting the cooperage and the curing yards run by the Pate brothers Jacob MacFarlane expressed his approval.

'It's only a matter of him having the papers he wants drawn up, and by Ne'erday we'll be in partnership.' Gil was so excited that he could scarcely keep still for more than one minute at a time.

'It's like having three bairns in the house instead of two,' Bethany complained as he came up behind her while she was peeling potatoes for his dinner at the sink, wrapping his arms about her waist.

'So you think I'm a bairn, do you?' His beard rubbed the soft skin below her ear and his hands crept up to toy with the buttons of her blouse, while his body pressed tightly into hers, forcing her against the stone sink. 'Do I feel like a bairn?' he asked, his breath hot on her ear.

'If you don't leave me alone your dinner'll be late.'

'I'm not bothered.'

'Gil!' She pushed his groping hands away. 'The wee ones are just in the next room. They could come in at any minute.'

'I'll be quick.'

'Not as quick as I'll be with this knife if you don't leave me in peace.' She tried, with great effort, to keep her voice light. 'You should know by now never to pester a fisher-lassie with a good cutting knife in her hand.'

For a moment she thought he was going to defy her, but just then Ellen came trotting into the kitchen. Gil sighed and stepped away from his wife. 'Tonight, then.'

'Tonight,' she agreed, glad that her back was to him and that he could not see her face.

The days when the fisher-folk of the Moray Firth celebrated the turn of the year with burning torches, and offerings of food and drink to the sturdy boats they relied on for their livelihoods, were gone. Now Ne'erday, the first day of the new year, was marked by more sedate customs. In the morning the children opened the gifts brought during the night by Santa Claus, the benign being who visited English children on Christmas Day, and at night families and friends gathered together to share their Ne'erday dinner. It had become a tradition for the Lowrie family – Meg, Albert and Mowser included – to eat at Weem's home on Ne'erday, and although he was no longer there Jess insisted on keeping the custom going. This year Albert was visiting with his latest lady love, but with Zelda and Jacob invited as well there were ten adults to cater for, as well as five children.

'Your mother's taking on too much, feeding us all,' kind-hearted Stella fretted to Bethany. 'We'd be better calling on her in the afternoon, then going back home to eat our dinners.'

'She'd not have it any other way.' Bethany had no wish whatsoever to be part of a family gathering, but she knew that Jess was determined. So was Gil, who planned to use the occasion to make an official announcement about his new partnership with Jacob MacFarlane. 'And it's not too much for her, she's as strong as a horse.'

'Right enough, Mr MacFarlane's done her the world of good.'

'You think so?'

'Oh yes. Since he's come back to Buckie the years have just fallen away from her.' Stella hesitated, giving her sister-in-law a sidelong glance. Bethany was not one for confidences, or gossiping, but after all Jess was her mother. Stella decided to risk it. 'I'm beginning to wonder if he's got a fondness for her.'

'For my mother?' Bethany's knitting dropped into her lap and she gaped at the other girl. 'You're havering.'

Stella smirked, delighted to have startled her cool, self-possessed sister-in-law for once. 'He scarcely left her side all those weeks you were in Yarm'th. They grew up next door to each other in Portessie, you know. My da says they were sweethearts once.'

'If they were, why did she marry my father?' Bethany scoffed.

'Because she loved him more, but seemingly Mr MacFarlane's never married. Mebbe when he lost her he decided there could be nobody else.' Before marriage and motherhood claimed all of her time Stella had enjoyed reading romantic novels; now her cheeks were pink with excitement at the idea that she might at that moment be watching a real romance from the sidelines.

'That's because he had more sense.' Bethany's knitting was in her hands again. Her needles raced along the row, turned, raced along the next row. 'There's other things in life besides marriage.'

'I can't think of any.'

'Aye well, you're lucky. You've got everything you want.' Bethany knew that her voice was too sharp, but she couldn't help it. She had not set foot in James's cottage since her return from Yarmouth and the two of them had made a point of avoiding each other. She would have preferred not to see Stella either, but the woman called in almost every day and the sight and sound of her, the way she talked incessantly about James, were almost more than Bethany could bear.

She was surprised now as her sister-in-law said hesi-tantly, 'I wish I did have everything I wanted. Then mebbe James would be happier. He's been like a different person

since he came home from England. He's got no interest
in anything.'

'It's always the same between seasons,' Bethany told
her shortly. 'The men don't have enough to do. He'll be
his old self once the boats start going out again.'

'I seem to be always annoying him these days and I
don't know why. If I just knew what I'm doing wrong
I could stop it, but I don't.'

'You knew when you married him that he was thrawn.
Mebbe you should have had more sense at the time.'

'Sense doesnae come into it when you love someone.'
Stella looked at her sister-in-law. 'I wish I was more like
you, Bethany.'

'Me?' Bethany felt a guilty flush rise up the smooth
column of her neck, and she began to look for an imaginary
dropped stitch as an excuse to keep her head bent.

'James admires you; he always has.'

'He thinks I'm an outspoken interfering bitch.'

'Mebbe that's why he admires you. I'm too . . . too
nice.'

'So I'm not nice?'

'I didn't mean it that way! If I could answer him back
and argue with him, the way you can, he might respect
me more. But it's not in me to do that. I think,' Stella said
miserably, 'that he'd be happier if he'd found a lassie like
you to marry.'

'For any favour!' Bethany shot out of her chair. 'I've
never heard such nonsense in my life.'

'You've dropped your knitting. Look, the stitches have
all come off one of the wires . . .' Stella fell to her
knees and began to gather up the bundle of wool and
wires that had fallen from her sister-in-law's lap. 'What
a mess . . .'

'Leave it, I'll see to it later.' Bethany snatched the
knitting from Stella's hands. 'Is it not time you were
home? You'll not sweeten James's temper by being late
with his dinner.'

When Stella had gone she went out to the wash-house at the back, where she paced up and down, muttering, 'Stupid bitch. Daft wee fool!'

No wonder James was short-tempered. Who wouldn't be, married to a simpleton like Stella? She raged at her brother for his stupidity in marrying the lassie, and at Stella for running to her, of all people, in search of advice and sympathy. Adding to Bethany's pain, reminding her day after day of what had happened at Yarmouth, and what could never happen again. And what might have been, if only Stella could have been his sister and Bethany old Mowser's daughter.

Sobs began to rise in her throat and she put both her hands tightly over her mouth to stifle them. But she couldn't stop the tears that, as she paced and turned, paced and turned, kept spilling over her fingers.

Thanks to the good herring season 1913 was welcomed in grand style along the Moray coast. The boat crews and the fisher-lassies had come back from Yarmouth with gifts squeezed into every spare inch they could make in their kists, and when the children rose before dawn on Ne'erday they found their home-knitted woollen stockings, normally the least interesting garments they possessed, stuffed with good things.

While they squealed their delight over apples and oranges, chocolate money and sugar mice and pigs, games and dolls and toy soldiers, their elders made preparations for the first day of the year.

From mid-morning at the latest the streets were busy with folk calling on their friends and relatives with gifts of drink, food and the essential lumps of coal, which signified a wish for warmth and prosperity for the household throughout the new year. All were welcome, though dark-haired men were in particular demand, with their special ability to bring luck to a house simply by being the first of the year to set foot inside the door.

Stella and Bethany went along in the morning to help
Jess prepare the Ne'erday dinner. Vast quantities of potatoes and turnips, carrots and onions had to be peeled and
chopped; pastry had to be made for the two large steak
pies; and there was chicken broth to make. By the time
they arrived, bringing their children with them, since
James and Gil would not have dreamed of looking after
their own families, Jess had already mixed the clootie
dumpling, tied it up in clean sheeting and set it to simmer
all day in a huge pot of water.

An hour later, deserting the oatmeal stuffing that she
was mixing in order to rescue Stella's protesting baby from
Ellen, who was trying to carry her about the kitchen, Jess
secretly wished that she had been left to see to the entire
feast on her own.

'We'll put her down on the rug, pet. She's happier
there.' She found something else for Ellen to do, then
used the back of her hand to wipe the sweat from her
forehead before returning to her work. 'I wonder if I
should have asked Albert's family for their dinner?'

'How could you, when none of us knows how many
he's fathered?' Bethany asked tartly, and Stella gave a
shocked giggle.

'I meant the lads that work with him and James on the
boat. And I should mebbe have asked Nathan and Gil's
mother.'

'You've got more than enough already to see to,' Stella
pointed out, while Bethany snorted at the idea of sharing
Ne'erday dinner with Phemie Pate.

'She'd just ruin the day for the lot of us, with her evil
tongue and her black looks. She'd not have come anyway.
We'll have to go to her in the afternoon, for a wee while
just, but we'll be back in time for your dinner. Where's
Innes?' Bethany asked as the children's noise rose an
octave, shrilling through the adults' ears. 'We could fairly
be doing with him here to keep that lot busy.'

'He's gone to fetch Zelda.'

'D'you think we're going to see a wedding this year?' Stella wanted to know.

'I'd not be surprised.' Jess would be more surprised if there wasn't a wedding, and the sooner the better. She was no fool and Innes, unlike his brother and sister, was an open book to her. A book that over the past few months had made interesting and disquieting reading. In the autumn, while the boats were all away at the English fishing grounds and she was looking after Meg, he had been so happy that he almost gave off a glow; but over the past week or two his exuberance had dimmed. He had started working all the hours he could and on the rare occasions when he was at home he either hovered maddeningly on the verge of blurting something out or was so absorbed in his own thoughts that he was no company at all. Zelda, too, had become more withdrawn, as though she was trying to shrink into herself physically and become small enough to escape notice.

Jess knew that feeling, for she had experienced it herself when she first discovered that she was carrying James. She, too, had tried to make herself unnoticeable until the day when Weem, by sliding a gold band on to her finger, had blessed her with marriage and respectability. Then, and only then, had she been able to walk tall, proud to be carrying her first child and happy in the knowledge that the bairn would be born within wedlock.

She longed to tell the young couple this, but she could say nothing, for the secret was theirs, not to be spoken of until they decided to confide in her.

Before the bowls of chicken broth were emptied that night Jess, eyeing her elder son's downbent head, was wondering if she had insulted him by inviting Jacob, an outsider, to share their Ne'erday dinner. She had been careful to seat James in his father's former place at the head of the table and put Jacob several places down at

one side, crammed between Innes and Meg. Even so, it
was Jacob who dominated the meal.

'This,' he said with satisfaction as he relinquished his
empty soup bowl, 'puts me in mind of my mother's table
in Portessie. D'you mind those days, Jess? It was a grand
life, was it not?'

'And yet you went away from it,' Meg reminded him.

'And did better for yourself than you would have done
if you'd stayed,' Gil added. A permanent smile seemed
to be pinned to his flushed face and it was clear that he
had had a fair drop to drink before his arrival. 'You've
done very well for yourself.'

'Mebbe so, but mebbe I lost more than I gained.'

'Never! See's that bottle over here, James.'

'Don't you bother yourself, James, the man's had
enough already,' Bethany said sharply from the stove,
then bit her lip as her brother, paying her no heed, thrust
the bottle at Gil.

'To tell the truth, Meg, now that I'm back I do regret all
those years away. Young folk often have the wanderlust
in them, but going away from your own folk can be a mistake.' Jacob leaned forward so that he could look along the
table at James and Innes. 'If you two lads take my advice,
you'll stay right here on the Firth where you belong.'

'I intend to,' Innes told him while James, slouching in
his chair and staring at the table, said nothing. Bethany,
safe in the knowledge that he would not look up, shot
swift, anxious glances at him.

'At least I'd the sense to come back, even though I
took so long about it. And now I'm in a position to be
able to help some of my own folk.' Jacob eyed the steak
pies that Jess and Stella were placing on the table. 'I tell
you, nobody the world over knows how to welcome the
new year in the way the Scots do.'

'You're right there!' Gil patted his wife's backside as
she leaned across him, a bowl in each hand, to reach
the table.

'D'you want these tatties set in front of you or emptied over your head?' she asked sharply.

'Ach, what's wrong with you, woman? It's Ne'erday, and surely a man can give his wife a wee cuddle now and again.'

Bethany clattered the bowl of potatoes and a bowl piled with mashed turnips, better known as chappit neeps, so hard on to the table that Jess feared for her good china dishes. 'Not in front of company.' Her face, already flushed with the heat from the stove, was scarlet and there was an ominous, steely gleam in her grey eyes.

'Now then . . .' Jess, anxious to draw attention away from the little domestic squabble, seized a knife and cut into the domed golden pastry covering the nearest pie, releasing a gush of aromatic steam. 'James, pass your plate down. Stella, there's more gravy in that pot over there, mebbe you'd bring it to the table.' If only, she thought as she piled wedges of pastry and chunks of steak and sausage on to plate after plate, they could all forget their differences and put a good face on it for Ne'erday, for her, for their guests.

But apparently not. James continued to scowl, despite Stella's anxious attempts to bring him out of his shell, and Gil's attentions had sent Bethany into a huff. She sat silently, picking at her food, and even Innes was quieter than usual while Zelda, close by his elbow, was like a little mouse.

By the time the clootie dumpling had been served and eaten Jess was worn to the bone with the effort of trying to pretend that this was a normal, happy family occasion.

Gil scraped his spoon noisily round his plate to trap any crumbs that might be lurking unseen, then re-filled his glass once again before pushing his chair away from the table and levering himself with some difficulty to his feet. 'Quiet now, I've an announcement to make.' His words were slightly blurred round the edges. 'I am proud to announce that me and Nathan and Mr MacFarlane here are setting up in business together.'

'In business?' Jess echoed, bewildered. She had heard nothing of any business deals. 'Jacob . . . ?'

'Aye, indeed we are,' he confirmed smilingly. 'I've need of good fish for foreign markets, and who better at catching and curing the silver darlings than our own local men? So from now on I'll be buying all the salted and pickled herring that Gil and Nathan can give me. And now that your announcement's been made, man,' he added easily to his new partner, 'I'd advise you to sit down before you fall down.'

Gil collapsed back into his seat, lifting his glass in a toast. 'Here's to 1913, and here's to your good health, Jacob MacFarlane.'

'And yours.'

'Well, I certainly wish the new venture success,' Jess said briskly when the toast had been drunk. 'Now it's time to get these wee ones to bed, then we'll have a cup of . . .'

'Since it's to be a formal occasion, I've a wee announcement of my own to make.' It was the first time James had spoken since his arrival and all heads immediately swivelled to where he sat, hands planted on the table and head up at last. 'You're not the only one who's starting the year with a new partnership, Gil. I'm thinking of doing the same thing myself. I might well be going to crew on Davie Geddes's boat.'

'What are you talking about?'

'Did I not say it clearly enough for you, Mother?' James leaned forward, his eyes – so like his father's – fixed on hers. When he spoke again it was directly to her, as though they were the only two people in the crowded room. 'Then I'll explain. I've finished with the *Fidelity*.'

'But . . .' Her head was beginning to ache and she was aware of Jacob, the stranger in their midst, following every word, bright-eyed with interest. 'This isn't a subject for our Ne'erday dinner. Bethany, Stella, help me to get the bairns to . . .'

'Don't be daft, man,' Meg boomed, ignoring her sister-in-law. 'The *Fidelity*'s a Lowrie boat. You cannae leave her, to crew for someone else.'

'I can do whatever I want,' James told her icily. 'Davie's looking for a good man to run his boat for him. And I'm looking for the chance to be my own man. I'll not have to work with Uncle Albert any more.'

'And who'll take on *Fidelity* after Albert's done with the sea?' Mowser had been concentrating on eating and drinking until then, leaving the conversation to others. Now that fishing was being discussed he began to take an interest.

'Charlie, mebbe, or Jem.'

'But they're nowhere near as good with a boat as you are,' Meg protested. 'Everyone knows that.'

'Albert doesn't, and I'm not waiting any longer for him to find out.'

'But James, what would your father . . .' Jess began, then stopped short.

'What would my father say?' James's face was as still and pale as marble in the gaslight; only his eyes were alive, glittering at his mother, mocking her. 'Ask him the next time you climb up that hill to keep his grave nice and tidy. Ask him – but I doubt if he'll bother with an answer, since he's done with both the *Fidelity* and the sea himself!'

'That's enough,' Jacob said quietly. 'You've no right to speak to your mother like that in her own home, or to run your father down when the man's not here to defend himself.'

James blinked, then rallied. 'And who are you, Mr MacFarlane,' he spoke the name sneeringly, '. . . to tell me how to speak in the house I was raised in?'

'A friend of your mother's and your father's from long

before you ever knew them. I don't like to hear them
miscalled by anyone, so sit down, man, and let us end
this evening in friendship, the way it should be.'

'James . . . ?'

Stella put a hand on her husband's wrist, but he pushed
his chair back sharply, ignoring her, then grabbed his
jacket and charged out of the house. As the heavy wooden
door crashed shut behind him wee Ruth started to cry
and the other children immediately joined in, without
knowing why.

'Well!' Meg was outraged. 'What does that laddie think
he's doing, behaving like that in his own mother's house?'

'He's upset, just,' Jess cut in swiftly, rising to her feet.
'And these bairns are worn out. Stella, Bethany, bring
them to the back room and we'll tuck them up in the bed.
Zelda, mebbe you'd make some tea while Meg butters the
currant loaf and fetches out the wee cakes. Sit down at
the fire, the rest of you, and we'll have our tea in just a
minute.'

'I don't know what's happened to James,' poor Stella
said, bewildered, when the younger members of the family
had been tucked into bed like a row of rosy-cheeked
sardines.

'Don't you fret yourself, pet, he never could abide
family gatherings. He'll just be needing a wee while
to himself, that's all. Would you go and help Meg and
Zelda?' Jess suggested, and, when the young woman
scampered off, glad of the chance to make herself useful,
'She's right, I don't know what's got into James. Do you
know anything about it?'

'How could I, when we never have anything to do with
each other? He's had enough of Uncle Albert, that's all,
and mebbe enough of this place and everyone in it, just
like me! But he's a grown man and he'll have to fend for
himself – just like me!' Bethany said, and opened the door
with such force that it would have rebounded against the
wall if Jess hadn't caught it.

21

In the kitchen Zelda was making tea while Meg set out plates loaded with slices of currant loaf, biscuits and cake. Gil, Jacob, Innes and Mowser Buchan were smoking their pipes around the fireplace and the storm caused by James's outburst seemed to have settled.

Although everyone but Mowser, who had a prodigious appetite for a man of his age, protested that they were too full to eat another mouthful, the plates cleared quickly and the big teapot was re-filled several times. The rest of the evening passed uneventfully and ended when Stella and her father collected the three little girls and set off home. Meg went with them, and immediately afterwards Bethany and Gil left too, Ellen cradled in Bethany's arms while Rory sprawled bonelessly over his father's shoulder, still sound asleep. Then Innes took Zelda back to the farm, leaving Jess alone with Jacob who, after seeing the others out, settled down by the fire and re-lit his pipe.

She stood over him, hands folded across her waist. 'Jacob, James is my son and this is the house he was born and raised in. It was not your place to chastise him tonight.'

'Not my place? Someone had to say something, and since Gil kept his mouth shut it was left to me. It fair angered me to hear that lad speak to you as he did. Anyway,' he went on calmly, 'there was a time when I thought that it was going to be my place by rights; when I thought that your bairns would be mine as well.'

'Well they're not yours, and there's no sense in trying to rake the past up again.'

'I know well enough that they're Weem's, and not mine. I think of that every time I set eyes on them. And I regret it, Jess. All right,' he went on as she began to speak, 'I'm not going to keep hankering after what's gone, and I'm sorry if I vexed you in front of your family by speaking out of turn tonight.'

'It wasn't all your fault, I suppose. It's just James – there's never any way of knowing which way he'll jump.'

'D'you think he means it about leaving the *Fidelity*?'

'Mebbe. And mebbe he was just trying to upset me and Bethany . . . her more than me, for that boat means a lot to her. She should have been born a laddie, then she could have gone to the fishing and worked on the boat herself.'

'That would have been a waste of a beautiful woman.'

Jess gave him the ghost of a smile. 'Better not say that to her. Being a woman's a curse as far as she's concerned. Jacob,' she went on as he picked his pipe up again, 'I don't want to be uncivil, but it's been a long day . . .'

'And you need to get to your bed.' He started tapping the pipe out on the grate, just as Weem used to do. 'Of course you do and I should have realised that for myself. My only excuse is that I enjoy your company so much.'

He went, and at last Jess was free to restore her kitchen to order. When Innes came in she was still working.

'Are you not in your bed yet?'

'Is that not what I'm supposed to say to you?' she asked drily. 'Put that cloth down, you've got your work to go to in the morning.'

'I can't go to my bed knowing that you're still busy.' He picked up a plate and dried it as he spoke. 'Two of us can get the work finished in half the time.'

'Zelda got back to the farm all right?'

'Aye. She fair enjoyed herself.'

'Good. I thought,' Jess said carefully, 'that she looked a wee thing pale.'

'Did you? She's fine as far as I know.'

Tell me, Innes, Jess thought. Talk to me and between us we can work out what to do. But he said nothing and so she, too, had to keep quiet.

'Mr MacFarlane?'

'Mrs Pate.' Jacob turned from his contemplation of the *Fidelity*, lying at rest in the harbour, and touched his cap. 'Good morning to you. A fine brisk day, is it not?'

'Well enough.' The sky overhead was blue, with what clouds there were racing across it before the wind.

Jacob bent to chuck Ellen under the chin and shake hands with Rory, then straightened again. 'I was just admiring the lines of the boat. She's a fine vessel – your father did well when he bought her.'

'He was proud of the *Fidelity*,' Bethany acknowledged, falling into step with him as he began to pace back along the harbour wall. 'Mr MacFarlane, I was wondering if I could have a wee word with you?' Her heart was thumping hard and she was glad of the keen January wind that had given both children bright-red cheeks and noses, for its sting would help to explain the high colour rising to her own face.

'It would be my pleasure. What can I do for you?'

'Mebbe you'd come along to the house and have some tea? We can talk in comfort there.'

He cheerfully agreed and as they walked together he talked about his enjoyment of the Ne'erday dinner they had shared at her mother's two days earlier. Only when the children were settled with their toys, and the tea made and set out along with a plate of shortbread fingers, did he ask, 'Now then, what can I do for you?'

'It's about my brother . . . about James.' She almost had to force the name past her lips, and a sudden darkening of the green eyes holding hers and a discernible tightening of Jacob's lips beneath his moustache made her mission all the more difficult.

'Ah yes, your brother. And what might we want to discuss with regard to him?'

Bethany took a sip of tea, realising only when it scalded her lips and the roof of her mouth that she had forgotten to put milk in. Seeing her wince, Jacob tutted, then took his own saucer and poured some milk into it from the jug.

'Drink this, it will soothe the sting.' While she emptied the saucer hurriedly he poured milk into her tea and stirred it. 'Now, take your time.'

Bethany had never been fussed over in her life, and it did not help at all, but she had been planning this business for two days and two sleepless nights, and had seized her chance when she saw the man standing alone on the harbour wall. Having taken the first step, she must go on.

'It's about what James said at Ne'erday about leaving the *Fidelity*. It's not what he wants, Mr MacFarlane.'

'Your mother seemed to think that he didn't mean it. That he was only trying to upset her, and you.'

'He does mean it, and it's got nothing to do with upsetting folk. It's our Uncle Albert: he's not half the skipper Da was, and James can't stand to see the boat wrongly used.'

Now that she was into the situation Bethany found things a little easier. Leaning forward, her tea left untasted, she explained how she and her mother and Innes had refused to hand over their shares in the boat to James in order to give him more say.

'We were just being thrawn and none of us realised how miserable James has been with the way the boat's being run. When I did find out I offered to let him have the use of my share, and to talk to Mother and Innes, but by then it was too late. I think,' she finished miserably, 'that he felt we'd betrayed him. And so we have in a way.'

Jacob had been watching her with that disconcertingly intent stare she had noticed the night he came to talk business with Gil. Now he asked, 'And what has this got to do with me?'

She bit her lip, realising that the hardest part was about to begin. 'I thought, when you took Gil and Nathan on as partners . . . They use all the fish the *Fidelity* catches, and James is right when he says she would do even better with a good skipper. And I wondered . . . Uncle Albert likes money better than he likes working, and if someone offered to buy some of his shares I'm sure he would sell them. Someone sympathetic to James's ideas. He is a very good fisherman,' she added hurriedly, 'and if the person who bought Albert's share was willing to make him the new skipper I'm certain he'd do well.'

'And you think I could be that someone.'

'None of us could afford to buy Albert out.'

'My dear young woman, what would I do with shares in a Buckie fishing boat?'

'What would you do with shares in the Pate businesses?'

'I expect . . . I intend,' MacFarlane said with emphasis on the last word, 'to make a deal of money from that arrangement. And so will your husband, which should please you. But a few shares in one fishing boat . . .' He shrugged, spreading his hands out. 'I'm not sure they would be of much use to me.'

'You could give them to my mother as a gift,' Bethany said without thinking. 'I'm quite sure that she would use them to help James.' Then, realising that she was speaking out of turn, 'I mean, you're old friends and it's plain to see that you like her, so . . .'

MacFarlane settled back in his chair. 'Has Jess ever talked to you about me?'

'No,' she answered, then wondered when she saw a sudden blankness in his eyes if she should have been kinder and lied.

'We grew up together. We'd have wed if she hadn't met your father.'

'You and my mother?' She could scarcely keep the astonishment out of her voice. So Stella's romantic notions had been right after all.

He leaned forward. 'Is that so surprising? I was a deckhand on another man's boat, and Jess was very beautiful, even as a child. You're like her,' he said. Then, as she merely looked at him as though he was talking nonsense, 'Oh, you're Weem Lowrie's daughter all right. You've his eyes – and his nature too – but you're fortunate in having your mother's fine bones.'

He reached out and touched one temple lightly; she stiffened but held still, without flinching as his fingertips traced their way down the side of her face, over the cheekbone to the point of her chin.

'You have the best of both of them,' he said, more to himself than to her. It was a relief when he sat back in his seat again, his voice taking on a business-like note. 'To be honest with you, Mrs Pate, I'm not of a mind to do anything to help your brother after the way he behaved in your mother's house the other night.'

She bit her lip, then said, 'You're right, he spoke out of turn, when he should have had the sense to hold his tongue, but that's not the way he really is, as you'll find out if you stay on here for long.'

'He's very fortunate in having such a loyal sister.'

His piercing gaze was disconcerting, and Bethany busied herself with pouring out more tea. 'We were close as bairns, James and me. And if you knew what had happened to him once he grew up you'd understand him better,' she said desperately; then as Jacob raised his eyebrows, clearly waiting to hear more, she threw caution to the winds and went on to tell him of the way her brother had been married off to Stella so that Weem could gain ownership of Mowser Buchan's sailboat.

'So, that's why he has such a grudge against the world?' Jacob asked when she had finished. 'And what about you, Bethany? What did Weem gain from your marriage?'

'Nothing.' She got up and began to collect the cups together, knowing that she had already said too much. His hand landed on her wrist, gently but with enough pressure to ease her back into her chair.

'I believe that Gil and Nathan Pate made an agreement with your father to buy all the fish the *Fidelity* catches.'

'Yes.'

'An arrangement made round about the time of your marriage, I'll be bound. Eh? Weem,' Jacob MacFarlane said when she kept silent, 'was more astute than I've given him credit for.'

'He was one of the best fishermen and sailors on this coast, and my brother James is every bit as good, as you'll find if you buy into the boat.'

'I'm sure he is.' Jacob got to his feet and began to shrug his coat on. 'It has been an interesting talk, and I'll certainly think over what you have said. But it might take a few days before I can come to any decision.'

'You'll not let Gil or James know we've been talking, will you?'

He gave her one final piercing look as he picked up his hat. 'Of course not. Thank you for the tea, my dear, it was very warming on such a cold day. And it was very kind of you to take pity when you found me shivering in that cold wind.'

As soon as he had gone Bethany wished that she had chewed her tongue out rather than spoken to him. She wanted to help James, but instead she had probably made things worse. She had even told family secrets to this man who had suddenly appeared from her mother's past, and in return she had discovered that Stella's romantic notions about Jacob MacFarlane and Jess Lowrie had been right after all.

It was a pity that she would not be able to tell Stella that.

Innes trudged along the last part of the lane that led to the Mulhollands' cottage. Anxious to get the evening's business settled, he had started at a brisk jog, but had been forced to slow down as the lanes became steeper. Clouds had come in from the north during the afternoon and now icy, sleety rain danced at him from the darkness, stinging his face. Down on the coastline angry great waves were crashing on to the shore and even the boats in the protection of the harbour shifted nervously at their moorings, crowding together as though for warmth and comfort.

For the moment at least the lane's high banks protected Innes from the wind that had been buffeting the village when he left. It was with this harsh winter weather in mind that the fishing folk who lived at the water's edge had positioned their homes with the windowless gable ends facing the winds and the spray.

Despite the chill bite that reddened his face, Innes perspired inside his best clothes, from nervous anticipation as much as from hurrying uphill. Tonight he and Zelda were going to tell her parents about their marriage plans. He thought that the Mulhollands, who treated him civilly enough when he visited their home, would be willing to accept him as a member of their family. Even so, the prospect of facing his intended's father and asking formally for her hand was an ordeal for any young lad.

'And not a word about the bairn,' Zelda had impressed on him at their last meeting. 'They'll mebbe accept you well enough, but I can't let my father know what we've been up to.'

'You make it sound dirty, and it wasn't! Not for me,

anyway,' Innes protested, and she went into his arms, hugging him fiercely.

'Nor for me. It was the happiest, most wonderful thing that ever happened to me! But I doubt if my father would see it that way. He says that purity's the greatest gift a woman can offer to her husband when they wed. That's all me and my sisters heard from him and my mother when we were growing up.'

'You offered your gift to me and I'm going to be your husband, so what's the difference?'

'Oh Innes, if you don't understand that you'll never understand my father. Just say the right things and keep away from the wrong ones. And you'll have to promise that we'll go to the kirk every Sunday when we're man and wife.'

'I don't go to the kirk.' Having been raised by parents who were rarely away from their church, Weem had turned his back on religion as soon as he was old enough to control his own life. Meg attended Sunday services, as did Albert, held up as an example by Weem to his children. 'If a man like my brother, with his carnal tastes, can walk into a church without it falling about his ears, then there can't be much to this God business,' Innes had heard him proclaim again and again.

'You'll go with me when we're wed,' Zelda ordered. 'And once we get married it won't matter about him finding out about the bairn, for then I'll belong to you and not to him.'

The shepherd's house was a matter of fifty yards in front of Innes now; he could see the light from the kitchen window, a pale glow that winked and fragmented, then disappeared and appeared again as the wind-lashed trees round the small building tossed their branches about. He would be glad to get indoors and sit by the fire and drink some hot tea. And see Zelda again.

Footsteps scurried down the lane in his direction; as he peered into the darkness, hoping that she had come to meet

him, a small figure ran full tilt into him and clutched at his
knees for support. 'Innes? Is that you?'

'Daniel? What are you doing out on a night like this?'

'Ma sent me,' Zelda's small brother panted. His face
was a dim grey blob in the darkness. 'You've to turn
round and go home right now, she says.'

'Why?'

'I don't know, but Da's in a rage and he's leathering
our Zelda. Ma sent me to tell you not to come . . . She said
not to!' Daniel squeaked as Innes began to run towards the
cottage, towing the lad by the wrist behind him.

'Never mind what your ma said!' All Innes could think
of was getting to Zelda. He charged along the last section
of the lane and started hammering on the thick timber
door with both fists, yelling out her name.

22

Innes was so busy attacking the door that when it opened he might have fallen into the stone-flagged kitchen, had Mr Mulholland not caught him by the collar, dragged him inside, then pushed him against the wall so hard that the breath was driven from his body.

'You dare to come knocking at my door after what you've done to my daughter?' Mulholland's face, just inches from Innes's, was twisted and so engorged with angry blood that his eyes stood out in their sockets.

'Mr Mulholland . . .' Innes's stunned lungs were still fighting to fill themselves again, and his voice could scarcely reach above a whisper. 'I love Zelda. I'd never harm her!'

'And you think that getting her with child, shaming a wee innocent lassie who's never known the marriage bed, isnae doin' harm tae her?'

Innes had managed to catch his breath. 'But I want to marry her! I came here tonight to ask your permission.'

'Marry, is it?' Mulholland turned away from him, easing his grip without releasing it. 'Grizelda, ye shiftless whore that ye are, bring my belt through to me. And there's a gentleman here with a proposal of marriage for you! Are you not the fortunate lassie?'

As the man shifted position Innes saw beyond him to the rest of the small kitchen. Mrs Mulholland, expressionless, sat in a corner with the two youngest members of her brood on her lap, while the others, including Daniel, who had managed to slip through the door unnoticed, were gathered round her in a tight group. The children were wide-eyed and white to the lips, and one or two were weeping silent tears of fright.

Innes only had time to glance at them before the door to the cottage's other room opened and Zelda appeared, her hair wild and her eyes red. A scarlet mark blazed across one cheek; her two hands, clenched before her breast, held the broad leather belt, decorated along its length with brass studs, that her father always wore about his waist.

At the sight of her all Innes's inhibitions about retaliating against an older man, the father of his future wife, vanished. Rage gave him the strength to throw Mulholland off and, as the man staggered aside, he reached Zelda, pulling her into the room, examining the welt on her face with his fingertips. 'Zelda . . . What in God's name d'you think you're doing to her, man?'

'How dare you use your filthy mouth to soil the name of the Lord!' Mulholland thundered behind him. 'I know all about you!'

'You told them?'

Fresh tears welled up in Zelda's dark eyes and she shook her head, biting her lower lip hard to stifle the sobs that were beginning to shake her shoulders.

'She,' her father stated contemptuously, 'said nothing. It was the farmer's wife who was the one to tell me that my daughter – my own child that I raised in God's light, and fed and housed and clothed, and guided along the path of righteousness – had shamed me before the whole community and pledged her soul to the devil as a whore!'

'Don't you dare say that about Zelda! She's a decent lassie; she's been with nobody but me, and that only because we're to be man and wife.'

'So you're proud of what you've done to her?'

'No, I'm not,' Innes said between set teeth. 'I lost my

senses and I behaved badly, but we'll be wed within the month. Surely you can find it in your heart to forgive us . . .'

'Only the Lord can forgive the sins you've committed against me and my blood, and I'm certain sure that He never will. Get out of my house,' Mulholland ordered, jerking his head at the door. In desperation Innes looked at Zelda's mother, who had always welcomed him into her house and treated him kindly. She had, after all, sent young Daniel to warn him to stay away. But she looked back stonily, tightening her grip on her youngest, and he realised that when it came to discipline and punishment her husband ruled the family and she agreed with all that he said and did. He and Zelda could expect no mercy or understanding from anyone in this house.

'I'm going, but I'm taking Zelda with me.'

The man shrugged his heavy shoulders. 'She's no daughter of mine now, you can lie with her in the pig pen if you've a mind. She's not worth any better than that.'

As Zelda made a small choking sound and tears poured down her white face, Innes swallowed down his rage. The important thing was to get her out of here as quickly as possible. 'Come away with me, we'll go to my . . .'

Putting a hand on the girl's back to urge her forward, he felt dampness against his palm just before she winced and pulled away, the breath hissing sharply between her teeth. 'Zelda?' He took her shoulders and turned her about, then exclaimed as he saw the blood seeping through the material of her blouse. It was then that he realised the meaning of the belt that her father had left in the inner room. The belt that was never away from his waist unless he was sleeping – or chastising one of his children.

'Dear God!'

'I told you!' Mulholland took a step towards him. 'I'll not have His name in your vile mouth!'

'It's safer in my mouth than it is in yours. Call yourself a man of religion just because you go to the church every

Sunday and say your prayers every day?' Innes faced him, feet apart and fists clenched. 'I'll tell you this, Mr Mulholland, I'd rather be a blasphemous sinner than worship any god willing to heed the prayers of a man who bullies defenceless lassies in the name of religion!'

With a low roar Mulholland seized him by the upper arm with one hand and snatched the belt from Zelda with the other. As he was hustled out of the cottage Innes heard the girl shout his name. Twisting round to look at her, he saw that her attempt to follow him had been foiled by her mother who, thrusting the little ones into the arms of two older children, jumped up and pulled her back.

That was the last Innes saw of her before the door slammed and he and her father were outside in the bitter dark night.

Mulholland propelled Innes down the dark lane, their booted feet scuffling and scuttering on the small stones and stumbling over the ruts. Below the sound of the wind and his own panting breath, and the older man's steady, animal grunts, Innes heard thin ice crackling beneath their weight as they splashed through puddles. He had no idea where they were going, and knew only that if Mulholland had some thought of running him off the area it would not work. Not until he got Zelda out of that house.

The man pushed him unexpectedly to one side of the lane, releasing his arm at the same time, so that Innes stumbled and almost fell over the raised banking. His attempts to remain upright took him up the slight slope and down the other side, but just as he managed to regain his balance Mulholland gave him a hefty push. Innes staggered, tripped over something and fell, pain jarring through him as his shoulder glanced off the trunk of a tree. He only had time to grasp that they were in some sort of clearing by the side of the lane before Zelda's father was on him, dragging him up by the jacket with one hand while he drew the other fist back. Then the world exploded and everything seemed to vanish for a matter of seconds.

When he regained his wits Innes found himself down on the ground, his body twitching in rhythm to the solid, throbbing pain of booted feet lashing into his sides and his stomach, and his back and his shoulders. His first instinct was to curl himself into a ball in order to protect as much of his body as possible, but realising as his brain cleared that he could not afford to let the fight become too one-sided, he managed to roll off to one side and regain his feet with the help of a sturdy bush.

As he turned, the moon, in a brief appearance between ragged, racing clouds, showed Mulholland facing him, moonlight glinting on the brass studs of the belt he had looped about his neck in order to leave his hands free.

'Have you had enough?' he asked thickly.

'I'm . . .' Innes, wincing at the pain in his jaw, spat blood and tried again, 'I'm not wanting to fight with you, Mr Mulholland. I just want to marry Zelda, and look after her and the bairn the way I should.'

'You keep away from her.'

'If I do that will you leave her alone?'

'That's none of your business. She's my daughter and it's my name she's brought down in shame. I'll deal with her as I see fit.'

'You'll not,' Innes said, and went in fast and low, tucking his chin down so that he could use his skull as a battering ram, well aware that the other man had the weight advantage and that he himself would have to use other tactics. The whoosh of suddenly expelled breath as he connected with Mulholland's midriff cheered him on and gave him added strength. Twisting, he forced his left shoulder into the man's hip, while both hands found Mulholland's left knee. He pulled hard and Zelda's father, already winded, went down forcefully. Innes followed and the two of them grappled, rolling over on the cold, stony ground.

It was inevitable that Mulholland's weight would eventually give control of the situation back to him. Even so, every time he tried to throw the younger man away Innes held on, his hands seeking a good grip. He was fighting for Zelda now rather than for himself. As Mulholland got to his knees, Innes caught hold of one end of the belt and pulled, with some idea of yanking it free and using it as a weapon.

The other end, with the big buckle on it, did not come loose as he had expected; instead, Mulholland's flailing hands slipped away, trying to reach the belt. Innes managed to hold on until Zelda's father, seemingly giving up the fight, fell on to his face, writhing and gurgling. Only then did Innes realise that the buckle had somehow caught in the man's clothing and, with the belt pulled tight beneath his chin, the man was slowly being strangled to death.

'Dear God!' He let go of the belt at once and started tugging at the body, trying to turn it over. 'Mr Mulholland!' For a moment there was no sign of life, then as he dragged on the man's shoulder Mulholland suddenly swung over and his two large hands reached up and clamped themselves about Innes's neck.

'Try to choke me, would you?' the man hissed into his ear as he scrambled to his feet, pulling his victim up after him. A knee jabbed fiercely into the pit of Innes's belly and pain radiated to the very tips of his toes and the ends of his hair. 'Now,' he heard dimly as he sank back on to the ground, 'you'll get the thrashing you deserve!'

Then Innes screamed as the belt buckle scythed viciously out of the darkness and slashed across one cheek. Another blow followed, then another and another, until he was too busy trying to scramble out of reach to count. Mulholland followed him, hauling him back each time he showed signs of hiding beneath a protective bush. Again and again the buckle landed on his head, his face, his arms, legs and back until finally a well-placed blow brought the metal down hard on one temple, and as far as Innes Lowrie was concerned the fight was lost.

Jacob rattled the poker between the bars of the fire, stirring the glowing coals into fresh life. The kitchen was snug and cosy, despite the wind that beat against the door in gusts. 'Your daughter took pity on me today when we met, and invited me in for a cup of tea. She's a fine bonny lass, Jess.'

'She was bonny from the very moment of her birth.' James and Innes had come from the womb red and wrinkled and squalling, but Bethany had been born with skin like porcelain, a silky covering of reddish-brown hair on her small skull and clear, calm grey eyes. Jess had thought as she held her new baby for the first time that a daughter would be special, but as soon as she was on her feet, two months before her first birthday, Bethany had scorned everyone else in favour of James, toddling out of the door after him and the other laddies whenever she got a chance. It was then that it had begun to dawn on Jess that her new baby's calm gaze had reflected a total lack of interest in the woman holding her, rather than serenity.

Jacob dropped the poker, settled his backside comfortably into the chair that had been Weem's and stretched his legs across the hearthrug. 'She's a right mixture of the two of you.'

'You think so? I only see her father in her.'

'She's got his eyes, his strong chin and his nature too, from what I've seen and heard of her so far. But that bonny sheen to her hair, like well-polished mahogany – that's his colouring darkened by yours. And she's got your womanliness.'

'That's something she couldn't have got from Weem,' Jess acknowledged, smiling. 'But I can't say I've seen it in her. She was always a tomboy, and although she makes a good fist of looking after Gil's bairns there's no motherliness about her.'

'That wasn't what I meant. I'm talking of the womanliness that sets a man's heart racing and his mind dreaming of what might be.'

'Don't tell me you've a fancy for her yourself?' She looked at him from beneath raised eyebrows. To her surprise, her teasing ruffled him.

'Not a bit of it! You know fine that there's only one woman I'll ever fancy. I'm just saying that she's got something that not many women have. And she got it from you. To tell the truth, I don't know what she saw in that lump Gil Pate.'

'That's for her to know. None of our business.'

'Aye well, there's no accounting for the world,' Jacob agreed. Then, after a short silence, 'She seems to be bothered about your James wanting to leave the boat.'

'I doubt if it's a matter of wanting. He and Albert just don't see eye to eye. When Weem was in charge of that boat she was always the last into harbour. Many's the day I've spent straining my eyes for a sight of her, and many's the time I almost gave her up for lost before she appeared. I've seen her come in so low in the water with the fish she carried that it was a wonder she didn't sink.'

'He was a good fisherman, was Weem,' Jacob acknowledged.

'James is just like him, but Albert's cautious. He's more likely to scurry back to harbour at the first sign of poor weather with the holds only half-full.' A gust of wind rattled at the door and Jess glanced at the clock. Innes should be back soon, no doubt chilled to the bone after his long walk down from the shepherd's cottage.

'Why did James not take the boat over when Weem died?'

Jess stared down at her knitting, then said, 'Men always think they'll live on for ever and Weem was the same as the rest of them. He made no plans for the future.'

'Will you be as bothered as Bethany if James leaves the Lowrie boat?'

'I'll be sorry about it, but he's a grown man and he must make his own choices. It's none of my . . .' She stopped as someone gave three hefty knocks at the door. 'That'll be Innes. I latched the door against the wind. Let him in, will you, while I make some tea. He'll be frozen through.'

As she busied herself with the kettle a blast of cold air swept around her ankles from the open door. There was a muttered conversation, then Jacob called to her, a note of urgency in his voice, and she turned to see him disappearing into the darkness, leaving the door swinging open. Following, she found him and another man lifting a large bundle from the back of a farm cart.

'What is it?' She wrapped her arms tightly about her body, shivering. Then as the men upended the sack between them she saw, in the light from the open doorway, that it wasn't a sack at all but a man hanging limply from their grasp, head lolling. 'Innes? Innes! Dear God, what happened to him?'

'All I know is that the shepherd brought him to the farm and the master told me to take him home,' the carter said, while Jacob ordered, 'Go on ahead, Jess, and we'll follow.'

Once Innes had been deposited on the bed in the small downstairs room, the carter made himself scarce while Jess and Jacob set about undressing the youth. He came to as they worked on him and feebly tried to fend them off, muttering at them through puffed, bleeding lips.

'What happened to you, son?' Jess asked frantically, shocked by the sight of him. His face was caked with blood and even the hands pushing at her were bruised and cut.

'Zelda,' he said in reply. One of his eyes was swollen beyond opening, but the other was suddenly wide, sweeping round the room. 'I have to fetch Zelda!' He tried to raise himself up, groaning and panting with the effort, but Jacob pushed him back.

'We'll fetch her in the morning. Just be at peace for now and let your mother tend to you.'

As they removed his filthy wet clothes Jess exclaimed again and again over each fresh bruise, while Jacob's hands moved over the younger man's chest, back and limbs, checking for signs of broken bones or internal injury. Then he fetched a towel and began, as gently as he could, to rub warmth into the chilled body, while Jess ran to warm a clean night-shirt before the fire and fetch a basin of hot water and some cloths.

Once washed from head to toe, Innes was a sorry sight. He was covered with welts and bruises, one eye was closed and there were cuts all over his face and hands. Only one of the cuts, from cheekbone to chin on the left side of his face, was still seeping blood.

Jacob applied a cold compress to both it and the swollen eye. 'He's going to be sore and stiff for a good few days to come, but no bones are broken and nothing seems to be hurt inside. He'll recover.'

'But what happened to him?'

'He's taken a good beating; feet as well as fists, and something else that caused those welts. But he fought back . . .' Jacob lifted Innes's right hand and pointed to the bruised, scraped knuckles. 'There were mebbe more than just the one man against him.'

'Who'd do such a thing to a laddie who's never lifted a hand to a living soul?'

Jacob shrugged. 'He's not your wee laddie any more, Jess. What he gets up to is his business, not yours or mine.' He eased the compress back and peered at the cut. 'It's stopped bleeding. Put your hand there, lad.' He lifted Innes's hand and placed it on the compress over his eye. 'It'll help. You'll mebbe have a scar on your cheek to show for the night's business, but that's of no importance,' he said calmly. 'We'll get you into your night-shirt now and I've no doubt your mother'll fetch you some food.'

Innes plucked at the bed-clothing, then peered round the

room. 'This isnae my bed,' he said, his voice smothered by his bruised, split lips.

'You're in the wee back room, for you're not fit to manage the stairs.'

'Should I mebbe send for the doctor?' Jess asked Jacob when she joined him in the kitchen later, having left Innes to drink a bowl of soup.

'Not at all. I've seen cuts and bruises and broken bones often enough in my time, and I've seen men coughing and spitting blood from hurts inside too,' he added, 'so you can take my word for it that your Innes has nothing like that. We've done all the doctoring that's necessary. Now,' he levered himself to his feet, 'I'd best be getting back to my lodgings.'

'I'm glad you were here,' she said as she saw him out of the door.

'I could always be here, if you just said the word, Jess,' he replied, and went into the night, shoulders hunched against the wind.

23

Zelda arrived early the next morning. 'Where is he? Mrs Bain says their carter brought him here last night. Is he all right?' A livid red welt on one cheek stood out against her white face.

'He'll mend. What hap . . . ?'

'Zelda?' Innes called from the back room and the girl rushed to him, halting in the doorway, her hands flying to her mouth as she took in the sight of his bruised face and swollen eye.

'Oh, Innes, what did he do to you?'

'Never mind me – what did he do to you?'

Zelda glanced over her shoulder at Jess, then went forward primly and sat on the end of the bed, hands knotted together in her lap. 'He was all right after . . . after he came back in, though he'd not tell me what had happened between the two of you, or where you were. It was as if it was all over and done with. Then when I got to my work this morning, the mistress told me that he'd carried you to their door and asked for someone to take you home. Mrs Bain was kind, she let me take time off to see you.'

'Who are you talking about?' Jess asked. Then as they glanced at her, at each other, and then away, like naughty children sharing a secret, she moved to where she could lift the girl's chin and study the damaged face. 'Was it your father, Zelda? Poor wee lass, is this what he did to you?' Turning to her son, her anger mounting, she added, 'And to you . . . all because of a bairn?'

This time they looked at each other, then at her. 'Who told you?' Innes asked.

'I could see for myself. Not because of that, lassie,' Jess added as Zelda's hand instinctively went to her flat belly. 'Because I know my lad here. Three months ago he looked as if he'd been given all the riches of the world, but for the past few weeks he's looked as if he had exchanged those riches for all the burdens. I've been waiting for the two of you to tell me, so's we could make plans.'

'We were going to, once we'd told her parents. But her father didn't take it very well,' Innes said.

'I've brought shame on him,' Zelda explained earnestly, 'and he's finding it hard to forgive me. But I think he's sorry for last night. My mother says he was on his knees most of the night, praying.'

'If I get my hands on him he'll be on his knees again, but only because he'll not have the strength to stand up,' Jess said fiercely, but Zelda had turned her attention back to Innes.

'Are you sure you're all right? Your poor eye looks terrible.'

It did. The area around it was puffed up and coloured dark blue, shot through with yellow streaks. What could be seen of the eye itself was a fearsome sight, since the white was now an angry red.

'I'm fine now that I know you're safe.'

'Oh, Innes!' Tears began to spill down the girl's cheeks. Heedless of Jess, she reached out to stroke her lover's battered face with the tips of her fingers. At her touch, Innes lurched forward on to his knees, pushing the bed-clothes aside, and Zelda went straight into his open arms.

To Jess's irritation, only Stella was in agreement with her desire to see Zelda's father punished for what he had done to Innes.

'It's at such times,' the younger woman said in a low voice, 'that I'm glad I only have lassies. Imagine seeing one of your own in a state like that!'

But when Jess turned to Bethany for understanding all she got was a robust, 'Good for Innes, he's got some gumption after all.' Meanwhile Jacob said, 'I told you, Jess, Innes is a grown man now and he must fight his own battles.'

'A boy who's never fought in his life, up against a big man with a belt in his hand?' Jess had finally got Zelda to tell her what had caused the cuts on her son's face and hands.

'There are no rules in that sort of fighting. Innes has to learn that next time he should make use of whatever comes to hand. I've seen a wee slip of a laddie besting a man twice his size, just because he'd the sense to pick up a length of iron chain from a quay. That was a grand fight,' Jacob recalled nostalgically. 'They ended up in the water and we nearly lost the two of them, for the big fellow cracked his head against the hull of a boat and the wee one wouldn't let go of the chain and got carried to the bottom by the weight of it.'

The following day Jacob called on James. 'You'll know about your brother's wee misunderstanding with his lassie's father.'

'I heard something of it.'

'His poor face is in a terrible state,' Stella chimed in.

'It'll mend,' Jacob assured her, then chuckled as old Mowser said sorrowfully, 'I wish I'd seen it . . . I've not seen a good fight in many a year.'

'Mind the time the new fishing season had to start with blood-letting for good fortune? Fine fights we used to see on the harbourside in those days, eh?'

'You're right there. It was a grand chance for men who couldnae stand each other to do something about it.' Mowser nodded vigorously. 'I got the season off to a good start myself many a time. I mind once when I was a deckhand just made up from being the new lad, and we'd this mate with a right sharp tongue. He'd never let a man get on with his job in peace, that one, and he'd a real down on me, being the youngest. Come the start of the new season, when I was bigger and a lot stronger than I'd been the year before, I made sure the rest of them would keep their hands in their pockets, then I went up to this mate of ours and "Just for the sake of the fishing", I said to him, all polite. Then I took my fist and knocked him arse over tit across the harbour.' Mowser cackled in delight at the memory. 'He made my life even more of a misery after that, but we'd the best damned season in years.'

'That's enough, Da,' Stella cut in, then to Jacob, in a whisper, 'I'd appreciate it, Mr MacFarlane, if you'd not encourage such talk in this house.'

'You're quite right, it's not what I'm here for at all. James, I thought you should be the first to know that your uncle's just agreed to sell his share in the *Fidelity* to me.'

James Lowrie had been sitting at the table, paying little heed to the conversation, but now his dark head jerked up. 'You've bought into the boat?' he asked incredulously, while Stella came to stand behind him, one hand on his shoulder, her face filled with apprehension.

'I have indeed. But it won't make any difference to you or the other shareholders,' Jacob nodded reassuringly to Stella, 'except that I hope you've not promised your services to Davie Geddes, for the *Fidelity*'ll be in need of a good skipper.'

Watching closely, he saw sudden hope spring to James's face, then it was forced out by suspicion. 'Why should you buy into the boat?'

'Because I used to be a fisherman in this district myself and coming back's given me the notion to be part of that life again. Though you need have no worries on my

account,' Jacob added swiftly, 'for I'll not be interfering
with the way you handle her.'

'Oh, James!' Stella, her face radiant, squeezed her
husband's shoulder, but he ignored her.

'You must have offered Albert good money, since he
didn't even have to think about it. Is my mother behind
this? Did she ask you to do it, to stop me crewing for
Davie Geddes?'

'You've either got a very poor idea of me as a businessman or a very good opinion of your mother's powers of
persuasion,' Jacob said evenly. 'Jess might be a good
friend of mine, but I don't seek her advice when it
comes to spending my hard-earned silver. I bought into
your brother-in-law's business because I expect to get a
good return from my investment and I bought into the
Lowrie boat for the same reason. I'm hoping you'll be
her skipper, but if you don't care for the idea I'm sure
I can find someone else.' He rose and picked up his hat,
nodding first to Stella, then to Mowser. 'Mrs Lowrie, my
apologies for having intruded into your home like this. Mr
Buchan, good day to you.'

'James . . .' Stella said again as the door closed behind
their visitor.

'I'll not have my mother using the likes of him to make
up to me for what she did to my father.'

'She did nothing to your father!' Stella spoke out for
once, goaded beyond caution by the way he had just
questioned a good opportunity. 'It was her right to bury
her own man. And she'd never ask Mr MacFarlane to
buy Albert out of the boat just to make you happy.'

'Even if she did,' Mowser said from his corner, 'what
difference would it make? You want the boat and now's
your chance. Don't be so thrawn, laddie!'

James hesitated, looking from one to the other, then
went out of the house. Jacob MacFarlane was walking
briskly away, but he stopped and turned when he heard
the clatter of iron-clad boots at his back.

'James Lowrie. Have you decided?'

'I'd like time to think about your offer.'

'Twenty-four hours and no more. I'd say,' Jacob said with a hard edge to his voice, 'that that should give you enough time.'

'Time for what?'

'To find out for yourself that I do not take my instructions from your mother.'

'You've taken a right beating there,' James said half an hour later. Innes, embarrassed, fingered his swollen mouth gingerly.

'It looks worse than it is.'

'It always does. Next time you'll be more ready, eh?'

'There won't be a next time, please God,' Jess said tartly from the stove, where she was using a large spoon to skim fat from a pot of mutton broth. 'Don't encourage the laddie, he's not a fighter and never has been.'

'He should have learned to use his fists when he was younger. God knows I tried to teach you,' James said to his brother.

'I never thought I'd have the need.'

'You know better now,' James said flatly; then, 'I want you to have a look at the boat's engines on Saturday. I don't think Jocky makes a good enough job of cleaning out the tubes and she needs a proper overhaul since there's a chance she might be doing some line fishing.'

With the advent of better weather some of the drifters had started fishing with long lines for haddock and codling, which were either treated in the smokehouses and sent to the markets or sold locally to housewives, who cooked them from fresh or smoked them on the triangular frames that hung on the outer wall of most cottages.

Innes's stomach muscles, still tender from his beating, twitched uneasily at the prospect, but he said aloud, 'I'll do that for you.' After what he had been through he was sure he could manage to go on board the boat again, as long as she was in the harbour.

'You've talked Albert into going after the white fish?' Jess was surprised. The *Fidelity* had not gone line fishing since Weem's death.

'It's nothing to do with Albert.' James watched her closely as he spoke. 'If she goes out, it's me that'll be taking her.'

'You?'

'Are you surprised? You must know that your friend Jacob's bought Albert out of the boat,' he said, and the spoon slipped from Jess's fingers to disappear beneath the soup's bubbling surface.

'He's done what?'

'He's bought a third share of the *Fidelity* and asked me to be her skipper. You knew nothing about it? And here was me,' James said, 'thinking that the two of you were close.'

She ignored the veiled taunt. 'But why would he do such a thing?'

'He says it's for the same reason he's become a partner in the Pates' business. The man likes to make money,' James went on as the door flew open and his aunt hurried in.

'Jess, wait till you hear . . .'

'I think I just have, Meg.'

'Ach! And here was me running all the way through the town to tell you.' Meg collapsed into a chair, fanning herself with a large scarred hand. 'I just met our Albert with a grin on him big enough to swallow a yacht.'

'So it's true that Jacob's bought his share of the *Fidelity*?'

'So Albert says.'

'How could he do such a thing?'

'You know our Albert – he's never been over-fond of the sea, or of hard work. Now he can be a man of leisure . . . Until he's spent every penny of the money he's getting.'

'Which he'll do as soon as he can,' James pointed out.

'As long as he enjoys the spending . . . You'll be the new skipper now, James?' his aunt wanted to know.

'Mebbe,' he said thoughtfully. Then, straightening his shoulders, 'Innes, I'll see you down at the harbour on Saturday.'

This time, possibly because the cuts and bruises on his face earned him grinning respect from those crew members on board, Innes found it easier to go on to the *Fidelity*. Jacob MacFarlane was there too, watching closely as Innes went over the engine, methodically checking and testing each part before he and Jocky cleaned out the tubes leading from furnace to smokestack. Because sea water was used in the boiler, the tubes salted up quickly and had to be scrubbed out regularly with wire brushes. It was a difficult, dirty job and when it was done both men were filthy and exhausted from working in the cramped conditions.

'I suppose you'll be looking for me to buy you a drink now?' James asked when his brother arrived back on deck.

Innes grinned, wiping his hands on a piece of rag. 'I'd say I've earned one.'

'You surely have, and it's her new skipper who'll be putting his hand in his pocket to reward you, eh, James?' Jacob said, and led the way from the boat. Innes took a deep breath and followed, hiding the panic that quivered deep within him each time he had to step from one boat to another over a sliver of dark harbour water. Knowing that his brother was watching closely, he refused to let his fear show.

'You know your business,' Jacob said admiringly when Innes had slaked the worst of his thirst and cleared the taste of grease and salt from his mouth.

'Each to his own.' Innes looked beyond the older man to

his brother. 'Eh, James?' His cut lip, still healing, smarted from the salt crystals and his bruised body ached from working in the tiny engine room, but he was pleased with what he had achieved.

'I suppose so.'

'It's a pity you didn't become an engine driver,' Jacob went on. 'You'd have been good at it.'

'He would that,' Jocky agreed generously.

'Ach, I much prefer land engines like motor-cars and motor-cycles. I'd not mind working in a wee garage, or mebbe even owning one some time,' Innes said easily. He downed the last of his drink and pushed the glass towards his brother. 'I could manage another.'

When he finally returned home, cheerful but not as drunk as he had been on the last occasion, he announced to his mother's dismay that he was going back to Zelda's home after work the following day to seek permission, once again, for their marriage.

'It's only right,' he insisted when Jess tried to dissuade him. 'I don't want any quarrel to hang over my marriage. Zelda deserves better than that.'

'And what about me having to clean up the blood and tend to the bruises when you're brought back home? Do I not have my rights too?'

'I don't think it'll come to that. From what Zelda says, the man regretted his behaviour almost as soon as it happened. He carried me all the way to the farm, remember, and saw to it that someone brought me home, when he could just have left me lying where I fell. And I still need to know that we've got his blessing and that there's not going be any more trouble for Zelda.'

'If you're going to that house I'm going with you, and that man'll get his head in his hands to play with if he tries to lay a finger on you!'

'For any favour!' Innes protested, horrified. 'Whoever heard of a man taking his mother along with him to ask for a lassie's hand?'

So Jess stayed home, fretting and worrying, and if Jacob hadn't arrived she might have followed Innes at a discreet distance.

As it was, the sight of Jacob pushed her worry about Innes into the background for a moment. 'You never said you were thinking of buying Albert out of the *Fidelity*,' she accused as soon as he came into the house.

'Who told you?'

'James, and Meg right behind him. And a few other folk, when I went out and about. It's a pity,' she said with an edge to her voice, 'that you couldn't come to tell me yourself.'

'I would have, but I'd to go to Aberdeen to sort out the money to pay Albert. I'd thought that he might take time to think about it, but instead he agreed at once, then he wanted the deal done quickly. Mebbe it was as well you heard the news from James, for when I first asked him to be skipper he seemed to think that the idea had come from you.'

'As if I'd ever suggest such a thing. That's men's business, not women's.'

'As a matter of fact, it was your Bethany who first suggested it as a way to keep James with the *Fidelity*.'

'Bethany?' Embarrassment turned Jess's face poppy-red. 'She'd no right to ask such a thing of you! Wait till I get a hold of her . . .'

'Now then, Jess, I'm only telling you because I'd never want to keep secrets from you. I was pleased that your Bethany had the wit to put the idea into my head, for since I came home I've had such a yearning to be part of the fishing again. And now I am, thanks to the *Fidelity*.' He spread his hands out. 'Everyone's content. There's Albert on shore with enough money in his pocket to last to the end of his days if he's sensible, and James running the boat. And even if I'm away in Germany or The Netherlands, or Russia, I'll know that part of me is still here on the Firth where I belong. We're all well satisfied with what's happened,' he said. Then, peering into her face, 'You're not angered with me, are you? You're pleased to know that your James is staying with his father's boat?'

She wasn't angry, but she was disturbed, for events were moving too fast for her. 'Yes, I'm pleased about that, but it seems to me that you're spending altogether too much of your silver on this family, Jacob.'

He leaned across the table and touched her work-roughened hand briefly. 'I'll not make myself into a bankrupt, have no fear of that. And I'm certain sure that James, Gil and Nathan will earn my money back for me, and a bit over besides, once the herring start to move again.'

'Aye well, I suppose you all know your own business best.' Jess got up to re-fill the kettle. 'It's surely time Innes was home.'

'It's early yet and I'm sure that now he's made his protest, Zelda's father won't cause any more bother. Even if he does, Innes has to deal with his own life as he thinks fit.'

'I know, but it doesn't stop me fretting about him, because he's always been the gentle one of the three.'

'I'll tell you one thing,' Jacob said firmly, 'you're right when you say he's not the coward Weem took him to be. That lad of yours is a talented engineer, and after that beating he had from Zelda's father he's gone off to take another, if he has to. He's got his own brand of courage, Jess.'

'I can't help thinking that cowards don't get hurt.'

'And they don't win bonny lassies like Zelda Mulholland, either. Where are they going to live when they're wed?'

'Here, with me, until they can save the money for a place of their own. The sooner that lassie's got a ring on her finger the better, and Innes's room upstairs'll easily take two folk. I'll not mind having Zelda under my roof, for she's got a pleasant nature.' And the thought of having a new-born in the house again, with its mewling cries and its dependency and its sweet, milky baby smell, warmed her heart. But what would any man, especially a bachelor like Jacob, understand of that?

'And I'll tell you another thing. You might say that Innes is the one you worry about, but it seems to me that you fret just as much over James.'

'I do not!'

'I'm glad to hear it, for I don't think he deserves it. I've not forgotten the way he behaved at your table at Ne'erday. He doesn't give you the respect you deserve, Jess . . .' Jacob began, but was interrupted by Innes and Zelda, hand-in-hand, their damaged faces glowing. At the second time of asking Will Mulholland had been gruff and terse, merely saying when Innes faced him with his request for a blessing, 'I suppose she could do worse. And what other man would have her, in her condition, anyway?'

'I could have hit him for that, but I didn't,' Innes assured his mother. 'I suppose when I think of it that he's right enough.' Then he yelped as Zelda dealt him a skelp on the ear.

'That's no way to speak of your future wife,' she said, her eyes bright with laughter and love. Watching them, Jess felt that this, at least, was a union she would not have to worry about.

Come to think of it, it was the only marriage that Weem had not arranged to suit his own purpose.

24

Ever since she had spoken to Jacob MacFarlane, Bethany had been uneasy. It was almost impossible to keep secrets among such a tight-knit community, and since she didn't really know the man well, how could she be sure that he would keep their conversation to himself?

When Gil brought home the news that Albert had sold his share in the *Fidelity* to MacFarlane, and when Stella, bubbling with happiness, confided that James was to become the new skipper, Bethany managed to look suitably surprised, but her unease persisted. When, a week later, she opened the door to find James on the step, glowering at her, she knew why he was there.

'Gil's not in,' she said, and began to close the door. He blocked it with his sturdy boot.

'I know, he's in the public house and likely to stay there for a good while.' He forced the door open again, pushing past her and into the kitchen. 'My business is with you. What d'you think you were doing, running to Jacob MacFarlane to beg favours for me?'

She thought briefly of trying to deny it, then decided that there was no sense in blustering. 'I might have known. Men can never keep their tongues still once they've got a drink in them.'

'Never mind blaming MacFarlane, Bethany, he let it slip without thinking. He believes,' James sneered, 'that you're a fine woman with a fine brain. He was pleased that you put the idea into his head, but I'm not, for I never liked meddlers.'

'Keep your voice down, there's bairns sleeping through in the back room. I only said to the man that it was a shame you had to seek work elsewhere, just because you were unhappy about Uncle Albert.'

'I've always known when you were lying, Bethany, even when you were a wee skelf of a thing. You got in my way then and, by God, you're still doing it!'

The colour that had rushed to her face when she opened the door to him now deepened angrily. 'All right, mebbe I did ask him to buy Albert's share of the boat so that you'd be able to stay on as skipper. What's wrong with that? You know you'd not be happy away from the *Fidelity*.'

'Happy?' He spat the word out. 'What's happiness got to do with it? Folk like us aren't supposed to be happy . . . Though mebbe I'd be a step nearer it if you could mind your own business!' He paced the kitchen like a caged animal while she watched, silent. 'You think I could take the boat now, knowing that you'd arranged it for me?'

'Stella said you'd agreed to it.'

'I've changed my mind and I'll tell Jacob that first thing tomorrow.'

'If you do you're a fool!'

'And if I don't I'd be an even bigger fool, letting a woman interfere in my life! D'you not think my father caused me enough misery, without you putting your neb in as well?'

'Oh, poor wee laddie, was his daddy cruel to him, then? It was you that stood in front of the minister with Stella, not him, so stop girning like a bairn that's dropped its toffee-apple.'

James had never taken kindly to being made a figure of fun; it was a weakness that Bethany had exploited cruelly time and time again in their younger days. 'You're a bitch, Bethany Lowrie,' he said now. 'A conniving, interfering . . .' he sought for more adjectives and, finding none, had to content himself with '. . . bitch!'

'That's better than being a fool. D'you know what I'd give to be in your shoes? It's all I've ever wanted, to be out there on the sea, hauling in the nets with a good boat like the *Fidelity* under my feet, instead of having to clean bairns' backsides, and cook and wash and lie with . . .' She broke off before her tongue gave her away, and began to pace the floor in her turn, wrapping her arms tightly about herself in a vain attempt to hold back the torment within. 'Sometimes the hunger and the longing near drive me out of my mind. It's what I was born to do!'

'Don't be daft, how could a woman ever crew on a fishing boat?' James asked, then stumbled back against the table as she suddenly spun round, the flat of her hand cracking across his cheek with all the force she could muster behind the blow.

In the old days her action would have been the signal for him to launch himself at her. They would have fought tooth and nail with grim, silent determination until one or the other admitted defeat. Now, as he peeled himself away from the table, one hand to his face, she gritted her teeth and set her feet slightly apart for extra balance in readiness. The blow must surely have hurt him, for her hand was stinging and burning with the force of it.

But all he did was examine his fingers, as though expecting to see blood. Then he said, amazed, 'What did you do that for?'

'Because you sound just like the rest of them – just like Gil and Father. I looked for something more than that from you, James. I thought we understood each other.' Tears prickled at the corners of her eyes and she had to struggle to keep her voice level. 'I'll never be at peace, because I was born a woman and can't do what I want to do more than anything in the world. And here's you . . . you've got everything, and you're throwing it away just because you're too thrawn to reach out and take it!'

Then, as he stared, the imprint of her palm and fingers clearly marked in deep red across his tanned skin, the anger drained out of Bethany. He was just like any other man, after all.

'Stay with the *Fidelity*, James,' she said, tired to her very bones now. 'I had to force myself to ask Jacob MacFarlane to help you. I'd to beg for the first time in my life, and the last. Don't let that go to waste.' She gave a shaky laugh. 'We're right miserable souls, aren't we, you and me?'

Then as he continued to stare at her, she swallowed hard and said, 'Come and put some cold water on your cheek. It'll ease the bruising.' She went towards the small sink. 'There's a clean cloth . . .'

'Bethany,' James said in a voice that was part-whisper, part-groan. 'God help me, Bethany, I've not been able to get you out of my mind since that night . . .'

The light in his eyes, hot and hungry, sent a tremor down the length of her. They were on dangerous ground, the two of them.

'You shouldn't have come here tonight,' she said, her voice shaking with the effort of hiding her own hunger.

'Aye,' he said. 'I should. I should have come to you sooner than this. But I'm here now, my lass.' He reached out to her and, tired of fighting her own instincts, tired of trying to do what was right for Gil and Stella, instead of what was right for them – for herself and James – she went into his arms, the tremor shuddering through her again as he bent his head, the red mark on his cheek like a warning flag, to kiss her.

When James had finally gone, slipping out of the front door as silently as a wraith, Bethany hunted out all the pins that had been scattered carelessly across the floor, then brushed her hair and pinned it up neatly. She shook out the rug where they had lain together and, as she laid it carefully back in place, the thought suddenly came to her that if Molly Pate had any notion of what had just taken place on the rag rug she had made, the poor woman must surely be birling in her tidy grave.

A giggle bubbled to her lips at the idea; she pressed them together tightly to smother it, then had to put a hand to her mouth as another followed, then another. She might have become quite hysterical if Ellen hadn't begun to whimper in the back room. She refused to settle down again and finally Bethany picked her up and looked at Rory, on his stomach as usual, with his head twisted at an uncomfortable angle and his pursed mouth making a soft popping noise with each outgoing breath. Carrying Ellen into the kitchen, she gave the little girl a drink, then settled in a chair by the fire with the child in her lap.

When Gil arrived only minutes later Ellen had already fallen asleep again, her thumb in her mouth. At the sight of him Bethany began to struggle up, but he put out a hand to stop her.

'Stay still and don't disturb the bairn.' He sat down opposite, still in his heavy jacket and boots. 'It's grand to come home to such a sight. I'm a fortunate man, Bethany.'

'And a drunk one too.'

'Just a wee celebration of the way things are going for us these days,' Gil said, then, almost shyly, 'I've been thinking, Bethany, would it not be nice to have a bairn of our own?'

'A bairn? But we've already got two.'

'Aye, but I'd like fine to have a wee lassie with your bonny colouring. Or a wee laddie would be even better. And when we move to one of those nice big houses on Cliff Terrace we'll have room for half a dozen more, if we want them. I'd like that.'

Bethany's skin, still tingling from James's touch, James's kisses, crawled at the very thought.

On a crisp, sunny day in February Innes Lowrie and

Grizelda Mulholland stood before the minister and made their marriage vows. Afterwards, both families squeezed into Jess's small kitchen for a wedding breakfast.

Still simmering with rage over the beating her son had taken, Jess had not been happy with the thought of having to entertain Will Mulholland and his wife in her own home. 'If I'd my way of it,' she told Meg hotly, 'that man would have his food thrown over him, instead of put down to him in a civilised way, after what he did to our Innes.'

'What's done's done,' her sister-in-law said calmly. 'The young ones are getting their own way and you'll have another grand-bairn to look forward to. Anyway, I doubt if Innes would thank you for losing your temper on his marriage day.'

Throughout the day the shepherd was remote and expressionless, saying little and keeping himself in the background. His wife, on the other hand, brought a large basket containing fresh farm eggs, a fresh-baked loaf, a pot of home-made jam and a large piece of cold mutton, 'Just to thank you for your hospitality,' she said as she handed them over. Then, removing the clean apron that had been tucked over the top of the basket to protect its contents, she tied it around her waist and added, 'Now then, just you tell me what needs doing and I'll see to it.' In the face of her clear determination to make amends for what had gone before, it was impossible for Jess to bear a grudge.

In any case, there was plenty to do and the more willing hands, the better. The table was swiftly covered with food donated by friends and family: steak pies and yellow fish, trifles and home baking. Most of the china and cutlery had been borrowed, for no housewife ever accumulated enough to supply a large gathering and there were plenty of folk happy to play their part in making the wedding a success. In deference to the Mulhollands' religious beliefs, there was no alcohol at the wedding party, but nobody – other than Albert and Gil – seemed to miss it.

Jess had spread a pretty lace tablecloth over the wall-bed and set out the wedding presents on it for all the guests to admire. There were four lavishly decorated cups and saucers from Bethany and Gil, a beautifully embroidered tablecloth from Stella and James, and a set of dishes from Zelda's parents. Jess had already promised the young couple the few pieces of furniture from Innes's room for their new home when they found it, and had also offered to buy a new bed. Albert contributed some china and Meg gave a pretty set of bed-linen.

'It came from Harry's mother when we were wed, but we werenae together long enough to get the use of it,' she said when she brought it to the house. 'Anyway, ordinary bedding suits me best.'

'It's beautiful!' Zelda marvelled over the pillowcases and sheets, trimmed with crochet so beautifully done that it looked almost like lace.

'Harry's mother did that, God rest her soul. She was grand at the fancy sewing, though I never could do that sort of thing myself.' Meg was delighted with the reception that her gift got, but to Jess she confided in private, 'I doubt if I could ever have slept on fancy sheets and pillows like that, but I never told Harry.'

'Zelda will make good use of it. It was kind of you to give it to her, Meg.'

'Mebbe it should have gone to Bethany, but she married into a house that had everything she needed, and Stella had all her mother's things. Best give it where it's most needed. I met your Bethany on my way here,' Meg added. 'She's looking right bonny these days.'

'She seems to be happier with her life since Ne'erday,' Jess said with relief.

Although it was the tradition that only close family gave gifts, Jacob MacFarlane had bought the young couple a

canteen of cutlery, so handsome that Jess had no option
but to give it pride of place in the centre of the bed.
There were some raised eyebrows when folk realised
who the donor was, but Zelda, still slender enough to
look attractive in her new blue dress, was thrilled with
it.

'I've never had so many pretty things in my life before,'
she said to Innes as they inspected their presents. Then,
squeezing his hand tightly, 'And I've never been so
happy, ever!'

Watching the way Innes was enjoying every moment
of his wedding day, Jess wished that the same could
have been said for her two elder children. Both had
been silent and expressionless during their wedding parties, though Weem had more than made up for them.
Remembering how vibrantly alive he had been, how
invincible, she had to swallow back a sudden rush of
hot tears.

Jacob arrived by her side just then. 'Everyone's having
a grand time, Jess. You must be proud of Innes this
day.'

'I am that.'

'You women,' he teased gently. 'I never can understand why you cry when you're happy as well as when
you're sad.'

It was late when the wedding party broke up and the
Mulhollands went off home. Will left without a backward
glance, driving his younger children before him as if they
were a flock of sheep, but his wife lingered with her
daughter.

'I'll see you both at the kirk on Sunday?'

'Of course,' Zelda assured her. It was the custom for
the bride and groom to lead the congregation into church
on the first Sunday after their marriage for their 'kirkin'
– a final blessing on their union.

'And mind and visit us once a week.' Automatically

Mrs Mulholland reached out and smoothed back Zelda's curly hair.

'Ma!' The girl flinched away, embarrassed. 'I'm a married woman now!'

Tears sparkled in her mother's eyes. 'So you are, pet, so you are!'

Innes put an arm about his new wife, who was beginning to snivel a bit at the sight of her mother weeping. 'I'll take good care of her, Mrs Mulholland.'

She gave an almighty sniff and blinked rapidly. 'I know you will, son. She's found a good man and that's all I can ask for her. Here.' She dug into her coat pocket, then thrust something into Innes's hands. 'That's for the two of you. No need to say anything to . . .' she cast a nervous glance at the dark night outside, where her husband and their other children waited for her, then went on, '. . . anybody. Goodnight to you, Mrs Lowrie, and thank you for your hospitality.'

As she closed the door, Jess said, 'I might not be so fond of your father, Zelda, for very good reason, but I like your mother. She's a decent body.'

'So's my da when you catch him in the right mood. Let me see . . .'

Zelda, unable to contain her curiosity, took Innes's hand and uncurled his fingers. Then she gasped at the sight of the two banknotes.

'Look at all that money! It must have taken her years to save it. Oh, Ma!' The tears filled her dark eyes and brimmed over.

Innes held her close. 'We'll put it in the bank, eh?' he suggested. 'Save it towards our own wee house. Then your mam can come and visit us there.' When she nodded, he drew her head in against her shoulder so that she could cry in peace and privacy.

The sight of them together stirred so many memories that Jess's heart turned over in her breast. She had had more than her fair share of loving and being loved and,

now that her own day was done, she hoped that for Innes
and Zelda the path through life would be just as enjoyable
as it had been for herself and Weem.

'I'm ready for my bed,' she said. 'We can clear this
place up tomorrow.'

As she unpinned her hair, still long and silky though now
well sprinkled with grey, and began to brush it out with
long, hard strokes from root to tip, Jess heard the faint
murmur of Innes's voice from above, followed by a soft
laugh from Zelda. Innes had found the right person and
the contentment needed to safeguard a marriage, but it
was different, she thought as she brushed and brushed,
for James and Bethany.

She had not been overly concerned about James's marriage, for Stella clearly adored him and a man needed to
have his own home and his own wife, but she wished she
had opposed Weem more forcefully where Bethany was
concerned, for it had been clear to her that the girl had no
desire to be tied down to domesticity. But he had scoffed
at her attempts to remonstrate with him.

'You were mother to two bairns at her age. What makes
her so different?'

'I married from choice.'

'And a good choice you made.' He gave her that swift,
mischievous glance that had always made her go weak
at the knees with wanting him. Even the memory of it
more than a year after his death brought a surge of heat
to her belly.

'Bethany's not like me.'

'More's the pity. It's time she started behaving like the
woman she is. She's been spoiled, that's her trouble.'

'And whose fault is that? You'd never let me scold her
when she was wee. She could wrap you round her little
finger – and she did, time and again. You made her think
she was special.'

Weem had the grace to look ashamed. 'Mebbe I did,

but she was easy to spoil. D'ye no' mind her, Jess, such a bonny wee lass with as much courage in her wee body as James. And a damned sight more than the other one,' he added sourly.

'It's not Innes's fault that he wasn't meant for the fishing life,' she flared, always ready to fly to the defence of her beloved younger son. Weem raised his thick, greying eyebrows and gave her a triumphant smirk.

'Who's doin' the spoilin' now?' he wanted to know. Then as she bit her lip, furious with herself for having fallen into his trap, 'I'll have no more of your fussing, Jess. Gil Pate's desperate to marry with our lass and he'll be a good husband to her. You know what they say: better an old man's darlin' than a young man's fool. Not that Gil's old.'

'Older than her by a good few years. And the father of two bairns already.'

'Carin' for them'll help to bring her round to the ways of a housewife all the sooner, and if Gil's willing to take all the fish the *Fidelity* can catch into the bargain, then that's fine with me. The matter's closed,' Weem said and snapped his newspaper open, always a signal that he wanted to be left in peace.

So Bethany had promised herself to Gil for the rest of her life, and now she and James were both tied to people who, decent enough though they were, could never satisfy their stormy, restless natures and the aching need Jess sensed in both of them. They were still drifting, each of them in danger of finding elsewhere the comfort they hungered for. The very thought of the unhappiness that could cause made Jess shiver.

Before getting into bed she knelt on the cold linoleum, hands clasped together and eyes tight shut against the dark, and prayed for the protection and happiness of her two older children. Then she flicked back the single long plait that kept her hair neat overnight, put out the light and got into bed.

*   *   *

The wedding was a torment for Bethany, who found it almost unbearable to be in the same room as James for so long, without being able to touch him. Since the night he had come to her door, blazing with rage at the way she had persuaded Jacob MacFarlane to buy Albert's share of the *Fidelity*, James had become the centre of her life. When they were apart it was as though the colour had been leached out of her world; when they were together in company, and unable to touch, she itched with need for him.

They were careful to avoid each other all through the wedding party, afraid of betraying themselves to watchful eyes, but inevitably the moment came when they met in the crowd.

'I'll see you tonight?' he said, low-voiced.

She had managed to get away from the house only two nights earlier to spend precious time with him. It would be hard to find an excuse to go out again tonight. But she no longer had any choice.

'Aye.' She spoke on a soft breath. 'Tonight.'

25

James was already down in *Fidelity*'s cabin when Bethany arrived, waiting at the foot of the ladder to draw her into his arms and kiss her, a deep, strong kiss that made her lips melt against his.

'I can't stay long, for Gil wasnae very happy about me going out again. He thinks I'm seeing too much of my mother these days.'

'I don't know what I'd have done if you hadn't, after being forced to keep my distance from you all afternoon.' He drew her down to sit on the bunk by his side, his mouth mapping out the shape of her face from forehead to eyes to nose to chin with tiny, light kisses. 'I'd probably have come knocking at your door,' he said against the corner of her mouth, 'telling Gil he must let you come to me.'

'I can just see you asking if I could come out to play, like a bairn,' she said, and felt a laugh ripple through him.

'Aye,' he agreed, then drew her closer, lowering her on to the bunk and leaning over her, enfolding her body with his. It was too dark to see his features, but she could feel his breath warm on her face, and when he said huskily, 'Will you, Beth? Will you come to play with me?' she reached up to draw him closer, more than ready to do his bidding.

Lusty though it was, Gil's lovemaking within the comfort of their bed was solely for his own pleasure. Even though she went to him a virgin, Bethany had always found his attentions tedious and unexciting; she had thought the fault was hers, since she assumed that Gil, already once-married, was experienced in the ways of pleasuring women. But with James she had learned that not all men were alike, when it came to knowing how to make a woman catch her breath in delight, and cry aloud, and play her own part in the loving. Just being together was a pleasure, which, had they both had their way, would have gone on for ever, but all too soon her sharp ears caught the sound of one of the church bells ringing the hour.

'I have to go.'

'Not yet . . .'

'And so must you. It's time we were back where we belonged.'

'I am where I belong, with the *Fidelity* and with you. Am I being too greedy, Beth?' James asked against her hair. 'Wanting both of you?'

'Gil must be wondering where I am.' She fumbled in the dark for her clothes, muttering her irritation. 'Put the lamp on.'

'Someone might see it and wonder who's working so late at night.'

'They'll wonder even more if they see me going ashore dressed in your clothes and you in mine. I can't see a thing, James!'

'A match, then, but not the lamp.'

Although they gave only a tiny flame, several matches provided light for long enough to let Bethany sort the scattered clothing into two piles. Once that was done they were able to dress in the dark.

'You go first and I'll follow in a wee while,' James said low-voiced, though there was nobody to hear them. Then as she turned to the ladder she felt his hand on her shoulder, turning her round to face him. 'I'll be here every night, waiting for you,' he said. 'Come to me as often as you can get away.'

Hurrying along the harbour wall towards the town lights, she knew that she would be back as soon as possible. No matter how wicked it was, she had committed herself to James and even if there had been a way to turn the clock back, she would not want to do so.

Once his ring was on Zelda's finger, Innes seemed to grow to manhood before his mother's very eyes. As the son of the house he had rushed in from his work to eat what was put before him before, as likely as not, rushing out again. Now he spent his evenings at home, sitting in the chair that had been his father's with a newspaper in his hands, reading out an occasional item to Jess, who was busy in her usual chair with her knitting wires, and Zelda, perched between them on a stool, stitching away at some small garment for the coming baby. On most evenings Jacob called in to make a foursome.

'When's he ever going back to wherever he lives?' Innes asked his mother after one of Jacob's visits.

'When he's good and ready, I suppose. He's got interests here, now that he's gone into partnership with Gil and Nathan and bought Albert's share of the boat.'

'Aunt Meg says you and him were sweethearts once.'

'Your Aunt Meg's got a long tongue,' said Jess, vexed.

'Were you?' Zelda butted in, eyes bright with interest.

'Mebbe. A long time ago.'

'You don't think . . .' Innes began, but Zelda nipped in sharply.

'Don't be daft, Innes, there'd never be anything like that now,' she said with the amusement that young folk showed towards any suggestion of romance between their elders. She was putting on weight swiftly, and now that she had stopped working at the farm she and Jess were in each other's company for the best part of each day. They divided the housework between them amicably enough and on the surface things worked out well.

'Though I do feel my nose being put out of joint a wee

bit when she tells me what Innes would and wouldn't like for his dinner,' Jess confided in Meg. 'Me that's raised him near on eighteen years.'

'Wives aye like to think that nob'dy knows their men better than they do. It'll not be long before the two of them find their own place.'

Zelda, too, was finding the domestic situation hard to take. 'We need a house of our own,' she told Innes in the privacy of their bedroom.

'I thought everything was working out fine here.'

'Aye, you would, for you're the one that gets the best out of it, with two women to run after you. Innes, you'll never grow up while you're biding in your mother's house. I want us to get a wee place of our own before the bairn comes.'

But when Innes started working longer hours in an attempt to make more money she was still not pleased. 'It's no sort of life, sitting around the house with your mother, waiting for you to come home,' she grizzled.

'If we were in our own house you'd not even have her for company.'

'But it would be different, d'you not see that? It would be ours, just for us. Mebbe we could find somewhere near my mother, or near the Bains' farm. Then I'd be close to folk that I know.'

At his wits' end, Innes went to Stella, who was more domesticated than Bethany, for advice. 'Mebbe you could help me to understand how Zelda feels, for I'm lost,' he said wretchedly, sitting in her kitchen with Ruth on his lap and the twins climbing all over him.

'She's from a big family and she's homesick, just. It's natural,' she assured him. 'I tell you what, I'll take the bairns along to your mother's more often and I'll ask Zelda if she'll start visiting me.'

'I'd not want her to know that I spoke to you about this.'

'She won't. I'll say it's for the company, now that James

is skipper of the *Fidelity*. It'll not be a lie, for even though the line fishing doesn't take him away for long at a time, he spends hours fussing over the boat when she's in harbour. He's like a bairn with a new toy.'

'I'd best be going.' Disengaging himself from the twins and handing Ruth over, Innes took a closer look at his sister-in-law. 'You look a wee bit pale, are you keeping all right?'

'I'm fine, just kept busy with the wee ones. You'll soon know all about that.'

'I'm looking forward to it,' Innes said, beaming.

'It makes a lot of sense,' Jacob MacFarlane urged. 'For one thing, the crew would be sure of a proper wage coming in. You'd not deny them that, surely?'

'But what about the bad seasons?' James, confused, scowled at the figures on the paper that the older man had pushed across the table towards him. 'How could we afford to pay them a set rate then?'

'That would be my problem, not yours. Each to his own strengths, James: you seeing to the boat and me to the money, that's what we agreed. Ask them,' Jacob urged when the younger man chewed on his lower lip. 'Just you ask them what they would rather have, certain money in their hands every week of the season, or having to wait till it's over before they find out how much they'll have to see their families through the winter.'

'I'll think about it.'

'We could tell them together, then I can explain . . .'

'I said I'll think about it. Leave it with me for now,' James said firmly, and Jacob had to be content with that.

'A steady wage to take home to the wife . . . that's somethin' fishermen have never known before,' old Mowser said when Jacob had gone.

'You're right there, Da. It'd mean a lot to the women-folk to know how much money was going to come into their houses, James.'

'I'm not sure, and even if I do agree it won't happen in this house. You heard Jacob proposing that, as the skipper, I would still take my share at the end of the season.'

'We'll do well enough with that. Won't we, my bonny lassie?' Stella cooed to the baby on her lap. 'If your daddy wasn't the fine fisherman he is we'd have nothing to eat at all. Then we'd mebbe have to eat you all up for our dinner.' She grabbed a fat, flailing leg and pretended to gobble it, while Ruth crowed with laughter. 'Yes, we would, and there's enough here to go round the neighbours too, wee fatty-bannocks.' Stella hoisted the little girl into the air, laughing up at her. 'You're a fatty-bannocks, aren't you?'

'D'you have to talk to the bairn as if she's a fool?' James snapped, and the smile was wiped from Stella's face as swiftly as if he had taken it off with the back of his hand. Mowser stared fixedly into the fire while the twins, playing amicably together on the floor, looked up at their father apprehensively.

'It's just the way folk talk to weans. She likes it.'

'How d'you know what she likes, when she's not got the words to tell you?'

'I just know,' Stella said feebly, bewildered by the sudden attack. She laid Ruth down on the wall-bed and began to push the twins into their jackets. 'I'm away along to your mother's to see how Zelda's feeling today. You'll be able to think clearer when we're out of the way.'

'You might as well stay here, for I'm going to the boat.'

'I was going anyway.' Stella wound a long scarf about Sarah's head, crossing it over the little girl's chest then knotting it at her back. Then she began to do the same for Annie. 'I promised Innes I'd keep an eye on Zelda.'

James, hauling on his long, iron-studded sea-boots,

gave her an exasperated look. 'Can Innes not look out for his own wife? And is my mother not capable of it too, since you seem to think that Zelda's in need of special help?'

'It's just that with this being her first bairn, and her own mother not being close to hand . . .' Stella wrapped a shawl about the baby, working quickly, anxious to get out of the house before the tears thickening her throat began to fill her eyes. 'There's a stew cooking, I'll be back in good time to dish it up to you.'

As the door closed behind his daughter Mowser cleared his throat, spat into the fire and made a show of combing his fingers through his luxuriant moustache. 'It doesnae seem right, somehow.'

'What doesn't?' James asked belligerently, wondering why he couldn't keep his tongue off Stella. It wasn't her fault that she wasn't more like . . . He forced his mind away from thoughts of Bethany.

'Now I come to think of it, the idea of a regular wage doesnae seem right for the likes of us. Fisher-folk arenae like factory workers or farm workers. We've our own way of doing things.'

'Times are changing and we need to change with them. I don't know . . .' James stood up, pushing the sheet of paper into his pocket. 'I'll have to think about it.'

Bethany, unable to stay for long in her own home these days, was already in Jess's warm kitchen when Stella arrived.

'You've not been to the house recently, Bethany.' Her sister-in-law loosened the shawl that held Ruth close against her. 'You and James haven't had a falling out, have you?'

'How could we, since we never see each other?' Bethany's voice was sharp and Jess, rolling dough at the kitchen table, saw Stella flinch slightly. Bethany herself must have seen it, for her voice became softer as she said, 'Wee Ellen wasn't herself for a wee while and I thought she might be sickening for something. I didn't want your bairns to catch it.'

Stella cast a doubtful glance at Ellen, who was rolling happily on the floor with the twins, the very picture of health, then she sat Ruth up on her knees and began to play the baby's favourite game.

'Knock at the doorie,' she crooned, tapping lightly with her knuckles on Ruth's forehead; then, touching a fingertip to each of the baby's eyelids in turn, 'Keek in, lift the sneck . . .' Finger and thumb gently tweaked Ruth's snub little nose, then Stella eased a forefinger into the little mouth, wide open in helpless laughter, with a loud 'And walk in!' She bounced Ruth up into the air several times.

'You'll make her sick if you keep doing that,' Bethany told her.

'Ach, she's got a stomach made of iron, her. Everything that goes in stays in, no matter what. Is that not right, my wee birdie? You've got your daddy's appetite.' Stella hugged the baby. 'And she's got his eyes, more than the other two, d'you not think so?'

'I don't see it myself.'

'You must see it, Bethany,' Zelda chimed in. 'She's more like her daddy than the twins.'

''Specially when she's thinkin',' Stella agreed. 'You know the way James goes all quiet when he's puzzling over something, as if he's looking right through you and seeing something that nobody else can.'

'How is James these days, Stella?' Jess swiftly cut the dough into rounds, using the top of a cup, and began to put them on to a baking tin. 'He must be happy to be in charge of the *Fidelity*.'

'He is,' Stella said, then her face clouded and the worry-lines appeared again between her eyes. 'Though it means more work, for it's an awful responsibility. And now there's this new ploy of Mr MacFarlane's for him to think about.'

'What ploy's this?'

'He wants James to pay the *Fidelity* crew set wages every week, instead of giving them a share of the takings at the end of the season.'

'James is surely never going to agree to that!' Bethany said.

'You don't think it's a good idea? It means the men'll get regular money coming in, no matter how the fishing goes.'

'And they'll never get the good big payment if the fishing goes well. They'll never be any more than hired hands, with no chance of ever getting their own boats one day.'

'I never thought of that.'

'I hope James does. If you take my advice, Stella, you'll tell him to think twice about it.'

'Why would he listen to me? I'm not clever when it comes to that sort of thing.'

'You're as wise as anyone else,' Jess assured the younger woman, taking a tray of golden-brown scones from the oven and putting them on the table to cool. 'You're doing a grand job of running a house and looking after two men as well as your bairns.'

'It's not the same, though,' Stella said wistfully. 'James never talks to me about his work, or asks my advice, because he knows I'd not be of any help to him. I wish I was more like you, Bethany.'

Bethany flushed. 'That's nonsense!' The sharp note had returned to her voice. 'You know me and James never see eye to eye.'

'You used to be as close as two peas in a pod. I mind those days, for seeing the two of you together made me wish I was as near to one of my own brothers. And James thinks highly of you even yet. He's always telling me I should be more like you.'

'Is he?' Bethany gaped at her, completely taken aback, as Innes came in, home from work early for once.

All the children greeted him with squeals of pleasure, but just as they were settling down to a rowdy game with him on the kitchen floor, Bethany jumped to her feet. 'Ma, would you keep an eye on these two for a wee while? I've to go to the shops.'

'These scones are cool enough to eat now, and I'm just going to make a fresh pot of tea,' Jess protested, wiping flour from her hands.

'I've my messages to get yet, and the dinner to start. I'll see to that, then come back for the bairns,' Bethany said, and hurried out of the cottage.

Without her in it, the room seemed to Jess to be dimmer than before. There was a glow to Bethany these days, as though a lamp had been lit within her. Briefly Jess wondered if her daughter was expecting at last, but she dismissed the thought almost as soon as it had arrived. A child, Gil's child, would not make Bethany as happy as she was at the moment. Possibly it was because of the partnership between Gil and Jacob, though why that should please her so much was a mystery.

Compared to Bethany, Stella looked wan and worried, but then life with James could not be easy. Jess put an extra layer of butter on the girl's scone, and an extra spoonful of sugar in her tea for added energy.

'Is Mowser in?' Bethany asked as soon as James opened the door.

'He's down at the harbour, and Stella's . . .'

'I know where Stella is, I've just left her there.' Bethany pushed past him and into the kitchen, which was filled with the aroma of the stew Stella had put in the oven earlier. Her knitting and some of the children's toys were scattered about the room, which looked cosy and welcoming.

James closed the door and turned to his sister. 'Is this a good idea?' he asked, though his eyes were burning and his hands already reaching out towards her.

She stepped back, out of his reach. 'Stella tells me that

Jacob MacFarlane has some daft notion about giving the
Fidelity's crew a wage instead of a share in the catch.'

'That's right. What's it got to do with you?'

'It's got everything to do with me. I'm a Lowrie, and
part-owner of the boat. You're not going to agree to it,
are you?'

'I've not decided.'

'Use your noddle, man.' It was something she had said
to him on countless occasions over the years, and a smile
quirked the corner of James's mouth.

'Jacob's mebbe right when he says they'd be better off
with regular money coming in.'

'They might be better off for now, but tell me this –
have you ever met a guttin quine who owns her own
house or employs other folk?'

'No, but what's that got to do with it?'

'It's got everything to do with it!' Bethany said impatiently. 'Every man who owns a boat here in Buckie got
it by working hard, and saving hard, but fisher-lassies
never become employers because they're lucky if they
make enough to live on. There's no saving from their
wages, no money to put behind them so that they can
start out on their own. They have to work for other folk
all their lives, and the same'll go for the *Fidelity*'s crew
if Jacob MacFarlane has his way. If you pay your crew set
wages, no matter how the fishing goes, they'll be crewing
for the boat for the whole of their lives.'

'That wouldn't be bad as far as I'm concerned. I've
got good men there and I'd not want to lose them.'

'That's exactly the way Jacob sees it: fishermen who
can't leave one boat to set themselves up with another.
That means fewer boats and more fish for the boats already
going out. D'you not see that?'

'I suppose I do,' he said slowly.

'Then tell him you'll have no truck with the idea. Why's
he telling you what to do anyway, when he only owns a
third of the boat?'

'He put in a fair bit of money to buy Albert off and he's really taken to the idea of being part-owner of that boat, Bethany. He's even had a man down on the harbour painting her.'

Bethany tutted. 'Waste of money. *Fidelity* doesn't need painting, she's always been kept smart.'

'I don't mean that sort of painting. I mean he's got someone painting a picture of her.'

'A picture? Why would he want such a thing?'

James shrugged. 'There's some do it.'

'More fool them, wasting good silver like that. And there's another thing,' Bethany suddenly remembered. 'You know that you're making Stella miserable?'

His grey eyes, which had become smoky with desire once the matter of the crew wages was out of the way, suddenly hardened and chilled. 'What's she been saying to you?'

'That you tell her she should be more like me. She says you get impatient with her.'

'She's got no right to talk about me to anyone!'

'For goodness' sake, man, it's what women do. What else do we have to talk about when we get together?'

'I'll not discuss my wife with anyone, Bethany, not even you,' James said stiffly.

'I'm not interested in discussing Stella, I'm just saying you should guard your tongue when you speak to her.'

The anger went out of his face, to be replaced by naked misery. 'She's not you,' he said, low-voiced, 'and that's what's eating away at me every time I look at her, every time I have to touch her. If it could just be us, Beth, me and you . . .'

She swallowed hard and fisted her hands. 'It can never be like that.'

'Why not?'

'For pity's sake, James . . . you know full well why not!'

'I can't think how we happened to be born into the

same family,' James said bleakly, 'for we were meant to be together, you can't deny it.'

Her eyes prickled and she blinked away a threatened rush of tears. 'If we were truly meant to be together we'd not have been born to the same parents,' she said. Then, dragging her eyes from his, 'I have to go. I shouldn't be here.'

'I'll see you tonight?' he asked as she stopped on the doorstep, glancing up and down the empty street.

'Not tonight, Gil's beginning to wonder why I'm going out so much.'

'As soon as you can, then. I'll be waiting.' The wind blew an errant strand of her glowing chestnut hair across her mouth; James reached out to smooth it gently behind her ear and on an impulse, without thinking where they were, she reached up and held his hand against her cheek for a brief, precious moment.

'Oh James,' she said, 'why did we ever let this start?'

'D'you regret it?' When she shook her head silently he drew his fingers from beneath hers. 'Go away, woman,' he said, his voice husky, his eyes making love to her. 'Go away before I pull you back inside and shut the door and be damned to the consequences.'

26

When Stella prepared to go, Innes offered to walk back home with her. 'You look wearied,' he said when she tried to object. 'I'll carry the wee one.'

'You're not bothered about being seen with a bairn in your arms, then?' she teased as they left the house.

'No, why should I?'

'There's some would think it's not manly.'

'Like our James, you mean?' He set Ruth on his shoulder, one hand balancing her securely, and slowed his usual long stride to accommodate Stella and the twins. 'It doesnae bother me one bit what some might say.'

'You'll make a good father, Innes.'

'I mean to do my best,' he said. 'Thank you for taking the time to befriend Zelda.'

'I enjoy her company.'

'If I could just find a wee place for the two of us before the bairn comes she'd be content.'

'Your mother's very happy to have the two of you under her roof and I know she's looking forward to the baby.'

'She's good to us, but Zelda's impatient for a place of her own. I wish I could earn more money.'

'Have you thought of trying to find work with one of the boat builders? James said you were good with the *Fidelity*'s engines. Better than Jocky, he thought.'

'Did he now?' Innes glowed; he had never been praised

by James before. 'I never thought of working for a boat builder.'

'You should try it,' Stella said, then as they turned a corner, 'There's Bethany coming out of our house.'

'She'll be looking for you.'

'But I saw her already today, at your mother's,' Stella said, then caught at his arm and put out her other hand to hold Sarah and Annie back, when they would have scampered ahead. 'Quick, round here.'

Innes, confused, had no option but to follow as she ducked back round the corner. 'What . . . ?'

'Shush! Bethany was in a right taking with James earlier and I doubt if her temper's improved much. We're playing hide and seek with Daddy,' she told the twins, who giggled and hopped about on the cobbles. 'Don't let him see us, mind.' Then to Innes, 'I told her about some ploy Mr MacFarlane has for the *Fidelity* and she wasn't pleased at all. She must have come straight here to lecture James about it. I don't want to be caught in one of their quarrels.'

She reached up for Ruth who, unwilling to leave her exalted position, held tightly to her uncle's hair. 'Let go of poor Innes, you wee monkey! There now.' She gathered the little one into her arms. 'Peep round the corner, Innes, and see if she's gone yet.'

Amused, he eased himself carefully round so that he could see without being seen. Bethany was still at the door and she and James were talking earnestly, heads close together.

'She's still there.'

'Are they quarrelling, d'you think?' Stella's shawled head bumped against his arm.

Innes stared as James's hand reached out to smooth a strand of hair away from Bethany's face. 'They don't seem to be quarrelling,' he said hesitantly. Stella began to ease herself in front of him and he made a move to block her, but it was too late. He heard the breath catch in her throat and felt her stiffen against him as Bethany put her hand over James's, holding it to her cheek. He bent his head closer to hers and said something, then Bethany released his hand, turned and almost ran along the street, fortunately in the opposite direction from where they stood.

James, his head turned away from the spectators, watched until she was out of sight before turning back into the house.

Sarah and Annie were dancing about, tugging at Innes's trousers and Stella's skirt, demanding to know when their daddy was going to get on with the game. 'Daddy doesn't want to play any more,' Stella told them, her voice bleak, all the earlier mischief gone. 'We'd best let you get home for your dinner, Innes.'

'Stella . . .'

'I'll see you again, Innes.' She kept her face averted from him, hugging Ruth tightly and urging the twins ahead of her. 'Thank you for your company.'

As Innes turned homewards he was confused; James and Bethany, once as thick as thieves, hadn't seen eye to eye for a good long while and these days a meeting between them, as his mother was wont to say, was like striking a match in a room full of gunpowder. But for those few moments at the street door they were like . . . like a couple, he suddenly thought. Then as the enormity of what he had just thought hit him, he stopped walking. James and Bethany were not a couple, they were brother and sister; his brother and sister.

He shook his head as though to clear it, and started walking again. He had been imagining things. Of course he had.

But still, he wondered. And when he reached home he said nothing of what he had seen to his mother or to Zelda.

After settling the children Stella began to make the dinner, marvelling at the way her hands and body worked as efficiently as ever, though her head felt as light and empty as a room that had been stripped of its familiar furnishings.

Her father came in, chattering about the men he had met at the harbour and what they had all said to each other. It was a daily ritual and she was able to reply at the right time, ask the right questions and nod when he paused for a response, without actually having to listen to a word he was saying.

While the pots simmered on the stove she fed and changed Ruth. Today, the innocence and trust in the baby's eyes, the smiles that showed four perfect little white teeth, flooded Stella with so much emotion that she had to fight to keep the tears at bay. One day, she thought, wee Ruth would have to find out for herself that the world was a frightening place where nothing – not even trust – could be taken for granted. Stella hoped that when that happened her beloved daughter, at that moment kicking her plump bare legs and babbling to the ceiling, would not hurt as badly as she herself was hurting now.

As soon as Bethany left, James went out the back door to the lean-to wash-house, where he stripped off his jacket, waistcoat and shirt, then pumped cold water into one of the two big stone sinks before dousing his head and shoulders over and over again.

Gasping, he straightened and scrubbed himself with an old towel until his skin glowed and tingled, then put his clothes back on and combed his wet black hair roughly with his fingers, sleeking it down against the shape of his skull.

When he returned to the kitchen it was to find Mowser in his usual chair, a twin on each knee, while the baby chattered to herself in her little crib. Stella, as serene as ever, was ladling stew into some plates. All was calm, all was as it should be.

Apart from the occasional comment from Mowser or

from one of the twins, they ate in silence, James pre-occupied with thoughts of Bethany and unaware of the sidelong glances that his wife cast him from time to time. After a while he pushed his plate away and sat down by the fire, using an open newspaper to shut himself off from the rest of the household. Mowser, always hungry for some man-to-man talk, made several attempts at conversation before giving up and going off to his bed. Stella settled the children for the night then sat down opposite her husband, her fingers busy with her knitting.

'Are you not going out tonight?' she ventured at last.

'No,' he said curtly, then when she stifled a yawn, 'You should go to your bed.'

'In a minute.' The fire had died down and she knelt to poke it back into life. Looking at her downbent head with its brown hair sleeked back into a neat bun, James recalled what Bethany had said about his treatment of Stella. He leaned forward and took the poker from her.

'Get to your sleep and let me see to the fire,' he said with gruff gentleness. Startled, Stella relinquished the poker and rose, but instead of doing as she was told she stood looking down at him. His hair had curled at the ends, as it always did when it was drying; she longed to touch it, knowing that it would feel soft and springy beneath her fingers. Instead she put her hands behind her back and said, 'I met Bethany at your mother's today.'

She was sure that her husband's broad back stiffened, though his voice was casual when he said, 'Oh aye?'

'I told her . . .' Her voice cracked and she had to clear her throat and try again. 'I said about Mr MacFarlane's idea about paying wages to the crew.'

He kept his gaze fixed on the fire, the poker rattling against the bars as he prodded and prodded at the coals. 'I know, she came to see me about it. You know what she's like, always poking her neb into things that don't concern her.'

She thought of the way he had smoothed the lock of

hair away from Bethany's face, and of her hand touching his. 'Did you quarrel, the two of you?'

'You know that we always quarrel when we meet up. Nob'dy can reason with Bethany.'

'I'm sorry if I caused any . . .' Stella paused, swallowed, then went on, '. . . any trouble between the two of you.'

James sat back on his haunches so that he could look up at her, his face flushed with the heat of the fire. 'You didn't cause any trouble that wasn't already there,' he said, then his gaze dropped away from hers. 'It's me that should be saying sorry. I've been hard on you lately and it's not been your fault at all. It's . . .' He hesitated and for a terrible moment Stella thought that he was going to say something she didn't want to hear. Her hands instinctively went up, ready to cover her ears, and her body tensed, but he only said, 'It's been a difficult time, with Jacob become part-owner of the boat, but I've no right to take my worries out on you.'

'I'm your wife, James, who else would you girn at?' She tried to make it sound like a joke, but to her own ears it came out as more of a plea. She prayed that he would stand up and take her in his arms and make everything all right, but when he did straighten he turned towards the door, saying over his shoulder, 'Get some rest, I'm just going out for a breath of air.'

'James.'

'What is it?'

'Don't leave me,' Stella said, and he spun round.

'What?'

'I meant . . . it's late to be going out.' It wasn't what she had meant at all.

He stared at her, then said gruffly, 'I'll not be long.'

She had forgotten to put the stone water bottle in earlier, and when she got into bed the sheets were icy against her bare feet. She shivered as much from fear as from cold, wondering where James was going and who he might be meeting. But, true to his word, he returned in a few minutes, blowing out the lamp as soon as he came in.

Stella lay rigid, listening to the rustle of clothing as he undressed in the dark. James Lowrie was her man, her wedded husband, and she loved him even more than she loved the children he had fathered on her. She wanted to sit up in bed, to ask him outright what he and Bethany had been saying to each other when they loitered on the very doorstep she herself brushed every day and whitened every week. 'Nob'dy can reason with her,' he had said of his sister, and, 'You didn't cause any trouble that wasn't already there.' But from what she had seen in that brief peep round Innes's arm, there had been no quarrel between James and Bethany.

When he finally came to bed they lay side by side, silent, for a long time before Stella summoned up the courage to move her hand across the cold, rough sheet to clasp his fingers. She heard a faint catch in his breathing, then after a moment he turned to take her in his arms.

It was what she wanted, and yet it was not what she needed. Even though his body merged with hers, a chasm still yawned between them and, much as she yearned to, Stella could not bridge it.

'Innes Lowrie,' Zelda raised herself on one elbow and peered down at him, 'don't tell me you're asleep already!'

'Of course not, I was just thinking.'

'Thinking about what?'

About James and Bethany, and the way they had lingered on the doorstep together, and the way . . . 'Nothing.'

'You're not here to think about nothing, or to sleep for that matter. I've been in this house all day with your mother, waiting for you to come home to me, and now that we're finally all alone in our own wee bed you're wasting time in thinking?'

The room was dark, her face in shadow, but her long,

loose hair tickled his throat and the dim glow from the small window highlighted one bare, rounded shoulder. He reached up and stroked her smooth skin. 'You're cold.'

'You're my husband, it's surely your duty to do something about that,' she said, and bent to kiss him, her full soft breasts deliciously cool against his chest. As he drew her beneath the blanket and wrapped his own body about her to warm her, it occurred to him that in the dark, with faces shadowed, a man was a man and a woman a woman. Even when they were blood-kin.

'What in the name of God's that din?' Meg cocked her head. 'It sounds like one of these newfangled motor-cars.' Then, as the noise stopped, 'Have a keek out the window and see what's going on.'

'You have a keek, I'm not bothered.'

'You're no' a real woman, Jess Lowrie,' Meg grumbled, levering herself out of her chair. 'You're no' nosy enough.'

Just as she got herself upright, Zelda came flying down the narrow stairs.

'For any favour, lassie,' Jess squawked at her in horror, 'will you watch what you're doing! D'you want to trip and break your neck and kill the bairn into the bargain?'

'I'm fine, I'm fine. It's Innes and Mr MacFarlane in a motor-car!'

'What?' Jess and Meg reached the window at the same time. 'What do they think they're doing, giving me a showing-up in front of all the neighbours? Zelda, pay no heed to the two of them!'

But the order came too late; Zelda was already opening the door, and by the time Jess and Meg got to the pavement it seemed that the entire street was already there to marvel at the gleaming chocolate-brown car. Innes, beaming so broadly that his face was almost cut in two, jumped down from the passenger seat and hurried round to where his wife hopped about on the pavement like an excited child.

'D'you like it? It's Mr MacFarlane's. I've just been with him to buy it.'

Jacob climbed down from behind the steering wheel, grinning at Jess. 'Your carriage awaits, my lady.'

She cast a horrified glance up and down the street. 'What are you talking about, man?'

'I'm saying fetch your coat and we'll take you for a drive. And you as well,' he added to Zelda and Meg, 'there's room for all of you.'

'I'm too busy.'

'Och, you are not, Jess.' Meg's eyes were gleaming. 'We were just having a bit of a gossip and we can do that any day of the week. I've never been in a motor-car before.'

Betrayed by her sister-in-law, fuming and embarrassed, Jess had no option but to fetch her coat.

'You'll sit by me in the front,' Jacob said, but she shook her head firmly.

'I'm affronted enough without that. What made you bring such a thing right to my front door for everyone to see?'

He looked hurt. 'I thought it would please you.'

'Please me? I don't know where to put my face!'

'Wait till you try it, Jess, it's grand to be able to up and go whenever you feel like it.'

'I already do that,' Jess said, 'only I use my feet. I'll sit in the back with Zelda.'

'I'll go in the front with you, Jacob,' Meg offered. 'How d'you get into the thing?'

After swinging the starting handle until the engine roared into life, Innes joined his wife and mother behind Meg and Jacob, and finally they moved off with a blare of the horn and a cheer from the neighbours. After driving inland for a while they stopped by a pleasant field. While the others found seats on a fallen log, Jacob and Jess strolled towards a stand of trees.

'You're vexed at me – and I thought you'd be pleased with the car.'

'It's got nothing to do with being pleased or not. If you want a motor-car then that's your business. It's just that I didn't like being driven along the street I've lived in all my married life, with folk standing at their doors and keeking through their curtains, and all the bairns too wee to be at the school running alongside.'

'They all wished they could be sitting there with you.' Jacob jerked his head, indicating the gleaming car by the roadside. Innes, too excited to sit still, had returned to it and was busily inspecting one of the wheels. 'Your lad's fair taken with it. He was a great help to me when it came to finding the right motor-car.'

'Innes has an eye for that sort of thing. I've been hearing,' she said, 'that the *Fidelity*'s crew's going to be paid proper wages during the next season instead of a share when the fishing ends.'

'Aye, they were all for it.'

'Not all, surely,' she said. Then when he raised his eyebrows at her, 'Stella tells me that James wasn't best pleased at you speaking to the rest of them before he'd the chance to think it over.'

'Time's moving on and the April herring fishing's almost on us. I began to wonder if the man was going to speak to the crew at all. Someone had to do it.'

'Behind his back, and him the skipper?'

He gave her a sidelong look. 'I felt that he had to be hurried along. Your James is a wee bit old-fashioned, Jess, he spends too much time wondering what his father would want him to do.'

'I hope the two of you aren't going to fall out about this.'

'No fear of that. He cares for the boat too much to

leave it and I know I've got one of the best skippers on the Moray Firth.'

'*We've* got one of the best skippers,' she said tartly. 'Me and Bethany and Innes own a share of her too.'

'Of course you do,' he said heartily, putting a hand beneath her elbow to assist her over the rough ground as they entered the shadows beneath the trees.

27

The new motor-car had certainly made a difference to Innes. He had had the time of his life helping Jacob to decide which one to buy and he was charmed by the way the older man had insisted that he inspect the engine of each model carefully before offering advice.

'He wants me to learn how to drive it, and he's asked me to look after it for him, because he trusts me,' he boasted to Zelda in the privacy of their bedroom.

'Of course he does, who wouldn't trust you? Innes . . .' she said, linking her arm in his. 'It was awful nice, riding along and looking out at all the folk. Could we not have a motor-car of our own one day?'

'Of course we can,' he said confidently, then, remembering the showroom in Elgin with its row of brand-new cars for sale, 'P'raps I'll even set up in a garage of my own. I could sell cars as well as repairing them.'

'We could have a nice wee house beside the garage,' she said at once.

'Aye.' He hugged her, loving the way there was more of her to hug these days.

'But when will it be, Innes?'

'Soon,' he promised rashly. 'Soon.'

James Lowrie would never forget the embarrassment of his brother's first trip on the *Fidelity*. It was no shame to the lad that he had been violently sick, for it was an experience that most new crew members, even James himself, had to go through on their first trip. He could still recall the gut-wrenching spasms and the great thick slice of salt pork that his father had forced him to eat.

'It'll come back up again before it's had time to start spoiling in your belly,' Weem had said candidly as his son, green round the gills, chewed manfully on mouthfuls of the fibrous stuff. 'But it'll cure you and you're better to have something to bring up.'

He was right: once the pork was over the side of the boat James began to feel better, and he had never been troubled with sea-sickness again. The problem with Innes was that he kept on being sick and nothing, including the salt pork, seemed to put an end to it. On the rare occasions when he wasn't hurling his guts overboard, the boy had been of little use and James had had to work twice as hard to make up for him, as well as suffering the jeers and taunts of the other crew members, who seemed to think that it was his fault that he had a weakling for a brother.

And now here was Jocky, his engine driver, flopping in his bed like a netted herring and suggesting that Innes should take his place on the *Fidelity*'s forthcoming trip.

'Are you sure you can't manage yourself tomorrow?' he asked in despair. 'It's only the line fishing and the Firth'll be like a millpond.'

'Can you not hear him wheezing away like a squeakin' gate?' Jocky's wife Nell asked sharply. 'The man's lungs is in a terrible state. He's not fit to walk to the privy, let alone go out on the boat.'

'The sea air'll do you good, Jocky.'

Nell folded her arms beneath her generous bosom. 'What sea air's that you're talking about? The man spends all his time down below with the engine. That's what's given him the bronchitis – all that steam and oil and stinking air. It's all right for you, James Lowrie, up on deck with the wind in your face.'

'D'ye think, lass, ye could fetch a drink of milk to ease my chest?' Jocky asked hoarsely, and when she had gone off with a bad grace he said apologetically to his skipper, 'I'm awful sorry, James, but the woman's right, I can scarce put one foot before the other. The way I am I'd be more of a hindrance to you than a help. I'm sure Innes'll go out with the boat if you ask him. He's a decent lad, and to tell the truth . . .' he broke off to deal with a fit of coughing that shook his skinny frame like a dog shaking a rat, 'he's a better engine driver than I am.'

'You suit me well enough, Jocky. Could you not just give it a try in the morning?'

'And have Nelly chasing me down the harbour, screamin' like a fishwife? No, no. And anyway, I know by the way I feel now that even if the bronchitis is liftin', tomorrow I'll be weak as a babby.'

James chewed his lower lip then said, 'Mebbe I'd be better to just keep the boat in the harbour tomor-row.'

'And hold the rest of the men back from earnin' money on the last trip to the line fishin'?' In his agitation Jocky reared up in bed and clutched at James's sleeve. 'They'll put the blame on me and I'll never hear the end of it! Fetch Innes, he'll do it for you . . .'

He went into another fit of coughing so severe that he couldn't catch his breath at all. As he thrashed about in the bed, whooping and choking and going purple in the face, James yelled for Nell, who rushed in, thrust a cup into his hand and went to sit on the bed, rubbing her choking husband's back.

'There now, there, my wee mannie,' she crooned. Then as Jocky drew in a shuddering breath that sounded like a bagpipe lament attempted by an untalented beginner, she glared up at James. 'Can you not see for yourself the state the man's in? Give me that milk. There'll be no line fishing for him tomorrow, and mebbe no more fishing at all if I can't get him out of this state!'

'Get Innes,' Jocky croaked feebly as James withdrew. 'He'll do it for you. After all, he's your own brother.'

When James arrived at the house to tell him that he was needed on the *Fidelity*, Innes at first thought that his brother was talking about another engine check in the harbour. He agreed jauntily enough, but as James went on, 'Be down at the harbour at five in the morning so's we can catch the tide . . .' his jauntiness disappeared like a puff of smoke.

'You're wanting me to go out with the boat?' He was aware that his mother, washing the dinner dishes, had paused and turned from the sink.

'That's the way we usually do it. We don't just stay snug in the basin and throw the lines across the harbour wall for the fish to catch.' James was as tense as his brother, and when Jess began to speak he tossed a quick, contemptuous look at her. 'The lad's a married man, he can speak up for himself. And if it's that weak belly of his you're worried about, we'll not be away more than twenty-four hours, so he'll not have the time to start spewing.'

'But Jocky Mason . . .' Innes protested.

'Jocky's got the bronchitis and he cannae manage this last trip before the herring fishing. It was him that said I should fetch you instead. He says you'd make a good engine driver, and it'll be a chance for you to see how the engines are running before we're off to Caithness with the nets.'

Innes's mouth had gone dry. 'I've got my own work to do. Surely someone else can go out with you.'

'We're not the only boat short of an engine driver,' James said, his voice taking on a sharp edge. 'There's three or four of them havin' to stay in port for lack of a man this time. But I'm damned if I'll miss out on one more catch of white fish when there's a decent enough driver in my own family. As for your own work, you can surely manage to get a day off. I'll pay you forty-six shillin' for the one trip; I'm sure that's more than the smith gives you for a week's work.'

'You'll do it, won't you, Innes?' Zelda interrupted, beaming. 'I'll go to Mr Gordon myself in the morning and say you're not well. He can surely do without you for one day.'

James grinned at her. 'You've got a good lassie there, Innes. You're a fortunate man.' He gave his brother a hearty slap on the shoulder. 'Tomorrow morning then, and don't be late for we've a tide to catch.'

'All that money for one wee trip,' Zelda gloated when James had gone. 'More to put in the bank, Innes.'

'Aye.' He shot a warning glance at his mother and she folded her lips tightly, waiting until Zelda had gone up to bed before she said quietly, 'You've not told her, have you? You've not told that lassie what you went through the time your father tried to make you into a fisherman.'

'There was no reason to tell her. Anyway, I didn't want her to think me a coward.'

'You're not a coward, Innes! You proved that when you took a beating from Will Mulholland, then insisted on facing up to him again to ask for his blessing on your marriage. The sea made you ill and now here you are agreeing to do it again.'

'James needs me.'

'What's James ever done for you?'

'He's my blood-kin and I can't let him down,' he said doggedly. 'And, Zelda's right, it'll mean more money towards getting a place of our own.'

'You know you're welcome to stay here for as long as you like – the three of you.'

'Aye, and it's good of you to put up with us. But I'm a married man now, Ma. My wife wants her own wee house and it's my job to provide it.'

She seized his arm as he tried to go past her to the stairs. 'Just because you're wed doesn't mean that I can't worry about you.'

'And just because I'm wed doesn't mean that it's easy to keep the peace between my mother and my wife,' he said with the ghost of a smile. 'But it's something I have to do, just like going out tomorrow on the boat.'

'You're a cheeky monkey, Innes Lowrie!' She swiped at him with the dishcloth in her free hand and he ducked away, grinning, relieved to have managed to dredge up some humour to ease the situation.

'I'd best go up to Zelda. Don't worry about me, Ma, and don't you get up tomorrow. I'll see to myself.'

'Innes . . .'

'I'll be back before you know it,' he said, and disappeared up the steep wooden stairs.

Although he was silent as a cat when he crept downstairs at four o'clock in the morning, Jess heard every movement because she was still wide awake, lying as stiff and straight as a poker in the bed. She had put out a good selection of bread and cheese, and scones and pancakes, for him to take with him, and left the kettle on the stove so that he could make himself some tea before going out.

She listened to him moving carefully around the kitchen, heard the soft clatter of the kettle against the teapot and the sound of water being transferred from one to the other. When the street door opened, then closed, she held her breath for a full minute, listening for movement, hoping against hope that he might have changed his mind and was still in the kitchen; but when she finally gave in to her anxieties and got up, Innes had gone, leaving behind half a mug of cold tea. At least, she thought bleakly, he had taken some food with him for later. Unable to go back to bed, she dressed and began to work on her knitting wires.

Several hours passed before Zelda came downstairs, her face still puffed with sleep, her hair tousled. 'I never even heard Innes getting up,' she said, yawning. 'Is there any tea? My throat's parched.'

'Sit down at the table and I'll pour it for you. I heard

Innes going out in good time. He'll be at the fishing
grounds by now.'

Zelda peered through the small window. 'It looks like
a decent enough day.'

'That doesn't mean they'll have good weather at sea.
Innes never spoke to you about his trips on the *Fidelity*
after he left the school?' Jess asked as she set a plate of
porridge before the girl.

'He said his da had wanted him to go to the fishing,
like James, but he didn't take to it.'

'He was awful sick . . . so bad that I knew he'd die if
he tried to keep at it. So I put a stop to his father taking
him to sea again.'

'Surely you can't die from sea-sickness?'

'Mebbe you can. I wish,' Jess said, unable to hold her
tongue any longer, 'that he'd said no to James.'

Zelda, who had always had a good appetite, scraped her
spoon around her plate to catch the last of the porridge.
'Och, he'll be fine. He's a man now, not just a wee laddie
like before. And it's just for the day; he'll be back in no
time at all.'

The moment he arrived in *Fidelity*'s engine room, Claik,
the trimmer, began to talk.

'Can you smell the reek of the fish?' he demanded as
soon as his foot left the ladder. Then when Innes, trying
hard to concentrate on the reassuring, familiar smell of
engine oil, shook his head, 'There must be somethin'
wrong with your neb then. My stomach never gets used
to that stink. The sooner we're at sea, the better, for a
few big seas'll wash the bilges out.'

In an area where most folk were named for their habits,
rather than by the names their parents had given them,
Claik had earned his nickname at school, where he had
been known as a telltale, always running to the teachers
to denounce small, scabbed-knee wrong-doers. Regular
playground beatings had failed to persuade him to mend

his ways and hold his tongue, with the result that he had retained both the nickname and, Innes soon discovered, his fondness for talking, even when he was hard at work shovelling coal into the ever-hungry furnace.

'That's us off, then,' he said while Innes tried hard to ignore the clatter of iron-studded boots on deck and the swinging, lurching movement that indicated *Fidelity*'s turn away from the harbour wall. Then, as the boat began to dip and roll, 'That's us out the harbour now.'

He kept his chatter up on the way to the fishing grounds, seemingly oblivious to his companion's silence. Innes was concentrating hard on convincing himself that James had merely asked him to see to the engines, as before, while *Fidelity* lay in the harbour, but as the boat began to lift and fall to the heavier seas out in the Firth, he quickly discovered that deception was impossible. Despite all the oaths he had sworn and the promises he had made to himself, he was back at sea.

At first, shutting his ears to Claik's babbling, he concentrated hard on the engines, making mental notes of things to be checked when the boat was being made ready for the start of the new herring season. Then he pondered over Stella's suggestion that he should think of trying for a job in one of the boatyards. Every community along the coast, large or small, had its share of yards but until then Innes, because of his fear of the sea, had never thought of working in one of them. The more he thought of it, the more the idea appealed to him. He determined to approach George Thomson of Buckie, and if that yard had no need of him there was Smith's of Buckpool, Herd and McKenzie of Finnechtie, and yards at Cullen or Portessie that any man would be proud to work for. This would be the time to make the change, he decided; a new wife and a new career, all in the same year.

Listing the yards where he might be able to find work kept his mind occupied and kept Claik's voice in the background while the engine, running sweetly enough, carried the *Fidelity* towards the fishing grounds.

When he had run out of boatyards, Innes turned his thoughts to Zelda, which was a mistake since it filled him with a yearning to be with her, or at least to be in his small workshop hard by the smiddy, safe in the knowledge that within a matter of hours he would be returning to her.

He would still be home with her by bedtime, he reminded himself firmly. Boats at the line fishing only stayed out for a day. Just then *Fidelity*, meeting with a steep wave, climbed it with ease before her bows dipped forward and she began the slide down the other side. Innes's stomach suddenly seemed to turn to stone; then, as the boat hit the valley before the next wave with a thud, the stone turned to liquid that boiled up behind his breastbone and into his throat. He had to swallow several times to keep it from reaching his tightly closed lips and splattering between them.

Claik, stripped to the waist and already running with sweat, merely mumbled a curse round the cigarette he had placed between his lips and juggled deftly with the shovelful of glowing coals he had just scooped from the furnace. It was a tricky moment, but he managed to keep the embers balanced on the shovel, and as the boat began to climb the next wave he used them to light his cigarette before tossing them back into the furnace. Then he peered over at Innes, his eyes startlingly white in his soot-streaked face.

'Are you all right? Your face's the colour of a fish floatin' belly-up.'

'I'm fine,' Innes said through clenched teeth.

Claik inhaled a great lungful of tarry smoke, then blew it out in a cloud that filled the small space and returned to the back-breaking work of shovelling coal from the bunker into the roaring furnace.

'Here,' he suddenly remembered, 'did you not have to give up the sea because your guts couldnae take the

motion of the boat?' When Innes, unable to trust himself
to speak, gave a nod, Claik said comfortingly, 'Ach, that
was a while ago. You'll feel different now, eh?' Then,
peering again at his engine driver, 'Mebbe no', though.
Here . . .'

He put the shovel down for a minute to rummage in a
corner, giving a grunt of pleasure when he unearthed a
grimy bucket. 'Stick that down beside you just in case.
But try not to use it, for the reek in here's bad enough.
Would you like a smoke? That always settles my belly
when it feels wrong.'

Innes shook his head, convulsively swallowing again
and again as the boat started to clamber up the side of
another big wave. She began to skim down towards
the trough earlier than he had expected, catching him
unawares. He staggered, and had Claik not put out an
arm to hold him back he might well have fallen against
the red-hot furnace.

'Hold on there, man, we don't want you burnin' yourself before we even get to the fishin' grounds,' he said
amiably, exhaling another lungful of strong-smelling
tobacco smoke. Then, as Innes grabbed at the bucket, the
battle lost, 'God,' he went on mournfully, 'just when that
stink from the bilges was gettin' washed out, too.'

It was full daylight when they reached the fishing grounds.
At James's shouted orders Innes stopped the engine, then
the mizzen was set to hold the *Fidelity* head to wind while
the lines went overboard. The task was lighter than shooting
the nets, but even so it was time-consuming, for there were
five lines for each of the seven men in the crew, and each
line held about a hundred and twenty baited hooks.

With the engine stopped, Innes at last had a chance to
get on deck for some fresh air. 'Not already,' James said
when he saw his brother emptying the bucket overboard.
'The water's scarce got a bit of movement on it.'

Innes, his stomach raw with continuous retching and

his entire body aching from the need to adapt his footing all the time to counteract the heavy rolls and pitches of the boat, glared at him.

'You'd be sick if you'd to stay down there, breathing in that poisonous air.'

His brother grinned. 'Am I not lucky being a fisherman instead of an engine man like yourself? We've got good fresh air to breathe up here,' he said. Then, recalling that the boat could not have put to sea without his brother's help, he added in a more friendly tone, 'You can stay on deck while we're putting the lines out, but just keep over there, out of the way.'

The fresh air and the cold wind were both welcoming after the stuffy engine compartment with its obnoxious fumes, but there was nothing stationary, Innes realised wretchedly, to fix his gaze on. The sea rolled and tossed and heaved; the cork float thrown overboard to mark the site of the lines bobbed and bounced in a way that made him feel worse; the horizon swung crazily; and even the clouds overhead raced across the sky, never staying still for a moment.

When the lines were shot and the men went into the galley for their meal he followed them, clinging to the thought that under cover there might be some stability. But in the enclosed space the boat's tossing, lurching motion was made even worse and the smell of the food only added to his misery. Seeing the sense of the adage that it was better to have something in his stomach than nothing at all, he tried to eat a mouthful or two of soup and bread, only to find that he had to rush out on to the deck almost at once, followed by a gust of laughter.

'You've not changed, have you?' James said when he came on deck later to find his younger brother leaning over the side and retching helplessly. 'Da thought you'd grow out of it, but you'll never make a seaman.'

Innes straightened, wiped his mouth on his sleeve and stamped back to the engine room without a word, but even with the engines stopped the place was uncomfortable and claustrophobic. He was soon back on deck, huddled miserably in a corner, yearning with all his heart for land, and home and Zelda.

28

Bethany and the children had almost reached her mother's house when they met Stella and her small family walking in the opposite direction.

'Your mam's not in,' Stella said. 'Mr MacFarlane's taken her out for a run in his motor-car, Zelda says.'

'Are you all right, Stella?'

'I'm fine.'

'You look awful pale. D'you want me to carry wee Ruth for you?' The sleeping baby, plump and rosy, looked far too heavy for her wan young mother.

'Leave her!' Stella said sharply as Bethany reached out to take the little girl. 'And you can leave my man alone, too!'

Bethany felt the colour drain from her face. 'James? I don't know what you're talking about.'

'You know well enough what I mean.' Stella slapped each word down on the air between the two of them; they sounded to Bethany like coins ringing on a wooden counter.

Her mind worked swiftly, desperately. 'James told you about me asking Jacob MacFarlane to buy Uncle Albert out, so's James could be skipper?'

Stella, caught by surprise, blinked at her uncertainly. 'He said nothing about that.'

'I tried to keep it a secret, but he found out and was real vexed with me,' Bethany prattled on, 'but at least he agreed to stay on with the boat, so no harm was done.'

Stella eyed her narrowly. 'Not long ago I might have wondered why you did such a thing,' she said, 'since you and James quarrelled every time you met up with each other. But I know now what was behind it.'

'I just felt that he should stay on the Lowrie boat. It's what Da would have wanted.'

'You're always on about that father of yours, you and James both. Always on about what he'd want.' Stella's eyes were burning now, like two red-hot coals. 'And are the two of you what he'd have wanted, Bethany? You and my James, brother and sister, sinning together?' she asked softly, and the blood froze in Bethany's veins.

'Don't be daft!'

'I must have been daft not to have known why he started spending even more time on the boat, and why he began to go on about me not being as clever as you. But I'm not daft any more, not since I saw the two of you together.'

'When . . . where?' Bethany asked in a panic, and could have bitten her tongue out as the final word left it.

'A week or two past, on my own front doorstep, when you thought I was safely out of the way at your mam's house.' Two bright-red blotches were beginning to stain Stella's sallow cheeks. Red for anger, Bethany thought. And red for danger.

'Och, that? I only went to see James about Jacob's daft plan to pay wages to the crew instead of . . .'

'I saw you,' Stella forged on over her sister-in-law's protestations. 'I saw him touch you and I saw you . . .' Her voice failed her, but the way she put her own fingers to her cheek, gently, as though caressing another hand that had paused there, told Bethany everything. 'How could you – with your own brother? It's a sin against God and a sin against nature,' she said vehemently. 'And it's a sin against me and my innocent wee bairns. I've been lying awake at nights wondering what to do about it, so I'm glad I met you today. Stay away from my man, Bethany, and stay away from me.' Her voice was menacing now, her anger so strong that the air about her neat brown head seemed to vibrate with it. 'Stay away, or I swear to God that I'll tell Gil and your mother what I saw. I'll tell the whole coast.'

Bethany attempted a laugh. 'You think anyone would believe such nonsense?'

'Oh, I think they would. I'm not the only one who saw you.'

'Who . . . ?' Bethany's throat was so closed up with shock that the word barely managed to squeeze out.

'That's for me to know and you to wonder about. But you'll know soon enough if you try to come between me and James again,' Stella said and pushed past her sister-in-law, scooping the twins before her. Bethany stared after the woman. Then, sick with shock, she blundered towards the refuge of her mother's house.

Ellen, used to being towed everywhere by the hand and panic-stricken to find herself adrift in the street, followed as fast as she could, bleating like an abandoned lamb until Rory took her arm and pulled her with him. They caught up with Bethany as she fumbled with the latch, so disturbed by the scene with Stella that her fingers were unable to make sense of the simple, familiar mechanism. When Zelda, alerted by the rattling sounds, opened the door from inside, Bethany almost fell into the kitchen.

'You're white as a sheet . . . What's happened to you?' the girl asked. Bethany pushed past her and reached a chair just as her knees threatened to give way beneath her.

'I'm fine, I just took a dizzy turn as I was coming along the street.' Bethany clutched at the edge of the table, squeezing her eyes tightly shut and lowering her head to her knees as the room slowly revolved about her. Dimly, she could hear Zelda talking to the children, settling them down on the hearth rug and giving them

something to play with. Then she jumped and gasped as
something cold and wet touched her forehead.

'Water, just,' her new sister-in-law said briskly. 'Hold
the cloth to your head while I make some tea.'

The cold compress and the hot tea worked their magic,
but when Bethany set out for her own home Zelda insisted
on going with her.

'You still look awful pale. Mebbe you're sickening for
something.'

'I'm never ill.' Now that she was beginning to feel more
like herself Bethany was anxious to be on her own, with
time to think.

'Mebbe,' Zelda said, 'you've a bairn coming.'

'What? Of course it's not a bairn!'

'You've been wed long enough. I know that when I
first fell with this one,' Zelda patted her rounding stomach
complacently, 'I fainted once in the dairy at the farm and
I was awful sick too. That's how the mistress knew I was
expecting. It was her that told me, for I knew nothing about
these things. You won't either, since Rory and Ellen aren't
your own . . .'

Her voice went on and on; she was as bad as Stella,
Bethany thought, and suddenly recalled Stella's face as
she had last seen it, ashen apart from the bright-red spots
on her cheekbones and the diamond brilliance of her eyes.
Stella knew, and according to her someone else knew too,
and nothing would ever be the same again.

It was a relief when they reached the house and Zelda,
refusing a half-hearted invitation to step inside, hurried
away. At last, Bethany thought, she had a chance to think
over what had happened. But when she went into the house
Gil was there, having finished work early for once and
waiting impatiently to tell her that he had just put down
the deposit on one of the big houses being built on Castle
Terrace, an area in the upper part of Buckie, overlooking
the Firth, where the old lighthouse stood.

'You'll feel like a lady there, Bethany,' he exulted.

'Mistress of a fine house, and with a bonny garden as well. I'll plant potatoes and grow kale and neeps for the kitchen. We'll mebbe be able to manage a lassie to help you with the heavy work.'

He kissed his wife soundly, while Rory looked on in shocked disapproval and Ellen jealously clamoured at her father's knee for attention.

'In a minute, henny, in a minute,' he said amiably, then picked Bethany up and swung her round. 'Mr and Mrs Gilbert Pate of Castle Terrace. Does that not sound grand?'

'Aye, it . . .' Bethany said faintly, her head whirling. 'Gil, could you put me down now?'

And when he did she ran out the back and only just got to the privy in time.

At almost the same time Innes – having decided that the fisherman's adage about full bellies emptying easier might be true – was in *Fidelity*'s galley, grimly forcing food down his throat. The place was empty, for the crew, having eaten and rested, were out on deck now, bringing in the lines. Soon they would be turning for home. Soon his ordeal would be over, but as the end approached, Innes, sore inside and out, stiff and bone-weary, decided that it was time for one last attempt to defeat his fear of the sea.

Elbows on the table, he chewed and swallowed, chewed and swallowed, his eyes firmly fixed on the opposite wall. The sea had calmed now and the boat's motion was more even and at first, when he pushed the plate away and leaned back in his chair, he felt better for the food. Energy began to pulse through his body, and he breathed deeply and stretched his arms high above his head. Perhaps he had won, at last. That, he thought with a grin, would make James eat his words.

It proved to be an unfortunate turn of phrase, for within seconds a stirring in the pit of his belly sent him lurching across the small galley to where the bucket waited.

It had been a good fishing, though there was nothing to beat drift-nets glittering with the silvery shimmer of the herring. As the lines came inboard almost every hook carried a fish, and James was exultant as he watched the sea-harvest being emptied into the baskets and lowered down to the hold. This was the last of the line fishing; within the week work would start on rigging *Fidelity* out for the new herring season. There was a lot to be done after the near-inactivity of the past three or four months.

His good nature ebbed at the sight of his brother shambling out of the galley door, staggering slightly as the boat lifted on a wave. James, his own booted feet set firmly on deck and balancing his body easily against the vessel's movements, groaned and then shouted hastily as Innes headed to one side, 'Port, man, port! Can you not tell what way the wind's blowing?'

As Innes turned a pallid face in his direction James stuck one finger in his mouth, then held it up in the air as illustration. 'Empty that bucket against the wind and you'll get it all back to do again,' he roared, and some of the men sniggered.

'Here . . .' Jem, younger and more compassionate than the others, took the bucket from Innes and upended it over the side, letting the wind carry its contents away from the boat. Then he picked up a piece of rope, looped it through the handle, caught both ends in one hand and dropped the bucket down into the waves. Bringing it back up again, he swilled the salt water around before tossing it overboard.

'That's it all cleaned. Best get back into the galley, Innes, or down to the engines,' he said kindly. 'We'll be heading for home soon enough. You'll be glad of that, eh?'

'You might as well stop now, Innes,' James yelled just

then from the bows. 'We've got all the fish we want for this trip, no need for you to go on feeding them.'

As another spatter of laughter passed through the crew, Innes, who had turned towards the galley, set the bucket down again and headed for his brother instead, clutching at handholds as he made his way along a deck slippery with bloody fish-slime. His face was white, but determined, and his voice when he yelled, 'Shut your mouth, James,' was strong enough to be heard along the length of the boat, even above the strong slap of the sea against her hull.

'What?'

Innes came to a stop within arm's length of his tormentor. 'You heard me. Shut your mouth and keep it shut,' he said, a clear, cold rage beginning to bubble up within him. 'You've had your sport with me and it's time to let it be. D'you not think it's bad enough to be spewing up my guts on this . . . this washtub, without you jeering and mocking and making a fool of me for their amusement?' He threw out an arm to indicate the gaping deckhands, then shouted at them, 'Never mind sniggering at me, get on with what you're paid to do, so's we can get off this damned Firth and back to land!'

'Get below,' James ordered his brother as the crew hurriedly turned back to their work.

'No.'

'Do as I say. Start the engines, we're turning for shore.'

'You and me have business between us first.'

'It can keep until we're back in harbour.'

'No,' Innes said. 'It can't. We'll turn for shore when I've had my say, and not before.'

James's expression moved from astonishment to anger. 'I'm master aboard this vessel!'

'Aye, and I'm the engine driver. The boat stays where it is until I choose to take it back to Buckie.'

'You defy me before my own crew, Innes, and I'll . . .'

The boat dropped suddenly beneath Innes's feet and he

clutched at a rope. Fortunately for him it held, allowing him to adjust his balance, but the sudden shudder in the deck beneath him was enough to bring a spurt of bile, hot and sour-tasting, into his mouth. He turned his head and spat it out with enough force to send it flying over the bulwarks and into the surging sea beyond.

'I've just discovered what caused my belly to go bad on me all these years ago, and again on this trip,' he told his brother conversationally. 'It's disgust, James, and contempt; and mebbe a dash of pity as well.'

'Eh?'

'Contempt and pity for you, James, and for our father and the way the two of you kept on and on, all the years I was growing up, about how the only fit place for a man to be was on the sea and how the only decent work was to be found on the fishing boats.'

'Claik!' James thundered. 'Get below and start the engine!'

'He doesnae know how, James. He's the trimmer, not the driver. Claik,' Innes shouted, his eyes steady on his brother's face, 'get everything ready. I'll be with you when I've got this business sorted.'

Stella came into his mind, her small face ashen after the two of them had seen her husband with Bethany, her eyes huge and blank, her voice flat as she told the twins, 'Daddy doesn't want to play any more.' It wasn't just for himself that he was angry; it was for her as well.

'Neither of you ever tolerated the idea of any other life, did you?' he asked James. 'The sea suited you both, but for me there was always more than following the herring. And just because I thought that, the two of you – and Bethany as well – made me feel for all those years that I must be lacking in some way. But all the time, James, it was you who was lacking.'

He spat again and this time the wad of phlegm landed neatly on the deck between his brother's feet.

James looked down at it in disbelief, then in one

movement he snatched at the front of Innes's jacket, twisting his hand tightly in the material so that Innes was dragged towards him. 'Get below and get these engines started right now or, so help me, I'll put you overboard!'

A terrifying memory of being held out by his father over the racing black sea below flickered into Innes's mind, but he found the strength to kick it out again before it could take root. 'Put me overboard . . .' half throttled as he was, he had to jerk the words out between gritted teeth, '. . . and you'll have to stay here until someone comes to tow you in, just like a bairn dangling from its mother's hand. Does that thought not make you wonder just who's the most important of the two of us right now? Anyway, d'you really think that Charlie and Jem and the rest of them would stand by and watch you drown me?'

While talking, Innes had managed to get his fists between himself and his brother and now he pushed upwards with all his might, forcing James to release him.

'Get on with your work,' James yelled at the others. Then to Innes, 'What in God's name's got into you, man?'

'I've had enough.' As the boat shifted unexpectedly, Innes rocked back on his heels, then managed to balance himself. 'Enough of your swaggering and your need to make other folk feel small.'

A sneer twisted his brother's weather-beaten face. 'You're parroting Zelda now, aren't you? If you ask me, she's just what you've been needing, Innes, a nebby wee wife sharp enough to put words into your mouth.'

'Zelda knows nothing of this, though you're right, she would probably say the same thing herself. We're fortunate men, you and me, for we both wed good women, women who love us no matter how many faults we have. I think the world of my wife and I'm determined to make her happy, but I'm heart sorry for yours, for she deserves better than she got.'

'You've not been wed above five minutes and here you are, presuming to interfere between me and Stella? I'll not have that, Innes. Mind your own business and get to the engines!'

'Not until I've had my say,' Innes repeated. He settled himself more firmly on to the decking, for he was beginning to understand the movement of the boat beneath him and recognise a pattern to the sea. 'What's going on between you and Bethany?'

His brother's eyes bulged with sheer shock. 'What nonsense is this you're on now?'

'There's something happening between the pair of you, something that's not right. Something that's not natural. For God's sake, man, she's our sister!'

James's weather-beaten skin had taken on a grey tinge. 'You're haverin'!' he exploded. 'All that vomitin's emptied your skull as well as your belly!'

'I know what I saw, and I saw the two of you on your own doorstep a week or two back. I saw you touch your own sister in the way a man touches a woman when he cares for her.' James opened his mouth to speak, then closed it abruptly when Innes went on, 'Stella was with me, for I was walking her home. She saw it too.'

'She didn't . . . she couldn't!' James babbled. 'She would have said . . .'

'Said what? When have you ever listened to your wife, James? The whole town knows that you only wed her just so's you and Father and Uncle Albert could get your hands on Mowser's boat. You've never cared about the humiliation that caused her, because you've never taken the time to wonder how your wife feels about anything. You don't even see that she's got more self-respect and more pride than you could ever have, do you? Stella would die for you, James, but she'd never allow herself to tell you that, or to beg for the love she's desperate for. Now I come to think of it,' Innes said slowly, coldly, 'I don't want to know anything about whatever's between you and

Bethany, for the two of you disgust me. And now that I've
had my say I'll start the engines and get you safely back
to harbour.'

He turned away, then turned back to say into James's
shattered face, 'I was right when I said that it was the way
you and our father treated me that stuck in my craw. All
gale-force wind with no substance, James, and now that
I've vomited it out all over you it's gone. I feel fine. My
mother'll be pleased.'

Zelda and Jess were both waiting on the harbour wall when
the Buckie boats came skimming over the dark seas, lining
up to come through the harbour entrance one by one, the
light on each masthead twinkling. *Fidelity* was one of
the last; as her crew took her to her usual place by the
harbour wall and the holds were opened, Jess anxiously
scanned the deck for Innes. James, setting up the deck
derrick and seeing to the removal of the baskets of fish,
glanced up once, his eyes raking the ranks of the people
waiting above, then looked away without acknowledging
his mother or sister-in-law. Gil was there, waiting for
the fish to be landed from *Fidelity* and the other boats
contracted to him and his brother, but there was no sign of
Stella. Given the late hour, with the children and Mowser
probably abed, Jess had not expected to see her.

'D'you see Innes yet, Zelda?' she asked, her heart in
her mouth.

'He'll be down below seeing to the engine,' her daughter-
in-law said comfortably, then her voice soared into a squeak
of childish excitement and she clutched at Jess's arm.
'No . . . there he is!'

As soon as he came through the galley door Innes
looked up. A broad grin split his grimy face at the sight
of his wife and mother waiting, and he waved and paused
to wipe his face on a large wad of rag pulled from his
pocket before making for the iron ladder set in the stone
wall. James, busy at the hold, didn't look in his direction

and Innes himself paid no heed to his brother. Charlie found a moment to catch at his arm as he passed; Innes listened, then shook his head and gave his cousin a quick slap on the back before climbing the ladder swiftly, though clumsily. The grin was still plastered on his face as he reached the top.

As soon as he was safely away from the drop to the harbour and the boats below, Zelda flew into his arms. 'I missed you!'

'Ach, I wasn't away all that long,' he said casually, winking at his mother over his wife's shoulder. He looked fine, Jess thought with astonishment. Tired, as was to be expected after a long, hard day at sea, but nothing like the ashen, exhausted lad who had twice returned to her from trips with Weem.

'You're all right, son?'

'I'm fine, Ma,' Innes said. 'I hope you've got some food ready for I'm starving.'

'It's being kept hot for you, but are you not wanting to go for a drink with the rest of them first?'

He shook his head and put an arm about Zelda. 'I've got all I need at home.'

'You smell,' his wife said as they set off along the street. 'Fish and oil and goodness knows what.'

'At least you're smelling the reek of it in the open air. Think what it's been like for me, stuck in that tiny engine room most of the day. You've got oil on your face now,' Innes said tenderly.

Zelda insisted on going with him to the outhouse while he washed and changed. A lot of giggling went on, and Jess had to call them three times before they finally came into the kitchen, Innes scrubbed clean and Zelda with her hair damp, both of them tousled and glowing.

They could scarcely keep their eyes off each other during the meal. Jess felt like an outsider in her own home and it was almost a relief when Innes pushed his empty plate away and announced that he was going to his bed.

'You should mebbe go to bed too, Zelda,' Jess suggested to her daughter-in-law. 'You look tired tonight.'

'You're right. I'll just do that.' Zelda bounced up from the table and almost ran up the steep, narrow stairs ahead of Innes. Left alone, Jess washed the dishes, damped down the fire and retired to her own bed with a cushion to put over her ears.

She was asleep long before Zelda, relaxing with a sigh of contentment against her husband's shoulder, said, 'If that's what going to sea does to you, Innes Lowrie, I'll have to send you out on the boat more often.'

'It's what you do to me.' He was drifting off to sleep, but he roused himself enough to kiss the end of her nose. 'And I'm done with the sea. I'll never go back, not for as long as I live.'

29

James stayed behind on the *Fidelity* long after Innes and the rest of the crew had gone ashore. He poured water into the small tin bowl, then stripped and washed himself as best he could before putting on the clean clothes he had stowed in a locker. He needed to see Bethany, to be with her and to talk to her about Innes's revelation, but time passed and there was no footstep on the deck overhead, no voice calling his name quietly from the galley.

He waited in the darkness, chewing at a thumbnail in an agony of worry. Their affair, the wondrous thing that had suddenly made his life worth living, no longer belonged to just the two of them. Decisions had to be made, hard decisions.

Finally he went ashore, heading for the pub and the companionship of the other men. Glancing in at the lit window as he passed, he saw that they were all there – Charlie and Jem and Claik and the others, and Gil was with them. That was why Bethany had not been able to get down to the harbour.

He passed the door quietly and hurried up the hill to Gil's house, keeping to the shadows, although the streets were quiet and many of the houses dark, the folk within already abed for the night.

The door was unlatched; he pushed it open slightly and said through the crack, 'It's me', before sliding in and closing it behind him. Bethany, ready for bed and caught in the middle of brushing out her long, curly hair, spun round, her grey eyes wide.

'James? What d'you think you're doing, coming here at this time of night!'

'It's all right, I've just seen Gil in the pub with a full glass before him.' His limbs went weak at the sight of her in her long white gown, the lamplight mining gold shimmers from the depths of her brown hair. 'Oh God, Bethany . . .' he said, and went to her.

The hairbrush fell to the floor as she melted into his arms, as hungry for him as he was for her. They kissed and kissed again, clinging together as though they had not seen each other for a very long time, or as if they were saying goodbye for ever.

Finally, reluctantly, she drew away. 'You'll have to go.' Her eyes on his face, and her hands tangling themselves in his hair, belied the words. 'He might be back at any minute.'

'I've something to tell you . . .'

'I've something to tell you too,' Bethany interrupted. 'Stella knows about us.'

His arms fell away from her and he felt the blood drain from his face. 'She's spoken to you?'

'More than that, she's told me never to go near you again, or her, or she'll tell Gil and Mother and everyone. And she says someone else knows too.'

'She's right there. It's Innes.'

Her grey eyes widened. 'Innes!'

'He told me when we were out at the fishing grounds. He said . . .' James choked on the memory of his younger brother's anger and contempt. 'Never mind what he said.'

'That's it, then. It's over.'

'No, it's not!'

'See sense, man. Stella and Innes both know about us. We can't go on as we have been.'

'We could go away together, somewhere far away

where we could live as man and wife with nobody know-ing any different.'

'You'd leave Stella and your three bairns?'

'For you I would.'

'James, we're brother and sister!'

'But we were never meant to be brother and sister. We can start again somewhere else – Jacob MacFarlane did it and so can we. Tonight, before Gil comes home . . .' Fired with the need to act quickly, he caught at her hands. 'Get dressed, Bethany, and pack some things.'

Her hair swung softly round her ashen face as she shook her head. Her eyes reminded him, now, of a cold grey mist on the sea in wintertime.

'No, James, I'm not coming away with you. Fishing's all we know, the two of us. I don't want to spend the rest of my life hiding, and wondering if someone we've met before in Caithness or Yarm'th or Lowestoft'll turn up on a boat with you, or working the farlins with me.'

'Take a day or two to think about it. I'll be on the boat every night, same as usual, waiting for you,' he said desperately.

She reached up to touch his face, her fingers as gentle as the touch of a moth's wing. 'Best go home to Stella now, before Gil comes back.'

When he took her in his arms again she clung to him and kissed him with passion, before pushing him towards the door. As he left, he heard her latch it behind him.

He had only passed a few darkened houses when he heard heavy footsteps at the other end of the dark street. James ducked into a doorway and flattened himself against the sturdy timbers, listening to a deep voice singing tune-lessly, mumbling the words and breaking off occasionally to curse, as Gil – for James recognised the cursing – missed his footing and stumbled.

When his brother-in-law had passed by he slid out of the doorway and made his own way home.

*   *   *

Ruth, fed and warm and dry, was crooning sleepily to herself in her little crib while Stella sat by the fire, her hands busy with some darning.

'There's water heating for you.' She nodded at the big pot on the range as she put her work aside and rose.

'I washed on the boat.'

'Was it a good trip?' She wrapped a cloth about her hands before opening the oven door.

'Aye, good enough. Did Gil bring the fish I set aside for you?'

'A while since. You'll have seen him in the pub, surely.'

'I didn't go to the pub, I wanted to put the boat to rights.'

'On your lone?' Was it his imagination, or was there a strange note to her voice? He glanced at her, but her eyes were averted, her head turned from him as she took a plate piled with food from the oven.

'Of course on my lone. D'you think the rest of them would stay on when there's drink waiting for them on shore?'

She said nothing, but the silence roared in his ears. While he ate, the food tasteless in his mouth, he waited for her to say something, wondered if he should speak first, decided that it was safer to hold his tongue, then began to wish that she would say something – anything – to break the terrible silence between them. If only Mowser was still up, filling the void with his usual aimless chatter.

Stella did not seem fazed by the silence. She moved calmly about the kitchen, taking the girls' small garments from the clothes-horse and folding them neatly, calming Ruth when she began to whimper, crooning to her until the baby finally fell asleep, then re-arranging the fancy gilt-edged dishes, presents from Yarmouth, Lowestoft and Grimsby collected by her and her mother and kept on display in a corner cabinet. When she finally spoke it was to ask, 'How did Innes do?'

'He seemed to manage. You've got a right fondness for Innes, haven't you?'

'He's a pleasant lad, and he's always been kind to me and the bairns. There's more if you want it.'

Looking down at his plate, he was startled to find that it was empty, though he had no recollection of eating the great mound of meat and potatoes she had given him. 'No, I'm fine,' he replied, and she put a mug full of scalding black tea before him and said, 'I'll away to my bed then.'

Later, as they lay side by side in the wall-bed, James reached out a tentative hand towards her. 'Stella . . .' he began, but she immediately cut across the words that were about to pour out.

'I'm tired, James. Whatever it is can wait till morning,' she said, and turned away from him.

She had never spoken to him like that before, never turned from him. It was as good an indication as any that all at once things had changed between them, and would never be the same again.

James lay listening to the faint, regular snuffle of Ruth's breathing, waiting for daylight to lighten the window.

'Your mother tells me that you're giving up your work here.'

'Aye, that's right.' Innes's voice was muffled because he was halfway under the bonnet of Jacob's motor-car. He emerged, closed the bonnet and wiped his oily hands on a rag. 'I've been taken on at Thomson's yard.'

'I thought you didn't care for boats.'

'I've no interest in fishing,' Innes was able to say it now without feeling ashamed, 'but steam drifters have engines and that's what I'll be working on. I'll make more money there – but don't you worry, Mr MacFarlane, I'll still be looking after this motor-car for as long as you want me to. You can try her out now.'

'You try her out, since you're the one who's been

working on her.' Jacob climbed into the passenger seat while Innes, flushing with pleasure, started the engine. It ran sweetly and when the motor-car moved off with the younger man at the wheel Jacob suggested, 'You should work in a garage.'

'That's what Zelda says, but there's no work to be had locally and I don't want to be too far away, with the bairn coming.' Innes gave a sudden laugh. 'Zelda's got it into her head that one day I'll have a garage of my own with a nice wee house beside it.'

'It's good to have an ambition ahead of you when you're young.'

'Aye, it is, but right now I'm kept busy enough trying to raise the money for the house, let alone a garage. Though it'll happen one day.'

'I'm sure it will,' Jacob said. 'I know from my own experience that you can do whatever you put your mind to. Well,' he added, with a sidelong glance at Jess's youngest son, 'you can achieve most things, if you put your mind to them.'

To Jacob's annoyance, Jess continued to be uncomfortable with the idea of his motor-car, and on the few occasions when he persuaded her to go for a run in it she insisted on meeting him outside Buckie, rather than being collected from her own home.

'What's the sense in you walking half a mile or more to where I'm waiting, instead of just stepping out of your own door and into the motor?' he wanted to know as they bowled through the pleasant town of Fochabers on their way to Elgin.

Jess, uncomfortably aware of the attention that the smart motor-car was attracting, plucked at the rug he had tucked over her knees. 'I can't get used to the idea of the neighbours seeing me in a contraption like this. Of anyone seeing me,' she added.

'You're an awful woman, Jess Lowrie,' he sighed, and

said it again later as she sat bolt upright on her chair in the hotel where they were having afternoon tea. 'Can you not just relax and enjoy yourself?'

'It's all right for you, Jacob, you've got into the way of these places.' She kept her voice to a whisper, her eyes darting nervously round the fine room. 'But I'm not used to it at all.'

'You could get used to it, same as I had to.'

'I doubt that. Anyway, your livelihood depended on it. I've no such need.'

'But I could show you such sights, Jess.' He leaned across the small table, his eyes taking on an emerald glow. 'You should see Russia, and Germany, and the Niagara Falls in Canada. And the Flemish tulip fields in the springtime, and the windmills . . . you'd enjoy all of those.'

'Mebbe I would, and mebbe the ordinary folk who live there would enjoy seeing the boats coming home in the dark with their lights all twinkling. Mebbe they'd like it on an autumn evening, seeing the sky the colour of an old pewter plate and the wee bit of mist far out on the sea, and the water all the shades of grey and looking like ruffled silk, and the dolphins playing as they go up the Moray Firth. But they'll never see that,' Jess ended briskly, 'just as I'll never see their countries, for people like us don't go travelling all over.'

'I did.'

'I keep telling you, man, that you're different. You've got more courage than I have.'

'It had nothing to do with courage and you know that better than anyone else,' Jacob said with a hard edge to his voice. Suddenly Jess recalled a much younger Jacob, bewildered, asking, 'Why, Jess? Why him and not me?'

'Madam?' A waiter had arrived from nowhere.

'What did you say?' she asked, confused, wrenched from her memories.

'Hot water, madam. Do you require more?'

'No, thank you.'

'Then more tea? It's been standing for a while, it must be quite strong now.'

His hand was outstretched towards the pretty silver teapot when Jess said firmly, 'No, leave it. I like it good and strong.'

As the man bowed and retired Jacob chuckled. 'You're coming out of your shell, woman.'

'I've never been in one, as far as I know, even though the furthest I've ever travelled is the Shetlands and Yarmouth for the fishing,' she told him, picking up another scone. 'And that did me well enough.'

'Aye, well,' he said quietly to her bent head. 'We still have time, you and me. Who knows what might happen yet?'

There had been a time, before the last Yarmouth fishing season, when Bethany and James had rarely set eyes on each other from one month to the next, but now she seemed to see him at the far end of every street she turned into, or passing every shop she was about to leave. She seemed to spend some part of every day avoiding him.

The nights were the worst, when she fidgeted and shifted in her chair, thinking about James, longing to go to the harbour to see if he was alone on board *Fidelity*, waiting for her. Gil, unaware of her misery, spent every evening now talking endlessly about the wallpaper and furniture they would have in each room of the new house, and the bushes he was going to plant in the garden.

Occasionally she was jerked from her own thoughts by some new inflection in his voice, some unexpected comment. Tonight it was, 'Imagine being able to go to the privy without havin' to step outside your own back door.'

'What?'

'You're away in one of your dreams again, aren't you?' He thrust the paper he had brought home with him that night under her nose. 'Look at that: a water closet with a mahogany surround, and a fine big bath, both in the same room. And a sink to wash your hands in, too. Wait till my mother sees it all!'

'She'll not approve. She never approves of anything.'

'That's what she'll say to our faces, but she'll enjoy boasting to the neighbours about us. And she'll not miss the chance to visit, either,' he added, and Bethany groaned inwardly, then forgot all about Phemie Pate as Gil went on, 'We'll be well moved in before the bairn comes.'

'What bairn?'

'The one you're carryin'.' He grinned. 'You thought I didn't know about it, didn't you? It might be your first, but it's my third, don't forget.'

'I'm . . . I'm not even sure that I am expecting.' Bethany's mouth was dry with shock. Zelda's innocent comments the day she had taken a fainting turn near her mother's house had been ringing in her ears ever since, but she had refused to accept them, or pay heed to the slight sickness she felt some mornings. She had never fancied the idea of having a child of her own, and she had more or less made up her mind to try to get rid of it. There were women who could perform that service, but she didn't know of any and she daren't ask anyone about them.

'Ye must be. Ye've not had any of that . . .' even Gil balked at mentioning a woman's monthly cycle, '. . . that business for a wee while, have ye? Ye've had a right struggle to make your belly behave itself when you're cooking my breakfast, and you've been as fidgety as a hen on a hot griddle. And in bed at night, when I touch ye here,' he leaned forward suddenly and took a firm hold of one breast, then grinned as she flinched away from his hand, 'ye're feelin' awful sore, aren't ye?'

'Yes.' It was true, but she flinched anyway whenever Gil touched her. It had been bad enough before James, but now . . . She forced all thoughts of him away.

'When'll it be?' Gil asked, then as she sat and looked at him foolishly, he counted swiftly on his thick, stubby fingers. 'October, I'd say, just before the boats go south. So I'll be here.'

October. Now that she had been forced to look at her pregnancy as definite, rather than possible, Bethany also had to accept that the child could have been fathered by either Gil or James. She shivered, suddenly cold although she was close to the fire.

'I'm right pleased, Bethany,' she heard Gil say. 'It's long past time we had a bairn of our own. Another wee laddie, mebbe, to play with . . .'

His voice faded away behind her as she got up, clapping a hand to her mouth, and rushed to the privy at the back of the house.

A mere week after he started work at Thomson's boatyard Innes came home in great excitement to say that he had just been offered a job at Webster's garage on the High Street.

'Seemingly Mr Webster's heard that I'm a good mechanic.'

'Has he now?' Jess said. Then, turning to Jacob, who had insisted on carrying her shopping home after meeting her in the town, 'Did I not see you talking to Mr Webster today?'

He looked embarrassed. 'The man was just saying what a fine motor-car I had.'

'And you told him that Innes looked after it for you.'

'It's only the truth.' The man looked over at Innes. 'I told him what a good mechanic you are.'

'And you asked him to take me on.' Innes's voice was tight with disappointment.

'I did nothing of the sort. As I said, your name came up in conversation. Anyway, you want to work in a garage, you told me that before.'

'That's right,' Zelda chimed in, her eyes blazing with excitement, 'and here's your chance.'

'I'm promised to the boatyard. What'll they think if I just walk out so soon after starting? Or have you had a word with Mr Thomson, too?' Innes asked the older man levelly.

'Of course not. It's something you'll have to work out on your own, if you decide to take up Webster's offer.'

Innes hesitated, looking from one face to the other, then said, 'I'll sleep on it and I'll make my mind up in the morning.'

Later, when Jacob left after enjoying one of Jess's fine dinners, he had only gone a hundred yards or so along the road when he heard Innes calling his name. He stopped to let the younger man catch up.

'About that job in the garage . . .'

'You'd be a fool to turn it down, when it's what you want and what you'd be best at.'

'I know that, and I'm not daft enough to say no to it just because you put in a word for me. But before I decide what to do,' Innes said, 'I think it's best to warn you that I'm not James.'

'Eh?'

'Just because we're brothers doesn't mean we're alike. You worked things out so's he could become skipper of the *Fidelity*; but I'm not looking for any favours like that.'

'Favours? But . . . but . . .' Jacob knew he was spluttering, but he couldn't help it. He had never known Innes Lowrie to be so coldly determined. Only James had seen that side of Innes, during their confrontation on the deck of the steam drifter. 'You think I bought your uncle's share of the boat just as a favour for your brother?'

'I never said that. You're a businessman, Mr MacFarlane, and I know that you intend to get a lot back from the silver you spent, mebbe even more than money,' Innes said cryptically. 'But I doubt if you'd have bought into any boat other than the Lowrie boat. And you'll benefit from me working at the garage, for now I'll have the proper tools to hand for your motor-car.'

'So you've decided to take up Webster's offer?'

'Probably, if I can leave Thomson's yard without any ill-feeling. I want that job because I know I'll be good at it, but since I minded telling you my dream about having my own garage with a wee house nearby, and since me and Zelda are looking for a house, I thought it wise to tell you that, as far as I'm concerned, your generosity's gone as far as it should. I'll get what I want one of these days, but I'll get it in my own way. Goodnight to you, Mr MacFarlane,' Innes said and strolled back to the house, leaving Jacob with his mouth hanging open.

30

The first thing that James noticed when he went aboard the *Fidelity* was the strong reek of carbolic, even out on deck. When he went into the galley his nose wrinkled and, as he began to descend the ladder to the fore-cabin, the smell became so strong that his eyes began to sting.

'James, stop where you are,' Stella said sharply from below. 'You'll crush the wee one's fingers, for she's trying to climb up. Ruth, will you get away from there!'

As he froze, scared to move in case his heavy boots crushed his youngest daughter's fingers, he heard the splash of a scrubbing brush being dropped into a bucket of water, then a yell of protest skirled through his head.

'No, Ruth, you're not going up there on your lone. Come on now and let your daddy into his own boat! See, here's a liquorice strap for you. And there's one each for you two as well, so let's have some peace here.'

He reached the foot of the ladder to find the cabin filled with his womenfolk. The twins were jammed together on one bunk with their rag dolls, and now Ruth was on another, chewing hard with her new teeth at the thick liquorice strap with which she had just been bribed. Stella, having restored peace, was on her hands and knees, scrubbing the floor. There was no sign of his mother or, he noted with disappointment, of Bethany.

'God save us, Stella, this boat stinks of carbolic!'

'It's a better stink than the one that was here when we

first came.' The words were jerked out of his wife's throat in time to the brisk rhythm of the stiff-bristled scrubbing brush. 'It was a disgrace, so it was.'

'We've been too busy catching fish to do much house-work.'

'So I notice. Sit down, man, and get your feet off my clean floor,' she ordered, then as he did as he was told, 'And keep an eye on Ruth for me, she's like a barrowload of monkeys, that one. She should have been a laddie.'

As nineteen-month-old Ruth, taking her mother's criticism as a compliment, beamed at her father, her grey eyes – Lowrie eyes, he realised for the first time – sparkled with mischief. She took the liquorice strap from her mouth and offered it to him, then rammed it back into her smeared little face when he shook his head.

'I'm nearly done.' Stella's head was at a level with her husband's knees. 'The cupboards are cleaned out and the new mattresses are waiting on the deck. You can help me to shake them out then bring them back down.'

'Is my mother not helping you? Or Bethany?' He had not seen her since the night she had refused to leave Buckie with him, and he was sick with longing for a sight of her.

'Your mother was here earlier, but she had other things to do so I didn't let her stay for long. She's not getting any younger and I don't want her making herself ill over work that should be my responsibility now, not hers.' Stella's voice was brisk, and as she sat down on her heels and ran the back of a hand over her damp forehead, her glance about the spotless cabin was proprietary. 'You can help me with those mattresses since you're here. Stay where you are, girls. Sarah, Annie, you make sure Ruth behaves herself. After all, James,' she went on, when she had managed to clamber up the ladder and they were both on deck, shaking out the chaff mattresses, 'you're the *Fidelity*'s skipper now, and I'm the skipper's wife. I should be the one responsible for seeing that she's cleaned out and victualled.'

'Bethany usually helps with the boat . . .'

Stella frowned her displeasure at hearing the name on her husband's lips. 'I thought it best not to ask for your sister's help this year, because she's busy getting ready to move into that fine new house Gil's bought for her on Castle Terrace,' she said in the chilly voice she now used if she had to mention Bethany. 'Anyway, she's probably better not to be doing too much hard work in her condition.'

'Her condition?'

'Oh, did you not know?' The frown vanished and she beamed at him, just as Ruth had beamed earlier, though in Stella's case her face was smeared with dust and not liquorice. 'Bethany's expecting a bairn . . . at last.'

The harbour took a sudden lurch to one side, then almost at once it righted itself again. But it couldn't really have moved, James thought, feeling sick and confused, since Stella seemed unruffled, and work was going on as usual on all the other boats, where the menfolk were busy painting and caulking while their women scrubbed, dusted and polished.

'Expecting . . . Bethany's having a bairn?'

'I thought your mother might have said.' Stella's voice came from a distance.

'I've . . . not seen her for a while. Or Gil.'

The brittle new confidence she had developed since the day of the last line fishing, the day that James had taken Innes to sea as his engine driver, caused her voice to ring out like crystal in the clear, sunny April air. 'Gil's fair pleased, I've heard. That's to be expected, for a marriage isn't a marriage without bairns, is it?' Then, as all the indications of a full-scale battle broke out below, 'Bring those mattresses down, will you?' she said, and fled into the galley.

Bethany – expecting Gil's child. So that was the end of it right enough, James thought drearily as he gathered up the chaff mattresses. She would never go away with him now.

It wasn't until he was halfway down the ladder, several mattresses over his shoulder, that he realised that the child she was carrying might well be his.

He arrived at her house just as she was leaving it. At the sight of him she began to duck back in, but he reached the door in time to put his foot on the step and prevent it from closing.

'Gil's not home and I can't think of any other reason for you to come here,' Bethany said from behind the door.

'I can think of a very good reason.' He pushed the door open with the flat of his hand and marched into the kitchen.

'I'm on my way to Mother's to fetch the bairns home. She'll be expecting me.'

'She can wait. Stella told me about . . .' He glanced at her trim waist, then swallowed hard, but the words refused to come.

Her face, which had been very pale, flushed and she put a hand to her stomach in the instinctive age-old way of women carrying a new life within them. 'What about it?'

'Why did you not tell me yourself?'

'Why should I?'

'For God's sake, Bethany, it might well be my bairn!'

'It's not,' she said at once.

'How d'ye know?'

'I just know. It's Gil's and he's pleased about it, and that's an end to it.'

In his exasperation James wanted to take her by the shoulders and shake the truth out of her. After that, he wanted to hold her and never again let her go. Instead he folded his arms firmly together to keep them from doing something foolish, and took a deep breath before saying as calmly as he could, 'You've been married to Gil Pate for the past two years with no sign of a bairn. We've . . . you and me . . . it's been five months since Yarm'th. And you're certain sure that it isnae my child?'

'I'm sure.'

'I don't believe you. I think it's mine, and that's why I want you to come away with me so's I can look after you, both of you.'

'I've already told you that I'll not do that. What was between us ended when Stella and Innes found out. We knew it was going to have to finish one day.'

'But not yet, not like this! Bethany, I'm sick with wanting you and not even being able to look at you or talk to you.' He had never begged before; had never in his arrogance believed that he would ever have to stoop to such a thing. But now he was driven by sheer desperation. 'Please,' he said, his arms slack by his sides now, his face bleak.

His misery broke her heart but she knew, even if he had not yet accepted it, that there was no going back for either of them. 'James, I have to go and fetch the bairns. Let me go.'

'If I can't have you in my life I don't want anything.'

'You've got a wife, and three bairns. And the boat,' she said with a trace of bitterness creeping into her voice.

Given the opportunity, she would still exchange everything without a backward glance – James, her unborn child, all that she had – for the *Fidelity*. But unlike James, she did not have that option. The thought kindled the old resentment into a little stab of anger that hardened her just enough to propel her forwards, going past him without touching him to open the door.

'I have to go,' she said again. He hesitated, opened his mouth, closed it again, then went past her and into the street.

Bethany followed him out, heading in the opposite direction though it meant taking a longer route to her mother's house. She had not gone far before an elderly neighbour stopped to congratulate her on the coming child.

'You'll be lookin' forward to welcomin' this one,' she said. 'The first's aye special.'

Bethany nodded and smiled and went on her way. She believed that this baby would be special, and that it would be a boy, the one thing that Stella did not have. He would be a fisherman.

Like his father.

When he left Bethany, James went to Rathven grave-yard for the first time since the day he had seen his father buried there. For a long time he studied the stone and the flowers and the neat patch of grass, then he sucked the saliva into his mouth and spat hard on to the grave.

'That's what I think of you, Weem Lowrie,' he said grimly. 'You ruined my life, though I suppose even you couldnae have foreseen what was going to happen, or prevented it. That was down to me and to her. But at least I'll make a better ending than you did. I'll see to that for myself.'

'This,' Jacob said, laying the large square parcel on the table, 'is for you.'

'What is it?'

'A present, just.'

'For me?' Jess, unused to receiving gifts, eyed it with suspicion. 'Why?'

'Because I want to show you how much I value your friendship. Go on,' he urged, 'open it.'

Nervously, unsure how to deal with this unexpected situation, she removed the string and unfolded the brown paper, and found herself looking down at a handsome framed painting of the *Fidelity* at sea, her mizzen sail hoisted and a puff of smoke floating from her stack.

'Goodness,' she said, at a loss for words. Then, realising that Jacob was waiting for more enthusiasm than that, she summoned up, 'Who painted it?'

'A man I heard of in Aberdeen, who does bonny paintings of boats like this.'

She recalled, now, that Meg had mentioned something about seeing an artist on the harbour wall, sketching the boat. 'You paid him to do this?'

'Of course I did.' His eyes crinkled with amusement. 'You didnae think he came all the way here to do it for nothing?'

'It's an awful waste of good money.'

'Not if you like it. Do you?'

'Well, he's got the boat just right,' she said slowly, her eyes on the picture. Time and time again she had seen the boat coming home, looking just like that. 'You'd almost expect her to sail right out of the frame.'

He rubbed his hands, grinning. 'That's what I thought. You could hang it over the fireplace, where you can see it every day.'

'Jacob, I can go down to the harbour and see her every day if I've a mind to . . . unless she's away at the fishing.'

He gave her a long, hard look, then shook his head. 'Jess Lowrie, what do I have to do to get you to change?'

'Nothing, for you can't teach an old dog new tricks.'

'You're not old,' he said, then rushed on as she opened her mouth to argue, 'You're months younger than me and I refuse to be old, so you can't be, either.' Then, on a more serious note, 'We still have a future before us, Jess.'

'You're going away from Buckie.' Now she saw the reason for his gift. She had become used to having Jacob in her life again and she would miss him sorely.

'As it happens, I am, in a week or two, for I'm needed elsewhere. But that's not what I meant about the future.' He took her hand in his. 'Being with you again, Jess, has been like getting the chance to live my life all over again.'

The door was unlatched, as always. Anyone could blunder in and see the two of them standing there, hand-in-hand, Jess thought, embarrassed. Under the pretext of

folding up the brown paper strewn over the table, she
eased her fingers from his grasp. 'That's a chance none
of us ever get.'

'There are ways and means. Marry me, Jess.'

'What?'

'Marry me. We can have the banns called and the
wedding over before I have to leave Buckie. Then you
can come with me and see some of the places I've learned
to call home. I'll bring you back here, don't fret about
that. I know you'd not be happy if I kept you away from
Buckie for too long.'

'I've never heard such a nonsense,' Jess said feebly.

'Where's the nonsense in it? We're hale and hearty
yet, with me still a bachelor and you a widow. What's
to stop us?'

'Weem.' The name was out before she had time to
think. 'Weem,' she repeated, quietly. 'Even though he's
gone, he's still my husband.'

'I'd not ask you to forget him and the years you had
together, but I'm offering you a different life, the like of
which Weem could never give you. You and me, Jess –
together, the way it was meant to be.'

Jess's fingers played nervously with a corner of brown
wrapping paper. 'Jacob, I'm very fond of you, but I'm
still Weem's wife, even though he's lying up the hill in
Rathven and I'm down here in Buckie. I've been a Lowrie
for most of my life and I'll die a Lowrie, with no man's
ring on my hand but his.'

His face tightened, but he kept his voice under control
as he said, 'I've mebbe been too quick with my proposal.
You'll want time to think it over.'

'No, I don't. You've had my answer.'

Now the anger began to show itself as an emerald glitter
in his shrewd eyes. 'So even now he's dead you prefer
Weem Lowrie to me!'

'Is that what it's all been about?' Jess asked, very
quietly. 'I wondered, when you stayed on here longer

than you'd expected to, and when you bought a share in Gil's business.'

'What are you talking about?'

'And then you bought Albert out of the Lowrie boat so's James could be the skipper, even though you don't care for him.'

'There's nothing wrong with your James that a wee bit of maturity can't cure.'

'And Innes . . . letting him help you choose that fine car of yours and look after it for you. Finding work for him in a garage. What was going to be next, Jacob: a wee house for him and Zelda? A nice wee garage of his own?'

The arrogance that had helped him survive and prosper in the years since he had been forced far from the Moray coast, by Jess's love for Weem, now surged to the surface. 'You're haverin'!'

'And then there's me.' Jess indicated the fine painting on the table between them. 'Giving me a picture of the Lowrie boat that's part yours now, asking me to be your wife, offering me a such grand new life . . .'

'Because I love you, I always have. You know that!'

'I know that you once loved me, and that I hurt you. But it's not me you want now, Jacob. Not Jess Innes, that used to bide next door to you. It's Jess Lowrie, Weem's widow. That's why you came back, isn't it? Weem's children, Weem's boat, his wife. You couldn't best him in life, so you set yourself out to best him once he was dead.'

'That,' Jacob said, his face almost purple and his voice thick with anger, 'is the daftest thing I have ever heard!'

'I hope it is, for it's the worst thing I've ever had to say,' Jess muttered wearily.

When he had gone, taking the painting with him, she sat down in her usual chair by the fireside, staring at the larger, empty chair opposite. Even now she could see Weem in it puffing at his pipe, rustling his paper, glancing up to give her the look that always made her weak with wanting him.

She picked up her knitting wires and got on with the tiny jacket she was knitting for Zelda's baby. When it was completed there was knitting to be done for Bethany. Life went on, no matter what.

'Thinking of putting yourself over the side?'

Startled, James spun round to find Jacob MacFarlane standing by his shoulder. 'Why should I want to do that?'

'The way you were leaning out over the water had me wondering if you'd some notion of putting yourself where you thought your father should have gone. Taking his place.'

'You've got a fanciful mind, Mr MacFarlane.' And a shrewd one, James thought uncomfortably, for the man was quite right in what he said.

Jacob chuckled, the strong-smelling smoke from his pipe curling up and away into the grey dawn light, leaving behind only a faint aroma. 'I've been accused of plenty in my time, but nobody ever thought me fanciful. Mebbe it's the fish stew we had for our supper that's done it. It's sitting in my stomach like ballast.' He belched slightly. 'A sleep might have helped, but it's a while since I'd to share a wee cabin with other folk. I'd forgotten how loud snoring can be.'

'That's why I prefer to be the one standing watch when the nets have been shot,' James said, and Jacob chuckled again.

'You'll be hauling the nets soon.'

'When I'm good and ready. We'll let more fish swim into them first.'

The *Fidelity* was off the Caithness coast, on her first trip of the new herring season. Although April was coming to an end, the early morning was chill and sharp, with a wintry feel still to it. The night had been clear and frosty, the sky massed with stars, echoed on the seas by the masthead lights on the great fishing fleet spread for miles around them. It was a fitting time, James had been thinking before he was interrupted, for a man to take leave of the world. Now he wished he had made his move sooner. If his unwelcome passenger would just go below now, before the others woke . . .

But Jacob seemed to be quite settled. 'I came on this trip because it's the last I'll manage before I'm on my way: Holland next, and mebbe Germany after that. I might catch up with you in Yarm'th at the end of the season.' He put the pipe into his mouth, then took it out again to say, 'You know, James, you could be an even better fisherman than your father, if you'd just put your mind to it properly.'

'What d'ye mean by that?'

'I came on this trip because I wanted to get the chance to speak to you before I left Buckie. Married or none, lad, you've had the look lately of a man who's got himself tangled up with some woman he can't have.'

'You're talking nonsense,' James told him roughly.

'I'm entitled to talk nonsense at my age. I was in the same state once over a woman,' Jacob said thoughtfully. 'But I couldnae have her, so I put my mind to other things instead. And d'you know what I discovered? That women age and women can change their minds, but money's aye faithful when it's in the right pocket.'

'I doubt if I'll ever see the proof of that one for myself.'

'Now that's where you're wrong, for I've invested a fair bit in you already, and I intend to see that I get a good return on it. And if I do well, then so will you.'

'I never asked you to put money into this boat, Mr MacFarlane, and I'm not interested in dancing to any man's tune. I thought you'd have realised that by now.'

'You're Weem's son all right. All I'm asking is that you stay with the *Fidelity* and sail her well, and make a fortune for the two of us. And get rid of any romantic nonsense that might be getting in the way,' Jacob said, then he sniffed the air. 'I think your cook's up and about, and I do believe that the fresh air's settled last night's fish stew.'

James glared after the interfering old fool's retreating back. The sooner he made enough money to buy Jacob out, he thought, the better. He cast one final look over the water to where he could see the nearest boats beginning to take in their nets, then went down to the galley for some food. The *Fidelity* would be the last to start hauling and the first to the nearest port to unload her catch, of that he was certain.

Later, as the capstan took the strain and the messenger began to lift towards the boat, water pouring from its length, James dug one boot hard into the angle between bulwarks and deck, and leaned out over the water. At first all was black, apart from flecks of foam, then the first milky tinge appeared far below. It turned to a definite grey stain approaching the boat, and then, as the sun lifted over the horizon and the first net came closer to the surface, it became an unmistakable shimmer of silver.

James let out a yell and leaned even further forward to dig his hands into the mesh breaking through the waves. The herring was there, in abundance. The silver darlings were back, and what more could any man want?

Bibliography

Auchmithie Album by Margaret H. King, published by Angus District Council Libraries and Museum Service

Buckie in Old Picture Postcards by Eric Simpson, published by European Library, Zaltbummel, The Netherlands, 1994; reprinted 1996

Collected Poems and Short Stories by Peter Buchan, published by Gordon Wright Publishing, Edinburgh, 1992

Fishermen and Fishing Ways by Peter F. Anson, first published by George G. Harrap, 1932; republished by E.P. Publishing, Wakefield, 1975

Fishing Boats and Fisher Folk on the East Coast of Scotland by Peter Anson, published by J.M. Dent, London, 1974

'The Fishing Industry' by Malcolm Gray, from *The Moray Book*, edited by Donald Omand, published by Paul Harris, Edinburgh, 1976

The Fringe of Gold (The fishing villages of Scotland's East Coast, Orkney and Shetland) by Charles Maclean, published by Canongate, Edinburgh, 1985

How It Was, leaflet by Isabel M. Harrison

Living the Fishing by Paul Thompson with Tony Wailey

and Trevor Lummis, History Workshop Series, published by Routledge & Kegan Paul, London, 1983

The Moray Journal – various newspaper articles

Northern Fishing Ports (From Whinnyford to Portgordon) by James and Liz Taylor, published by Visual Image Productions, Fraserburgh

The Silver Darlings, leaflet by Isabel M. Harrison

'The Story of Buckie', article by Peter Bruce in *The Leopard*, published by the Mill Business Centre, Udny, Ellon, Aberdeenshire, July 1994

That's Fit I Can Mine (That's What I Can Recall) – growing up in Buckie in the 1930s, a collection of poems by Isabel M. Harrison, published and reprinted 1992, second edition, 1995

Women's Contributions to the Fishing Communities of the North East of Scotland, 1850s–1930s, thesis by L.A. McAllister MA, University of Aberdeen